J. Evan Johnson

When It's
ALL
that's
LEFT

A Novel

20 Theory Books

Chapter One

His breathing is fast and it seems the more he tries to control it, the more constricted his lungs feel. Sharp pains rage around his chest from his bruised and battered ribs. For this very reason, he hates those moments alone. His thoughts contend with one another until they blend and he can't figure out where one ends and the other begins. He holds on to his Bible, staring at his reflection in the mirror, wondering what kind of man he has become.

He wants to step out of the bathroom, primarily because the odd smell of cleaning chemicals is making him nauseated, but he is paralyzed; he's paralyzed with fear, with pain, with guilt. Beads of sweat form along his brow. He moves a shaky hand to the paper-towel holder to grab something for his face. Incrementally, his breathing gets back to normal, and he wipes droplets of sweat away.

Not thinking, he had run into the bathroom and never checked any of the stalls to see if anyone was there before he locked the door. He snaps around quickly, looking under each stall, thankfully finding no one. He unlocks the door and starts out the bathroom, unsteady at first, but now regaining his balance. After a few more deep breaths, the panic subsides. He looks down the hall, then behind him.

No one is around.

Mark Cooke makes his way to Pastor Brentwood's office for the first of what he assumes will be many meetings of counsel in trying to deal with the evil that has befallen upon his family recently.

"Does she know you still think about me?"

Mark freezes. His shoulders slump; he hangs his head.

"I mean, if my spouse were thinking of another woman as much as you think of me, I'd feel a bit angry. Maybe even disappointed, you know, given the circumstances."

Mark turns around to see Alicia. She looks just as he remembers her: soft, radiant, and full of life. He looks at her as she partially hides in the dark area of the hallway.

"I wore your favorite color today."

"I noticed." His voice comes out deep and hoarse.

"And do you like my hair?"

"Yeah."

"Then why don't we go out for a couple hours? Just me and you."

"I shouldn't even be thinking of you."

"True. But you are. I see it all over your face."

"I can't."

She shrugs her shoulders and turns her back. "So I'll see you at home for dinner tonight?"

"No. I'm going to the hospital."

She hesitates for a few moments. "I'll just see you when you get back. Give Jade my best."

Mark watches her walk down the hall and out the church.

"Mark?"

Mark turns around to see Pastor Brentwood eyeing him curiously.

"Everything okay?"

"Uhhh, yeah. Everything is fine."

"Shall we?" Pastor motions toward his office.

Mark follows Pastor Brentwood into his office and takes a seat. "I kinda feel like I've been in here way too much . . . like this is my home now." He gives a weak smile at his even weaker attempt at a joke.

"Well, much has happened to you, Mark. And sometimes having someone to talk to about these things helps."

"I just don't get why." He stares at the new-looking carpet he's never noticed until now. "Why did all this happen to my family? Why me?"

"Mark, who were you talking to in the hallway?"

The abrupt change in conversation catches Mark off guard. "Sir?"

"It sounded like you were having a conversation . . . but you weren't on the phone."

"Praying. I was praying."

Pastor nods but doesn't seem convinced. "It's a tough question to answer, the one you asked before I interjected. God's ways are mysterious, and many times hard to follow . . . hard to understand. But keep your faith. Stay close to Him. He won't let you down."

"What if He already did?"

"You can't believe that. Do you?"

Mark leans forward in his seat. "Can you do me a favor?"

Pastor blinks. "What do you need?"

"Don't talk to me like you're a pastor. You're close to Jade, too. Don't talk to me like I'm on the edge and anything that isn't Jesus-centric will send me backsliding. Be straight up with me. What happened to us . . . it's messed up. And God . . ." Mark sits back and thinks for a moment.

"I see where you are coming from. I understand the situation. It stinks, I know. And what stinks even more is it seems that God isn't there—for you, for your family. And out of all the people on the face of this planet, why did this have to happen to Jade? I get it. I'm angered by it. I'm scared of the results of it. Ever since we saw that news report, my wife and I have prayed, just looking for clarity. We would be foolish if we didn't admit our faith was shaken when we first heard the news. It hurts."

A silence permeates the air. Both men sit, each lost in his own thoughts for a moment. Mark shakes his head.

"I just don't get it. People every single day invite drama into their lives. They make stupid decisions and follow those up with even dumber ones. Some simply don't think, others just don't care, but none of them goes through what we are going through right now. And we're the ones who follow Christ. We try to be righteous. I prayed for protection, every single day . . . and that got us here. God is just, right?"

"Of course."

"God is good all the time, and all the time God is good. Isn't that how the saying goes?"

"Yes."

"So tell me, where is the justice in this? Where is the goodness? At the end of the day, why am I praying this silly prayer of protection when those who meant to harm us already did? Where was our Defender . . . where was our Protector then?"

Pastor stares at a sliver of empty space on his desk. "I understand where you are coming from. And I wish I could wipe this all away for you; for Jade; for your family. But I urge you to not lose hope. Don't let go of the belief that God has your best interests in mind. There is something to come of this. Something good, I believe."

Mark sits forward in his chair, eyes ablaze. "What good can come of this? If Jade doesn't make it, that's bad. If she does make it, she's more than likely going to have some limitations, and that's bad. Pastor,"— Mark looks down—"I killed a man. I took someone's life. And then I saw someone take their own life right in front of me. Her blood splattered on the window behind her. I will always remember that. I will always remember her. And now I am a murderer. And—" He becomes very reluctant to mention he still sees Alicia. "Where is the good?"

"Mark, in time, we will work through all of this, and I am confident God will show up. I expect it. But we have to stay prayerful. I'm in this with you. I will help you along the way."

Mark continues to look down as he feels tightness in his throat. He tries to rein in his thoughts and emotions, but everything becomes a jumbled mess. He feels that dark feeling settling on him again. "Sir," he barely gets out, "Can we pray now?"

"Of course."

Mark starts off the prayer with a simple word.

"Help."

⋅⋅⋅

Craig sits slumped in a large, cushioned chair, staring at a TV, stewing over Berta, thinking of his last conversation with Mr. Ramses. He appreciates what the man has done for him, but isn't too keen on being strong-armed into it. The Texas ranch is a huge and beautiful chunk of land, yet utterly lonely.

He had spent his first day simply taking everything in. Last night, he spent more than a few hours praying, even while feeling just as disconnected from God as he did when he was in jail. He even called Mr. Ramses a couple times just to see if any progress was made. Of course, none was.

Though the house was stocked with food and every household supply he could need, he had still gone out yesterday afternoon to shop at a small produce stand he saw on one of his excursions. The stand is about a couple miles away from the ranch property, a distance he had no problem walking. He had grabbed a few apples and cucumbers, then he made his trek back to the ranch. At first, it was strange walking along the dusty road in the blazing sun alone, but he got used to it and by the time he made it to the stand, he quite enjoyed it. He thinks it may have been delirium, but he still enjoyed it nonetheless.

When he first got to the stand, he knew he looked a mess. He was sweating, and smiling with a weird grin. The young woman who seemed to run the stand had a soft voice with a southern drawl that made his heart melt. He was always a sucker for the soft southern belle voice. That produce-stand lady could have asked him to jump off a bridge, and he would have obliged delightfully.

He chuckles at the thought as he reclines in the chair but stops, knowing there is no one around to laugh with.

He sits up in his seat and digs into his pocket, pulling out a dime. He flips the dime to the floor and swears he hears an echo that goes on for minutes. Desperate for some human interaction, he checks his wallet for some cash and finds a few dollars, but what he finds in one of the pockets forces him to pause. He finds a tattered business card with a phone number: Patrice Stafford's number.

Patrice is an interesting woman to him, one who would surely know some of what he is going through, but he can't bring himself to call her, for a number of reasons. For one, Mr. Ramses explicitly told him not to communicate with any client. Second, and more importantly, he feels he would be somehow cheating on Berta by contacting this woman who had been (maybe still is) clearly enamored with him. He paces back and forth, almost gone stir crazy. He knows the law firm would be able to cover up anything that might get out, and that's only if somehow Detective Simms found out he had contacted a client.

His next thought is on Berta. He is pretty sure she flat-out doesn't care what he is up to or what he does now. He remembers how her face looked when he had to leave. He remembers when he told her he killed a man. That look that's a mix of disgust, hatred, and fear, a man could not soon forget.

And with each passing day, the divorce process that seems to move at breakneck speed gets closer to completion.

He shakes his head, knowing she doesn't care about him. It hurts him to know that she may never care again. He stares at the card, thinking of Patrice again. She said she would always be there to answer. Throwing caution to the wind, he dials the number on his Ramses-given cell.

The call goes to voicemail.

ଔଓ

Berta lies in her bed, her back gently rising and falling with each breath. Her alarm goes off, causing her to startle awake. Wide-eyed, she stares at the clock that says 6:00 before she slams her hand on the top. She flips onto her back and stares at the ceiling. Though she has been in the bed alone, never has it felt as empty as is does now. She slides out of bed and slowly stands to get ready for her first day back at work. Unfortunately, her vacation—if that's what one wishes to call it—is over, and she must return to face her duties.

And Angelina.

She moves around the condo, hearing every single one of her moves echo off the empty walls, not so subtly reminding her that she is once again alone. Her divorce from Craig is moving as smoothly as things like that can go. Soon enough, she will no longer be Mrs. Barlow. Unfortunately, that means she will return to being Ms. DeVries, a name she holds even more disdain for.

She tries not to think too much of Craig, nor does she think of how something so wonderful with him became so poisonous. He was the man she essentially chased for ten years. Craig, the man who went to jail for a crime he didn't commit, though in her mind now, even that is questionable. Craig, the great lover. Craig, the most loyal man she'd met, she'd thought. Craig, the liar. Craig, the cheater. Craig, the . . . murderer. She bristles, realizing she went too far down her mental rabbit hole. Once again, she tries not to think too much of Craig.

After cleaning up and dressing, Berta goes to a small cafe not too far from where she lives and finds a small table in the corner to sit. She sips on a small latte while trying to steel herself to step into work. For a small cafe, many people are packed in. Only a few tables line the window side and those are taken up by people and their laptops. The front counter is crowded with more people rushing in to get their early morning fix.

Back to the daily grind.

She sits, staring off into space, still feeling numb from the recent whirlwind of events. Someone sits in front of her, pulling her from her trance. He has a short-cropped haircut and a face that looks carved from stone. She notices the dimple in the middle of his chin.

"May I join you?" he asks.

"You are?"

"Logan Simms." He puts out his hand, but slowly retracts it when Berta doesn't shake it.

"You were at the hospital, were you not?"

"Keen observer." He smiles a smile Berta finds to be genuine. "I'm Detective Logan Simms."

Berta tenses and hopes he doesn't notice. His disarming smile becomes a distant memory when she tries to figure out why he is sitting in front of her now. "What can I do for you, Detective?"

"Your husband, Craig."

"Ex-husband, sir."

"Ah. I did hear about the impending divorce. Listen, I don't want to take up too much of your time. I just have a few questions about Craig, if you don't mind."

"I do mind." She comes off more forceful than she wants. Her tone causes him to raise an eyebrow. She can't tell what his expression means.

"So, I'll keep it to one question. Do you know where he is?"

"We're in the middle of a divorce, Detective. Where he is, I would have no clue about."

"Fair enough. May I ask why you two are getting a divorce?"

"I thought you said you would keep it to one question."

He smiles again. Berta finds his smile to be genuine again, as if he is truly amused by her.

"My apologies. But just that last question."

She hesitates but finds no harm in a simple answer. "He just wasn't the man I married. And instead of growing together, we grew apart."

Simms nods and gets up from his seat. He pulls out a card and places it on the table in front of her. "Well, I'm guessing you already know I'm looking for him."

Berta stays silent.

"If he shows up, don't hesitate to call. You have a good day, Ms. DeVries."

She watches him walk away, and is left with an odd feeling. Something about him doesn't sit right with her. But then she finds herself intrigued.

⊗

Jade lies curled up in a ball, covered only by her blanket of memories that glows gold. She lays her face on what feels like a concrete floor and looks around. The memories that kept her warm are starting to fade. Some flicker out like a campfire flame in the morning. Others simply cut off as if by a switch. One by one, each memory fades until she is left in complete darkness. She sits up. She tries to make more memories appear by thinking of them, but she isn't able to. She stands and walks. Where to? She cannot tell. Each step feels like she's stepping in a small puddle of water so cold it stings. She regrets moving now, but she knew staying put wouldn't get her anywhere. Slowly, she takes a step and hears what she presumes to be water splashing around her feet. She stops.

But she still hears the splashing. Behind her.

Still unable to see anything, she starts moving faster forward, but as she picks up speed, so do the steps behind her. After only a few moments, Jade is out-and-out sprinting, but she is stopped in her tracks by a loud booming sound.

A gunshot.

Seconds later, she feels a burning in her back, then a searing pain. She falls to the ground, into the freezing water. She screams in agony, writhing in pain. The pain and the stinging cold wrap around her body, leaving her shaking and crying. The pain is so much for her, she doesn't notice she is able to see again. She slowly wipes away tears to see not another memory illuminating the area but a person . . . on fire. As the being steps closer to her, the frigid water she lies in evaporates. The being kneels down and lifts her off the ground with gentle ease. She stares in amazement, not understanding how the intense flames of the being aren't harming her as she rests in its arms. Furthermore, she realizes she no longer feels the pain in her back. The being is faceless, but she senses it staring in her eyes with a gaze so intense it feels like it is literally touching her soul.

"Who . . . who are you?"

The being speaks in a choir of voices, all sounding like her own, but all are distinct.

"I am you."

Jade doesn't understand, but she lets this being carry her away from the pain. Right now, she doesn't care where she is going; she just knows she doesn't want to feel that pain again.

Chapter Two

Mark gets home to a cold and empty house and walks to adjust the thermostat. He then finds his comfortable chair and gently sits. Next to the chair is a small stand with his painkillers on it. He stares at the bottle for a few moments but turns away in disgust. He buries his face into his hands.

"Are you hooked on those things?"

He looks up to see Alicia again. He repositions his face into his palms again, but finds it difficult to breathe without sharp pains running around his abdomen. He grabs the bottle and labors his way to the kitchen.

"You are, aren't you?"

Mark doesn't say anything.

"You don't need them, Mark."

"What I need is for you to go away." He grabs a bottled water and pops it open. He then gets two small tablets from the bottle and downs them with a few gulps of water. He simply stares at Alicia.

"Why would you say such a thing? You fought so much to have me here with you, and now you want me to go away. That hurts my feelings."

"You aren't real. I don't know what you are, but I know for sure you aren't real."

"So, more insults?"

"No." Mark advances toward her, but she steps back. "The truth."

She turns on her heel and dashes up the stairs. Mark labors after her but stops at the bottom of the staircase.

"Alicia," he calls out but hears nothing back. He slows his breathing to control the contractions his ribcage is making. He thinks to himself he saw her before he took the pain meds, so she wasn't a hallucination—at least not caused by the pain pills. He feels he can't stay in the house alone for fear of what he might do, so he decides to go check up on the kids before visiting Jade.

☙❧

Mark leaves and gets to Jade's parents' home, where Kalina, Charles, and Amber have been for a couple weeks.

"Shouldn't you be home resting? Least of all traveling long distances?" Jade's mother answers the door with a not-so-kind greeting.

Mark still smiles but knows there's a lot of unspoken of tension between them. "Hello, Joanne. I came to see how everyone is doing."

She stares at him long and hard. "You didn't call."

"I know. Each time I did before, you were all going out, or busy doing something or other." He returns the hard stare.

"Just trying to keep them busy. It helps keep their minds off things." She moves to the side to allow Mark in.

He starts past her but stops. "They are my kids," he says, not fully looking at her. "And they'll be coming home soon enough."

"I don't doubt it. But will my child go home? Will she?"

Mark looks down. "She will." Without going deeper into the conversation, he starts toward the back of the house. "Are they outside?"

"Yes."

"Thank you." He leaves her presence abruptly and walks to the patio door.

It doesn't take long for his emotions to crop up once he sees them: Kalina and Charles chasing each other around and Amber chasing something he can't see. He watches as Charles starts to show off, dodging around Kalina with his football moves. Kalina stops in her tracks and waits. Mark knows she's calculating Charles' movements. Then, like a flash of light, she lunges for him and tackles him to the ground. Charles gets up, clearly not liking what just happened, but says something and they do it again. Charles lays it on thick with the moves, and this time Kalina barely gets him . . . but she still trips him up. After laughing for a few moments, they end up sitting next to each other in the grass to watch Amber. They're talking, but he doesn't know what they're saying.

He steps out the house and gently closes the door. "You should have dodged left. She can't cover that side."

Both look back and as soon as they see him, they jump up and race toward him. Mark scoops both of them up in his arms, completely ignoring the shooting pain around his ribs. Then he winces a bit and has to put them down. As he does, he sees Amber rushing up to him but falling down as her little legs get caught in grass. He catches up to her and picks her up, kissing her on the cheek. He heads back toward the house with a noticeable hitch.

"Dad, why are you limping?" Kalina asks.

"I'm getting old."

"You were always that. I've never seen you limp like that before."

"I was always old, huh?" Mark smiles. "Sit. We gotta talk."

"Is Mom okay? We saw the news reports," Charles says.

"When can we come home?" Kalina asks.

Mark walks to the table, sits in a chair, and sets Amber in his lap. Kalina and Charles take seats next to him. He looks at them, not really knowing where to start, not really knowing what to say. He stares at them for a little bit longer as a tear falls from his eye. "Your mother is in a tough spot."

"Reports said she was kidnapped and beaten. They made it seem like it was really bad," Kalina says.

Charles looks down and plays with a stone at the table.

"The reports are a bit dramatic, but . . ."

"But true, right?"

"Yeah. She's . . ."

"On life support."

Mark looks at Kalina and sees a fire behind her eyes he doesn't think he has ever seen before. It bothers him a bit that a child her age would even have to think about things like this.

"And you? What happened to you?"

"I have a few broken ribs."

"Broken?" Charles says. "Who would do something like that to you and Mommy?"

Mark shoots a look over at Kalina before she blurts out who did it. She opens her mouth but pauses. "A very bad person," she says.

"How's school?" Mark changes the subject.

"It's fine," Kalina says.

"Think you would get used to the whole home-schooling thing?"

"No. It's not like on the commercials for home-school programs. But everyone is being really nice, though."

"That's a plus."

"Yeah. But I miss actually going to school."

"Yeah, me, too," Charles says.

Mark smiles. "Never thought I'd hear that one."

Charles smiles back, albeit weakly.

"Listen, we will get back to normal. Everyone is going to be okay. We have another hurdle to jump, but we will jump it. Just a little more."

"Wait, we're not going home with you?"

"Not yet, Buddy." He pats him on the leg. "Not yet." He looks around. "I haven't seen your grandfather. Where is he?"

"Not here," Kalina says. "He hasn't been since the first night."

"Really."

"Think he finally had enough."

"Enough of what?"

"Grandma. I heard them arguing, but they weren't yelling. Just a whole bunch of points that contradicted each other. At the end of it all, Grandma asked Grandpa what he wanted to do. He said he was doing it, and the next morning, he was gone."

"How do you know all this?"

Kalina looks down. "I was snooping."

"What did I tell you about that?"

"I know, I know."

He looks toward the sky, allowing a breeze to swirl around them. "You three better get in the house. It's starting to get cold. And I'm headed over to see your mama."

"Can we come?"

"Not yet, Sweetheart. Plus, I'm probably staying at the hospital for the night. It would be tough to manage all four of us on a hospital cot." He smiles but finds his joke hadn't landed.

"I don't mind," Kalina says.

"Neither do I, and I'm sure Amber wouldn't, either," Charles says.

"Listen, guys, I would love nothing more than to hang out with you tonight . . . to have us all together again, and that time is coming. Just not yet."

Both nod in understanding.

"You keep looking out for each other, okay? I'm going to talk to your grandmother for a few minutes. I'll be back in a couple days."

Mark gives hugs to each of his children and heads for the house, where he sees Joanne through the kitchen window, seemingly watching him with the kids. When he makes eye contact, she snaps her head away. Mark gets to the kitchen and stops at the entryway.

"Do you blame me?" he asks.

She gawks at him for a few moments before going to the refrigerator and pulling out a large Tupperware container filled with food. "You hungry?"

"I was going to eat at the hospital."

She frowns and waves off his answer. "Wash your hands. Grab a couple plates." She digs in the refrigerator and pulls out a few more containers.

He quickly washes his hands and grabs two dishes from the plate cabinet. She starts placing food on the two plates in a deliberate manner. Everything is separated; nothing touches or runs into the other foods. Mark smiles.

"Jade preps the same way. Still, to this . . . day."

She smirks. "I got so used to preparing her plates in this way. It never went away." Her smile fades a bit. "She used to hate . . ." She puts down the spoon she had been working with. "She *hates* when gravy, sauce, whatever gets to her bread and makes it all soggy."

"Don't I know it! I remember one time, I made her a sloppy joe."

"You got in trouble, didn't you?"

"Sure did. She looked at me like I was an alien." He chuckles, then pitches his voice up to imitate Jade's voice, "'Mark, Baby, what exactly do you want me to do with this?' and I answered, like an idiot, 'Eat it, I guess.'" He looks down and doesn't say anything. Both stand for an awkward moment of silence, lost deep in their own thoughts.

"I hope you don't mind it being re-heated in the microwave."

He tries to get out of his head. "No . . . no, I don't mind."

A few more minutes of silence and she has two warm plates of food placed on the kitchen table. They sit at opposite ends of the table.

"How are your ribs?" she asks.

"Getting better, I guess. It still hurts like crazy without the meds. Laughing, lifting, sneezing . . . it all hurts still. But I manage." He takes a bite of food. "This is good."

"Thank you." She takes only a bite before moving it around on her plate. "So to answer your question, I do blame you. But I know I shouldn't."

Mark stops eating, as he is losing his appetite rather quickly. He sits up tall because that's the only position that doesn't hurt right now. "Maybe you shouldn't. But I do. I blame myself every morning as I wake up and every night before I go to bed. If I hadn't . . . All I had to do was squash things with Alicia from the moment I saw her . . . I'm sorry."

She looks at Mark for a second and goes back to eating. "I am, too, Mark." She sighs. "It's tough for a mother to see her daughter in the shape Jade is in."

"It's tough for everyone to see Jade that way."

"I suppose it is. So much so, her father collapsed under the pressure."

"What do you mean?"

"He's hurting. He's hurting bad and I don't believe I was the medicine a good wife should be to her husband's soul."

"That's a way of putting it."

"You look at the role of a wife differently?"

"I mean, it isn't the only role, right?"

"Of course not." She fiddles with her fork. "I was too harsh, too abrasive, and I never really considered how he feels. So, he's gone. Where, I don't know. But he's gone . . . maybe for good."

"I hope he'll come back. Everything going on is a lot to take on alone. We all need to support each other."

"So who is supporting you?"

"Pastor Brentwood. I've been meeting with him. There are a lot of things I need to . . . sort through."

"I see."

He wipes his mouth and sets the napkin he used on top of his empty plate. "Thank you so much for the food. I better get going to the hospital." He grabs his plate to place in the dishwasher.

"You can leave everything there. I'll clean up later." She hesitates. "Have the doctors said anything about bringing her closer to home?"

"Yeah. I'm told it's too risky. Her doctor and a few others almost got into a fistfight on whether to transport her or not. At least that is what Dr. Chalmers told me."

Joanne looks down. "Well, you be careful. The trip is long. Just be careful."

He smiles and heads toward the front door, with her following closely behind. She opens the door to show him out.

"Listen, if it isn't too much on you, could you possibly come back tomorrow, or the next day, even?"

"Yeah, sure. I'll run by as often as these ribs permit." He smiles. "I'd better run. Thanks again for the meal."

"Sure thing. Mark?"

"Yes, ma'am."

"We were wrong to think you were wrong for her, to think you were beneath her. I know she must have told you that's what we thought."

"It came up. But no worries." He frowns a little. "You were right." He labors into his car, and after a final smile and wave goodbye, he is off.

◦◦◦

Mark gets to the hospital and heads straight to the elevator. Once he is let off on Jade's floor, he walks for a bit before coming to a nurses' station he knows well. Almost all the nurses recognize him and greet him with smiles. Mindy, his nurse when he was a patient there, smiles and asks him how his ribs are. He gives her an update on how he's feeling. He greets each nurse by name and talks to a few of them, primarily the ones on Jade's team. All the nurses on Jade's team are women. Most are Christian. They all have become counsel of some sort to Mark, guiding him through the finer points of his current situation. He appreciates each one of them.

He gets to Jade's room and Roz, a heavyset woman with kind eyes, opens the door for him.

"I've set up a cot for you, Mark. Bible on the nightstand. You hungry?"

"Thank you, Roz. I ate before I came."

"Well, you let one of us know if you need anything."

"I will. Thank you."

She leaves the room, gently shutting the door behind her. He stands in the middle of the floor, exhausted from his four-hour trek, and shuffles over to Jade's bed.

"Hey, Babe." He grabs the Bible from the nightstand. "Ready for prayer?"

೦೪೮

Jade sits by a fire covered only in a fleece blanket. She stares at the being of fire, who seems to stare back, though she doesn't see eyes with which that is possible.

The being carried her for what seemed to be forever to this particular site, which is really more darkness only slightly illuminated by a simple campfire.

"Thank you for getting me out of there. Whatever that was." She shivers under the blanket. "To be quite honest, I don't know what that was . . . or what this is . . . or what you are."

Again, in a choir of voices, the being responds, "What do we remember?"

"I was . . . I was taken. Taken from my home by a man. I saw his face once. Never seen him before that. But then I was thrown in this dark room, so I never really saw him after that, either. I was in the room for who knows how long and . . ." She stops. "Where am I?"

"We are safe."

"Okay, but where?"

"Safe."

"So this place of darkness is called 'Safe'?"

"There is light."

She pauses and gives a puzzled expression. "The only light is from this fire, from you, and from that dot off in the distance that looks like a star. Other than that, there is no light."

"So is Safe a place of darkness if there's light?"

She stares at the being. "Who are you, again?"

"We are the same."

"We as in me and you?"

"Indeed. Two sides, same coin."

"So wouldn't I know you if you were me? Wouldn't my questioning be redundant?"

"Very few of us know ourselves. You are no exception."

She shivers even more, though the being and the fire are more than enough to keep the surrounding area warm. She gets chills primarily because she's uncomfortable with this being saying it is her, or that they are one and the same. "Why am I here?"

"To be safe. To be saved."

"What if I don't want to be here anymore?

"We may go. But to where?"

She pauses, in thought. "Home."

☙❧

Craig wakes from his nap by the doorbell ringing. He takes a few moments to regain his balance and he stumbles to the doorway. He sees a shadowy figure at the door, and already knows it's Ramses. In an instant, he feels light on his feet. Maybe Ramses is here to tell him it is safe to go home. Maybe he is here to let him know that everyone is safe and in good health, that his friends are doing well, that Berta is waiting for him to come home.

As he steps closer to the door, and as the last remnants of a dream-filled nap fade away, his feet feel heavier. His chest aches somewhat as he opens the door to see a stern-faced Ramses. To most people, his cold stare alone would be intimidating, but Craig has seen him in the courtroom. In the courtroom, Ramses is nothing short of a beast—a beast that even he would fear if he ever had to judicially go against him. But today is a different day. Today, in front of him, Craig sees a surprisingly softer Ramses, which only means his stern face has softer edges.

He moves to the side to let the man in. "Is it good news or bad news?"

Ramses ignores his question and takes in the house. "You know, I haven't been here in years." He smiles at a few of the paintings on the wall. "Had it built for Janice. She grew up on a ranch, so for the most part, she designed the place." He chuckles. "Of course I had some say, but only on the smaller things like granite countertops and the stainless-steel appliances."

Both men walk to a set of stairs. Craig notices that Ramses revels in his memories of the ranch, almost to a point of seeming lost in them.

"She's big on natural light, if you haven't noticed."

"I have. It's very bright in here."

They begin walking up the steps.

"Yeah. If I had it my way, this place would have ended up a lot darker. No skylights. No floor-to-ceiling windows. It probably would have resembled a cave. But Janice wanted the light. She needed the light. She feels the light is important. It's her link to God, she says."

"I see. So where you live now . . . it's pretty open and well lit as well?"

"Nope. And she hates where we live now. She comes back here every spring. Like a retreat for her and God."

"Why are you telling me this?"

"Because I thought you should know why I sent you here. There's something about this place that's . . . healing. I wish I were able to come here more often, but that's beside the point. You need a lot of healing, Craig. You need to reconnect with God."

"You came all this way just to tell me that?"

"Not quite." He puts out his hand. "I need the cell phone. The burner."

"What?"

"The cell I gave you before you left. I need it."

"Sure." Craig pulls the cell from his pocket and hands it to Ramses. "But I don't understand what you ne—"

Ramses slams the phone to the floor, shattering it into pieces.

"I don't get it."

"Patrice Stafford."

That's all Ramses needs to say for Craig to look down. "She's one of my clients."

"Yet, I get the strange feeling you called her for something that wasn't work related."

"I guess."

Ramses shakes his head. "So what of Alberta?"

"What of her? She's divorcing me. I can't get anywhere to contest the divorce . . . what do you mean, 'what about Alberta'? What am I supposed to do?"

"Out of all the people you could have called . . . your current wife to try to patch things up, your friend who you call your best friend— whose wife is in the hospital . . . hell, you could have called me to see how I'm doing, but no, you call Patrice Stafford. Strange, Craig. Really strange. And stupid."

"I know. I—I don't know. I needed someone to talk to and I had her number and . . ."

"You are fond of this woman?"

"I guess. I mean, she's fond of me. And she's good to talk to, even if I can't quite tell her everything."

"Look, your best bet now is to get things straightened out with God. Everything else is showing itself to be a distraction."

"What's with all this God talk now? I never heard you mention God until now."

Ramses motions Craig back downstairs. "Who do you suppose I am?"

"I don't know. Lupo told me you are the game. People fear you."

"Correction: criminals fear me."

"But aren't you one of them?"

"Far from it. Take a seat."

Craig sits in the living room area.

"I go to church every Sunday. I'm on the board for three different charities."

"Sounds like Mr. V." He sniffs. "But that doesn't mean anything. Even Mr. V. fell into his share of dirt."

"He did. He wasn't any less of a good man because of those shortcomings, though."

"What's your point?"

"My point is I don't do the same things Raul has done. I don't own any shady businesses. All my deals are done in the light. What I do is use information from Raul as leverage. I have a lot of information on a lot of people. So all those idiots out there think I gain power through underhanded measures. All I do is keep each of them at bay. Fewer bad things happen that way. Clean and safe streets for my kids."

"I understand."

"That's what man I chose to be." He sits. "The question remains: What man do you choose to be?"

Craig looks perplexed. He knows he's heard that exact question before. "It's a good question. One I thought I had an answer to."

Ramses pulls out another phone and sets it on the coffee table in front of Craig. He gets up. "You're a grown man. I can't tell you what to do, but I've spent my life advising people. My advice to you is to pray, hard. Get right with God again. And stop making it more difficult to protect you."

"I understand, sir. I apologize."

"Not a problem we can't fix." He gets up from his seat. "What did you two talk about, anyway? I'm curious."

Craig shrugs. "Nothing. She never picked up. But we had a few good conversations before. She's easygoing. And she's strong in her ideologies. She's—"

"Just how Alberta was when you met her."

Craig chuckles, but doesn't remove his gaze from a speck on the floor. "I never looked at it like that."

∞

Berta gets to her office building questioning why she is setting foot into the building again. Her first day back, yesterday, was a dull one that seemed to pick right back up where she left things. Angelina was still working diligently at getting Berta fired or getting her to quit. John Bromley was still playing a massive amount of defense. Berta is tired of this dance and is thinking about just letting go and getting a new job. Part of her feels that God has placed her there for a reason, but the reason isn't as clear as it once was.

"Excuse me. Mrs. Barlow."

Just before she gets into the building she turns around to see Simms strolling up to her. "Detective?"

"Please. Call me Logan."

"What can I do for you, Detective?"

"A few questions."

"Again? I thought yesterday was enough. And how do you know where I work? Are you stalking me?"

Simms smiles and starts to speak but no words come out.

"I hope you don't plan on making a habit of this."

"No. Not at all." He shifts his stance. "Do you know a Patrice Stafford?"

"Maybe. Why?"

"We were able to get his phone records from his office, thereby a list of his current clients. Patrice is the most recent addition to his client list."

"So?"

"The timing is interesting. And I wondered . . ." He stops speaking, looking for Berta to ask him to continue. When she doesn't, he continues anyway. "I wondered if she was part of the reason you and Craig are getting divorced."

"What? Detective, I think you are crossing some boundaries."

"I just ask because maybe she would know of his whereabouts, especially if they were . . . intimate."

"Again, you are crossing the line. But as far as I know, they were not intimate."

"Thank you. And what about Angelina Crosby?"

Berta freezes. "What of her?"

"She's your supervisor, right?"

"Your point?"

"Was Craig intimate with her?"

"I don't believe he was. Look, are you going through his supposed list of hoes to see if he's hiding with them?"

"Just doing my job." He looks down. "Do you even know the kinds of things he's wanted for? The kinds of crimes we believe he committed?"

"No. And at this point, I don't care."

"Murder, arson, drug trafficking . . ."

"I thought I told you I don't care."

"I heard you. But I thought you should know."

"Now, let me ask you a question."

"Pardon?"

"I can ask you a question, right? Just one question . . . and I mean that."

He smirks. "I suppose."

"Why are you following me?"

"Oh, that's a simple one." He sticks his hands in his pockets. "You know more than you let on." He turns to walk away. "And until I know what that is, I will continue to show up." He nods. "Have a good day, Mrs. Barlow."

She didn't think about it before, but it occurs to her that when she first met him, he parted calling her "Ms. DeVries."

CHAPTER THREE

Jade walks side by side with the flame being through what seems to be endless darkness, covered by the fleece blanket she's had since the campfire. She feels her bare feet stepping along the cold pools of darkness, but she isn't bothered by it.

"So what can I call you?" she asks.

The fire being answers in what Jade perceives to be gibberish. She asks for the being to repeat.

"Ymen eeht mai."

Somehow, Jade begins to understand and nods. "Interesting name."

They continue walking.

"So what? Is this the scenic route?" She smirks, but turns serious again, realizing her joke didn't land with this mysterious being. She glances over her shoulder to see the star get smaller and smaller. She doesn't understand it, but she feels drawn toward that star.

Yet, she continues to walk away from it.

"What's up with that star? It's the only one out . . . It just looks strange."

"The star leads to a bad place. You wanted to go home. We are going home."

Jade takes one last glance at the star. "How do you know where we are?"

"I can see."

"How?"

"Do you wish to see?"

"I would like to see something other than this darkness, sure."

"The darkness emanates from your heart."

She stops walking. "What are you talking about?"

"The darkness around you proceeds from your heart. In order to see, you must eliminate the darkness of your heart."

"So we have to go to my *heart*? For me to . . . see?"

"Indeed."

She looks down in thought, knowing she must ask the question she feared all along.

"Did I die?"

Without hesitation, the flame being answers, "Yes."

"So what is this? What am I?"

"Do you remember what happens after death?"

Jade sits on the ground, holding herself. She tries to understand everything that's going on, but even more so herself. She died, and she doesn't know what she is now. A spirit? Is she in hell? Heaven? She looks up at the flame being.

"Are you an angel?"

"Yes."

"So this place . . . you called it Safe, but . . . am I safe here?"

"You are safe wherever I am."

"And if I died . . . and it's dark here . . . you're taking me home . . . is that heaven? No, it's dark here because of my heart, right? So . . . going to my heart . . . is that judgment for me? I'm so confused."

"To see, you must get away from star. The star leads to pit of flames. Pit leads to nothingness. But to get to brightness, we must purge away the darkness to see the way."

"What?"

The flame being sticks out its hand. "Allow me to show you."

☙

After another night sleeping on a cot next to Jade's hospital bed, Mark goes home to shower and change his clothes. On the drive back home, he figures he will stop by to see Joanne and the kids. He even decides to suggest she and the kids stay with him. It would allow the kids to be home in their beds again and for him and Joanne to keep each other company. If she will have it, they might even be each other's support like she spoke of yesterday.

He also has a meeting scheduled with Pastor Brentwood today. Part of him dreads the meeting, because he knows he hasn't been entirely open with him. There is much Pastor doesn't know about him. In fact, there's much most people don't know about him. Terrible things. Things he regrets. He's going to try to stay honest, nonetheless.

While getting a quick bite to eat, he hears the doorbell ring and, curious, he answers the door.

"Detective Simms."

"Hello, Mark. You sound none-too-pleased to see me."

"What can I do for you, Detective?"

"Straight to the chase. I get it. Listen, do you have a few minutes to talk?"

"Actually, I don't. I was on my way out."

"Listen to the man."

Mark sees Alicia come up in his peripheral vision.

"He probably has quite a bit to say," she says.

Mark fights the oncoming anxiety and allows Simms in. "Have a seat." His eye twitches and an odd feeling stalks its way into him. He's experienced a certain level of darkness taking over before, a depression of sorts. What he feels now is a new level of dread. He's having trouble focusing as he grabs the edge of the chair for balance.

"Are you okay?" Simms asks.

"Yeah," Mark says, "I'm fine. What do you want to talk about?" He sees Alicia standing in the corner, not saying anything, not looking in his direction.

"A couple things. We have a tricky situation with your friend here, Mark."

Mark jolts. "You see her, too?"

Simms raises an eyebrow. "See her?"

Mark quickly realizes Simms has no idea what he is talking about, but being the detective he is, Simms won't let on and will try to find out more information. "What are you talking about?"

"Craig." Simms leans back in his seat. "We have no idea where he is. His wife doesn't, either. At least that's what she says. Do you?"

"No. He didn't tell me much of anything before he left. Just that he had to leave. Business trip. I think he was trying to grow his company." *Bald-faced lie.*

"Trying to grow a company at a time like this? With his closest people going through hell, and his wife filing for divorce?"

Mark shrugs, but not without paying for it. Pain reaches around his entire abdomen. "Why are you looking for him?"

"I think you know why."

"I don't. Craig and I are great friends. He's my brother, basically. When he got home from jail, he turned his life around. I know he hasn't done anything to warrant police investigation." *Another bald-faced lie.*

"If only that were true. Have you talked to him recently?"

"No, I haven't. What's the tricky situation?"

"Well, it's simple. The longer he stays on this *business trip,* the more time he's looking at."

"Time? Time for what?"

"We have him linked to a few of our unsolved cases, and linked to a few more that were closed but were confusing."

"Linked?"

"Then there's your case. The brother of the dead man at the garage explicitly describes Craig as the killer."

Mark winces in pain. He looks around for his painkillers. "I see. Well, I haven't spoken to him. Is that all you needed?"

"Unfortunately not." He sits up straight in his seat. "You sure you're okay?"

"I said I'm fine. What else do you need?"

"Do you know of any places he may stay? Places outside of his normal home that he would presume to be safe?"

"No. I can't think of anywhere." He looks at Simms straight-faced.

"Okay. Listen, what I have to say next is sensitive information in a way. I'm not exactly sure how to tell you, but we scoured over every detail to make sure."

"Just tell me, Simms. Just another hammer to drop, right?"

Simms looks stumped for a moment. "Again, the main reason for my visit is to divulge a bit of information to you. There's not much I can say . . ." He pulls his wallet from his coat pocket and pulls out a card. "You remember when I told you Alicia was trying to ruin you?"

Mark tenses up. "I do."

Simms stares at Mark while sliding a shiny card onto the coffee table in front of him. "This was in your pocket when you first were taken to the hospital."

Mark snaps the card up from the table and scans what he determines to be a driver's license. He looks at it once, but isn't able to process what he sees. He looks up at the corner to see Alicia storm out the room. He looks back at the license.

"That's impossible," Mark says.

"I'm sorry, Mark. The coroner ran tests. We tracked history. It is the truth."

"I saw him, Simms. I saw him when we were . . ." He gets agitated. "You ought to do some more digging because this"—he waves the license—"*this* is a fake. Some kid's prank."

"Mark, it all adds up. I would have told you sooner, but we wanted to make sure."

"Okay, okay, slow this down. How did I get this?" His breathing becomes more labored.

"It was in your jeans pocket when we found you in the Langley house."

"So what does this mean?"

"Well, it means your brother was alive."

"No."

"He was the officer you tangled with at the mansion."

"The one lying twisted at the bottom of the stairs?"

Simms nods.

"So . . . I killed . . . my brother?"

"I'm sorry, Mark. From what we can tell, Alicia tracked him down and they worked . . . together."

"Against me? Why would he want to hurt me?"

Simms remains still. "Mark, are you here by yourself?"

Mark doesn't answer.

"Mark? It's probably not a good idea for you to be by yourself."

Mark's hand trembles. "There's no one."

"Well, if you don't mind, I'd like to sit with you for a bit."

"Not necessary."

"I know."

Mark looks at the license of his deceased brother. He places the card on the table, but doesn't remove his eyes from it. "I really have no idea where Craig is."

Simms nods. "I know."

"Tell me what you know . . . about my brother. Tell me what you know."

⚜

It's two in the morning, and Berta snaps up from her sleep. Another bad dream. It seems to be the norm for her now to wake up in a cold sweat and not get back to sleep until it's time to go to work. For the past week, she's been working off of three or four hours of sleep a night. She knows she can't keep going the way she is, but she doesn't know what else to do. She consistently tells herself to get up. She tells herself to get up out of this ditch she finds herself in. But divorce is usually not easy. And her divorce from Craig carries much baggage.

She walks to the bathroom and grabs a washcloth to run it under water and wipe the drops of sweat from her forehead. She stares at herself in the mirror. She observes the bags under her eyes, and the fact that she can even see the sadness behind them. She tries to tell herself she is worth something, but the pervasive thought in her mind is that she is far from priceless. She sets the washcloth down and sits on the edge of the tub. She starts up a few times to pray, but finds her attempts to be futile. She doesn't feel like praying. She doesn't feel like doing anything. Rather, she wants to curl up into a ball and die. Life isn't worth the struggle, the consistent battle. She shakes her head, trying to shake away the negative thoughts, to no avail.

A tear traces down her face, and before she realizes it, she is sobbing. Her sobs come out soft at first but increase in intensity as time goes on. Her movements are reminiscent of a boxer in a fight who's losing, the sobs rack her body so hard. She falls to the floor and curls up into a ball. She kicks the wall a few times, being so tired of crying, but she cannot stop the tears from falling. She cannot stop the sobs from violently jerking her body around. She kicks the wall again and hurts her heel. She stops and lets the throbbing pain in her heel radiate throughout her leg. Her sobs eventually subside, but the tears keep falling until she falls asleep on the bathroom floor.

⊂⊃

A round of loud knocks on the door coupled with rapid ringing of the doorbell wakes her from her uncomfortable sleep. Berta peels her face from the bathroom floor and stumbles to the bedroom. She glances at the clock to see she is four hours late for work. She finally gets to the door and groans when she sees who it is through the peephole.

"What do you want?" Her voice comes out groggy.

"We need to talk, Mrs. Barlow. It's important."

"I have nothing to say to you, Logan. Why are you at my home?"

"You're not at work today."

She sighs and starts to unlock the door. "You get five minutes. Nothing more. I need to get to work."

Simms enters the home with a smirk on his face.

"What's so funny?"

"You called me Logan."

"I'm half asleep. What do you want, *Detective?*"

"I need you to be honest with me."

"Okay." She turns to walk to the bedroom. She limps a bit. "I need to get ready for work."

"Is everything fine?"

"What do you think?"

"No. I mean your walk. You're limping." He walks over to her and grabs her hand.

"What are you—" She pulls her hand away and faces him. Both stare at each other for a few seconds.

"I'm sorry. Please, just sit down."

Berta eyes him curiously. She relents and takes a seat.

"What hurts?"

"What?"

"What hurts?"

"My—my heel."

"How did you hurt it?"

"Kicked the wall."

"Why would you do that?" He kneels in front of her and grabs her foot. He pokes around her heel.

She winces. "It doesn't matter." She jerks her foot away from him. "What do you need now?"

"Are you taking care of yourself?"

"Is that what you are here for? To check up on me?"

"Yes. No. I have more questions, but this is more pressing."

"More pressing than arresting my so-called criminal ex-husband?"

Simms stays in his kneeling position. They have another stare off.

Simms sighs. "Do you know where Craig is?"

"You asked me this before. My answer is the same. I have no idea."

"Are you positive? Do you have any idea on where he would go? Who he would go to for help?"

"None," she says in an annoyed tone.

"We are getting closer to linking him to some of these cases." He stands. "If we find that you had key information, we could—"

"What? Arrest me?" She puts her wrists out in front of him.

"This isn't a joking matter."

"Look, I've told you what little I know. There's nothing else for me to say to you." She stands and limps to her door. "You may leave now. And please do not come back. If you are finding it difficult to track some of this stuff to him, maybe he didn't do it."

Simms stares at her, but she can't tell if it is in anger or admiration.

"Why do you protect him?" he asks.

"I'm not. I want to be rid of him."

"I'm sure." He walks out the door. "Until next time, Alberta."

Berta shuts the door, angered by the way Simms said her name, though she didn't correct him at all. She makes a quick phone call to her job and explains an emergency came up, and that she is sorry. She assures Mr. Bromley that she will be in tomorrow. With haste, she gets dressed and leaves her home. She has a feeling that Simms is following her wherever she goes. In fact, she's hoping for it.

CS80

It doesn't take long for Berta to get to Lockram, Ramses, & Peterson. Getting a few minutes to talk to Mr. Ramses might prove to be a different story, but that doesn't bother her. She will wait all day if she has to. With this day being an off-from-work day, she has a sense of freedom she hasn't felt in some time. She considers this on a deeper level. She still doesn't have to work, and as time goes on, she finds it more difficult to do so. She has more than enough money in the bank just from what Raul left her. And she could make a little more from the business . . . the same business she and Craig grew when they took over. Craig would have to buy her out and rebuild. That's if he comes back.

Though, the money from both sources combined would be enough to retire on. She sometimes wonders now where the stacks of money came from, the money Raul left for her. She wonders if it was all from advising or if it came from other, more underhanded means. Maybe some of that money came from the graves of a bunch of innocent dead people. She shakes away the thought. Fortunately, it doesn't take as long to get to Mr. Ramses as she anticipated. He comes to get her personally and leads her to his office.

"I hope this is a better visit, my sweet," he says.

"We'll see. I need you to be honest with me, though."

"I always am."

Berta scrunches her face, though he doesn't see it.

"What can I do for you?" He asks.

Both sit by a window in his office on a cozy sofa. He offers her a drink, but she declines.

"Where is Craig?"

Ramses stares at her and smiles, a genuine one from what she can tell. She still doesn't like it, though.

"I'm sorry, Alberta, I cannot tell you that."

"But you know where he is, correct? He came to you to fix things for him, right? Or am I mistaken?"

"Did he tell you this?"

"No one did. It's obvious to me. You cleaned up things for Raul . . . you were basically commissioned to keep an eye on us . . . he got into trouble . . . you clean up his mess."

Ramses folds his hands and places them atop a crossed leg. "Okay. You surmised correctly. But I still cannot tell you where he is. Not yet." He gets up and walks to the window. "Is that detective bothering you?"

"Maybe. It depends on what you mean by 'bother.'"

"He's following you wherever you go." He chuckles. "Detective Logan Simms. Real big on justice . . . at least that is the way he wants to be seen. He's known for taking down the big guys. He's a supercop to some." He looks at Berta. "But he's anything but. You see, it's a funny thing, trying to take down a man with a past . . . especially when you have your own."

She feels somewhat guilty under his gaze.

"The moment he becomes too much to deal with, let us know."

"What exactly are you doing?"

"Cleaning up messes. Isn't that what you said I do?"

"Yeah, but . . ."

"We're cleaning up these cases they think they can link Craig to, including this most recent thing . . . that's so no one decides to pick up the mantle after we remove the detective from the picture."

"You're going to kill him?" Berta says, fearful.

"No. We are not criminals. We uphold the law, well, as good as lawyers can, really." He chuckles. "But no, we are not some thugs over here. He's going to bow out voluntarily once he hits all the dead ends. Which reminds me . . . I need you to walk out of this building with your divorce attorney. Go to the steakhouse down the street. The detective will think this is nothing more than a simple meeting to clean Craig out. Don't look his way."

"He's out there now?"

"I'm staring right at him. He drives a black sedan. No one really notices it; it blends very well."

"Fine. But I'm not ready to leave yet."

"What do you need?"

"I want to talk to him. Craig. I . . . want to talk to him."

"That can be arranged." He walks over to his desk and pulls out a cell phone. "I meant to tell you I talked to Izabel recently."

"Oh?"

"She's hoping for you to talk to her again."

"Are you going to start campaigning for her?"

"No. That's not it at all. I just know out of all the things that happened, she's probably the last to blame. You both are victims of some terrible circumstances. You should be leaning on each other for support rather than ignoring each other."

"I didn't ask for advice on this."

"But that's what I do. I advise. I clean up messes. I make things better for people." He sits at his desk. "But I digress. That CD you have from Marcy."

"She told you about that?"

"She told me a lot. But that CD; I hope you have it somewhere safe. Especially with the detective snooping around."

"I do."

"You should destroy it. Or give it to me and I'll destroy it. Either way, it shouldn't be in existence."

Berta glares at him. "Noted. Can you get me in contact with Craig now?"

"Ringing now," he says as he hands her the old-looking cell phone.

⋈

Craig is unable to move around the ranch house without noticing the beams of light shining in every direction. Ever since Ramses visited him, he's gone into this deep introspective mode, thinking about what type of man he wants to be, and what type of man God would have him be.

He thinks on how beautiful it is outside and decides to take a stroll. He knows he is supposed to keep a low profile, but if he doesn't get some more fresh air soon, he is sure to go crazy. Plus, he refuses to be cooped up in the house just because he is on the run. It's like being trapped in a box of his own sin. He steps outside and hears birds chirping. He smirks and then remembers the produce stand just a ways down the road. He checks his pockets for cash and starts on his way.

By the time he gets to the produce stand, he doesn't feel as energetic as he once did. He remembers a time when he could run two miles in thirteen minutes. It took him twenty-five minutes to get to the produce stand. He knows he should work out again, because he finds his performance on this walk unacceptable. He gets there, slightly out of breath, to find a small line in front of the stand. He looks to the opposite side of the dirt road to find cars parked. He stands in line observing the young woman running the produce stand. After staring at her for a little more, he realizes she isn't as young as he initially thought. The slight bags under her eyes and the slight wrinkles at the corners of them lead Craig to believe she is in her late thirties, maybe early forties. With each customer she serves, he notices another thing about her. When it is finally his turn, he simply waits for the petite woman to speak. He smiles in anticipation.

"Afternoon," she says.

Craig exhales. He can only stare for the time being.

"Sir, are you okay?"

"Yes, I am. Sorry. I"—he clears his throat—"I was looking to pick up a few apples and—"

"A few cucumbers?"

"Yes. I suppose you remember me?"

"The only one without a car on this road, yes."

"I guess it looks weird, huh?"

She nods and smiles.

"Well, yes, I would like a few cucumbers as well." He smiles. "I walk because I'm not that far away from here. I like the fresh air, well, the non-dusty parts."

She chuckles.

"So are all of these homegrown?"

"Sure are."

"And you travel how far? Because I see nothing but more dusty roads in the distance in every direction."

"I'm from town. You've never been?"

He shakes his head.

"Where are you from, exactly? I've noticed you have a strange accent," she says.

"I'm not from Texas. Actually, I'm along the East Coast, not too far from Virginia."

She waits for him to elaborate, but when Craig doesn't say any more, she nods and starts for the cucumbers.

"I . . ." He tries to find something else to say, just to change the subject, but decides to remain quiet.

She grabs a few cucumbers and Craig pays her for the food. "Thank you, Miss—"

"Addison." She sticks out her hand. "Addie for short."

"Thank you, Addie. I'll see you around."

"See you around." She grabs a few crates and stacks them on the back of a pickup truck.

He starts on his way when she says, "You never told me your name."

"Craig." He fears it is a mistake to tell this mystery woman his real name. He smiles and begins his trek back to the ranch.

A few moments later, he hears a truck starting, then stalling. He stops walking and looks back to observe Addie having trouble with her truck. She hops out and opens the hood. Craig starts on his way back to her to make sure everything is okay.

"Everything good?"

"Stupid truck is dead. My fault for squeezing the last little bit out of it."

Craig looks at the truck. "Look, I know nothing about vehicles and fixing them up. But I can grab—I can get my truck and help you out."

"You don't have to."

"I insist."

And just like that, Craig is off running down the dusty road back toward the ranch.

By the time he gets back to the ranch, he is gasping for air and drenched in sweat, but he throws his veggies on the kitchen counter and heads straight for the garage. Once there, he looks over the four vehicles Ramses has parked and picks the oldest-looking one, a Jeep Grand Cherokee that seems to be from the 90s. He walks around the garage looking for a key but realizes each of the vehicles has keys in them.

He hops into the truck but stops. *What am I doing?* He rests his hand on the steering wheel and catches his breath, taking a few more moments to think. He's definitely exposing himself way too much now. This woman Addie already has his name. Now, he's risking more exposure by helping her get to town. Wherever that is. Ramses told him to stay put, but he feels the need to help. She needs his help. Still, he exits the car and slams the door shut. He can't risk the detective tracking him. He's already shown enough. He takes a deep breath to calm himself, but the more he tries to calm himself, the more his stomach twists and ties in knots. He simply cannot leave her stranded.

◌◌

It only takes a few minutes for him to drive down to where Addie is, and when he pulls up, she smiles. He hops out the truck.

"You really don't have to do this, really. I can get the truck working again."

"Nah. By the time that happens, the rest of your goods will go. Plus, it's no big deal. I want to help."

She hesitates, but eventually starts pulling crates from her pickup and sliding them into the back of the Jeep. Craig grabs a few and places them in as well. Once everything is loaded up, they get in.

"So, given I know nothing around here, you're gonna have to direct me a bit."

"How good are you at following directions?"

"I'm okay, I guess. Why? A lot of twists and turns?"

"Well, here's how you get to town . . . you go straight."

"Okay. Then what?"

She laughs. "That it. It's just a straight shot for about fifteen miles or so."

"No stops or anything?"

"Nope. Just one long road and croplands on both sides."

He smiles. "I think I can handle that. Maybe."

"Thank you for doing this. I appreciate it."

"It's my pleasure. Plus, I get to see this town you talk of."

"It's wonderful . . . and I don't say that because I live there." She looks over to him and smiles. "Many of the town folk have been there for years."

After another fifteen minutes of driving, Craig notices the roads go from dusty to concrete and he drives past a sign saying, "Welcome to Silver Rock." He slows down.

"So is this town?"

Addie nods.

"Where to?"

"Hang a right." She seems to be preoccupied with something.

As he drives around, the first thing he notices is the diversity. People of all types move about their daily lives in a cohesive manner. He sees a bunch of shops, all looking like the classic mom-and-pop shops.

"Keep straight and then go around the circle."

"Ah. There's the silver rock."

In the middle of a traffic circle sits a giant silver rock. Once he drives around the rock, he sees a residential area. Just on the edge of the residential section, a tall church stands. The sun shines from behind the top of the church and leaves a shadow of the cross on the street. He looks at Addie to see her staring out the window.

"Hey. Everything good?"

She blinks a few times and her mood picks up again. "Yes. I'm sorry. Just thinking. You know, I didn't think you were actually coming back. I don't know why. I just . . . this is very nice of you."

"It is my pleasure to help."

"I'm the third house on the left."

Craig drives down a street filled with cottage-like houses, each on its own small plot of land. He pulls up to where Addie lives. Addie hops out and pops open the back to start pulling out the crates and the stand parts. Craig moves around the back to help her.

"I just need to get the things out of the truck. I can take them in the house."

"Okay. Not a problem. You going to set up shop tomorrow?"

"Sure am."

"You need a ride?"

"No. I can't ask you to do that. I know someone who will help me get my truck fixed up. I'll get on that tomorrow. Thank you again, Craig."

Craig eyes her a bit more before nodding and starting for the truck. "Sure. Not a problem. You be safe, Addie."

❈

Craig drives back to the ranch with an uplifted spirit. He barely remembers the drive itself, but he remembers the great feeling of helping someone. He takes a deep breath. There are still some things he has to face, and he doesn't know if things are ever going to work for him and Berta. At the very least, he feels himself being renewed. He looks on the counter in the kitchen where he left his apples and cucumbers to see his "super-secret" phone.

The screen lights up, showing three missed calls.

CHAPTER FOUR

She thinks she's crazy, or a sellout, or something worse. Berta gets back to her home on the verge of tears again, but maintains her composure. She sits on the couch, trying to stop herself from trembling. *What have I done?* She holds herself as the tears begin to flow.

After the three attempts at contacting Craig, she left Ramses' office feeling dejected, though her initial reasoning for showing up there had little to do with wanting to speak with Craig. After the failed attempts, she left the building with her divorce attorney to have lunch, as Ramses requested. She knew Simms had followed her and she easily spotted his car. The black Honda Accord had the tinted passenger window rolled down. She stared him in the eyes, looked away, then made eye contact again. She then looked back at the building from where she came. By that time, her attorney asked her a question she didn't hear at all, so she asked him to elaborate a bit, and they continued the conversation.

She buries her face in the palms of her hands.

"Lord," she calls as an attempt to pray. "I am a terrible human being."

Her phone rings. After a few rings she grabs it.

"I know you said you didn't love me anymore, but this?"

Her breath catches in her throat. She trembles even more.

"I don't have much time here, but I talked to Ramses. You want me to go away? You hate me that much?"

"What are you talking about?"

"Don't play games. You led supercop to Ramses because you knew he was the only one who could clean this stuff up for me."

"And."

Craig chuckles. "I'm amazed at you. You know Ramses can crush that guy, easily. Hell, I'm nowhere in the area and I could crush that guy."

"Then why are you running?"

"Because contrary to what you think, I am not that guy. I am not the guy who just crushes people who get in my way."

"That's what Raul, the monster, and Ramses said, too."

"So, are you my enemy now? Is that it? We're enemies? You want to see me go to jail for the rest of my life?"

"No." She sighs, exasperated. "I don't want to see that. I . . . I just know right is right and wrong is wrong."

"But what's right in this situation? You think it's right for me to go to prison for things I didn't do . . . again? Did you even look into what they're trying to pin on me?" He chuckles. "I bet you didn't."

She doesn't know what to say.

"Look, I have to go. I'll talk to you whenever I do, I guess."

And just like that, he hangs up, leaving her there speechless. She realizes Ramses saw right through her stupid attempt to help Simms. She believed she was right in helping, because what Craig has done has crossed the line. But then, there is still the question of what Craig *did* do. What exactly is Simms after Craig for? She kneels by her window.

"Lord, I am a terrible human being."

⋇

Mark sits in the same spot Simms left him in last night. Every hour or so, he would try to go to sleep, but would see flashes of his brother. He would immediately wake up.

He stares out into space. "Alicia."

Alicia comes out, but stands at the opposite end of the room.

"Let me explain. Please."

"How did you find him? How did you know he was still alive?"

She doesn't say anything.

"You wanted to explain. Go ahead."

She still remains quiet. He labors out of his seat and shuffles toward her until he is face to face with her.

"I'm sorry," she says. "I know it is going to be tough. I know. But you have to find a way to forgive me."

He looks away from her. "I hate you. I hate you with every part of my soul. And . . ." He turns back around and shuffles back to his seat. "Is there any more?"

"You and I both know there's more. There's a lot more."

Mark sits back in the seat and stares off into space.

The doorbell rings, snapping Mark out of his daze. He doesn't know when he blanked out; he just knows he must have sat in that chair for hours, just staring. He slowly gets up, letting his body adjust to finally standing up again. The pain shooting around his ribcage is almost unbearable, but he doesn't take any of his medication for it. By the time he reaches the door, he sees Pastor Brentwood turning away. Mark hesitates, but winds up opening his front door.

"Is everything okay, Mark?"

"I'm sorry. Something came up and . . ."

"We had a meeting scheduled for today, I believe."

"We did. I know. I apologize. I . . ."

"Do you need some help?"

"Sir, I don't know how much more I can take. I . . . I don't want to be here anymore." He doesn't know why he just said that, but saying it strangely makes him feel a little better.

"Here? Here in the house?"

"No. Here . . . alive."

"Mark, may I come in?"

"Of course."

Mark lets the man into his home.

"Sit. We pray, talk, and pray some more. Times like this you have to stay connected. You need to—"

"Have hope? Have faith? I'm out of both. Do you think Jade is going to recover? I don't. You think I'm going to have my sanity if she does? I don't."

"You can't let this beat you, Mark."

"Sir, I killed my brother." Mark tries to laugh away some of the pain, but his laughs come out sounding like cackles and slowly turn to sobs.

Pastor Brentwood allows Mark a few moments to calm. "I don't think I follow. Your brother was killed when you were younger, right?"

Mark shakes his head and grabs the license off the coffee table. He hands it to Pastor Brentwood. Mark notices his expression change.

"Dear God. Is this a joke?"

Mark shakes his head again.

"How?"

"The detective thinks Alicia was initially looking for my parents . . . and she stumbled on his info. But there's no way of really knowing . . . because she isn't here to say." Mark isn't so convinced of the second part. "I never looked for him. Not once. I always assumed he was dead. But I never looked to confirm that. I just accepted it and kept life moving."

"But you were a child when it happened."

"Yet, how many time have we as children remembered an event as one thing, though in reality it happened a completely different way?"

Pastor looks down. "Dear God. Dear God."

"I've been sitting here thinking. He had a child. He was a respected officer. It doesn't make sense for him to be a part of this . . . this whole thing of kidnapping Jade. We fought. He was trying to kill me. He had to have known it was me, right?"

Pastor continues to eye the license. "I don't know."

Mark scratches his head. "She wanted to destroy me. She plotted and planned for years . . ." He stares at Pastor with a fierce determination. "I have to find out what else she's done. We will never be safe."

"Mark, she isn't alive anymore. She can't do any harm. The police have dug into every possible angle. Isn't that what the detective told you? It's done."

"It's not done. I still see her."

"I know you may think she is—"

"No. I literally still see her. She is sitting on the couch now. Say hi."

"Hello, Pastor," Alicia says.

Pastor turns around and turns back to face Mark. "Mark, I think . . . I think we should slow this down a little."

He bites his bottom lip until it stings for him to stop. "You clearly don't see her. Do you?"

Pastor looks at him blankly. Mark looks down at his feet, seemingly in deep thought. He shakes his head.

"I have a massive headache. I didn't get any sleep last night. You think we can postpone our session?"

"Sure, Mark. Whatever you need. We should pray before I leave."

Mark nods.

"And you should really have someone here with you. Your ribs still hurt?"

"Even more so now. I stopped taking my medication. Too easy to get hooked. Don't want that. Thought . . ."

"I understand. Joanne mentioned to me that she wants to help. Maybe she's a good person to call."

"I will, sir." He holds in another wave of sorrow before continuing. "The detective reviewed every angle, you said?"

Pastor nods while looking at him strangely.

"I think I need to talk to him again."

☾☽

Jade eventually sheds the fleece blanket on her way to what the flame angel calls her "heart." She looks over at the flame angel often, but the being doesn't respond. In the distance, Jade finally sees something other than darkness. The two come up to a small lamp post that holds a small, dimly lit lantern. They stop at the post. The flame being points in the distance.

"We are almost there."

"Almost? I still see nothing."

"Just stay near me. You will see soon."

It only takes a few more minutes of walking before she sees a large shadow of a building. They get to a large metallic-looking door. The front of the door glistens as if it is wet.

"The outside of this place looks like a prison. This is my heart?"

"It is."

"So what do we do now?"

53

"We go in." The flame angel moves to press on the door. After a few seconds, it seems to lean into it a bit more, but the door doesn't budge.

Jade gets the feeling something isn't right. "Are you sure this is my heart? I mean, this sounds a bit weird, anyway. Though, all of this is a bit weird, but still. Maybe you have the wrong . . . heart."

She hears something in the distance. The flame angel places a firm hand on her belly to move her behind itself, such that her back is flat against the large metal door.

"What is it?"

The flame angel says nothing, but stares out into the total darkness. Jade faintly hears more noise accompanied by talking. The longer they wait, the more Jade can make out what is being said.

"Messengers," the flame angel says.

She listens a bit more to hear whispers and screams, all mixing into a chorus of obscenities. She looks as the flame being's light diminishes a bit.

"What are they?"

"Messengers. They bring the dead one."

A chill goes up and down her spine. "What do they want?"

"You." The flame angel presses her into the door. "You need to get us in."

"How? I can't move this door if you can't."

"Incorrect. You are the only one who can move this door."

The flame angel steps forward as its light diminishes even more. A loud squeal slices through the air before the entirety of the flame angel is consumed by darkness. Fear grips her as she is no longer able to see. She feels around the door and begins to push it open. To her surprise, she gets it open a crack, as she feels a rush of warm air breezing through. She pushes it open enough for her to slide in. She calls for the flame angel a few times before it comes crawling to the door. Jade slides back out to help the flame angel to the door. Just as she pushes it in, she feels a clawing at her leg. She screams and leaps for the partially open door. She gets in and pushes the door closed, still hearing the obscenities being shouted in the air. She then hears clawing at the door, and backs away. She tends to the flame angel, who lies on the ground.

"Are you okay?"

"I will be." It points toward the door. "A lantern. Grab it."

She looks to the large metallic door again, somewhat hesitant to step near it. Next to it she sees an extinguished lantern. She rushes to grab it and brings it back to the flame angel. It grabs the lantern and places a balled fist inside it. For a few moments nothing happens, until a bright light appears inside the lantern.

"There are more. Light them. This gets rid of the darkness of your heart."

"What about you?"

"I will catch up."

She looks for a few seconds before standing tall and starting down the dark corridor. She is able to get some faint light aimed at the wall to see a metal gate, like those outside a prison cell. She moves toward a cell, realizing she is in exactly what she said the place looked like.

A prison. Her heart, from which darkness emanates, is a prison.

⋘⋙

Craig sits outside with a blanket protecting him from the morning chill, watching the sunrise. He didn't get much sleep last night, his thoughts of Berta keeping his mind going. He just finds it difficult to wrap his brain around how easy it seemed for Berta to flat give up on him . . . on them. He takes a quick sip of his still-steaming hot coffee.

Part of him feels betrayed. When he called Ramses back, he had hoped for some good news, as that is how all their calls start. Craig has high hopes to come home; Ramses dashes those hopes with news of nothing going on. But this time was different. And he began to soar when Ramses told him that Berta was trying to get in contact with him. He didn't think for one second that something negative could come from her wanting to speak with him. After all, she said she didn't want to be near him or in any way associated with him. Why else would she call? Then, even harder than before, Ramses crushes his hopes, by explaining how Berta possibly pointed the detective in his direction. At first, he was incensed. He couldn't believe she would do such a thing. He took a few hours to calm down, then had Ramses get him in contact with her. Hearing her speak, and hearing the arrogance in her tone made him even madder.

Even as he thinks about it now, he feels his blood pressure rise. He closes his eyes and breathes some semi-cool air into his lungs, allowing the growing rays of sunlight warm his face. His mind drifts back to a time when he was still trying to make ends meet. He thought of himself as a broken man then. For reasons past his understanding, he vividly remembers a conversation he had with Raul Valencia. At the time, he was just getting into some of the shady underdealings Raul and Berta's biological father were a part of.

"What are you doing?" he said.

"What do you mean? I'm making a living for myself. This is the way the world works. Eat or be eaten."

"I know I must have said that a thousand times. But, what if I was wrong?"

"What do you mean?"

Raul smiled. "What if there is more to life than . . . eating? Think about it . . . I'm full . . . yet, I'm not."

"What's with the riddled talk?"

"Craig, I need you to get out of the game. Whatever it is you think you are playing, I assure you it is not."

"That's not what Mr. Morgan says."

"Mr. Morgan?"

Craig remembers how he felt then. He remembers the beads of sweat forming on his back under his silk French cuff dress shirt.

"Yeah," Craig said, "Mr. Morgan."

"Mr. Morgan, huh?" An expression of realization forms on his face. "Look. Let me tell you about Mr. Morgan . . ." His voice was strained and angry. "He's a gutless, coward of a human being who will go down as one of the biggest jokes in history. He is not a man. He's an egotistical prick. He—"

"—is your friend . . . So I was told."

"A business acquaintance from long ago. Nothing more. And what he has done to Alberta . . ."

"What has he done to Berta?"

Raul smiled. "Mr. Morgan is Mr. DeVries. Courtland DeVries."

"Oh my God, Berta's weirdo father?"

Raul nodded. "And he had you with something as simple as a fake name. One he's used many a time, in fact. That's why you aren't cut out for this. Truthfully, I'm not cut out for this anymore."

Craig remembers the bile rising up into his throat and the feeling he had. It was as if he betrayed Berta, and that wasn't his intent at all.

"*Sir, I will cut all communication.*" He stepped back a few steps. "*But I have to ask. How did you . . . How did you know? She asks all the time.*"

At the time, Raul was getting sicker so his movements were slow and labored, but he still found a way to get around. Most of the time it was with Craig's help. When Craig wasn't helping him around, Raul had a cane to manage.

Raul walked over to the window and stared out at the cityscape; a cityscape that changed over the years. "She was part of a scheme your newfound friend was starting up."
"*And?*"
"*And I bought her.*"

Craig remembers how shocked he was.

"*You mean—*"
"*I mean Courtland was involved in a sex-trafficking ring . . . and Alberta was to be his first major sale. I put up a large sum of money to subvert that and ensure her safety.*"
"*Why haven't you told her?*"
"*Because it would devastate her.*" He stared a hole right into Craig. "*And I expect you to keep this to yourself as well. She deserves a life where she doesn't have to worry about things like this.*"
"*Yes sir.*"
"*Plus, she can never find out what I was. I won't be able to take it if she saw me as . . . the same type of scum.*" He sat at his desk. "*You

see, Craig, we were nothing more than criminals . . . and we each have a set of things to answer for. I'm trying to make things right . . . but I'm running out of time."

"Sir, if I may . . . why don't I keep in contact with the scum. Maybe I can find a way to turn things on him."

"You can't. And it would be a waste of your time. Focus on improving yourself." He rested his hand on the top part of his cane. "Craig, what kind of man do you want to be?"

He considered the question. "I don't know, sir."

Now Craig understands a bit where Ramses' line of questioning came from, and why it sounded so familiar. He's convinced that Raul asked the very same question of him . . . maybe even the other way around. But he ponders for a few more moments and understands why he thought of that particular time.

That conversation changed his life.

As one of the last few conversations he had with Mr. Valencia before he died, that particular conversation ended with him doing a bit of soul searching. He decided on expanding the business he would eventually take over. He set aside the hustle. He set aside hurting people. He cut all communication with Berta's disgusting father. He decided it was time to settle down, but not with just any female. He needed the one. Many things changed for him after that conversation. Remembering that conversation changes things within himself now.

Berta isn't at fault, he figures. She is and was the victim. Truthfully, if justice were served, Craig would be in jail, locked away for life. He knows that now. He examines who he is, and figures Berta would be better off without him. He understands her actions much more now, for he believes she knows the same thing. He squints at the sun. Half of him says he's scared, and he knows he can't go back home. The other half says he should turn himself in.

Because he deserves it.

CHAPTER FIVE

Jade shuffles across the dusty concrete, her immediate area illuminated only by the lit lantern that she holds to the side and slightly behind her body. She passes a number of cells on her left and right, none of them with anyone in them as far as she can tell. She finally sees another lantern on the wall in between two cells. She gallops to it and quickly starts a small flame in the dormant lantern.

"One down."

As she turns to continue on her trek, out of the corner of her eye, she sees some movement in the cell. She takes her lantern and tries to illuminate the inside, but finds the lantern not strong enough to brighten the corners of the small space. She stands in place a bit longer because that is exactly where she thought she had seen movement.

"Are you just going to stare, Child, or are you going to let me out?"

Jade instinctively steps back. A dark figure moves toward the bars, stepping into the dim light.

"Mama?"

The once-soft-looking woman places her hands around two of the bars of the cell door. Jade notices the different cuts and bruises on her knuckles. She takes a step closer to the bars and brings the light to her mother's face. Her eyes look sad.

"Mama, why are you here?"

"Can you get me out? Please, get me out."

"I don't know what to do."

"There's an upper level. It has access to—wait. Where are your clothes?"

"I d—"

"How many times do I have to tell you?" Her voice shifts. "How many times? How many times?" She repeats herself a few more times. Each time, her voice goes deeper and deeper. "I told you, I always tell you. Stop looking like a little whore. Just like these little skanks in the streets. What is Kalina going to learn from you? How to be a slut. There it is. She's is going to be a slut, or a crackhead like her real mother, who's probably dead, by the way . . ." She continues to mutter. "Poor child. She will never learn anything good from her real mother, and she will learn nothing good from her fake mother, either. And to marry that man . . ."

Jade stands at the cell, horrified. "Where's Daddy?"

"HE'S GONE. But he will be back. Oh, and when he comes back . . ."

Jade slowly backs away from the cell and turns to walk away.

"Where are you going? You better be going to the room to get me out of here."

Jade ignores her and keeps walking. She hears her mother's screams down the hall. Eventually, her walking turns into running. Oncoming tears sting her eyes as she comes up on a speaker, the kind set up for PA systems. She faintly hears sounds from it that sound like more than static. She hears words, but none of them makes sense. She tries to make out the words, but finds them to be in another language . . . but she somewhat understands a few words. She passes the PA speaker and urgently tracks down the next lantern. When she gets to it, it doesn't take long for her to recognize the someone in the cell.

"Mark?"

ⳇ

Berta gets to a worn-looking door inside an apartment complex, thinking about simply sliding the package she wishes to deliver under the door and leaving. She decides against that idea simply because she feels in her gut that her anger shouldn't be directed at her mother. Part of her feels embarrassed for being so angry with her in the first place.

She knocks on the door. It takes a few moments but she hears shuffling in the background. The door cracks open, and she sees nothing but a shadow through the slit of light. The door slowly opens to a smiling Izabel.

"Alberta." She seems at a loss for words, with multiple attempts to say something. She opens her mouth to speak, but stutters each time.

Berta gives a sheepish grin and moves toward Izabel. She slides the package into her purse and wraps her arms around the older woman, embracing her. Izabel tenses at first, completely caught off guard by Berta's outpouring of emotion. Berta holds tighter until she feels her mother hugging her back. At this very moment, Berta realizes how much they really have in common, and how much they both have to gain simply by sticking together.

"I'm sorry."

"I'm—" Her words get caught.

Berta feels her mother shaking in her arms and realizes she is crying. Her eyes already hurt from the lack of sleep and the millions of tears she's already cried. "I don't want to cry anymore."

Izabel gently pulls away. "Yes. Of course. Please, come in. Take a seat."

Berta steps into the apartment and sits in one of the chairs, the same one, she believes, she sat in the first time she was there. She looks at Izabel, who strangely seems to notice the same thing. Berta looks down.

"I'll get some tea ready. Would you like some?"

Berta nods.

Izabel rushes to the kitchenette and fills a kettle up with water. She starts heating the water up on the stove and takes a seat.

"I have something for you," Berta says as she digs in her purse. "Well, it's kinda for us . . . I guess." She pulls out a CD and a set of papers. She looks to see Izabel's expression turn grim.

"You didn't destroy it?"

Berta shakes her head.

"Why?" She moves closer to the table where Berta placed the CD and papers.

"Part of me thought it was somehow going to tell me something new. I've finally come to terms with it not."

"Alberta, I am sorry. Truly, I am. I didn't know what to expect from the CD."

"Not your fault. I understand that. I just lashed out at you . . . I was wrong, and I am sorry. I brought this here because I thought we could both destroy it." She stares at the CD. "Call it silly, but I'm still looking for a way to move past all this mess."

"It's not silly at all. A lot has been heaped on your shoulders in the last while. You're handling it all admirably."

"I doubt that. Admirable probably isn't the right word to use."

"You're still here, aren't you?"

"Barely."

"People have killed themselves and others over less."

Berta looks up and finds her mother staring at her with one of the most caring looks she has ever seen. For the first time in her adult life,

Berta sees Izabel as her mother. "So I've heard." She looks back down at the CD. "I'm getting a divorce."

The air is cut by the whistling of the tea kettle on the stove. Izabel jumps slightly, and hops to the stove to pull the boiling water from it. Berta watches her as she places tea bags in the top part of the kettle. A few moments later, she has two steaming cups of tea sitting on a tray, and walks toward her.

"May I ask why? I didn't know your husband, but he seemed to be . . . secure, I guess."

"What do you mean?" She grabs the cup nearest her and brings it to her face. She allows the steam to rise into her nostrils.

"The only time I've seen him was at the funeral. But the way he looked at you . . . the way he was there for you. He seemed supportive."

Berta raises her brow. "Craig? Supportive?"

"I'm wrong?"

"Let me tell you who Craig is. My husband . . . soon-to-be-ex-husband, is . . ." She looks down at the CD again. "You listen to the entire thing?"

Izabel frowns. "I did."

"Even the end . . . after the five-minute wait?"

"Yes. Why?"

"The protege . . . whom Raul took under his wing . . . who apparently did some work that impressed the monster . . . that guy . . . the one who knew for years how Raul got to me, and never told me for one reason or another . . . that's Craig."

Izabel holds her cup of tea close to her face, staring at Berta through the steam over the cup. She slowly puts the cup down. "This is such a silly question . . . but are you sure?"

"I am. No doubt about it."

"But Raul said he isn't like them. He stepped away from his brief stint in that world . . . right?"

"Wrong. He went back to that world. I'm not so sure he left. He still had a way to contact these criminals."

Izabel looks like she is in deep thought. "I'm sorry to hear that. Again, I don't know him . . . but I still have to ask . . . are you sure he is like them? Even Raul had . . . a soft side."

"He's close enough. You know he's on the run now?" Berta takes a deep breath and exhales slowly, squeezing air from her parted lips. "I just can't live with that. None of this, really."

"I understand."

"You don't feel the same? Or am I reading your face wrong?"

"Well, we have no choice but to live with it. It is a part of us. It's part of what makes us, us. And we made it to the other side of so much . . . it's hard for me to be sad right now." She smoothes her dress over her crossed legs. "Don't get me wrong, I feel for you. I really do. But as far as myself . . ." She shrugs.

"That seems . . . odd."

"Alberta, Sweetheart . . . I just wanted to find my daughter. I just wanted to tell her how much I love and missed her. I got that. Everything else becomes noise to me." She grabs her cup of tea. "So Raul was a criminal. He treated us well. He protected us from things we couldn't protect ourselves from. He showed us what love looks like. At least, he tried. Your husband . . . let me just say that I saw a lot of similarities, good similarities, between him and Raul."

"In a few glances at a funeral?"

"More than a few."

Berta shrugs. "I don't know. I'm just so—"

"Angry, I know. Allow yourself to be that, but don't stay there. And for goodness sake, don't make decisions from there."

"So you're saying don't get a divorce?"

"No, I'm saying take some time to yourself to figure if that is the best option. Do you know why he did it? Why he lied to you? The fact that he did these things are bad and I agree, but were his *reasons* honorable?"

"Maybe. I don't entirely know. But, how does that matter? He lied to me . . . for years."

"Maybe what you think of him is important . . . and that would clearly change that. Raul acted the same way."

"Craig is not Raul."

Izabel smiles. "Maybe they're more similar than you think."

೮೪೮

Mark stands by the window awaiting the arrival of detective Simms. Once he sees Simms' car pull up into the driveway, he immediately opens the front door and stands by the doorway, signaling Simms to come in.

He walks in holding a manila envelope and a folder.

"Thank you, Detective."

Simms hands Mark the envelope. "Copies of the police reports."

"I really appreciate this." He takes the envelope.

"And, the case file." He sets the folder on the table. "You have ten minutes with this, and I'll need to be here as you scan."

"Perfect."

"Mark, what are you looking for?"

Mark tears through the folder, scanning pictures, memos, and newspaper clippings. "Answers."

Simms sits on the couch. "To what, exactly?"

"To what happened."

"Help me out here. What's in here that you don't already know?"

Mark grabs a paper and holds it up. "I don't know how she got to my brother."

"There's nothing here but phone records that prove conversation between the two . . . no transcripts or anything like that. No letters. No audio."

"But here's an address."

"We searched his apartment already. Nothing there."

"No, an address for his girlfriend. She could shed some light on this whole thing. I have questions." He looks down at the papers. "Apparently questions no one asked."

"We asked her a bunch of questions as is. She didn't have much of any answers for us. He wasn't living with her at the time."

"I have to try."

"Try to what? There is no tangible benefit to this. Why put yourself through more pain and drama?"

He slams the coffee table with his fist, making a booming sound. "Because I have to."

Simms looks at Mark and leans in. "Look, I understand this is a lot for you."

"No. No one knows how much this really is for me. You haven't the slightest idea. You know what she said to me before she pulled the trigger?" He slams the folder shut. "There are some terrible things she has done that are still hanging out there . . . some things were done to her . . . because of me, I know." He reopens the folder and scans more of the files, trying to absorb as much as he possibly can in the short time he has.

"Look, if you are seriously gung ho about this, you need to know a few things."

Mark gives Simms his full attention. "Like what?"

"First, everyone is keeping a closed lid on Bernard's identity."

"I wish they did that with me," Mark says sardonically.

"I understand." He slowly shuts the folder and pulls it toward him. "The guys in the media are working on a spin on the whole event . . . essentially trying to detach him from anything that happened. According to the force, he died in the line of duty. He died a hero."

"A hero?"

Simms nods.

"So his closest people don't know what really happened?"

"They find it odd, I heard. But no one is digging into anything."

"Why? Don't they care?"

Simms shrugs. "I just thought I'd help you with a bit of context." He pulls a card from his breast pocket and sets it on the table. "I had an off-the-record conversation with Alicia's psychologist. She will probably make things clearer for you."

Mark takes the card. "Thank you." He examines the card. "Why are you helping me?"

"I see it from a mile away."

"See what?"

"Your guilt is eating you alive." He stands and walks to the door. "And I'm hoping to get into your good graces."

"Why?" Before Simms can answer, he says, "Craig?"

Simms says nothing.

"But I don't know anything."

"I suppose I believe you to an extent." He opens the door, "I'll check up on you soon. Take care."

⚜

It's midday and Craig stands on the back porch of the ranch, a place that has become his favorite in the home. The sun is bright and beaming down on him, but he doesn't care. A breeze cools off the top of his head as he stares off into the distance, thinking. His burner cell buzzes in his pocket.

"Hello."

"Craig, do you have a few minutes?"

"Sir, is that a joke?"

"I'm sorry. That wasn't a joke, but it was still insensitive."

"No worries. What's up?"

"I have someone here who would like to speak with you."

Craig cringes. "It's not Berta again, is it sir? I don't think I can take another talk . . . not like the last."

"I understand. But no, it isn't Berta. It's her mother."

Craig's breath catches in his throat.

"Are you able to speak?"

"Sure," he finally gets out. "No problem."

A few moments later, Craig is greeted by a woman's voice that skips the pleasantries and gets right to a point. What that point is, he doesn't know.

"Hello, Missus—er—Miss . . ."

"Rego. Please call me Izabel."

"Hello, Izabel. What is this, a—"

"Tell me, Craig . . . do you love my daughter?"

Craig pauses, feeling his hands become clammy. "Ma'am, I don't think this—"

"Please just answer the question. Do you love Alberta?"

He sighs. "Yes. Yes I do. But I've done wrong by her. I've done some pretty bad things, ma'am. That's why this conversation isn't face to face."

"I understand. But why didn't you tell her?"

"I'm guessing you know the whole story already."

"I know enough."

"Well, here's the deal: I was told not to say anything. Mr. Valencia —"

"Raul."

Craig noticed the way she said his former mentor's name. "You two have history?"

"Indeed."

"Small world," he says in an annoyed tone. "Well, he told me not to say a word to anyone. So I didn't. He couldn't stand the idea of Berta looking at him differently, as if he was a—"

"Monster?"

"Yes. Like her biological father." He switches the phone to the other ear and takes a sip of water. "No one can understand why I stuck so closely to what he said. That guy pulled me out of a dark place . . . more than once. The least I could do was that . . . Even after he died, I wanted to preserve the memory of him."

"Oh, I understand. Honorable reasons."

"Something like that usually isn't tagged with honor." He pauses, wondering if he should ask the next question on his mind. "I can only assume he's done something for you?"

"You are correct in that assumption."

Craig nods, though no one can see him. "So what is this call for exactly?"

"I wanted to hear for myself . . . if you are a monster . . ."

"I can assure you, ma'am, I'm no monster."

"I figured that much when you decided it was okay to speak with you."

"I've just done some really bad things."

"And? We all have done something. Have you asked God for forgiveness?"

He's taken back by her question. "I guess. I mean for all the things in the past . . . yes."

"And what about now?"

"I guess not."

"Well . . . maybe you should."

Craig doesn't say anything. He takes a deep breath.

"Ma'am, though God may forgive me, I doubt your daughter will."

"Maybe she will. She just needs time to cool off."

"So what are you saying?"

"It sounds silly, but this time apart might be good for you two. Both of you need some space to figure things out. I believe when you get those things figured out, all paths will lead back to each other."

Craig chuckles. "I don't mean to put a damper on this optimistic thought you're having, but I'm on the run, ma'am. I've got a detective on me and I could go to prison for the rest of my life. I will be an example . . . easily. I'm not really thinking of making it back to her as much. This is survival now."

"I have full confidence Ramses will be able to clear everything for you."

"And there within lies my problem. *Should* everything be cleared? I deserve to lose her. I deserve to go to jail. I deserve . . . what I've done to people . . . I deserve death."

Long silence. A few moments later Ramses speaks on the phone.

"Craig, I will give you a call later."

"Okay." He frowns. "She just hops off the phone. Not another word?"

"She seemed to be a little upset. Listen, you take it easy tonight. I'm making real progress . . . just a little bit more time."

"Thanks, I think. Real quick, could you check up on someone for me?"

"What do you need?"

"Can you check up on my friends? Mark and his wife. Let them know I'm thinking of them."

"I can. I'll let them know."

"Thank you."

The other end of the phone cuts off. He ends the call and places the burner phone on the table in the kitchen. He stops and stands in the middle of the kitchen.

"Lord," he says. "Please forgive me. I have done some terrible things, but those things . . . the actions I have taken were all with good intentions. We needed to get to Jade before it was too late . . . Mr. Valencia needed . . . I feel like I'm making excuses for my behavior."

He stops mid prayer, finding it difficult to continue. He feels a burning in his gut; something making him restless. He starts again.

"Lord, please forgive me for the wrongs I committed."

Again, he can say nothing more. He starts thinking of Addie, the produce stand woman. He shakes his head to shake out thoughts not centered on God. He tries to move forward in prayer again, but stalls . . . again. Thinking about it, he realizes he doesn't know if Addie ever got her truck fixed.

At odds with himself, he sits down, mentally forcing himself to not think of her, but the more he tries, the more difficult it becomes. He isn't able to finish his prayer anymore because his thoughts are consumed with her. He finds it strange. None of the thoughts are sexual in nature, but somehow he finds himself worried about her, and he has no real reason why.

"Lord, I ask that you look over Addie. Don't know if she believes in you, but I pray for her wellbeing regardless."

Addie is on his heart something heavy. So much so, he decides to check up on her. The produce stand is only a couple miles or so away, so he wouldn't be risking too much exposure. He goes to the garage and hops in the truck he drove before, to drive down to the stand.

Chapter Six

"Hey, Sweetheart." Mark seems weak, tired. "I was wondering when I'd see you again."

Jade stares at Mark in the jail cell. His clothes are tattered and they look burned, the edges turned black. He has cuts and bruises all over him. Jade stares at Mark in complete silence.

"Babe, why aren't you saying anything?" Mark asks. He rests his arms on the bars of the cell.

"What is there for her to say, Love?" Another voice comes from the cell.

Jade looks past Mark and appearing from the darkness in the same manner her mother did, is Alicia. Mark looks back and smiles. This makes Jade sick to her stomach. She looks at Alicia, who is carrying an object in her hand. It doesn't take long for her to realize Alicia holds a knife. The closer she gets to the cell door, the more she realizes the knife is dripping with blood. Jade steps away, but looks at Mark in shock. She refocuses her attention on the knife in Alicia's hand.

"You lost, Dear," Alicia says in a menacing tone. "There's always a part of him that will keep me safe. There's always a part that will reach back to me." She gently caresses the side of his face with her free hand. She then kisses him deeply, open-mouthed and full of passion. Mark begins groping her, removing tattered garments of clothing.

"Mark?" Jade whispers.

Mark doesn't hear her and continues kissing Alicia on her body. Alicia whispers something in his ear, and as if on cue, he presses her against the wall and thrusts himself into her. Jade stands there horrified and turns to walk away when she sees Alicia holding up the knife.

"Mark! Stop!"

With precision, Alicia digs the knife into Mark's side, but he doesn't react. He continues with his desperate thrusts with the sounds of his grunting outdone only by Alicia's wails of pleasure. Jade turns and lights the lantern next to the cell and makes her way away from Mark's cell until she can no longer hear their grunts and wails.

She eventually gets to a staircase leading to the upper cells and climbs the stairs, taking two steps at a time. She gets to the upper level to see a couple lanterns scattered on each side of the upper level. Going to the rail, she can see down to the first level and faintly see the lanterns she's already illuminated. She rushes to the lanterns, not stopping to look into the cells, and lights three of the four.

On her way to the last lantern on the floor, she passes a cell from where she hears whimpering. She slows, bracing herself for the worst. She steps closer to the cell to see Alicia sitting in the middle of the floor, sobbing.

"I'm sorry," she says.

Jade sets the lantern down next to her and grips two bars of the cell tightly. "How are you in here . . . and with Mark?"

"There's always more than what you see. That is a different side of me, one I regret." She stands. "Jade, I'm so sorry."

"Sorry doesn't begin to scratch the surface here. I'm here, wherever this is, because of you."

"You don't understand. I—"

"No, you don't understand. You snaked your way into my life . . . and destroyed it."

"But you have to let me out. You have to get me out of here."

"What?" She realizes the lantern down by her feet shines with a brighter flame. She looks at the other lanterns she's lit and finds each of those burning brightly. "You're lucky I don't torture you like you did me."

"Just up ahead is a room."

"I don't want to hear it."

"Please." She runs to the front and grabs the bars. "Up ahead is a room with controls to all the cells. Just flip the switch to let us free."

"Why would I do that?"

With tears streaming down the sides of her face. "Because you can never be free if you don't."

⁂

It's a rainy morning, but Berta still gets out early to get to work. Lately, she hasn't been as committed to her position, and that makes her feel like she's taken advantage of the opportunity John Bromley has given her. A while back, he suggested she take some time off to clear her mind, and to get some personal matters straightened out, but she's sure he had no idea the amount of junk she still has to sort through. She feels she should have just resigned when she was originally going to.

When she gets to her desk to find John standing there waiting for her, she already knows her time is up. She smiles and nods in his direction.

"Mr. Bromley. Good morning."

"Good morning, Berta. I know this is very last minute for you, but I was hoping you could block off some time to have a quick sit-down."

"Sure. Right now?"

"Please, get settled first. When you're ready, just stop by my office."

Berta takes a few moments to drop her stuff off and freshen up before heading into John's office. He motions her to close the door and have a seat.

"Berta, today is a very good day."

She frowns. Apparently she prepared for the worst for no reason. "Why's that?"

John turns to face her and smiles. "She's gone." He hops up and looks out the window. "May as well be sun shining and chirping birds out there, 'cause it is a wonderful day."

"She who? Angelina?"

"Yup." He walks to the edge of his desk and sits. "The Wicked Witch of the West is dead."

"What . . . what happened?"

"Don't know exact details. I just know she's gone. She's outta here." He makes motions with his hands as if he were an umpire for a baseball game. "Great job."

"Great job? I had nothing to do with this."

John looks straight-faced for a second, then smiles. "Oh, I get it . . . plausible deniability."

"No, sir. I really don't know what's going on."

He reads her face for a few long moments before going behind his desk and taking a seat. "I thought you had something to do with that detective coming by."

"That detective?" She leans back in her seat. "What does he have to do with anything?"

"He came by to ask her a few questions. But afterward, she was really out of sorts . . . said she should stop blocking you from being your absolute best. Not even a day later, my boss comes in and says she's on her way out. Next day, the day you took off, she's packing her things and she was gone."

"But why do you think I had something to do with it?"

"Well, you know this detective, right? You were talking to him right out front here." He points out his window. "I'm sure no one else really noticed. I just happened to look out while in deep thought about . . . I don't remember exactly what. Anyway, I looked out and saw you talking to the same guy who showed up to see me and her."

"He spoke with you as well?"

"Yes."

"What about?"

"You. What type of employee you are. What type of person you are. Any trouble with anyone other than Angelina?" He looks at her plainly. "You're not in trouble, are you?"

"No. I'm not."

He pauses, lost in his own thoughts. "Good. Didn't think you were. But you had nothing to do with the detective showing up?"

"None, sir."

He smiles. "That can only mean that she-devil got herself into some risky business practices." He laughs a hearty laugh. "It's all caught up with her. Serves her right. Oh, and that promotion that was supposed to happen after your performance review is going into full effect. It's a new day, Dear." He pauses in his celebration. "Why do you not seem so happy?"

"I don't know. I wonder what this detective did. What he was look-ing for. Why Angelina left."

"Does it matter?"

"For me, it does."

John looks at Berta, then down at his desk in shame. "Shoot. Look at me. Gloating. I've never been one to enjoy another's misfortune, yet here I am . . . like a little school boy . . . laughing and giggling. You know"—he leans back in his chair—"she looked scared, Berta. When she packed her things and held that box in her hands . . . I saw it."

Berta nods. "You know, I've been waiting for a day like this for so long. But now that it's here . . . I find it hard to celebrate. Everyone else sees some sunshine now that the dark cloud is gone. I wonder why the dark cloud existed in the first place."

"Yeah. I get it. That's not where I am with all of this, but I get it."

She nods. "Is that all, sir?"

"It is for now. Quick recap at the end of the day?"

She heads to the door. "I'll have my notepad ready."

◌◦◌

Later in the evening Berta paces the floor in her home. She walks back and forth sorting through her thoughts and her feelings on everything she's learned today. A knock comes at her door. She races over to answer it, knowing already who it is. She opens the door wide.

"What the hell did you do?" she says.

"Good evening, Berta. Never known you to use such language."

"You don't know me at all."

"I know more than you think. And what do you mean what the hell did I do?" Detective Simms stands with a smug look on his face.

"Angelina."

"I questioned her for her possible involvement with your ex-husband."

"So why did she leave so abruptly? And you spoke to my boss about me. What did you do?"

He smirks. Berta notices how calm he is.

"I don't think I said anything funny."

"No, but you did ask me a bunch of questions at once. Which do you want answered?"

"Stop playing games. Explain. Now."

"You know you're cute when you're demanding. I never saw it before, but the corner of your mouth slightly ticks up when you're really pissed."

"Hardly appropriate, Simms."

"That's fair." He jams his hands into his pockets. "I talked to her simply based on her supposed connection to Craig."

"And?"

He shrugs. "He was sleeping with her."

Berta stands flat footed. Her jaw becomes slack. "What?"

"She told me presumably the same thing she said to you. Then she went on to tell me about a time he visited her in the middle of the day . . . right after you left for the day."

"She's a liar, you know."

"Yeah, I know. But the security tapes don't lie . . . and they didn't. He was there. She said she slept with him back in the day . . . and that he couldn't resist taking another shot at her when he found she was so close."

Berta sits, confused.

"She was very forthright with information . . . once I applied some pressure."

"Pressure?"

He takes a few steps toward her. "Living life the way that she did . . . one is bound to have some skeletons in their closet. She was blackmailing quite a few people."

"Was she blackmailing Craig?"

He stares her in the eyes. "No. He was with her willingly."

"How do you know?"

"Again, if she's lying, she has way more to lose."

"But she quit. She's likely gone."

"The info I know about her, she doesn't want to get out."

Berta stares off into space. "He's really a monster, isn't he?"

"It seems so."

"What are you after him for? I mean, what did he do?"

"You sure you want to know?"

Berta nods. "Please."

"There is the current case . . . murder . . . in Philly. The only thing is the sole witness isn't talking. Then there are a few past cases that we thought were closed. One in particular is disturbing."

Berta looks at him with eyes that beg him to tell her.

"Four murders, again in Philly. Back then, a cash reward was offered for any information leading to an arrest."

"How much cash?"

"Fifteen thousand dollars."

She gawks.

"Yeah. Crime hit a peak then. Each of the murders had someone who had information that led to an arrest . . . so someone walked off with fifteen thousand easily. I can't tell you much more, but I will say this. I've found a link that places Craig as a primary suspect for each of the four murders."

"So you think he worked the system in a terrible way."

"Possibly. There's a lot involved here; Money laundering . . . extortion . . . drug trafficking. He's a crime boss . . . or he was . . . and he never paid for the crimes he committed." He moves a step closer to her. "But I need you."

She snaps her head up. "What?"

"I can't do this without you. If you know anything . . . big or small . . . about where he's hiding, please let me know."

"I let you know already."

"The law firm?"

She nods. "That's the only connection I know."

Simms looks visibly frustrated. "That's a tough egg to crack. And I'm running out of time."

"What do you mean?"

He sighs. "Cases are disappearing. People aren't talking. Ones I got to talk, now recant their testimonies. I'm losing traction. And I'm losing it fast."

"There's not much I can do. I told you what I know."

"Do you have a way of reaching him?"

Without hesitation, she says, "No. And even if I did, he wouldn't want to talk to me."

"Well, if there's anything you can think of, don't hesitate. Call me."

Berta nods quickly, still maintaining a far-off look.

"Look, I feel that I need to say this. I—"

"What did you say to her to get her to leave?"

"Pardon?"

"Angelina. You pressed her for some information, fine, but I don't see how that made her leave." She looks up at him. "What else did you do?"

"Convinced her that was best for her."

"Why?"

"I was hoping to get in your good graces." He shuffles. "I dunno. You could use a break."

"Is my life that bad?"

"I'm not saying that. But the way things have been . . . they seem kinda rough."

"Do you know what that means for her, though?"

"I honestly don't care." He heads to her door. "I need to go. If I overstepped, I'm sorry."

"But you're not . . . sorry. Are you?"

"I suppose I am not."

He leaves Berta's home, with Berta sitting in the living room. She waits a few minutes to make sure Simms is gone, before dashing to her cell phone and rapidly tapping at the screen. She waits a few seconds, tapping her foot, becoming more and more anxious. Someone on the other line picks up.

"Hello. Is Mr. Ramses in today?"

CX80

After only a few minutes of driving, Craig gets to the produce stand and finds it mostly deserted. Only a single person looks around, but only for a few seconds before getting back in their car and driving off. He sees her truck still parked in the same position it was in when it stalled. He pulls off from the stand and heads to Silver Rock.

It doesn't take long to reenter the town and he slows down to keep with the speed limit. He tries to remember where he dropped her off but doesn't come up with much. Passing on his right is a restaurant that he pulls into. He takes a deep breath, and gets out the truck. *Big risk, guy. Big risk.* He's somewhat fidgety and he tries to calm his nerves to not seem weird. He heads into the restaurant and heads straight for the bar section. The portly bartender eyes him curiously.

"New around here?" the bartender says, while drying a large beer mug.

"Yeah. Why?"

"I notice everyone who walks in here. It's always the same people. Never noticed you before. Anyway"—he smiles—"didn't mean to come off menacing if I did. What can I do for you?"

"I'm looking for someone."

"Okay."

"A woman."

"Look, I can help, but if you're here to cause trouble—"

"No. I'm just checking on her. I haven't seen her in a couple days . . . don't really have a good feeling about it."

"Does this woman have a name?"

"Addie."

The bartender sets the mug behind him. "I know nothing of an Addie."

"But she lives in this town . . . and you notice everyone that walks in here, right? I'm sure she—"

"Look, I don't know who you are. Quite frankly, now I don't care. Best advice I can give you: leave her alone. Go back to wherever you came."

Craig keeps his cool. "Look, I'm just looking for a few cucumbers."

"Now you lie?"

"I dropped her off in this town a couple days ago because her truck stalled."

The bartender's eyes get wide. "Get out. Leave now before I call the cops."

Craig doesn't need much more of a cue than that. He puts his hands up and backs away from the bar. Within a few seconds he's out the restaurant and back in the truck. He taps the steering wheel driving by the church. He's telling himself to leave the town and go back to the ranch, but he feels something deeply troubling in his heart. The bartender's reaction when he said her name doesn't help matters, either. As he drives by the church, he notices for the second time the shadow the steeple makes on the street below. He continues driving to see if a drive by the houses can jog his memory.

He drives for a few minutes before finding the home he believes to be Addie's. He vaguely remembers dropping her and her things off in front of this house. Craig parks and cuts the truck off. He gets out and stares at the cottage-looking home with a fence around the small front yard. He strides toward the front door of the house and rings the doorbell. He rings it a few more times, but no one comes to the door. He gives up and heads back to the truck. Just before he passes the fence, he hears the door creak open.

"Can I help you with something?" the old woman says.

Craig gets a good vibe from the older woman and flashes her a genuine smile. That seems to put her at ease. "Sorry to disturb you, ma'am; I'm looking for Addie. I think she lives here. Correct?"

"No, she doesn't. You better leave." She starts to close the door.

"Wait, ma'am. Please. I don't know what's going on, but all I'm doing is checking up on her. I dropped her off here." He points to toward the street. "It was a couple days ago."

The woman squints. "I remember you. She told me about you."

Craig doesn't know what to say. "What did she say?"

"Son, a word of advice. Leave this town. Don't come back."

"Trust me, ma'am, I'd much rather be back home . . . but that's not an option. I'd rather not be in this town . . . but the more people seem to want to push me away, the more I feel the need to stay. What did she say?"

"You are far from home. You are the nicest man she has ever encountered." The old woman scoffs. "But she felt you carry a heavy burden of some sort."

"So you've spoken to her recently. Is she okay?"

She looks at him with a cold stare. "No. She isn't okay." She shakes her head. "But there isn't anything anyone can do about it. I beg you, please . . . just leave." She looks out to the street.

Craig turns around to see a police car whooshing by. By the time he looks back to the old woman, she is closing the door. He doesn't want to push any further, and he definitely doesn't want to make a scene with the cop car going by. He gets back to the truck and starts the engine. His mind is spinning with information, and he is uncertain of his next move. He's even more uncertain of what this town called Silver Rock is all about.

He drives for a few minutes to the only place he believes would offer any real help: the church that casts a shadow of the cross with its tall steeple. He gets to the large classic-style double doors and is greeted by a feeling he usually doesn't feel when stepping into a church.

Dread.

He walks around the single-room church, looking for someone to talk to, but he hears not a peep. He stands in the middle of the sanctuary and waits. He hears some creaking and cracking of the wooden parts of the church, but nothing by way of human movement. He turns around to leave the church.

"May I help you?"

Craig turns around to find a man wearing a blue dress shirt buttoned all the way to the top, slacks, and patent-leather shoes. He has a comely face, but his eyes tell some other story. The man's eyes are unsettling.

"Yes. I'm looking for someone. Her name is Addie." Craig immediately notices the slight twitch in the man's eye. "Do you know her?"

"I do. I've seen her a few times in here before. Are you a friend of hers?"

"Yes. And I haven't heard from her in a few days. I'm a bit worried."

The man squints. He sticks out his hand. "I'm Reverend Sally. Benjamin Sally."

Craig shakes his hand, but internally regrets doing so. "Braylon."

"Well, Braylon, it is a pleasure to meet you. Unfortunately, I can do nothing to help in terms of your finding Addie."

"Do you know of someone who could? I just want to know how she is doing."

"Unfortunately, I don't."

Craig eyes the reverend for a few seconds, but is unable to figure him out. "Well, thank you for your time."

"Indeed."

Craig cautiously exits the church and hops into the truck. He figures he better not press his luck, and should head back to the ranch. This visit to Silver Rock has left him worried. Something is wrong with Addie, but he is inclined to leave everything alone and never return to the town again. That's safer for him.

After all, he is still on the run.

◌◈◌

Mark finds himself back in Philly, sitting in his parked car on a small side street of row homes. He's sat for a half hour now, watching various people come and go from the address written on a piece of paper. His palms are sweaty, and he feels like he blinks a thousand times a minute. He first must do something before he loses his nerve for it as well. He pulls out his cell phone and the card Simms gave him with contact info for Alicia's psychologist. Eleanor Bixby is the name—her name—he keeps in his mind, hoping she picks up the phone. She doesn't, but he leaves a message.

Once he's done leaving a message, he hangs up and gets out the car. His stomach starts doing flips, but he moves to the front door anyway. *I should be good. No one knows who I am. I should be good.* He gets to the front doors and knocks on the screen door.

No answer.

He sees a doorbell and tries that a few times before waiting. The door slowly opens to a petite woman with caramel-colored skin. She looks worn, presumably from crying.

"May I help you?"

"Ummm. Yes. I'm . . ." He can't find the words to say. Behind the woman, he sees a bunch of people talking, some sitting around, others seemingly crying. "I . . ."

"One of Bernie's friends?"

Mark nods and looks down. She ushers him in.

"There's food in the kitchen. Help yourself."

"May I talk to you for a moment?"

The woman looks confused. "I guess."

"I . . ." Mark realizes he hasn't thought this plan all the way through. "How did Bernard pass?"

"What?"

"I'm sorry if this is too much for you, but—"

"What do you mean, 'how did he pass'? He was killed in the line of duty."

He sighs. "Do you believe that? Can you say that is a fact without a shadow of a doubt?"

She takes a step away from Mark and looks toward the dining room. Mark glances to see two men who may have a few pounds on him sitting, watching them.

"Who are you?" she asks.

"A friend."

She squints. "I don't think I believe that."

"Fine. But we were close. Look, I just need to know if you've ever seen this person." He pulls out a picture of Alicia that he took from Simms' case files. "There's more to Bernard's death than you think."

"I don't know who you are, but I know for sure you weren't close to Bernie. No one calls him Bernard."

Mark notices the two men have somehow moved closer to him without his knowing it. At this time, everyone in the house is staring at him. He looks up toward the kitchen and makes eye contact with a woman who instantly recognizes him. She moves a few people from her path to get to him.

"You can't be," she says. "You can't be here."

The caramel-skinned woman looks more confused by the second. "You know him?"

"Yes Stephanie, I know him." She steps closer to Mark. "You never forget some people, no matter how much they change . . . especially if that person is your son."

CHAPTER SEVEN

Mark stands in the middle of the floor, feeling like he's on display, with everyone's eyes on him. He feels a mix of sadness, anger, and anxiety rise up as if a cloud, hanging over everyone's head. He stares at the woman who claims to be his mother, knowing it's her, hating that it's her.

"Mark?"

He doesn't say anything.

"I know . . ." She steps closer to him, but he backs away. "How did you . . . Where . . ." She holds her hand to her mouth.

"Mark . . . as in Bernie's brother, Mark?" Stephanie says. She steps around into his vision and gawks at him. Tears start streaming from her eyes, and before long, every woman in the house is crying. "He looked for you," Stephanie says. "He looked for you for so long. We all did. You . . . disappeared."

Still staring at his mother, he sidesteps Stephanie's outpouring of emotion and cuts to what is angering him at the moment. "He wasn't dead."

His mother shakes her head.

"And no one thought to tell me."

"We couldn't. By the time we found out, you were gone."

"Who's we?"

She motions to a few people sitting at the large dining room table. They all look at Mark with remorse in their eyes. These people, Mark presumes, are his family.

"Much like your return now, he returned to us. He was looking for us . . . to forgive us."

"No. He was in my arms that night. I held him that night . . . DEAD . . . in my arms." Mark is finding it difficult to keep his composure.

"No. He was alive, barely. Of course, I thought the same. He was gone." She wipes her face. "I snuck him out to the hospital with help from the neighbors. Was back home before Jack could wake from his stupor."

"And you just . . . dropped him off?"

"I was . . . I was messed up on that stuff. And I knew I couldn't stay too long for someone to get a really good look at my face. Didn't want Child Protection Services on me . . . didn't want to lose you, especially after already thinking I lost Bernie."

"But why didn't you tell me at least that? Why keep me in the dark? Why let me suffer?"

"No one knew, including myself."

"What do you mean no one knew? You knew. You're the one who dropped him off, right?"

No one says a thing. No one moves.

"This has got to be the stupidest . . . I'm calling your bluff. That's not the reason. What is the real reason?" His eyes are ablaze. "What is the real reason? Why didn't you tell me?"

She looks down. Her voice comes out quiet and suppressed by on-coming sobs. "That is the reason."

"You lie." He steps forward, fists balled, veins stretching across the side of his head. "What is the reason?"

He feels a firm hand placed on his chest. One of the big men holds his hand to Mark's chest. "Hold up, Baby Cuz."

Mark glances at the man, then keeps his intense gaze locked on his mother. "I'm only going to say this once. Get your hand off me or I swear on everything that is holy and true, you will not have a hand to take back." He snaps his stare to focus on the man with his hand to his chest. Slowly, the man lets his hand fall to his side. Mark once again retrains his focus on his mother. His voice becomes gravelly. "The reason?"

"Mark, you left without a word. By the time we found out about him, we couldn't get ahold of you. We contacted the college and everything . . . but we never could find you."

"But you had to have known . . . that he was alive somehow . . . back then."

"How? He was comatose when I took him to the hospital. We mourned like he was gone. But he found us and we thought it to be a miracle when he did. I've never seen a miracle before that . . . and not one after . . . until today. You coming home . . . it's . . ." She walks away to the dining room with someone helping her.

He looks around. Everyone still stares at him. He glances at Stephanie. She gives him a look as if she's trying to understand him. At the moment, Mark is trying to understand himself. He knows he came here for a reason. He must find out where and how Alicia comes into play. He shuffles toward Stephanie, but before he could pull out Alicia's picture again, as if she were reading his mind, she says, "Her name is Jasmine. The woman in the picture you showed me."

Mark processes what he was just told. "That's the name she told you?"

"Not hers?"

He shakes his head.

"I knew something was up with her." She looks around as she wraps her arms around herself. "Do you want something to eat?"

"I shouldn't."

"Please," Mark's mother interjects, "please stay. Can we all just talk? I know you're mad . . . but please, let's just talk. Mostly everyone is leaving soon anyway. It will be just us three."

"I didn't come here to forgive you."

"But it can't hurt to ask."

Mark looks around and sure enough, people are filing out the house. Some go to the kitchen quickly to grab a plate of food, but most of them excuse themselves by Mark and head out the door. The entire moment feels surreal, and a large part of him wants to follow right behind everyone who is leaving the house, but he looks at Stephanie. She looks worn and tired. He can easily sense the pain that resides behind her eyes. He keeps his gaze on her to avoid making any more eye contact with his mother.

"Please sit down," Stephanie says. "Make yourself comfortable."

Mark takes a few cautious steps toward the dining room table and takes a seat. He doesn't look at his mother still, but he knows she watches his every movement closely.

"Are you at all hungry?" Stephanie asks.

"Honestly, I'm not. I just . . . I need to know who Alicia . . . Jasmine is to you."

"Is that her real name? Alicia?"

"Yeah."

Stephanie takes the seat next to him and stares at him for a few long and awkward moments. It seems no one knows where to start.

"I told you the truth," Mark's mother cuts in. "About why I didn't tell you. I didn't say anything because I couldn't say anything. Didn't know he was alive. Didn't want to lose you . . . so I didn't search to find out."

Mark looks down, having already heard enough of his mother and what he hears as excuses. He digs in his pocket and pulls out the picture, and slams it on the table. He glances at Stephanie. "You said her name was Jasmine. That was the name she gave you. How did she show up?"

Stephanie looks at Mark's mother. The old woman nods.

"Jasmine came out of nowhere. Me and Bernie were dating and we were having troubles. I was . . ." She tries to hold in tears. "I wanted him to stop being a cop. I told him it was too dangerous. That he had to consider the kind of future he wanted for us . . . for his child."

"You were pregnant then."

She nods. "And he didn't want a child. So we were a bit rocky, but I thought we were okay. We were working things out . . . but then she came along." She looks down. "I was about set to have Kayla . . . we were out walking . . . went to the 'burbs to walk on their track. She was there jogging. Said she went to school with him. They had a nice conversation or whatever." She shrugs. "I never thought anything of it. Never thought he would leave me . . . and Kayla . . . for her."

"Did you notice anything strange about that first interaction?"

"No. Not at all. But ever since that interaction, he acted funny . . . different." She looks him in his eyes. "But what does this have to do with Bernie's death?"

Mark looks down and clears his throat. "She was heavily involved in his death."

"As in she killed him?" Her eyes light up as if a match were behind each eye.

"No." He continues to look down. "She set him up."

"But why?"

He looks at her with caring eyes, at least as caring as he can muster, and says, "To get to me."

"Wait, hold on now," Mark's mother jumps in. "How would she even know?"

"Sounds crazy, I know. A lot of pieces would have to fit in order for her plan to work . . . but it almost worked."

"And the story the police told us?"

"Fabricated. They needed him to look like a hero. I've been told it's because the way the police force looks right now."

"Where is she?" Stephanie asks.

"Dead. She killed herself."

Everyone sits in silence trying to absorb what they just learned, but as time goes on, each person's face twists.

"What did he say about me? Bernard."

Stephanie takes a few moments to come to before answering. "He simply wanted to be reunited with his brother . . . his one-time protector."

He looks at the floor. "Did he say anything . . . negative?"

"No. Never. At least not to me."

Mark brushes the top of his head. "Are you sure?"

"I'm absolutely positive." She gets up from her seat. "How do you figure she was trying to get to you? What happened?"

"Alicia and I have a history . . . a pretty tainted one. He helped her . . . do some pretty bad things to me."

"So what are you saying?"

Mark looks back and forth between Stephanie and his mother. He stands. "That detective questioned you . . . He leave a card?"

"Yeah."

"Call him. Ask him exactly what happened. Tell him you met with me. He'll tell you."

"Why aren't you telling us?" his mother asks.

He heads toward the front door, looks at them, shakes his head, and leaves. He walks out knowing he won't ever find out what his brother's motivations were. Whether he operated freely . . . or was under duress . . . or hated him . . . or loved him. Those questions will forever go unanswered.

He gets in his car and checks his phone. He has a few missed calls and a voicemail. He thinks it's the psychologist calling him back, but listens to the voicemail and realizes it's the hospital. He quickly calls them back and gets in contact with Jade's doctor.

"Dr. Chalmers. Mark Cooke here."

"Yes. Mark." Long pause. "You should come to the hospital. We've some things to discuss."

"Like what? Is everything all right?"

"Mr. Cooke . . ." Another long pause. "Jade's vitals are slipping."

"What do you mean, slipping?"

"Her . . . brain activity . . . took a sharp dip today. Heart rate is slowing. You should get here to talk."

"I'll be there. I'll be there in a couple hours."

⚮

"Why do you tell me this?"

"Because it's the truth. You can never be free unless you free us. We are all a part of you . . . even if you don't want us to be." Alicia lets her grip go a bit as her hands slide down the bars. "We can't stay here."

"I don't understand. I don't understand any of this. I was led by this guy who was on fire to this . . . prison. He said it was . . . or is my heart. I just need the darkness to go away so I can see where I'm going."

97

Alicia looks at Jade in confusion. "You may see where you're going, but do you know where you're going?"

"Is this a philosophical debate?"

"No . . . though, that's what it always seems to turn into for us . . . right?"

Jade says nothing.

"Look, Jade, I need you to get me out of here. All of us . . . we need to be free . . . in order for you to be free."

"Why do you make it seem like you're doing me a favor? Like you care what happens to me."

Alicia moves away from the bars and sits back in the middle of the floor. She weeps again, and through her sobs, Jade hears her somehow get out, "You don't care. You never did. Never will. And for that . . . you will die here."

Jade moves away from the cell, realizing she has lit all the lanterns in the building. She waits a few moments for something to happen, but nothing does. Still, the only light in the entire surrounding area comes from the lit lanterns. She looks at the one she carried around with her, finding it extinguished. She starts on her way back downstairs to meet up with the flame angel when she sees what everyone she's encountered talked about: a small space not blocked by bars. She assumes it holds the control panel to open the cells. She turns her back to the area and continues walking back to the flame angel. She has no desire to let any of them free. In fact, she believes they all deserve to be in the cells they are in. *They all deserve to rot in those cells. They deserve to die.*

She stops, pausing to try to figure out where that line of thinking came from. She shivers as the sheer intensity of those thoughts scares her. She gets to the top of the steps, but before walking down, she takes a last glance toward the lanterns. She waits, but nothing moves. Nothing makes a sound. She finds that even more unsettling.

She looks to her side, to grab the single lantern when she realizes it's not at her side. She looks around and finds it in front of the last cell she was in front of. She steps her way to the lantern and takes one glance into the cell to find someone else other than Alicia.

She rocks back and forth, holding herself, whispering something Jade is unable to hear. She doesn't know what to say, so she asks a simple question.

"Are you okay?"

The being turns her head and at that instant, Jade knows who she is.

She is her.

Jade looks at her doppelganger in shock. The "other" her turns to face her. "To let me go," she says, "you must let them go."

"What good would that do me? I've come here to light the lanterns, and that's what I have done."

"Yet nothing changes." She looks at Jade with imploring eyes. "Do I deserve to rot in here? Do I deserve to die?"

Jade steps back. "Why are you here in the first place?"

"I've been here the longest. Why, I cannot say."

"How long have you been here?"

"Years . . . decades."

"But . . ." Without another thought, she rushes past the cell and heads toward the control room. She stops at the complicated-looking panel looking for a switch but having no luck. She finds a key sitting on the panel and scoops it up. She studies the panel for a keyhole and finds one, jams the key in, and twists. An electrical buzz and a loud beep later, the cells open. Jade sees Alicia, coming from a different cell, not bothering to look back. She also sees Karen and Calvin, both scurrying back downstairs. But as far as her doppelganger; she is nowhere to be seen.

Jade makes her way back to the cell to see her doppelganger still sitting there, now gone back to her mutterings. Jade walks into the cell and touches her shoulder.

"I opened the cells. You are free now." She pauses to hear what she is saying. "Hey, what are you saying?"

The doppelganger points to the wall of the cell. Jade moves up to the cell wall and observes what she deems to be gibberish written—rather, clawed—onto the wall. Jade looks at the doppelganger's fingers to see them bloodied. She turns back to read what's on the wall.

"Ymen eeht mai," the doppelganger repeats.

"I don't get it," Jade says. "What are you saying?" Then, she remembers. "The flame angel's name?"

She nods and holds up her bloody pointer. Jade looks at the wall, then back at herself. The woman stands to her feet and moves to the writing on the wall to point . . . the opposite way of normal reading. She keeps pointing until Jade figures it out.

"I . . . am . . . thee . . . ne . . . my?" She squints. "What does that mean?"

The doppelganger returns to her spot in the middle of the floor. Jade looks at the writing again.

"I . . . am . . ." Jade looks scared. "I am the enemy."

"Flame angel . . . bad," the doppelganger says. "The flame angel wanted me here . . . wanted you here. The flame angel . . ." She looks up at Jade with fearful eyes. "I'm so sorry."

Jade grabs the woman's hand. "It's okay. Let's get out of here. We can make it without it. Just me and you. We can make it."

The doppelganger shakes her head. "We can't. I already know how this ends." She gives Jade a hug. "I'm so very sorry."

Jade feels someone behind her and snaps around.

The flame angel stands at the cell opening.

ᏣᏚ

Only a day after his solo visit to Silver Rock, Craig sits in the garage in the truck with the burner phone up to his ear, set to go again. He speaks to Ramses, concerned still about Addie.

"So what am I gonna do?" he asks.

"Stay out of it."

"But something's wrong. One of the residents told me."

"Some old woman who probably doesn't remember what happened to her five minutes ago."

"But still. Why did everyone shift as soon as I mentioned her name? Not a coincidence."

Craig hears Ramses sigh over the phone. "From your current position, what exactly do you plan to do?"

"I don't know. I didn't get there yet."

"Well you better . . . and soon."

"Have you ever noticed anything strange when going into the town?"

"No. But then again, I was never the one going into town. Janice was. But she never mentioned anything strange."

"Well . . . I dunno . . . I need to find out what's going on with her."

"Now you *need* to? Craig, what is really going on here?"

"I care about her well-being. And I can't stop thinking about her." He sighs. "Now, I know how that sounds, but I don't mean it in a sexual manner or anything. I just . . . I've been praying a lot . . . at least a lot more than I did when I first came here. Addie came up in my prayers.

101

She's on my heart something strong. I feel like I'm being urged by God to move. Not for my sake . . . but for hers."

He hears Ramses sigh loudly. "Do you have to get into trouble wherever you go?"

Craig chuckles. "Seems like it."

"Look, there isn't much assistance I can offer here."

"I'm not asking for any. Plus, they don't seem too fond of visitors."

"All the more reason to be extremely cautious." He clears his throat. "But why get involved? All this work I'm doing here . . ."

"It all could be for naught, I know. But believe me on this, I truly appreciate what you have done for me."

"Almost done. The only case open is the most current."

"That's it? Then I can come home?"

"Indeed."

Long pause.

"Do you think I deserve it? To be a free man after what I've done?"

"I don't believe your mistakes should be the end of you."

"And if you can't clear the case? If I go to trial?"

"It was self-defense. That's why I deliberately decided on cleaning that one up last. If you got snagged on that one, that's likely the easiest to defend. The others, not so much."

"Self-defense? I knew before I even got there it was going to come down to someone shooting at someone. I could lie to the courts and be fine with it . . . but I can't lie to God. I wanted to take them both out. I wanted them to feel pain. I wanted them to die for what they've done to my brother. I came in there with intent and a gun." He pauses. "I mean, I killed some mother's baby boy. Some woman's husband or boyfriend. I should be in prison, shouldn't I? Isn't that justice being served?"

"You've never expressed this to me before."

"But shouldn't I? Shouldn't I be thrown away to pay for the things I've done?"

After a long silence, Ramses says, "Maybe."

"Look, you asked me what kind of man I wanted to be. I figured it out. I just want to be honorable. At the end of all this, I may not be remembered as such . . . but I hope God would see me as such. So, I ask you, what is the honorable thing to do here?"

"I don't know."

"I have an idea. I'd bet a small fortune you know as well, and you don't want to say it."

"Look, is it honorable that you served time in prison for crimes you didn't commit?"

Craig doesn't say anything.

"Because if I recall, you already did that. A friend, your best friend, your brother, asked for your help in extreme circumstances. Would it have been honorable to say no to him, even if it was well within your means to help?"

"It wouldn't have been, but—"

"Then stop beating yourself up, Kid."

Craig dismisses the conversation with a melodramatic sigh. "Did you ever get a chance to deliver that message . . . to Mark?"

"Not quite yet. Can't seem to find him. He hasn't been at the hospital . . . he hasn't been home. We'll get to him, though. No worries."

"Could you deliver another message?"

"You could always deliver it yourself."

"I could. But what's the fun in that?" He chuckles. "But seriously . . . could you tell Berta . . . tell her that I love her. I won't be able to stop doing that. Tell her that the man she knew . . . is the man she knows . . . and that I'm sorry for not being completely upfront with that part of my life . . . with that part of her life."

"I can deliver that."

"Thank you, sir." He sighs. "I'm going to get out of here. Head back to this town to find Addie."

ﭢ

"Very well," says Ramses, almost in a disappointed tone. "I'll talk to you soon. Be careful."

Berta watches Ramses hang up the phone after having listened to his entire conversation with Craig. They stare at each other for a few moments before he speaks.

"Did you get all that?"

She nods. "He's beating himself up again." She taps her fingernail on the wooden arm of the chair she sits in. "I would normally be there to talk him through."

"You can still be there. It just takes a call."

"Yeah." She frowns. "He talked of justice."

"Something on your mind?"

"I believe in justice. But what is that really? You do wrong, and then get punished for it? You do right and get rewarded for it? Is justice just that and that only?" She looks at him inquisitively.

"That's what justice is legally."

"But biblically?"

"It's a bit more than that, I believe."

"You see, I'm starting to have a different understanding of justice. This detective, Simms, sees justice strictly as punishment for wrongdoings."

"And you?"

"After a talk with Izabel . . . she told me what he said to her . . . I believe there's more. I believe in the strong hand of God . . . but I also believe in the caring hand of God. I feel like . . . I let my anger get the best of me. But I'm so torn . . . and still angry."

"You still love him."

"That didn't sound like a question."

"Because it wasn't. I can see it. I can hear it. You still love him, but you are trying to reconcile the man you thought he was with the man the detective says he is."

She nods.

"I think you should give him a call."

"And who is this town chick?"

Ramses smirks. "Town chick?"

"Addie. That's what he said her name was. Who is she?"

"That one, I don't have an answer to. I wish he'd just stay at the ranch, but I can image he's gone stir crazy. I just hope he doesn't get himself into any trouble." He starts straightening up his desk. "You know why I help him?"

"Because Raul asked you to. You feel indebted to him, maybe?"

"I am indebted to him, but that's not why I help Craig. Craig . . . he . . . he deserves a break. Growing up the way he did. Still, he turned things around. I get he hit some major speed bumps, but . . ."

"Mercy," she blurts out.

"What?"

"Mercy . . . deliverance from judgment . . . God is merciful . . . and, like forgiveness, is required of us to show others." She stares blankly at the floor.

"Okay."

"Mercy and justice don't mix, right?"

"Again not legally."

"Because showing mercy at many times is at the expense of justice. In Craig's case, he committed a crime, and the just thing would be for him to go to jail. Or, we could have mercy on him and not send him to jail . . . but then justice isn't served. Right?"

"Right."

"Wrong. Did Christ die for exactly this?"

"I'm following."

"The sins of the world, before, during, and after the cross were put on his back . . . He was sacrificed. Justice was served then for all of our wrongs for all time . . . but mercy was shown at the very same time to all of us who believe. He believes." She looks Ramses in the eyes. "But I'm over here, literally judging him, and not in the discerning way. I was trying to throw him in prison."

Ramses folds his hands in front of his face and gives her a perplexed look. "What happened? I'm assuming more than a talk with Izabel."

"I've just been thinking, that's all. Or maybe I stopped thinking and started listening." She falls into deep thought.

"Listen, Alberta, you are just doing what you feel is right. We all are doing what we feel is right. No need to beat yourself up over it, but be flexible." He smiles. "Because at any given moment, we could be wrong."

She nods quickly and jumps to another subject. "I think the detective is getting desperate. That's what I came to you for. I need you to track someone down."

"Do you think he will become dangerous? The detective, I mean."

"I don't know." She says. "He very well could."

Ramses phone rings. "Excuse me, Dear."

Ramses answers the phone and gives a few curt uh-huhs before looking to Berta and saying, "Speak of the devil." He looks down at a few papers on his desk. "Call me when they leave." He hangs up and folds his hands. Berta waits for him to say something.

"The detective is searching your home."

"What? Why?"

"For something that will lead them to Craig, I'm guessing."

"Can they do that?"

"With a warrant, yes. But for some reason, I feel they don't have one."

"What makes you so sure?"

"Gut instinct."

"Is he searching . . . or is he putting something in?"

"Good question. I'll have someone sweep your place before you go back in."

"Why now?"

"Why is he searching your home now? I think you're right on him becoming desperate. His moves here on out may become . . . erratic."

Berta folds her hands as well, but to keep them from trembling.

Chapter Eight

Craig gets to Silver Rock again, but this time hopes to take a more cautious approach. The first place he heads to is the old woman's house, as he felt he got the most traction there. He hop steps to her front door again and knocks. After waiting a few moments he rings the doorbell. He hears a few of the locks unlock and the door slightly cracks open. A slender hand holds the edge of the door, and through the crack he sees a youthful face.

"May I help you?" a different woman's voice gives Craig a start.

"Hi. I was here yesterday." He pauses for a second. "I was looking for Addie."

"There isn't anyone by the name of Addie here."

"I know. I was told by the older woman who lives here."

"That older woman has a name."

"We never got that far in the conversation. Look, if she's here, could you tell her the man from yesterday is here?"

"Okay, Man From Yesterday, what is your name?"

"Braylon. Tell her I just need a few minutes of her time."

The doors shuts, and Craig waits outside for a few minutes. He watches people and how they operate in the town. They all look normal enough, but something in his gut tells him this place is off. The door opens again behind him. He turns to see a taller woman. Blond hair. Gray eyes.

"She says she remembers you. You weren't supposed to come back."

"I know. She told me to leave, but I can't. I have to find Addie. She told me Addie wasn't in good shape. She's the only one in this crazy town that said something that wasn't laced in weirdness."

The woman looks to the side and whispers something, but Craig is unable to hear. She nods.

"She says she wants to talk to you. But you could never come back to this house."

"That's fine."

The blond woman lets Craig in the house, then closes and locks the door. She slowly lets go of the lock as if she's unsure whether she's done the right thing. "This way."

Craig follows the tall and slender woman down a hallway covered with pictures. He sees one picture in particular with just the older woman and the younger hugging, smiling.

"She's your mother?"

"Yes."

Craig nods. He follows the woman until they get to a smaller room with the older woman sitting down, knitting. He smiles and is seated in front of her. His smile fades when he sees a handgun on a small table next to her. The younger blond sits next to her mother.

"I thought I told you not to come back. I begged you, actually."

"You did. I didn't listen . . . obviously."

She keeps her eyes focused on her knitting. "Your name isn't Braylon. Craig," She looks him in the eyes. "Isn't that your name?"

Craig nods.

"So you are a very interesting person, Craig. You come to this town, looking for Addie, giving fake names, and clearly"—she sets her knitting down—"you're not afraid of guns, which are illegal in this town. Imagine that, a small town in Texas where guns are essentially outlawed. Right to bear arms my ass." She shakes her head. "Anyway,"—she folds her hands in her lap—"what's your story?"

Craig freezes. "Wh—What do you mean?"

"Aha. There it is. So you're not afraid of guns . . . but you stutter on telling your story? Addie told me she felt you carry a lot of burdens. What are they?"

"Is it necessary to tell you?"

"If you want to know where she is . . . it is."

He nods, considering what he's going to say next. "I've . . . hit a few speedbumps in life. Hard. I've hit them hard. But I am always offered another chance to make things right. This time . . . I don't know . . . this time it's about the type of man I want to be."

"Too cryptic. Give me details."

"I can't. It . . . could put me in danger. This is all going pretty fast. Can we start over?"

"So you expect me to put my life in danger for you? A stranger who can't give me their real name?"

He pauses, noticing she isn't allowing a fresh start here. "I don't understand how you are put in danger."

"This town has gone to hell," she says. The wrinkles on her face become more pronounced.

"I've been trying to get her out of here for years now," her daughter cuts in.

The older woman pats her daughter's lap. "From the rock to the church to the very edges of this town . . . it's all gone to hell. Many moons ago, this town was wonderful. It was originally a Christian town, ya know. But now . . . there's this group that has their fingers pressed to all the goings-on in this place. And they care very little for the people. They care only for the illusion of power."

"You're telling me about cryptic?"

The old woman smiles. Slowly, her smile turns into a hearty laugh. "I like you, Craig. I get the same vibes Addie got. If circumstances were different, I'd have you take my daughter's hand in marriage."

"Mother!" Her daughter's face turns bright red.

"What? Am I the only one attracted to a strong God-fearing man?" She shrugs and smiles. "Anyway, Craig, what exactly do you want with Addie?"

"Ma'am, I just want to see if she's okay."

"But I already told you she's not."

"And I want to help."

"Do you love her?"

Craig is taken aback. "What? No. I just . . ." He looks squarely in the old woman's face. "You're a Christian. So you understand what it feels like to be led by God. It's a strange—"

"Tugging. A pulling from your insides. You feel it in your bowels and it's not because you ate something funky the night before."

"Yeah." He smiles. "I *have* to make sure she is okay. I've done my share of turning my back on God. I don't want to go down that road again . . . especially as I'm going to need Him a whole bunch and real soon."

"I don't know. I think you may have bit off more than you can chew here, Buddy."

"Understatement of the year. Listen, what do you want to know?"

"What has you in this town in the first place? It isn't quite a vacation spot."

"I'm staying not too far from here. I was first brought over by Addie. She runs that produce stand and her truck broke down. So I helped."

"And where you're staying?"

"Yeah. It's not my place . . . so I cannot say . . . but . . ." He looks back and forth between the two women. "I'm not from this state . . . or even this part of the country. But I had to leave my home because some guy . . . a detective . . . is trying to throw me in jail."

"So, you're on the run."

"For things I've done in the past mostly. But I went back to that tainted part in my life . . . because my brother needed me to."

"So you did some things . . . for family."

He nods. "I would die for them. But I severely wronged others."

"Like who?"

"Like my wife . . . soon-to-be-ex wife."

"I see. Is Addie your friend?"

"I don't really know her, honestly. Again, this makes little sense to me . . . but I'm not about to turn my back. Not now."

"I see. Seems to be a bit much if you ask me."

"There isn't much for me so . . . why not?"

"Well, let me tell you, Addie is family to us. Unfortunately, there isn't much we can do for her at the moment. I'm an old lady. All I do is pray for this town. I pray for her."

"That's a very powerful thing . . . prayer. Sometimes, that's enough."

"Apparently. You're here."

"Pardon?"

"You ever think you could change this town?"

"I doubt that."

"Well, I believe you are more powerful than you think you are. A man of God, following God, is more powerful than any structure, than anything the devil can throw at him." She pats her daughter's lap.

"Sweetheart, please show Craig where Addie is. Go out the back. Don't want anyone seeing you."

"Thank you, ma'am." He gets up and starts to follow her daughter out the back door. He stops. "Just one thing. Why do you stay in this town?"

She stands. "Someone has to pray for this place."

"But isn't that what the church is for? The one with the giant steeple and cross."

She smiles a weak smile. "That's what it's supposed to be. You two better hurry. My gut is telling me someone will be around to check up on your vehicle parked out front soon."

Craig nods and rushes to follow the old woman's daughter.

⊂⊃

Mark finally gets back to the hospital being somewhat thankful for not having to take a four-hour drive to get there. For the entire two hours, he replayed what Dr. Chalmers said to him and examined his tone, the inflection on certain words like "vitals" and "slipping." He feels many things are slipping, of which the primary things are his sanity and his wife. By the time he gets to the lobby of the hospital, he is so worn out from thinking, he almost stumbles into the elevator that takes him to Jade's floor.

Inside the elevator, he stares at his blurred reflection off the stainless steel doors. Even through that reflection, he can see the bags under his eyes. He licks his lips, but it feels like a dry sponge rubbing against sandpaper, his mouth is so dry. The doors open and he ambles toward the nurses' station in front of Jade's room. Roz sits on the computer, clicking away at the keys, but it doesn't take long for her to notice Mark approaching. She shifts her gaze to Mark, and that's when he notices it.

She's been crying.

113

Mark looks around to see other nurses busying themselves, but he gets the feeling it's forced. He looks back at Roz, and for a few seconds, holds her pained and watery gaze. He forces a smile, but he knows it looks more like a grimace. He nods, though she said nothing, and she immediately reaches for the phone to get Dr. Chalmers. He then heads into Jade's room and gently closes the door behind him. Seeing her in the shape she's in still shakes him to his core, so much so his breath catches in his throat. He holds his chest, right around his heart. Each time he steps into this room, he feels his heart breaking. He grabs his usual seat next to her with the nightstand with the Bible on it behind him, and he waits. He touches her hand gently.

"Hey, Babe. You hanging in there?"

He waits in silence, almost in reverence, trying to keep stable. His chin quivers a bit, but he staves off the urge to break down and cry. He hears a firm knock on the door, and Dr. Chalmers enters the room. Mark stands and shakes his hand.

"What's the news, Doctor?"

Dr. Chalmers rolls a stool over to Mark and sits. He starts to say something but pauses. He tries again. "Things are slowing down for her, Mark. We ran a few tests to determine brain activity and . . . that's going away as well."

"What are you saying?"

"We are going to get to a point at which we will be forced to take her off life support. That point, where there is no brain activity"—he clears his throat—"we would bring in a neurologist for a second opinion, but as it stands . . . it won't be much time now. We've done all we could."

Mark stares at Dr. Chalmers with a blank stare. "How much time does she have?"

"Not much. A week . . . a few days."

"So if that's the case, she's still dying . . . even though she's on this breathing machine and has this feeding tube." He feels anger rise in his chest.

"I'm sorry."

"Listen to me. Don't you dare take her off these machines."

Dr. Chalmers holds his hands up. "I will keep her on as long as I can, but you have to consider her needs . . . what she would want. There is a bit of pain associated with keeping her on these machines and her body isn't healing, not at a good rate, anyway. The pain only increases as time goes on. And eventually, the machines would be working, but . . . she wouldn't be at all. You should consult with family to decide the next steps."

Mark stares at Jade and takes in a slow and deep breath. "Thank you, Doctor," he says through a clenched jaw.

Dr. Chalmers nods and leaves Mark alone with Jade.

"Jade," Mark says, "I know it's hard. I know it's hard, but I need you to fight. We all need you to fight. Don't give up. I . . . I can't do this without you." He bows his head and starts to pray when he hears a knock on the door. It's Roz. He looks up at her.

"Do you need anything, Mark?"

He shakes his head and retrains his focus back on Jade. "What do you do when—when you've done everything?"

"Pardon?"

"Jade shouldn't be here. But even as she is here, I'm virtually powerless to get her out."

"I wouldn't say powerless. We are all connected to someone powerful enough to get her out."

"But I'm praying, Roz. Everyone is. We've done everything medically, spiritually . . . I mean . . . what's left? What more can I do?"

"You pray more. You pray harder."

"There's no such thing as praying harder."

Roz looks at Mark. "Then you have to endure."

He places a soft hand on Jade's. "I'm scared, Roz. I've never been more scared in my life."

Roz sighs. "May I pray with you two?"

Mark simply nods. Roz grabs a seat on the other side of Jade, and amid the sounds of the machines keeping Jade alive, she prays.

০৪৮০

Jade stands with her doppelganger pressed behind her. She stares the flame angel down, not flinching, but entirely fearful of what it may do next.

"What is this about?" Jade asks.

"You, Jade. This is all about you. Isn't that what you like to think?" The flame angel's voice still comes out as multiple voices at once, but now is accompanied by distorted sounds she hasn't heard before. Then it begins to laugh. "You still really have no idea what this is, do you?"

She thinks, but is still having a hard time trying to understand what is going on. Her face shows frustration.

"Such a child still. Even after all those prayers; all that time in a building meant for worship." The flame angel steps out the cell. Jade grabs her doppelganger's hand and pulls her forward, but the flame angel moves too quickly.

"Some time ago," it says, "I told you that you would die in a ditch, both you and Mark. You both thought there was a God who pulled you out and set you free." It slams the cell door shut. "He didn't."

"Come back here." She rushes to the cell door and tries it, but it is sealed shut. "Hey," she screams, but hears nothing in return. As the flame angel leaves, the light it produced does as well. She presses herself to the bars, trying to see down the walkway, and notices all of the lanterns she lit are now extinguishing.

Her breathing becomes heavy, and she feels a wriggling in her stomach. Before long, the entire prison is pitch black. She hears murmurings from her doppelganger behind her. Jade kneels and feels on the floor to start crawling to her. At Jade's touch, she jumps, but Jade pulls her in close and holds her.

"We're going to die here," the doppelganger says.

"No, we won't."

"You were my last hope. My last chance."

"Wait." Jade listens for a moment "Do you hear that?"

"No."

Jade remains quiet to listen. It comes faintly at first, but she hears it pretty clear. Screeching, laughing, obscenities being shouted in the air. "Messengers."

"What? What are those?"

"I was told they bring death." She wobbles to her feet. "We can't stay in here. We have to find a way out." She tries to see something, anything, but is confronted by more darkness that's seemingly darker than black. That wriggling in her stomach becomes greater.

"There's nothing we can do. Just accept it, Jade."

She flops to the ground. "I just want to go home."

Jade hears something else, even over the cacophony of screeches and howls. It sounds like a really loud whisper, but she hears it as if it were spoken directly into her ear.

Lord, we've done all we could.

In the darkness, Jade feels the warmth of light, because she hears Mark's voice.

We need you, Lord. We need you in a mighty way. We need a movement by you to pull Jade through this. It feels like we are running out of time. We humbly come to you, the Redeemer of time.

Jade tries to listen, but the whooping and screeching of messengers becomes too much. She feels a shaking from the floor and in an instant, a bright white light shines directly into the prison. She can't tell from where the light is coming. All she knows is it comes from above. The messengers continue with their screeching, but in a different tune, one of agony. The light dims a bit, but still remains as a beam shining through the roof, straight down the middle of the prison.

She doesn't hear any messengers, but she still hears her doppelganger crying. She blinks her eyes a few times to adjust her vision as she tiptoes to the cell door and places her hands on the bars. She stares at the beam of pure white light. Parts of the prison are destroyed, walls collapsed into cells, a giant hole in the roof, a massive crack in the floor.

Lord, if I may be a little selfish, I need her. The kids need her.

"That's Mark," Jade says. She turns around. "You hear him?"

Through sobs, her other self says, "His prayers will go unanswered."

Jade lets her hands fall to her sides and tries to read her doppelganger. "What's with you?"

"Do you see a way out of this cell?"

"I don't . . . but that there"—she points at the beam of light—"that is different. I feel . . . hope."

"Hope doesn't get you out. Hope doesn't free you."

"Doesn't it?" She walks back to her twin and sits next to her. "We're going to get out of here."

"Then what? You'll never make it in time."

"What do you mean?"

She doesn't repeat herself.

"Tell me, what are you talking about?"

"Why do you suppose the flame angel led you here, away from the star?"

Jade remembers the star and how strange it felt to walk away from it. "Is the star . . . is it heaven?"

"It is the way to life."

"So sitting in here . . ."

"Death, but life again."

"That's confusing." She looks at the cell floor. "How do you know all this?"

"I've been here, in this exact cell, in this position, for a very long time. For a lifetime . . . for your lifetime."

"So we just wait . . . for death, and life? I'm so confused."

"It will be a death of sorts for us, then likely life for you . . . but another death for me."

"But we are the same."

"In some ways." She looks up at Jade. "But not all."

The sound of Mark's voice fades from the beam of light, but the beam still remains.

⊂≳≲⊃

Berta sits in her car out in front of Izabel's apartment, waiting for her to come out. She stares out the window, falling into a daydream, an occurrence that happens often lately. More times than not, she daydreams about what life would have been like had she not met Craig. This time is no different. She imagines herself being so wonderfully single and devoted to ministry. She would travel the world and help children, primarily little girls who have a tough go at life like she did.

The strange thing about these daydreams is that they all end up in her meeting Craig. Once, she was in Brazil volunteering and he was from another church doing work there as well. Another time, she was at a fundraiser and he was more or less the main guy everyone was trying to get money from. One daydream she's had involved her marrying someone else and having kids but cheating on her faceless husband with Craig.

She shakes away her latest foray into a life far out of her reach as Izabel makes her way to the car. She gets in and gently shuts the door. They greet each other.

"Thanks for coming with me," Berta says.

"No thanks needed. But I am confused on where we are going exactly . . . and why."

"Her name is Angelina Crosby."

"And this woman is the one who was tormenting you at your workplace for years?"

"The one and only."

Izabel looks at Berta with a confused expression.

"I know. But hang with me here. She's built herself up to be this immovable object in that company, but it took one visit from this detective, and she's gone. Just like that."

"Detective?"

"Yes. The one who is after Craig."

Izabel sighs. "Taller? Hard face? Dimple in chin?"

Berta turns toward her mother. "That's him."

"He came to the library."

"For what?"

"He asked about you."

"But not about Craig?"

"Nothing about him. He seemed to want to get personal, but I kept it surface level. But all he did was ask about you." She presses her lips together for a second. "I don't know for sure, but . . . I think he is enamored with you."

Berta looks down. She's had inklings of the same thing, but never thought any more of it.

"So why are we paying this Angelina a visit?"

"I need to know if Craig really slept with her . . . what this detective said to get her to leave so quickly." She looks back up at her mother. "And I needed you to come with me to read her."

"Why would you need to know any of this? That makes no sense, and the woman likely won't have a thing to say to you."

"I just do."

"That's not a good enough reason to willingly put yourself, and myself for that matter, in harm's way. We don't know this woman. We don't know what type of shape she's in, what type of mindset she has. This is crazy."

"No crazier than going to the monster's funeral."

Izabel looks straight ahead in deep thought. "Do you feel you are being led? Like at the funeral, do you feel the urge to move?"

"A little. I just . . . I feel talking to her will bring some clarity. I'm not sure how. I just believe it will."

"Fine." Izabel fastens her seatbelt. "I'm with you."

Berta looks at her and smiles a weak smile. "Thank you," she says as she starts the car.

CஐஐD

Berta and Izabel make it to Angelina's home, a nice-sized house set in a nice development. Berta glances at Izabel, noting the unsure expression she wears. She pulls the car up to the curb, at the end of a long driveway, and parks.

"Why are you doing this again?" Izabel asks.

"The detective got her to leave somehow. And he told me she confirmed that Craig slept with her, and that he went back to her. Showed up at my office after I left for the day to see her."

"And you believe that?"

"No, I don't. But there's something eating at me, asking, 'What if it's true?'" She sighs. "And if we absolutely confirm it isn't true . . . then that means the detective lied to me. I mean, I can only think of a few reasons why, and they all scare me." She looks at the home, noting the white picket fence, the large front and back yard, the three-car garage. "But if we can somehow glean the truth from her, and that Craig did sleep with her, then this divorce is my final answer." She then sees the front door open and out comes Angelina walking hand in hand with a little girl.

Berta's jaw goes slack for a second as she watches Angelina in street clothes play with this little girl. The way she is with the girl tells Berta instantly that the girl is Angelina's daughter, and Berta second-guesses making this trip. Still, she didn't make it for no reason. She forces herself to get out the car and casually walks to the edge of the front lawn. Izabel stands behind her. It only takes a few seconds for Angelina to look up and lock eyes with Berta, a point at which she ushers her little one back inside.

She tries to read Angelina's expressionless face as she struts toward her near the end of the drive.

"What are you doing here and how did you find out where I live?" Angelina asks as soon as she is in hearing distance.

"Is that your daughter?"

"Again, how did you find out where I live? John tell you?"

"No. Look, I don't want to take up too much time—"

"No, no, no. You can't be here."

"Angelina."

"Don't."

"That detective that spoke to you before you left."

"I said don't." Her voice comes out a bit hoarse.

Berta stops speaking and observes Angelina. A quick gust of wind blows between them, causing her to wrap her arms around herself. She nods. "Okay. This was clearly a mistake. I apologize for wasting your time." She turns around to her mother and mouths "Let's go."

"Did you send that detective?"

Berta stops in her tracks, but she doesn't turn around. "No. Not at all."

"He seemed really interested in you."

Berta turns back around. "So is that what this is? You still need to have the upper hand. I can't ask you anything directly, but you can ask me whatever you want?"

"It's not like that. It's just . . . I'm not supposed to say anything to you."

She stares at Angelina, waiting for her to elaborate.

"He threatened me. Threatened my family."

Berta looks at Angelina's hand to see a wedding ring. "Never knew you were married. You . . ."

"Used my body in disrespectful ways? Isn't that what John said?"

"Something like that. Is he wrong?"

She wraps her arms around herself as well and looks down. She looks at Izabel, then back to Berta. "Would you like to come in? We can talk for a few moments before my husband comes home."

"Certainly."

Berta and Izabel follow Angelina into her home, noting how lavish the place looks on the outside, yet so terribly plain on the inside. They walk past a den-type area where the little girl she saw earlier sits and watches TV.

"Marilynne, what are you watching?"

"Cartoons."

"What cartoons?"

"The cartoons you don't want me watching."

"Then what are you supposed to do?"

"Vela said I could."

"What did I tell you about lying?"

Long pause. "Sorry."

"Vela, can you get Marilynne while I take our guests to the sun room?"

An older woman in plain clothes comes around the corner, startling Berta. "Of course," she says.

Berta and Izabel follow Angelina to a bright room full of books and plants. She offers seats. Each of the women sits and for a few moments they simply stare at each other.

"You're married. And you have a child . . . and a maid."

"Yes."

"And John was right."

Her expression goes blank. She seems to read Berta for a few long moments. "He was."

"But why?"

"There isn't a reason I can tell you that won't sound like an excuse. There isn't anything I can say that won't make me sound selfish . . . or devious." She rubs the palms of her hands on the front of her legs. "So I'll just say I did it to get ahead, because that's the most believable."

"Tell me the parts that aren't as believable. Tell me the parts that make you seem selfish or devious . . . because that's what I already think of you. So, my thoughts of you won't change for the worse. If anything, what I think of you will get better. Not that it matters what I think."

She sighs. "I needed to succeed. I needed to show everyone I can make something of myself."

"By tearing me down?"

"I am sorry for that. I just . . . once I went that path, I couldn't just step away. I knew too much. I still know too much."

"So what did the detective say to get you to leave so abruptly?"

"He threatened my family. He knew things no one knew. He talked of my little Marilynne. He knew of the blackmails. He knew . . . too much." She crosses her legs.

"So you left because you were scared."

"Wouldn't you?"

Berta presses the conversation forward. "So of the men that you blackmailed . . ."

"I already know where you're going with this, and the answer is no. Your husband is not one of them. I did not ever sleep with your husband. Not ever."

"That's not where I was going with that, but since we're here, the video of him in the office when I left that one day?"

"He wanted to know why, why I was doing what I was doing, why I was lying."

"The detective told me you said something different to him."

"We never even talked about your husband." She uncrosses her legs. "So he is clearly lying to you."

Berta looks at Izabel to see her nod. "I figured as much."

"So who is he?" Angelina asks.

"Who are you talking about?"

"The detective. He gave me the name Simms. Who is he to you that he would tell you about a separate conversation he had with me? Why did he ask me all those questions about you?"

"It's a long story . . . one I can't say too much on."

"Now hold on a second. I was forthright with what I know. It would be nice to be paid in kind."

Berta looks at Izabel before turning back to look at Angelina. "He's digging into my life . . . trying to find my husband."

"What did he do?"

"He has a past."

Angelina laughs. "We all do."

"Well, his past can send him to jail for a very long time."

"So that well-mannered, respectable-looking man has a thug side, huh?"

"That's not it."

"Then what is it?"

Berta shrugs. "I don't want to talk too much about it. If anything, it could get you into more mess."

Angelina stares for a moment. "Then say no more."

Berta stares at a speck on the floor, thinking about what Angelina told her.

"Well, sorry to cut this meeting short, but you will have to go. My husband will be home soon and well . . . it would be awkward."

Berta and Izabel rise. "Of course. Thank you for speaking with us."

"One last word of advice." Angelina chuckles. "Maybe this is the only real advice I'll ever give you, but be careful around that detective. Something is seriously off with him."

"I'm aware."

"You ought to be more than aware. You ought to be away. Far, far away."

Chapter Nine

Craig follows the old woman's daughter out the back of her house, on a hurried trek to Addie's home.

"I never caught your name," Craig says.

"I never gave it to you." She urges him forward. "Nor do I plan to."

He doesn't say anything in reply, taking it as a cue to be quiet, and follows behind her as they trudge through a bunch of shrubs and bushes. After a few minutes of traversing a heavily wooded area, there is a short clearing at the back of a small cottage.

"I'll go first."

And just like that, the young woman leaps from the bushes and dashes to the back door of the cottage. Craig wonders what all the sneaking around is for and finds it very confusing. Moments later, the woman comes back and slips back into the bushes next to him.

"She doesn't want to see you. She said you should leave and never come back."

Craig looks at her strangely. "I didn't do all this just to turn around. And why is everyone telling me to never come back?"

"Listen to me." Her voice becomes strained. "There are a lot of things you don't know about this town . . . there are a lot of things you don't know about how this place operates. No one rushes headfirst into this place."

Craig looks determined. "I. Don't. Care." He hops from the bushes and dashes to the back door to knock.

He frantically knocks until the door opens and he is pulled in. He braces himself against a kitchen counter before turning around and seeing Addie.

"What are you doing? Are you crazy?"

Craig looks in shock. "Addie . . . what happened to you?"

She barely stands, holding her side with one arm. The other arm is in a sling. Her left eye is swollen shut and her upper lip has a few dark marks on it.

He notices her voice comes out hoarse, and sees the bruises around her neck. He takes a step forward but she retreats.

"What the hell is wrong with you?"

"I came to see if you were okay."

"Well . . . you see? I'm not. So?"

"Addie, let me help."

"What—" Her voice comes out loud. She winces and tries again. "What can you do? Save yourself a lot of trouble. Just leave. I'll be fine."

"Who did this to you?"

"You haven't asked anyone else around here about me, have you?"

"I . . . I went to the restaurant at the edge of town . . . near the sign . . . and I went to the church. The old woman through the woods was helpful, though."

Another knock at the door. Addie struggles to get to the door. She lets the old woman's daughter in. The young woman stares at Craig with a piercing gaze. Her face slowly turns red.

"You must have a death wish."

He ignores her. "Addie, tell me what happened. Who did this?"

"Why?" She raises an eyebrow and gives him a stare before rolling her eyes. "So you can save me? Big strong man coming to save me?"

"I don't know where any of this is coming from."

"Typical. This is all your fault, you know."

"What? What do you mean?"

"Because he has nothing over you. He doesn't even know you. So he took it all out on me. All of it."

"What is happening here?"

"Just stay away. Don't try to help. Just leave me alone."

Craig stands there, stunned. He opens his mouth to speak but is interrupted by a sound in one of the other rooms.

"Oh, my God," Addie says. "My husband is home. Why is he home?" She looks to Craig and the other woman. "You two have to get out of here."

Without hesitation, the younger woman rushes out the door. Craig stands for a moment before jetting out the back door and into the wooded area. Dashing through the woods, Craig and the younger woman get back to the older woman's home and breeze in. Craig pants, trying to catch his breath.

"What the heck just happened?"

"You got your answer." She looks suspiciously toward the living room. She holds her hand out to quiet Craig.

When he brings himself to complete silence, he hears the old woman talking to someone. The young woman tells Craig to stay put, then she disappears around the corner. Craig creeps his way toward the front of the house and catches a glimpse of a few people standing at the door. He pulls back into the narrow hallway, trying to think of what to do next. He peers back out to see the older woman talking to what seems to be police officers. His stomach turns. He waits a few minutes for the officers to leave before he steps out. The old woman chuckles while taking a seat.

"Seems like our little town here is onto you."

"He went to Jared," the young woman says.

"Who's Jared?" Craig asks.

"The bartender at the restaurant," the old woman says. "I'm assuming you don't know what a snake looks like?"

"I don't understand."

"He's in with them. Jared is," the young woman says. "He's their eyes and ears. You must leave now."

"Now wait a second, Wren," the old woman says. "We can't let him go just yet. Those officers are still snooping around his vehicle."

"Mother."

"What? You were going to tell him your name anyway."

"No, I wasn't."

The old woman shrugs. "So, did you find Addie?"

"We did," Craig says.

"And?"

"She's in rough shape . . . but she had this fire in her. I don't know how to explain it."

"She's got spunk, that's for sure."

"But then her husband showed up, and she got really scared. I shouldn't have been there, sure, but there was something else with her fear." He looks back and forth between the two. "Did her husband do it?"

"If I told you yes," the old woman says, "what would you do? Because according to the cops I just talked to, the perp is still at large."

"If her husband did it, there's nothing much I can do. Why doesn't she just go to the police?"

Neither woman answers. He looks back and forth between the two again, swearing that he notices Wren shake her head slightly at her mother.

"It's been real, Craig, but you have to go," the old woman says while staring out the window.

"Wait. What aren't you telling me?"

"We've told you all we know. This is the part of the journey where you do some searching on your own."

"But I don't unders—"

The old woman pulls her gun on Craig. "Listen, you are a nice man. And we would love to help you further, but we cannot. I've already brought quite a bit of trouble to my doorstep. Now,"—she glances out the window—"while you still have the chance, I advise you to get in your vehicle and leave."

Craig stares at the woman and backs away slowly. "I understand. Thank you for your help." He starts for the door. "But there is no rest of my journey. I've found out what happened to her. She doesn't want my help. No one from this town seems to want me here, so . . ."

"The choice is yours; but do you really think God wants you to stop there?"

"Says the lady pointing a gun at me." He flexes his jaw muscles. "What else can I do? What else can anyone really do?"

The old woman shrugs. Craig, being exasperated, thanks the two again and leaves.

ೞ

"So if I stay, I die, then live again. I leave, I get to life," Jade whispers to herself. She turns to her other self. "But what if I don't want to experience this death?"

She looks up at Jade with solemn eyes. "It doesn't seem you have much of a choice."

Jade turns away and stares at the beam of light streaming through the roof of the building. She examines it, trying to understand what it is exactly, and how is it a source of light in this prison called her heart. She looks down at the bars, remembering she was able to open the door to this place, while the flame angel was not. The flame angel, she determines, doesn't have much power at all, but is deceitful. She wonders if she is able to move the cell bars like she did the doors leading into this place.

She squeezes the bars, warming the cold metal in her hands, and tugs at them, gently at first. She looks to the beam of light and focuses on it while pulling and pushing the bars with every bit of strength she has.

The bars don't move.

After a few more tries, her hands begin to hurt, so she lets her hands fall to her sides. She sighs in exasperation. She glances over at her other self to see her gawking at her. Jade rolls her eyes and continues to stare at the beam of light.

ଔଓ

Berta gets back to her home after dropping Izabel off at her apartment. All Izabel said to her is that she believes what Angelina said. This echoed Berta's opinion, and that put her in a deep thought zone. Both women stayed quiet for the rest of the trip back.

She gets to her elevator and presses the button to get to the top floor. A few moments later, the doors open to Simms leaning against the wall opposite the elevators. For a brief moment, Berta freezes, but she quickly regains her composure, hoping Simms didn't notice.

"Detective."

"Berta."

Both stare each other down, but Berta is the first to look away. She turns and heads toward her door. Once she gets there, she jams her key

133

into the lock and thrusts the door open. Simms casually walks in and gently closes the door after her.

"So you thought it was necessary to search my home, did you?"

For the first time Berta can remember, Simms looks shocked.

"What are you talking about?"

"Don't play dumb. I know when someone enters my home without permission. Did you find what you were looking for? Did you find your *smoking gun*?"

Simms sighs. "No. And I apologize."

"That's it?"

"What else do you want me to say?"

"Did you have a warrant?"

"Of course I did."

Berta stares at him, trying to determine whether he is lying. She automatically assumes he is, but decides to play things safe. She presses the issue no further, knowing that Ramses had her place swept for any listening or video devices.

"What do you want, Simms?"

"The same thing I've always wanted. Nothing's changed. Well, something changed. My ability to get that thing has significantly diminished. The goal, though, was always the same; it is the same."

"Why do you want him so bad?"

Simms raises an eyebrow. "Because he's a criminal. The ending to a long string of criminals, the way I see it." He smirks. "But I thought you knew that already."

"I do." She remains calm. "But what are the chances he didn't do any of what you think?"

"Slim. There are people out there covering it up for a reason." He takes a step toward her. "But if I'm not mistaken, it seems you don't agree?"

"Well, it seems like it's more than justice to you. I feel there's something else."

"Your intuition serves you well."

"Then what is it?"

He looks to the ground. "I spent most of my adult life being a cop. It's in my blood. When I became detective, it was one of the best days of my life. You know, that and the birth of my son."

"You have a son?"

He nods. "But when I became a detective, I"—he jams his hands into his pockets—"I felt like everything in my life, both good and bad, led to that moment."

Berta tries to read him. Knowing what she knows about him currently, she tries to understand his angle, because she knows there's more to this story than he's telling.

"I've had some cases . . . I treat them all as important, but one of the cases at the beginning of my career as a detective was to take down Bobby Newton and his entire network. He was a ruthless criminal. Drug dealer. It took a while and some help from the FBI, but we took him down. Locked him and his people up. Life in prison." He chuckles. "News spread fast. The streets were getting cleaned and one after another, crime boss after crime boss, we took them all down. Then, I ran into a different type of criminal. These ruthless crime bosses started becoming even more ruthless businessmen." He locks eyes with her. "And that's when I first ran into Calvin Gaffney." He walks to the window and stares for a few minutes. "Could never catch him. Not until Mark showed up."

"I don't understand how this is supposed to lead me to a greater understanding of why you want Craig so badly."

"Craig solved the case, Berta. Not me. He went around the law and got to Mark's wife before any of us could even . . ."

"Is this about jealousy?"

"No."

She waits for him to speak again.

"We do things by the book. We do things the right way." He shakes his head. "And to find out his connection to one of the absolute most elusive crime bosses this town has ever seen . . . Raul Valencia is the guy we could never catch."

"So if he were alive still, you'd be after him?"

"If he were alive, he'd be in prison by now."

"You know you're talking of my stepfather."

"I do." He slowly turns to face her. "I still have trouble reconciling."

"Reconciling what?"

"How someone so beautiful can get caught in something so dirty."

She feels her pulse quicken. Not lost upon her is the fact that Simms has mentioned nothing of the monster. "I think you should go."

"I'm sorry. Did I offend?"

"I'm married and you are after my husband. Yes, you offended me."

He starts a staredown, but Berta averts her eyes.

"Well, I wanted you to know . . . I wanted you to know that there aren't any more cases left."

"What do you mean?"

"All the previously unsolved mysteries have been solved. Craig's latest foray into crimeland, well—" He pulls out a picture and hands it to Berta.

She nearly vomits at what she sees. "Why would you show me this?"

"Because I need to know where he is. I need to know where Craig is."

"Who is this?" She waves the picture.

"That's what's left of the witness to the murder in Philly. Do you know where Craig is?"

"No."

"But you have a way to contact him. Tell me the truth." His eye twitches.

"No. Now take this"—she presses the picture to his chest hard —"and get out of my home. Don't come back."

She notices, as he leaves, that he wears a pained expression on his face. She also has a bone to pick with Ramses, knowing he's the one who is cleaning things up for Craig. She finds his actions toward that witness deplorable. She slams the door shut and forces herself to breathe.

"Something is off about him. He mentioned nothing of Dad."

Berta snaps around, pressing her back to the door.

"Jennifer."

She comes from the back rooms. "Sit. We need to talk."

☙❧

After a day of staying and praying over Jade, Mark gets home to change clothes and shower. Plaguing his mind are thoughts of what to do with Jade, knowing he has to call everyone and let them know what's going on. As soon as he steps into the house, he is greeted by a cold emptiness. He looks around. No Alicia. He trains his focus on the bottle of pills sitting on a table next to his comfortable chair. He realizes he hasn't taken them for some time now. He's thankful the pain hasn't been as much. Certain movements still get him, but he is able to manage better. He digs into his pocket to pull out his cell phone. He calls Joanne, Berta, and Craig. No one picks up, so he leaves each a message. He trudges upstairs to the bathroom to take a shower.

When he gets out the shower, he strolls to his dresser.

"Make love to me, Mark."

Mark flips around from the dresser to see Alicia lying in the bed wearing a black silk chemise. She toys with her hair seductively. For a moment, all he is able to do is stare.

"Did you hear me?"

He grabs some clothes and heads back toward the bathroom. "I did."

"Mark, please don't go."

There's a softness he thinks he hears in her voice that gives him pause.

"Please don't leave me again."

He puts his head down. "I'm . . . I'm married. And I love her. You know that. I miss her. You know that."

"But that didn't stop you before. I just want to feel your touch. I just want . . . I want your body next to mine. You have the same look in your eyes you had those years ago."

"We never made love."

"It's me, Mark. I was there. You may tell that lie to everyone else, but I was there. I felt you. For that moment in time, it was just us. You can deny it to everyone else. You can deny it to save your marriage. You can even lie to your pastor about it, but you can't lie to me about it."

He considers what she said. "I'm sorry." He starts toward the bathroom again.

"Mark." Her voice comes out strained and high-pitched.

He turns around to see her sitting up, clutching a pillow to her chest. She holds her hand out, reaching for him. He takes a step toward her as she lies back. He stops just at the edge of the bed.

"Why are you here?"

She looks at him quizzically. "Why do you put me here?"

He stares for a few moments before looking away, being unable to hold her stare. The moment he looks back, she's gone. He hurries and gets dressed to rush downstairs en route to the hospital to get back by Jade's side. He gets to the front door as his cell phone buzzes in his pocket. He yanks it out, noticing the number.

"This is Mark."

"Mr. Cooke. This is Eleanor Bixby."

"Oh, hi." He tries not to sound so depressed. "Yes, Ms. Bixby—"

"Please call me Eleanor."

"Sorry, Eleanor, thank you for calling me back. I—"

"What exactly did you call me for?"

"I was given your number—"

"By the detective, I know. But why search me out?"

"I didn't really search you out . . . I just—I just wanted to speak with you about Alicia Langley."

Mark hears nothing, but he feels like he needs to prove his point more.

"The detective told me you talked to him off the record. I was just hoping we could talk under the same condition."

"You're asking me to just throw out doctor-patient confidentiality? Just turn my back on ethics, on my code?"

"Alicia is no longer alive."

"The rules still stand."

"But you talked to the detective."

"Sure. Only after being forced." She exhales loudly. "Look, I don't like any of this. I don't like it at all . . . but I've been given no choice."

"What do you mean?"

"You speak as if you don't know."

"I don't know. What *is* there to know?"

She chuckles. "You seriously have no idea?"

"None."

Her chuckles turn to out-and-out laughter. "Fine, Mr. Cooke. Let's meet up. You are a ways away from here, are you not?"

"I am. But I'm on my way up there, or past there."

"Fine. Take down this address. It's a small little dive. Meet me there tonight at seven."

Mark takes down the address and gets off the phone. He places a hand on the door.

"Where are you going?"

He doesn't turn around to look at her. "Out."

"Out where?"

"You know where."

"But what are you talking to her for?"

"What do you mean?"

"I mean why are you digging into my past now?"

"You said so yourself. There are things you've done, things done to you, that are bad. You said you were sorry. Are you?"

"No."

"Well . . ." He opens the door and leaves his home.

CHAPTER TEN

Berta sits down cautiously. "What's going on here?"

"Did you destroy the CD . . . and the files?"

"Of course. Why? Why are you here? And how did you get in here without being noticed? The police were here, no?"

"No, they weren't. Just your friend who just left. I waited until he was gone before getting in. You need better security. Anyway, they got us."

"They who?"

"I don't know yet. But they killed my mom. They almost had me, but I got away."

Berta starts and stops a few times before saying anything. "What happened?"

Jennifer starts pacing back and forth. "We were living life . . . weren't even in the U.S. Somehow, someone broke into where we were staying and they . . . they"—she pushes a few loose strands of hair behind her ear, then wraps her arms around herself—"they butchered her. These guys, they were professionals—the way they broke in, the organization they had. They burned down where we were staying." She looks at Berta.

"I'm so sorry."

"I will mourn properly when I find out who did this . . . and why."

"You think I have something to do with it?"

"I don't know. We took a big risk by giving you two that CD. We took a risk just by talking to you in the first place."

"I had nothing to do with it."

"What about who you associate with?"

"Like who? My mother? My soon-to-be-ex-husband? How about my pastor? How about—" A thought bounces around in her mind. Ramses knew about the CD. Ramses also, as Berta had just witnessed, will go to extreme lengths to keep Craig safe. What was on the CD wouldn't be a smoking gun for anyone looking to expose them all, but it would cause people to snoop around more. *But would he kill Marcella and Jennifer over a CD? Maybe it's more about what the CD represents as opposed to what's on it. Marcella and Jennifer presumably have access to a lot of information, information that could take down Ramses, Craig, and anyone else involved. So, did Ramses see that as a threat to Craig and himself? But then, because of the nature of the information they have, Marcella and Jennifer likely made a lot of enemies.*

"Who?"

She snaps from her trance. "I'm sorry, Jennifer. But anyone could have done this."

"What do you mean? There aren't that many people who could."

"Your mother killed the monster, no?"

"She never said that."

"She said she buried him. But we both know what that means. It's pretty straightforward to me. The thing is, that network he was running before ended up where?"

"In her back pocket."

"And I'm guessing the only card she had to play was to threaten to expose them, correct?"

"Yeah. What are you getting at?"

"I'm saying they would eliminate the last bit of their known connection with the monster, then live their lives as if nothing ever happened. The monster had his network set up so if one part needed to be eliminated, another part would do it. But he was always protected. That I know for sure."

Jennifer seems to ponder what Berta says. She digs in her pocket and pulls out a USB flash drive. She holds it in between her thumb and index finger, then flings it onto the coffee table.

"What's that?"

"Everything. His entire network. Names, addresses, events, and how they were coordinated. It's everything. This is where we pulled the CD information from. Little by little over time, Mom and I added to the file behind his back. Once he died, we were able to complete it."

Berta sits and thinks for a few long moments. "Okay, so?"

"I don't know." She holds herself tighter. "I have this information, but I can't do anything with it. Don't know who to trust. Don't know who to go to."

"But you seemed to have made it to my doorstep. How did you know where I live?"

She points at the drive. "It's on there. He was tracking you and your husband for years," she says matter-of-factly. She looks down to her side. "I wish I had a normal life. I wish he didn't take that from me." Berta notices a single tear drop from Jennifer's face, but Jennifer wipes it away quickly. "So here's what I'm thinking. Take the drive. I can't keep it. It would do no good with me, anyway."

"I don't want any part in this."

"You're already involved." Her eyes light up. "You have Raul's group still looking after you and your husband."

"Not so sure about that." She doesn't know where Jennifer is going with this, but she doesn't wish to reveal how much she knows of Raul's network.

"I am. It's in the files."

"And what would you do?"

"Well, I need a favor."

"What?"

"I need to stay with you, just for a little bit, while I figure out my next move."

"So you want to bring the monster's group of seedy individuals to my doorstep?"

"First, it will take time for them to find me. Second, even if that happened, they wouldn't do anything stupid because that would start a war in which they would lose. I just need a couple days."

"So,"—Berta stares a hole into her—"that's what you came to me for. Protection."

"Not the only reason. But it's an incentive."

Berta scoffs.

"Listen, I know you see it. This network is the last remaining piece of that sicko. We can destroy it and the memory of him. That's what Mom and I were trying to do. I know you and your mother want the same."

"What you are asking for is for me to participate in your revenge plan. To that, I have to decline. I'm not in the revenge business. I err on the side of letting God handle that part of life."

Jennifer chuckles. "You honestly can sit here and say you don't have the slightest desire to finish this?"

Berta shakes her head. "I just don't see it that way."

"Well, it's admirable"—she picks up the flash drive—"but I can't see it any other way. If something isn't done, nothing will ever be done . . . and I'll be dead."

Berta stares out the window, pressing her lips together in a grimace. She starts to feel nauseated thinking about her next course of action. At the moment, she believes Jennifer, and in that, briefly mourns the loss of Marcella. She wants to leave this all alone, but doesn't find herself in a position to do so.

Jennifer ducks behind the sofa for a second and stands with a bag slung around her shoulder. "I gotta keep moving." She starts for the front door.

"Wait." Berta gets up and begins pacing. "I can get you a couple days, I think."

"Thank you." She looks like she's on the verge of breaking down. "Thank you so much."

"I still don't know what I can do other than that."

"Don't worry. I just need some time to think . . . to breathe a little. I can't do that if I'm always running."

Berta shoots a look over to her. "But if you screw me over—"

"No. That's not why I'm here." She puts her hands up in retreating fashion. "You are my last hope."

φφ

Craig runs along a dusty road with the sun beaming down on him. As of late, he's taken to jogging a couple miles to the empty produce stand and back. He does it to get air into his lungs, to get moving, and to clear his mind. Why on earth would he venture into the unknown town of Silver Rock to help this mystery woman who clearly didn't want his help? He asks himself that question often and comes to the conclusion that it's from being restless and bored. He thought he was moved by God. But now he knows. He's not risking his life to help anyone who doesn't want it. And he is in no position to risk his life for anything anyhow. Still, what the old woman said to him rings clearly in his mind.

He once again gets to the produce stand to find it completely empty, and turns around to continue his jog back to the ranch. He begins to daydream again.

"I wanted to give you this," Raul said. "Let it serve as a reminder."

"Of what exactly?" Craig asked.

"Of what you came from. Of who you were. Of how much more you can be."

Craig looked at the leather-covered box for a few moments before opening it. He opened it slowly to a cracking noise, revealing a big-faced watch. He instantly recognized the watch as the one he tried to steal from Raul.

"Sir?" He looked up at Raul.

"It doesn't work. But it doesn't need to. Keep this with you always. You've come a long way, Craig."

"I'm a little slow to the draw here, sir. What is the significance of the watch I tried to steal from you, a watch that doesn't work?"

Raul smiled. "The watch serves as a low point for you. But it also marks a new beginning." He sat in his tall, leather executive chair, one hand propped up on his cane. "It's a reminder to never go back to that low point in your life."

"Thank you, sir, I think." Craig eyed the watch curiously. "Still, a pretty strange gift: a watch that doesn't work."

"Just look forward to seven forty-three."

"Huh?"

Raul said nothing more of it, and Craig knew right then, Raul's time was running short. A week or so later, Raul passed.

Craig gets back to the ranch and gets upstairs to take a shower. He digs through one of his bags to find the leather box, a lot more worn than what it was years ago. He opens it to a few more clicks and cracks of the hinges. The trinket that has been on his mind during his jog, the big-faced wristwatch. He rarely looks at the watch, and he has never thought to get the thing working again, but every so often, maybe once a year, he pulls it out to stare at it and remember Raul. It's strange to him that for most of the year, the watch is out of sight, out of mind, but today all he can think about is the watch and what it really means. He looks away thinking he is far more what he used to be than what he could be. He closes the box and sets it back in his bag at the moment his cell rings. He quickly picks it up once he sees that it's Ramses.

"I've got good news," Ramses says. "With a catch."

"That being what?"

"Well, first, your name is cleared."

Craig pauses for a long time before saying anything. "That's good news . . . right? What's the catch?"

"There are some things we still need to clean up here. Some causes for concern."

"Meaning I still can't come home yet. What are your concerns?"

"Well, for starters, the main witness to the garage incident is dead. But that's not of our doing."

"I don't understand."

"Quite frankly, I don't, either. But this is a gut call here. I think you should stay at the ranch until I can make some sense of this."

"And the detective?"

"Hopefully he'll back off. But he's already searched your home and the office."

Craig tenses. "Berta didn't take too kindly to that, I'm guessing."

"She didn't seem particularly bothered."

"Really?"

"Really. Anyway, I need to figure out what is going on. As for the detective, time will tell. He has no teeth now. He cannot touch you. But again, I need to make sure. Shouldn't take me longer than a few days."

"Thank you, sir. I appreciate all of this, all of what you've done."

"Of course, Craig." He ends his sentence as if he wants to say something more.

"There's more?"

"No." He clears his throat. "Just wandered into my thoughts."

"Never known you to be a daydreamer. That's my thing."

Ramses laughs. "Yeah. I suppose it is. How did things go with the Addie woman?"

"Not so well. I think. I'm actually not sure. I did find her, though."

"And?"

"And I was right. She was in trouble. Someone beat on her pretty bad. I think it was her husband. She didn't want my help, though. In fact, she wanted me to be far, far away."

"Domestic dispute. That happens sometimes. Hopefully this is the end of it."

"Yeah. I'm going to leave it alone. It's just weird, that's all."

"What? Her insistence that you stay away from her?"

"No. How I found her. So you remember the old woman I told you about?"

"Yeah?"

"She went on to explain that there's this group that seemingly controls things in the town."

"Every town has a government."

"No. She made it seem like something more devious."

"You ever think she was simply anti-establishment?"

"I haven't. I mean she did seem upset over some of their gun laws that seem to override state laws. I get the feeling she isn't talking about local government, though."

"Why?"

"Well, I came in looking for Addie. The old woman starts telling me about the corruption in the town. She believes I can fix that somehow."

"Was she drinking?"

"Seriously, I have a hunch that someone from this group harmed Addie."

"But you don't know for sure."

"I don't."

"And you don't know exactly what the old woman's motivation is."

"I don't."

"Well, you already know what I'm going to say."

"I know. You're going to say stay out of it. Trust me, I am. I'm so ready to come home."

"Well, just a few more days. Sit tight until then."

☙

Mark pulls into a small lot in front of a beat-down looking building and parks the car. Nervous ahead of his meeting with Eleanor Bixby, he takes a few deep breaths before stepping in.

The air is thick with smoke and moisture as he makes his way to a booth in the back. The lighting is low, so he doesn't worry much about being seen, but he avoids all eye contact nonetheless. He assumes this bar is a place where a lot of dirty deals occur, just based on how inconspicuous one could remain. He gets to the very back booth and slides in, nestling himself into the darkest part of the bar. An odd smell rises to his nose, which forces him to sit at the edge of the booth's seat. He doesn't want to know what disgusting things grow in the very corners of the bar.

He takes a few moments to observe who's in the bar before Eleanor shows up. He sees a man slouching so much his face almost touches the table in front of him. Every so often, the man takes a long draft of his beer-filled mug. He looks at two people—one male, one female—sitting three booths ahead of him. She gets up to grab some drinks at the bar. She wears tights, Uggs, and a low-cut sweater. The man is partially covered in darkness, but it looks like he wears a ragged jean vest and plain t-shirt under. Mark observes both of them, not realizing the guy stares right at him. Mark diverts his attention. A few moments later, Mark sees growing movement in his peripheral. The man and woman from three booths down slide into his booth, the man first, the woman after. Mark doesn't say anything.

"Two hundred for a few hours," the man says in a gravely voice. "Fifty for some under-the-table action."

Mark is appalled. "Sorry, not interested."

The man smirks and looks toward the woman. "You ever been with a white girl before?"

The woman starts making gestures with her tongue, flicking her tongue ring around. Mark feels a fur-covered Ugg boot moving around the inside of his thigh.

"Again, not interested. I'm actually waiting for someone."

The woman pouts.

"In here?" the man asks. He chuckles. "She can be everything and anything you want."

Mark looks past the woman and her pouty face to see a larger woman in a red business suit trotting her way toward him. She eyes him for a moment before stopping at the bar and grabbing two drinks. The woman with the tongue ring turns around sharply and then to the man.

"I think he likes them thicker."

The man looks toward the bar and grunts. He nods at the woman with the tongue ring and they both leave the booth and casually walk back to theirs. The woman in the red suit sits in front of him and places a drink in front of him. She takes a quick sip of hers and unbuttons her suit coat. Mark takes a couple seconds to figure her out, as it seems she tries to do the same. As she grabs her glass to take a sip, he notices a diamond ring on her ring finger.

"Married?" Mark asks.

"Next year," she says in a husky, almost bluesy voice. "Some advice. In dives like this, get a drink first. People won't bother you then."

"I see. Well, I don't usually go to dives like this, so . . ."

She nods and takes another sip. "Understood. So, what can I do for you?"

"I was thinking you could help me understand Alicia Langley a little more, but . . . you mentioned something about being strong-armed by the detective. I thought about that the whole way here."

"Ah." She smiles a wide smile. "You don't really know your detective friend, do you?"

"He's not really my friend."

"Well, he's dirty. As dirty as they come. He told me you would seek me out. He forced me to speak with you."

"How can he do that?"

"He has some stuff on me. That's all I'll say."

"Are you dirty as well?"

"No. I am not at all. I adhere to the highest professional standards. It's my personal life that's a mess. My personal life is what he used against me." She takes a bigger gulp of her drink. "So what do you want to know about her?"

"Listen, I'm sorry for what the detective has done. I did not ask him for this, and if you are uncomfortable with this—"

"Ha. You didn't come all this way, sit in this disgusting bar, just to tell me I can go about my business, pretend this didn't happen."

Mark stares her in the eyes for a long and awkward moment.

"She's right," Eleanor says. She takes a few long gulps of her drink, almost finishing it. "You do get lost in your eyes."

"Pardon?"

"Forget it. What is it you want to know about Alicia?"

"Okay. I don't know where to start. I mean, she told me, before she took her life, that she's done some things, some terrible things, all in an effort to destroy me."

"And you're coming to me because?"

"Closure, I guess. To see if there is anything more for me and my family to worry about."

"Closure?" She gives a smug look. "Mark, you do realize you virtually ruined her life, don't you?"

"I think we were both affected by a set of unfortunate events."

"My, my, aren't we political."

His voice is strained. "What do you want me to say?"

"I don't want you to say anything. In fact, I don't want to be here right now, but again, I was coerced. At the very least, if I'm forced to talk to you, I would like you to be upfront and honest."

He looks down at the golden liquid sitting in his cup, falling slightly into a daydream. "I've made some bad choices in life. All of this . . . my wife, my best friend, my kids—everyone I'm connected to—is feeling the negative effects of my actions."

"And you feel guilty."

He nods as if it were a question, though he knows it wasn't. "Everything I face right now is because of the poor choices I've made. I—" He thinks about what he just said in greater detail. "I've made bad choice after bad choice that dug me deeper and deeper."

"Into what?"

"Into hell."

She smirks. "Christians are so dramatic. Why did you make those choices?"

Mark pushes away his drink. "The why can come later, maybe. I didn't come here to be analyzed. I came here for information on Alicia."

"Can I ask you a personal question, first?"

"You can ask, but I may not answer."

"Well, if everyone around you is hurting because of your actions, why are you here with me?"

"I have no answer for that."

"Would you like to hear my hypothesis?"

"No."

"You're running. You're looking to shift some of this blame here, and while Alicia can be to blame for her actions, you set the wheels turning."

He doesn't want to think much more on it, and he feels he needs some control over the conversation. "Can we move on?"

She flexes her jaw muscles enough for Mark to notice. "Fine."

"So tell me about when you first met her."

Eleanor takes a final sip to her drink before slamming the cup down on the table. She doesn't seem drunk, but she seems to be a lot looser than what she was when she first got to the booth.

"She was scared. She was confused. She was hurt." Eleanor sighs. "She was in love. She was in love with you, but she hated you at the same time. For the first few weeks, she said virtually nothing. She resented me. But that doesn't matter. After a while, she was very open with me."

"And?"

"And what? Our first meeting was rough. It smoothed out after a little bit."

"What did she mention of me?"

Eleanor looks to her side, toward the bar. "One second." She gets up and grabs another drink. As she makes her way back, she shakes off her suit coat, revealing a black, sleeveless blouse. She takes a sip of her new drink and sits back at the booth.

Mark waits for her to get her thoughts together.

"Just to let you know, I am not an alcoholic."

"Never said you were. Plus, I'm sure it doesn't really matter what I think of you."

"It doesn't." She bores a hole into the wall behind him. "But it does."

He looks at her, confused.

"I sat with her three times a week for two years. A great deal of that conversation centered on you. I've come to know you, through her."

"I have to stop you there. You've come to know some of my actions, maybe, but you haven't come to know me at all."

"A fair statement." She averts her gaze. "So she mentioned a lot about you, about the times you two had, about the depression she fell into when you disappeared, and the joy she felt when she found you."

"So she searched me out?"

"After starting a family, she found herself comparing her current husband to you. He failed at every level, but only because she wanted him to fail. She wanted you. So for the years she was married, she focused most of her energy into finding you." She plays with her cup, sliding it back and forth across the wooden table, being careful not to spill any of the liquid. "And she eventually did."

"So it wasn't God, as she seemed to believe?"

"Wasn't God, fate, or any kind of coincidence."

Mark lets that sink in. He taps his untouched cup.

"You can guess what she thought about you from that point, the joy, the lust, the pain."

"What did she say about my wife?"

"Jade?"

Mark gets uncomfortable with her casual use of his wife's name. He nods.

"She hated her. Point-blank. She felt Jade was inept as a wife, and she wanted her gone."

"She felt so strongly about it, she thought it was a good idea to kidnap her and push her to the brink of death?"

"Alicia was sick. At the end of the day, she had issues that she could never get past, going back to her tortured youth. Isn't that what drew you two together in the first place? Rough youth?"

"Back then, maybe."

"And when she reappeared in your life?"

"She was someone familiar in a completely new land for me."

"The land wasn't that new. You were there for some time, no?"

"Please continue." Mark has had enough of her probing questions.

Eleanor nods. "She told me about the abuse, about your brother. I'm sorry for what happened."

"Did she tell you anything about him?"

"Other than the story, no. Nothing."

"Did she give any hint to her plans when she got out?"

"Somewhat. I didn't know she was going to take everything as far as she did. But she expressed her displeasure with what happened to her. She wanted to start anew."

"I'm guessing she maintained her innocence concerning the child-abuse case?"

"She did, but that's not all I'm talking about."

Mark looks at her, waiting for her to elaborate.

"I figured you didn't know." She becomes fidgety. "I don't know how to tell you this."

"If you're going to tell me you think she was innocent as well . . . I already know that. And I believe she didn't abuse her son."

She opens her mouth to say something, but it seems to get caught. She narrows her eyes and tilts her head to the side. "What do you mean?"

"Her ex set it up. At least, that's what he told me. I had no idea, but when I testified . . ." He looks down.

"I had no idea. But I wasn't talking about that." She leans on the table, obviously starting to feel the effects of her drinks. Her face turns bright red, forcing Mark to wonder if she is going to be sick. She takes a hard gulp of her drink yet again.

"Maybe you should slow down a little. Don't take this the wrong way, but it isn't a good look if I have to take you—"

"She was pregnant," she blurts out. "She was pregnant and she believed it was your baby."

CHAPTER ELEVEN

"She explained to me in detail what the night was like. You were supposed to be at the gym. Instead, you two had a date at her place."

Air gets caught in his throat.

"You had sex with her, didn't you?" She leans more on the table, slowly blinking her eyes.

"I—" He frowns.

"So I'm guessing she never told you. Mark? Mark?"

"How did she know it was mine?"

"She didn't, I suppose. But, she said she didn't do anything with anyone but you. I believed her."

Mark thinks for a few moments. "I don't."

"Well, she was definitely pregnant, and she definitely lost the baby. Those two things aren't left up to speculation."

"What do you mean she lost the baby?"

"Exactly that."

"Care to elaborate?"

"I don't. I have to get home."

"Please. I need to know. What happened?"

"But you don't believe the baby was yours, correct?"

"The baby was definitely hers. I just need to know."

She lifts her cup to drink more. Mark stops her, placing his hand over the cup and pressing it down. "You have to drive home."

"I'm a big girl, Mark. I can handle my drink. Not that you care."

"Just don't want that on my conscience."

"Right." She scoffs, letting go of her cup and pushing it aside. "She was beat up. She was beat up badly."

"Why? How?"

"Fresh meat in a hardcore prison system with a child abuse charge. Connect the dots."

"Why was she even with the hardcore offenders?"

"Good question. One I don't have an answer to."

"So they beat her . . . and she lost the baby."

"Your baby."

"Why should I believe you?"

"You don't have to believe me, even if I'm the one who tried to talk her through her pain. You don't even have to believe that you were the father. The medical records say enough, though."

"But there's no way I can get a look at those."

"Technically, there's no way we should be here talking now. Get your dirty friend to get those for you."

"I don't have a dirty friend. Plus, I have what I need."

"Do you? How has your situation changed now that you know this stuff?"

"It hasn't, really."

Eleanor looks at her watch. "I really must go." She puts her suit coat back on. "If you would be so kind as to let the detective know I upheld my part of this deal I never agreed to."

"Of course." He looks to his right at the man who falls asleep at his cup. "I'm sorry he threatened you. That's not what I'm about."

"Listen,"—she scoots out the booth and stands up—"I have a great idea on what you're about. I need not know any more." She begins striding away. "So long."

"Good night."

She leaves the bar with Mark watching her the entire way. He gets up from the booth to see the man and the woman two booths up, staring at him. He ignores them and heads to the hospital to be by Jade's side.

☙❧

Jade sits in her jail cell on the verge of tears. She stares at the beam of light in the middle of the prison, trying to understand what it is and where it came from. She feels unmistakably drawn toward the beam of light.

"You hear that?" she asks her doppelganger.

"No. What?"

"Sounds like . . . someone crying."

"I don't hear it."

"No. Listen."

Jade steps to the edge of the cell, right at the bars, and tries to calm her breathing so that the shifting of air into and out of her lungs is virtually quiet. She knows she hears it, and she swears it's Mark. She hears enough to know he holds in his tears.

"Just let it out, Sweetheart."

She continues to listen, as it sounds like there are words being said through the sobs, none of which she can make out. She feels strange, though, as if something wriggles in her gut, and she feels a burning in her chest. The beam surges brighter.

Lord, please, please bring her back. Lord, please. Please.

She hears Mark's voice (and his sobs) clearly. With that, the area begins to rumble again. It picks up intensity until she and her doppelganger are somewhat tossed in the cell. Jade is able to stumble back to the cell bars and hold on tightly as the ground under her rocks. A crack forms in the floor of the cell and after two hard rocks, opens up a hole big enough to fit through. After a few more moments, the shaking dies down, and Jade looks around to survey the damage. She crawls up to the hole in the floor to look down into the cell below them. Just barely, she can see that the bars to the cell below them fell in.

"There's a way out down there." She looks around to find a way down.

"Why leave? You don't know where you are going."

"I'm getting back to my family." She takes the thin mattress off the cot in the corner and flings it so it's flat just under the hole. She takes a deep breath, trying to brace herself for a tough fall.

"You're jumping?"

Jade looks up. "No choice. Can't think about it. Just gotta do it." She takes another deep breath. "No choice."She slides along the floor and along the inside of the hole of the floor, scraping her sides along the jagged concrete. Her eyes fill with tears from the pain. Once she gets into position, she lets go, trying to maneuver her body to lighten the impact of the fall.

She falls on an angle and lands with a hard thud. She screams in agony as an impossibly sharp pain runs from her right heel to her lower back. She rolls around for a few moments before attempting to stand to her feet. She's able to stand on one leg, but even that sends a burning sensation throughout her entire body. She hobbles toward the beam of light, but stumbles and falls hard on her side. She struggles so much to get to her feet again that she opts to crawl. Inch by inch, she gets closer to the beam of light until finally, she places her hand in the light. The first thought she has as she inches her entire body into the beam of light is that is it warm.

And her pain is completely gone.

It reminds her of when she first woke to this place. She was protected and kept warm by her memories of her family. She gets to her feet and closes her eyes. For a moment, she feels happy, and she finds that strange for the time being. When she opens her eyes, she sees a form not unlike the flame angel standing in front of her. She jumps, but the form doesn't move. She remains still.

"The star," it says in a choir of voices. "Do not be afraid."

Jade looks at the form, noticing that the flames which engulf this being are bright white.

"I don't trust you."

"A part of you does. If you trust Him, trust me. I can only do His will. You must go. Move forward, and don't look back." The being moves to the side, pointing in the direction of the entrance to the prison. Then, with great speed, it jumps into the air and higher into the beam, leaving her alone again.

She takes a few steps outside the light of the beam, walking toward the entrance of the prison. She looks at the cell from where she came and sees her doppelganger leaning on the bars, giving her an empty look. Slowly, her other self moves away from the bars until she is out of Jade's view. Jade understands that she could not bring her doppelganger with her, anyway.

As she walks away, Jade finds that she understands a few things about where she is. First, nothing is as it seems. Everything she sees is a representation of something else. She doesn't know how she knows this now, but she is absolutely positive of that notion. She picks up the pace to the entrance of the prison where she sees the large front door collapsed. She can see directly outside and at an impossibly long distance, she sees the star. Crawling to the entryway, shouting more obscenities in different gurgling voices, are messengers.

ೞ

Berta gets to Lockram, Ramses & Peterson with a mission on her mind. Ramses has quite a few things to answer to and as soon as she sees him, Berta starts in rapid-fire fashion asking those questions. She rattles off more than a few questions and at the end of it all, takes a few moments to catch her breath.

"Hello, Alberta. How are you? Me? I'm fine. My family? They're good as well. Have I lost weight, you ask? Why, yes. I've been going to the gym lately. I don't lift like I used to, but I still try to keep my heart healthy." He looks at her smugly.

"I'm not joking right now, Mr. Ramses."

"Well, Alberta"—he folds his hands—"what can I do for you? Please, take a breath this time."

Berta becomes slightly annoyed but continues anyway. "The witness. The final witness was killed."

"I know."

"Your doing?"

"No. Not at all. But who informed you of this? The detective?"

Berta stares at Ramses, reading his expression, looking for cues of lying. "Yeah. He was at my place not too long ago. He showed me a picture of the scene."

"Well, I can assure you we had nothing to do with that." He pulls off his glasses to clean them. "I'm growing increasingly more concerned about the detective." He looks up at Berta. "And I don't know why he would show you a picture of the man."

"He's become more desperate to find Craig."

"But that doesn't make any sense now. Craig could walk right into his office and do a dance in front of him, and the detective could do nothing." He slides his glasses back on. "He could do nothing. Why is he still pursuing this?"

"I don't know. But about that witness—"

"Again, I swear on everything that is just and true, we had nothing to do with the death of that man. In fact, we are trying to find out who did it. Only then can we make conjecture as to why."

"So it wasn't part of your keep-Craig-out-of-jail campaign?"

"No. Not in the slightest. Alberta, we deal in information. Everyone alive has a use. Dead people aren't leverage."

"Are you schooling me on this train of thought?"

"No. I'm trying to convince you that we aren't bad people like you seem to believe we are. We have families to take care of. We have hopes and dreams just like you have hopes and dreams; but I digress. My hunch is that the detective had something to do with it, but I just don't know what exactly. Maybe he knows he lost and he was upset."

"Upset enough to kill someone?"

"Maybe. Maybe not. I'm just throwing things out there. That one doesn't sound as likely."

"So how do you plan on finding out?"

"I have a few sources to go to. By the way, I told Craig his name is cleared. Unfortunately, I had to tell him to stay for a few more days while I figure out what's going on."

Berta nods but stays silent. She tries to tame the thoughts that run rampant in her mind.

"Alberta," he snaps her out of her trance, "are you sure you still want to go through with the divorce?"

"Why do you ask?"

"Well, you know I would do anything for you, as evidenced by getting the divorce set up and moved along. I just wonder if it is better that you two separate for a little before making the final decision."

"Have you mentioned this to Craig?"

"Listen, I've talked to Craig in depth about this. He obviously doesn't want to be without you. He's angry, of course, and he may have said some things out of anger, but that man loves you. He has and will continue to lay his life on the line for you. You are *the* reason he has to hurry back."

She begins to feel more irritated by the second. "I don't want to talk about this right now. There are more pressing matters at the moment."

Ramses sighs and bites his bottom lip. "Fine. What else is on your mind?"

"Marcella is dead." She waits to see a reaction, hoping to find a hint of recognition, something that would tell her that he's a part of it.

"That's very unfortunate." He looks confused more than anything. "How do you know this?"

"Jennifer."

He nods. "I'm sorry to hear that."

"Because of the CD, you think?"

"Don't know. How would anyone find out about that?"

"I don't know. As far as I understand, only three other people knew about the CD. Me, my mother . . . and you."

Ramses looks down. "Please don't tell me you think I killed her, too."

"I have to ask, don't I?"

"Look, as with the witness, we had nothing to do with her death. I feel there's more you're not telling me."

She thinks for a moment, knowing she has to trust Ramses at this point. He has offered nothing that would tell her he is lying, and even though she wants to believe he and his deceptive bunch had something to do with the deaths of the witness and Marcella, her gut is telling her they had nothing to do with them.

"Jennifer is staying with me."

"Why?"

"Because she needs protection."

"Presumably from the people who killed Marcella?"

"Yes. There's more." She digs in her purse. "She gave me this. I don't know what to do with it." She hands Ramses the flash drive.

"What's on it?"

"The monster's network."

Ramses' eyes get wide. "What do you mean?"

"I haven't looked at any of the data myself. I was just told that everything there is to know about his network is on that drive. They collected data over a period of time and had it saved with them."

"And you ask me if I killed Marcy?"

"There could be stuff on there about you. Apparently, there's stuff on me and Craig on there."

"Who else knew they put this together?"

"That I don't know. I'm guessing no one, but I really have no idea."

"Thank you for trusting me with this."

"Why are you thanking me?"

"Because I should." He dials on his phone and asks for a person by the name of Dexter. "I'll have my people look at this and I'll get back to you."

Berta stands. "She wants revenge."

"Who?"

"Jennifer. She wants to make sure even the memory of the monster is bad."

"And you? What do you want?"

"I don't care about the revenge . . . but I agree with her on one thing. People should know what a terrible human being he was." She smiles a mirthless smile. "Maybe that is revenge."

"Maybe this is out of bounds, but you must forgive him, Alberta."

"What?"

"Courtland. What he's done. It's wrong. It's deplorable . . . but you must forgive him. Real freedom is on the other side of that forgiveness."

"I have forgiven him. I've done that a long time ago."

"So why ruin his name? He's gone."

"That's not my main objective."

"Then what is?"

"There's something on that drive that people are willing to kill for. Something on there that could hopefully help Jennifer. Something on there will save her life. At least, that's what we are all hoping for, right? And there's info on there on all of us, apparently. We are all in danger . . . possibly."

Ramses nods in understanding, but he still looks at Berta with a discerning eye.

"I must get back home. Let me know if anything comes up."

Ϧʀϧ

After a night of packing, Craig wakes up energetic. He spends most of the morning imagining what he needs to do when he goes home. He can get Berta back. He can be a support for his friend.

He can get his life back.

The more he thinks of the good things that will happen when he goes home, the more he asks himself if he deserves any of it. He knows he doesn't. He prays a silent prayer thanking God, but not without feeling a bit guilty. With so much nervous energy, he decides to get his jog done early. He changes and heads out.

He sees it from a good distance away: cars at the produce stand. Part of him gets excited to see the produce stand up and running again. He sees Addie busying herself with her customers after giving him a quick glance. He then sees a large man, his head ducked under the hood of her truck. Craig wipes the sweat off his forehead with a towel he carries with him whenever he jogs, and gets in the back of the line. He stares at her the entire time, noticing she avoids making eye contact with him. When he finally is next in line, he doesn't say much.

"Nice, you have pears," he says to break the silence.

She smiles.

"Hey, I'm uhhh, I'm headed home soon."

"Are you? That's good. Hope you enjoyed your vacation."

Craig looks at her strangely. "Vacation?"

"Yes, vacation. You and your wife wanted to get some time away from the city life. Isn't that what you told me?" Her eyes are pleading.

"Yeah. I forgot I told you that."

"I still can't understand why you two would want to come to this part of Texas. There isn't much to do."

"That's why we like it here. It's very quiet. Peaceful." Craig notices the man who was under the hood of Addie's truck is now staring at him.

"Well, how about this?" She grabs a cucumber. "One on the house, so to speak."

He takes the cucumber and pays her for the pears. "Thank you. I'll see you around—er, I guess not. Take care of yourself, ummm. I never caught your name."

"Addison."

"Well, take care of yourself, Addison."

Craig turns and jogs away, thoroughly confused by the interaction. He played along because he feels she was trying to tell him something. He just has no idea of what.

He gets back to the ranch and places the things he purchased on the counter next to the sink to wash them. He washes the pears first and sets them aside. After cleaning the cucumber, he grabs a peeler to prep for a little salad he has planned. He starts peeling but stops, staring at marks made into the vegetable. It looks like they were done with a fingernail. The lines aren't straight but slightly curved, although it is clear to see. Etched into the skin of the cucumber are letters that form the phrase, "HELP ME."

Chapter Twelve

"I'm just delaying the inevitable," Mark says, devoid of any emotion. "She's not going to make it . . . and I'm going to have to make the call soon. This is all my fault. I've made countless terrible decisions, most of them stemming from my anger, and my selfishness—pride, even. My actions killed an innocent woman . . . and her child . . . my child. My actions sent my wife to the hospital to await death. My actions killed my brother."

"But somehow, you still feel like you've done the right thing."

Mark looks out his rearview mirror to see Alicia staring at him with an intense gaze, her arms crossed.

"I don't, actually. Not now. I did then. All I could do was the best I could do for the time."

"Sounds like another excuse."

"Think what you want." He puts the car in park. "I don't need to explain anything more to you."

"What? You ruined my life. You owe me—"

Mark flips around. "I'm sorry, okay? I'm so deeply sorry." He closes his eyes. "I'm sorry."

Once he reopens his eyes, he notices he is completely alone in his car. He sighs, unbuckles his seatbelt, and gets out the car. He walks to the large double doors to Jade's parents' home and rings the doorbell. When Joanne answers, all he can do is look. She looks at him with calm eyes, though he senses her pity for him through them.

"Is she gone?" she asks, looking like she doesn't want the answer.

"No, ma'am. But we need to talk."

"Please come in. Are you hungry?"

"No, ma'am."

"Your ribs good?"

"They're a little better. Not by much, but at least I can breathe a bit easier without the stabbing."

"Mark, you sound terrible."

"I know, ma'am. Where are the kids?"

"Upstairs." She yells upstairs, "Kids."

Kalina is the first to come to the top of the steps. Mark smiles at her and she returns a smile that warms his heart. She gallops downstairs and jumps into his arms. He holds her tight, and for the third time today, almost comes to tears.

"You coming to take us home?" she asks.

"We'll talk about that later. Let's just hang out for a few, huh? I miss you guys."

She gives him a discerning look. "You look bad."

"I know, Sweetheart."

"Grandma told us Mommy is getting better."

Mark glances at Joanne, but quickly refocuses on Kalina.

"Come here."

"What?"

"I want to look at your face."

"Kalina, what are you doing?"

"Just come here. Daddy, please?"

Mark reluctantly bends to her level. She grabs his face and looks into his eyes.

"Why do your eyes look like that?"

"Like what?"

Kalina stares for a few moments more. "Sad."

Mark stands up straight.

"If Mommy was getting better, wouldn't you look . . . wouldn't you be better, too?"

Mark opens his mouth to speak, but Joanne interrupts.

"There are still a lot of hurdles to jump, Dear. Your father has been doing quite a bit of running around, on little sleep, I presume. Everything is fine."

Mark can do nothing but nod. He smiles a weak smile before asking for Charles and Amber.

"We were all upstairs hanging out."

"I'll get some lunch together," Joanne says.

Mark follows Kalina upstairs to spend some much-needed time with his children. In the back of his mind, he feels a slight tugging for his child he has never seen.

∞

After spending time with his kids, helping with Charles' and Kalina's homework, and giving Amber a bath, Mark sits with Joanne in the study, sipping on a cup of tea.

"I'm sorry I haven't been able to stop by as often. Thank you again for looking after the kids."

"No need for thanks. They're my grandchildren. I love them dearly." She holds the cup of tea to her nose, taking in the steam. "Is this the talk? The dreaded talk I think we all were hoping to not have?"

"I think so."

For an extended moment, both sit, sipping on their tea, saying nothing. Mark doesn't know how to start and it is clear neither does she.

"There's no getting anything past Kalina, is there?" he asks.

"Nope. That girl is smart as a whip." She sets her cup down. "Especially when it comes to you."

"Yeah?"

"She's worried about you. I would tell her things are getting better so the future wouldn't be such a weight on her. She can think herself into some pretty dark places."

"Really? I never noticed."

"I think this is a new thing. It's tough for a kid to stay positive in situations like this."

Mark nods and lets another block of silence fill their conversation.

"I went to the hospital a couple days ago," he says. "They called me in to update me on Jade's condition."

"And?"

He shakes his head.

"What does that mean? Give me details."

"Her vitals are slipping. Even while being on the machines . . . she's still dying. Brain activity is reducing. The doctor said something about an independent neurologist to determine her condition, or something like that." He looks her in the eyes. "She's not going to make it. That's basically what he told me. And he suggested I talk to everyone close, to determine our next move."

"Like taking her off of life support?"

Mark nods. He sets his cup on the table and rises, trying to move around in an effort to relieve some tension. It doesn't help much, because with each step he takes, the urge to break down and cry increases. He looks at Joanne, noticing her eyes well with tears. With each second that passes, her demeanor becomes more downtrodden. Mark watches her as she melts into a pool of tears. He steps warily to her and kneels down.

"I'm sorry." He ends his fight with his tears, allowing them to flow freely. "All of this is my fault. I allowed this—" He looks down. After a few more moments, he gets up and sits back in his seat, lost in his own thoughts.

Both sit for a long time and cry.

After both are able to compose themselves, he speaks in a gravely tone. "I think it's a good idea to take the kids back home. Start to get them used to life . . . how it's going to be."

"I understand."

"You should come, too." He looks at her pensively.

"I can't. Plus, if Harold comes back . . ."

"Then leave him a note or something. You shouldn't be here by yourself no more than I should be anywhere by myself. We need to stick together."

"I see."

"And I think I'm going to need a lot of help . . . with the kids. They're going to be—"

"Devastated."

He nods.

"I'll go. Start packing tonight."

She gets up and grabs the cups of tea. "You should stay the night. It's late to be on the road . . . in your condition."

"Thank you, but I'll be fine. I'll come pick—"

"I wasn't asking." She gives him a hard stare. "Rest up. Another day tomorrow."

Once she leaves the study, he sits slumped in the chair, thinking. The edges of his vision turn black, and once again, he feels dread. Unfortunately, he is getting used to the feeling of dread. Dread follows him wherever he goes. He feels the tightness in his head that happens before a headache occurs. He takes a few deep breaths, realizing for the first time in a while that his ribs are sore. He gets up and grabs his cell phone, remembering a bit of business he needs to handle. He calls a number and waits for a pickup on the other end.

"Detective."

"Mark. All good?"

"Yeah. I just wanted to thank you for helping me. The info you gave me has been revealing."

"You visited his family?"

"Yeah. And I talked to Eleanor Bixby. "She," he hesitates, "informed me of a lot. She wanted me to let you know that she did what she was asked."

"Good."

Mark lets silence fill the line.

"Mark?"

"What did you do to get her to talk?"

"You ought not worry about that."

"What types of things are you into?"

"Why are you taking on this line of questioning?"

"Well, she didn't seem like she wanted to be there to me, and I wonder how you got her to speak on something she legally isn't allowed to."

"Did you find what you needed?" Simms cuts to the chase.

"I believe I did."

"Good. Listen, I better go."

"Sure."

Simms hangs up abruptly. Immediately thereafter, Mark calls Berta, silently thanking God for his call's going straight to voicemail.

◈

She takes a hesitant step toward the gurgling creatures, and as expected, they do not move. Jade takes another step, not looking at them, but staring at the star. The messengers call her all types of names. They disparage her. They make her feel worthless, but she takes cautious step after cautious step. Once she's a single step in front of them, she realizes how easily they blend into the darkness, being shrouded by shadow themselves. Still, she can see the star, and she takes a step into them. They finally part and allow her through, but to the sound of gnashing teeth.

She smiles for the first time since being here, as her understanding grows by just a bit. The fear she originally had of the messengers now no longer exists and she focuses even more on getting to that star. She picks up the pace, not looking back, and starts to run.

In a blink, she's transported to a bright area, an area she immediately recognizes to be home. She stops and stands motionless in the living room, hearing laughing from upstairs. Everything looks as she remembers it, and that scares her. She glances at the clock on the wall. It says *three forty-six*. She rushes upstairs to see Mark wrestling with Charles and Kalina acting as referee. Amber sits on their bed watching, laughing, making random noises. When she steps into the room, they all stop.

"Uh-oh," Charles says. "I think we're in trouble now."

"Hey, Babe," Mark says. "We were just passing time until you woke up. We tried to keep quiet, but I guess we failed on that one."

Jade stands there, stunned, not saying anything.

"Mommy." Kalina frowns. "Are you okay?"

"Yes . . . yes, I'm fine. I just . . ."

"Bad dream?" Mark asks.

"I think so." She walks to Mark and hugs him. Shocking to her is how real he feels. She wraps her arms around him, feeling his back. She gives him a kiss. His lips are warm. She looks into his eyes and sees what she has always seen: the best scenario of endless possibilities.

"You sure you're good?" Mark says.

"I think I am." She notices he smells just like Mark, too. "I think I will be."

"Kids, go ahead downstairs, okay? Let me talk with your mother for a few minutes."

Kalina and Charles oblige and as they leave, Jade gives them a tight hug.

"It's okay, Mommy. It was just a dream," Kalina says.

Once they're gone, Jade goes to hold Amber, scooping her up in her arms. It feels like she hasn't held her in forever.

"So what happened in this dream?" Mark asks.

"It's a lot, Sweetheart. There was this flaming angel, two of them, and my mother was there. Didn't see the kids, but it was in total darkness and you were there with Alicia." She notices she rambles. "You were there with Alicia."

"Alicia? You mean my ex-fiancee, Alicia?"

"Yes, and you two were in a jail cell . . . and she and you were . . . doing things . . . sexually."

"Wow. What a dream. A strange one, I'll say."

"Is it really that strange?"

"Well, yes." He smirks in confusion. "How would you know it was Alicia? Like, how would you know what she looks like? You've never met her."

"What do you mean? You . . . you were seeing her. We went through years of counseling because of it."

Mark's face gets serious. "Babe, Alicia died before I ever laid eyes on you."

⋞⊰⊱⋟

Berta gets home to find Jennifer curled up in a ball, resting on the couch. She has an afghan pulled over her. Berta winces at the handgun sitting on the coffee table in front of her. She's never liked guns, never had to deal with guns, and hopes to never have to deal with guns. Unfortunately, she realizes her life has taken a few odd turns. She looks at Jennifer, watching her body rise and fall along the waves of deep sleep and pities the young woman, her half sister. The sleep she is getting might be the first real sleep she's had since her mother's death.

Berta tiptoes out to the balcony, the place that has become her thinking spot lately. She takes in as much cool air as she can into her lungs and exhales. The slight rush leaves her feeling a bit lightheaded until she evens out her breathing again. She begins to pray, but knows not what for. She ends up simply standing there waiting, hoping.

"What did you do with the drive?"

Berta turns around to see Jennifer standing at the doorway, her arms wrapped around herself.

"Gave it to the only person I know who could do something with it."

"So now what do we do?"

"We wait."

Jennifer nods. "So, Sis . . . I guess there's a lot we should talk about." She looks down at the floor.

"I suppose." She feels Jennifer's eyes on her, but continues to look out into the distance.

"What was it like?"

"What?"

"Being raised by Raul."

She doesn't answer at first. After a few moments of reflection, she says, "It was . . . what I needed. I wouldn't be the person I am without him." She turns to look at Jennifer. "Even though I know he wasn't the best,"—she turns back—"he was the best to me."

"Raul sounded cool. At least whenever Mom . . ."

Berta looks over to see Jennifer trying to find the right words to say. Her face turns bright red as a small sob escapes her lips.

"I'm trying to keep going," Jennifer says with a strained voice. "I can't start thinking of her now."

"Hey, hey." Berta walks over to her and places her hands on her shoulders. "It's okay. It will all be okay. You need to get it out."

Her chin quivers. "I can't. Because once I go in, I will not come out." She shakes from Berta's grasp, turns on her heels, and heads back inside.

Berta allows her a few minutes before heading back in as well. She goes to the kitchen. "You hungry?"

"I am. But you don't have to make anything. I have some snacks in my bag."

Berta starts rummaging through the refrigerator. "You're a guest in my home. I'm making you dinner. What are you in the mood for?"

She sighs. "Chinese."

Berta stops her rummaging to go to the island and pull out a menu.

"Sesame chicken."

Berta stops abruptly.

"All those places are the same. I always get Sesame chicken."

She nods and places an order for them.

While waiting, Berta decides to pick the conversation back up again. "What happened to your brother?"

"He's with my aunt. He thinks he's just hanging for a little." She adjusts in her seat. "We couldn't bring him. Plus, we were supposed to come back for him whenever things settled down."

"But they never did."

"Obviously."

"Why did she drop him off to begin with? And why just him?"

"I was supposed to be with him. Mom . . . she initially dropped us both off. I followed. I just snuck back onto the truck. She didn't notice until she was grabbing her bags for a flight." She looks around. "You religious?"

Berta looks around, trying to find what made her ask that question. She finds nothing. "It depends on what you mean by religious."

"One of the things I saw on the drive was this church you went to . . . like, a lot."

"What else is on this drive, exactly?"

"It's a bunch of information on people, but it's detailed. There are some other parts, parts that Mom put on, that I never saw. But yeah, most of what I looked at was information on you."

"And that was detailed."

"Embarrassingly so."

"So the monster was following me. This entire time, for years. Why?"

"'Cause he was demented."

"Was there stuff on you and your mother there?"

"Nope. Nothing. Which pissed Mom off more than anything. He kept tabs on you, your husband, your mother . . . but nothing on us. Maybe because we were right under his thumb."

"But he struck me as paranoid. Why wouldn't he have stuff on you two?"

She shrugs. "So, back to my question: you religious?"

Before continuing the conversation, Berta ponders on why there is little information on the drive about Courtland's second family. "I believe in a relationship with a loving and caring God, yes."

"Still? After everything that has gone wrong in your life?"

"I beg your pardon?"

"Look, we're in very similar boats here. We were both abused in one of the worst ways. But with you, I mean, you were sold off. And your marriage . . . I know you have to wonder if you can have any real relationship, let alone a marriage . . . I wonder that all the time for myself, but I already know the answer. I can't. How can you still believe in a god—any god, really—after everything that went down? What good has your belief done you so far?"

"I'm sure life could have been a lot worse for me. I could have been killed. But I'm alive, and able to fight."

"But what did your belief get you? How do you know your life wouldn't be here no matter who or what you believed in? What if your belief is largely inconsequential?"

"It's not."

"How do you know?"

"One night, right after the monster"—she pauses in effort to hold back sobs—"finished doing what he did to me, I prayed. I didn't pray before that. I didn't even really know who I was reaching out to. I just asked God to save me. I wanted the monster to stop. The next night, I'm curled up in my bed, and I know he's going to come into my room and try something with me. I pretended to be sleep. It . . . just . . . went by faster that way. But that time, he didn't do anything. He stepped into my room, but he stayed by the doorway. After a few seconds, he left. I flip around, still pretending to be sleep, but sneaking glances at my door, when I see an angel sitting in the chair next to my bed."

"A what? You can't be serious."

"I am. I'm so serious. I stared at the angel until I fell asleep. A few hours later, I was being taken away by Raul."

Jennifer stares for a few moments. "I'm not sure what to say to that."

"Ever since that night, I believed, and I followed His will. It was a no-brainer for me. So, at times like this, I think back to that time, that time when all I had to ask was for Him to save me."

Jennifer's face contorts. "All you had to do was say 'save me'?"

"That's all I could do at the time."

"Well,"—she throws her hands up in the air—"save me." She lets her hands flop into her lap. She wipes her face and looks at her hand, almost shocked to see her fingers glistening from her tears. "Excuse me," she says and gets up to go to the bathroom.

Berta decides not to say any more, determining when Jennifer wants her help, she will come to her.

cs80

Craig speeds along the dusty road, determined to help Addie. He drives past the produce stand, which is completely deserted. He finds it strange she left so soon after he was there. He becomes intensely focused on freeing her and making sure she is safe. The idea forming in his head is for him to pick her up and take her from the town, just so she can hide out for a few days to come up with a more solid game plan.

He eventually gets to Silver Rock and drives to the first place he knows to go that's somewhat safe. He pulls up in front of the old woman's home and hops out the truck. With haste, he gets to her door and rings the doorbell. In only a few moments, the old woman answers the door and ushers him in.

"What did you do?" she asks.

"What do you mean?"

"Addie and some brute drove by here maybe ten minutes ago. Followed by a cop car."

"Is she home?"

"No idea where she is. Either way, I don't think it's a good idea to be here in this town. I get the feeling they are looking for you."

"I'm just looking for her." He paces back and forth. "If I don't get to her now . . . there's a chance I won't be able to. That is, if they are looking specifically for me."

"What do you plan on doing?"

"I need to go out back. If they come to your door, just buy me a little time."

"They're not going to come to my door asking questions. You do know that, right?"

"I won't be long at all."

He paces his way to the back door and ducks away from the house, rushing through the shrubs, trees, and bushes. He gets to Addie's home and waits. He remains perfectly still, waiting. A slight breeze blows through at his feet. He creeps up to her back door and knocks, but hears nothing. He slinks back into the brush and waits a few more moments. When nothing happens, he turns around and heads back to the old woman's home. He gets in and rushes through the kitchen and dining room to the front door, but stops abruptly.

"I said they weren't asking questions," the old woman says as she sits surrounded by officers.

Craig counts three, but he can tell the one who is leading the charge, so to speak.

"Well, if it isn't our mystery man," the lead officer says. "How are you doing today, sir?"

Craig says nothing.

"Well, here's the situation at hand. One of our wonderful Silver Rock townspeople has been assaulted. She was beaten pretty badly, and well . . . the offender is still at large."

Craig looks over the three cops, watching them become more and more antsy. One even goes as far as placing his hand over his gun in the holster.

"The victim is a longstanding member of this town. Everyone knows her, and she knows everybody. Needless to say, the townsfolk are taking this one personally." He stands behind the old woman and places his hands on her shoulders. "So what is your name?"

Craig still remains silent.

The lead officer smiles, but then an intense expression washes over his face. He squeezes the woman's shoulders hard enough for her to whelp. "Ma'am, if you don't mind telling me his name."

She grits her teeth and stares at Craig. "Braylon. His name is Braylon."

He releases his grip. "I think you just made a mistake, ma'am, I do. I thought his name was Craig. Never heard of this Braylon before." He takes his time and walks around to face her. He kneels down in front of her. "So how's Wren?"

The old woman spits in the lead officer's face. He snaps back slightly, but otherwise retains his composure. "I wish you hadn't done that." He stands and moves toward Craig. Swiftly, he punches Craig in the stomach.

Craig winces but doesn't move too much.

"On your knees. Hands on top of your head."

Craig tries to brush off the pain and scans the three officers. "No," he says. "You have no grounds."

"Let me see. We have reason to suspect you assaulted Addison Chapman. We just caught you trespassing on her property, *my* property, in search of her, and you assaulted an officer of the law. Myers, you know what to do."

"I did no such thing."

The officer who was closest to the door walks over to the lead officer and stares at Craig. In a flash, he punches the lead officer with enough force to send him to the ground. Then, the remaining officer rushes Craig and tackles him to the ground. All three officers proceed to beat Craig, kicking him and stomping him until he doesn't move anymore, until he can't move any more.

◌�◌

When Craig finally wakes up, he does so within the confines of a small jail cell. Every part of him aches as he stands to his feet. He shuffles to the bars to see something past the concrete wall that blocks most of his view, but gives up after a few. He grabs the bars and leans in.

"Lord, Lord, Lord," he whispers. The taste of blood still lingers in his mouth. "I just . . . I just."

He cannot find the words to say for his present predicament. Instead, he limps away from the bars and gingerly sits on the jail cell cot.

Chapter Thirteen

"She died in a car accident. One late night coming from her friend's apartment. Her friend, Rochelle, lived off campus, but only fifteen minutes away." Mark adjusts in his seat. "But it only takes an instant for things to change completely. One instant for life to change forever." He shakes his head. "But you know this already, no? We talked about all of this before."

"I . . . I remember something different."

"Babe, you sure you're okay?"

Jade sits on the edge of the bed while still holding Amber. The baby wrestles in her grip a bit before yawning.

"Looks like someone is sleepy," Mark says. "Here, I'll put her down for a nap. I'll be back in a few minutes."

Mark lifts Amber from Jade's arms and disappears out the room. Jade quickly takes the moment to rush to the window and look outside. She knows what she remembers, and it's nothing like what Mark said. She also knows that something is off. Her memories cut off at a certain point, and the more she thinks about it, the sooner that point becomes. Where she was before she was taking a nap, she has no idea, but she feels a tugging, a desire, a longing even, to simply look outside and find . . . something. She stares out at the sky. All blue skies, some clouds, bright and beautiful sun. *What am I looking for?*

"Beautiful day, isn't it?"

She turns her head to the side, still looking outside through her peripheral. "It is."

He walks up behind her and wraps his arms around her waist. She virtually melts into his body but catches herself. "Can you tell me . . . again?"

"Tell you what, Sweetheart?"

"What happened. All of it. All that stuff before we met. I just . . . it would do a lot for me and my mind right now."

"Those were some pretty rough times." His grip loosens. "I don't usually, you know, go back there."

"Please? For me?"

Mark releases her and moves around her to sit in the chair next to the window. He looks up at her.

"Of course. Anything for you. Are you looking for the abbreviated version? Because this story is pretty long."

"I have time." She smiles.

"Okay, well . . . Alicia was on her way back to see me, actually. This kid came through, a teenager who just got his license, and just . . . smashed into her. He shouldn't have been driving at night. He was trying to get his parents' car back home before they came back themselves. He was going fifty-five in a thirty-five zone. She died instantly. He was in the hospital for weeks before he was released."

"My God."

He winces. "Yeah. It was tough. I blamed myself for a while. I begged her to stay with me for the night. She was coming to see me because I wanted her near me. I hated myself for that. It took me even longer to forgive the boy who did it. I even hated his parents. But I moved past all that. It took a while, and some help. Holly had a big part in that, though."

"Holly? Kalina's mother?"

"Indeed. She led me through the darkness I was in. And we fell in love. We eventually had Kalina. The problem was, we knew it wasn't going to work out. A man is a different being when he's vulnerable and mourning. In this case, who I was really didn't fit with who she was really. So, we parted ways, but she stays active in Kalina's life."

"Wait. What?"

"Holly is active in Kalina's life. Something wrong with what I said?"

"No. Sorry. Just had a random thought."

"What's on your mind?"

"Just . . . what do you do for a living?"

Mark chuckles. "You're weirding me out, Love."

"What do I do for a living?"

"Are you serious?"

"I am."

Mark's face shifts slightly, but he still answers. "I'm an elementary school teacher. Been that for years. You run a pharmacy. You've done that for years."

"I run a pharmacy?"

"Yes, Dear." Mark looks around. "Are you playing a prank on me?"

"What?"

"The kids are going to come rushing in any moment now, aren't they?"

"What? No. I just . . ." She looks next to him at the digital clock on a stand in the corner.

He moves just slightly, so that he blocks her view of the clock with his head. He looks her in the eyes and smiles. She returns his smile.

"You know, maybe I could use a little more sleep."

"Well, let me set up the bed for you." He gets up and smooths out the comforter on the bed.

It's then that Jade gets a good look at the clock. It says *three twenty-nine.* She freezes.

"You okay?" Mark asks.

She turns around and smiles. "Of course. I'm just really tired."

"Well, get your rest. I'll worry about dinner."

"Thank you, Dear." She gets into the bed and lies down, turning her back toward Mark and the door. A million thoughts run through her mind as she tries to calm her breathing. *Okay . . . okay, just relax. Breathe. Three twenty-nine. Three twenty-nine. No, it was three forty-six. Time is going backward? Don't be silly. You clearly didn't see the correct time when you first woke.*

"Hey, Babe," she calls over her shoulder.

"Yup."

"Could you wake me up in twenty minutes?"

"Of course. You sure you don't need more rest than that?"

"I'll be fine. Twenty minutes, please."

"No problem."

She hears him leave the room and the door click shut. Her stomach is in knots trying to figure out what is going on. Something isn't right, this much she knows, but she has no idea what that is. Thinking about it, she has no idea what she was doing before she originally went down for a nap. She sits up in the bed.

"You're supposed to be getting your rest."

She jumps at the sound of Mark's voice and flips around. "Mark, you . . . wait, why are you . . ." She looks at his expression. She looks into his eyes. She has seen that look before. He takes a step toward her.

"Give me the phone, Jade."

"Mark, what are you doing?"

"I said give me the phone."

Jade leaps back, pressing her back against the wall as Mark jumps onto the bed, reaching for her. He stumbles but regains his footing on the other side of the bed. He reaches for her, but she scurries out of his grasp and dashes toward the door. He dives and catches her foot, sending her falling flat on her face. He moves in on her, towering over her and snatches her by her neck. She feels his cold grip tightening and her breaths become shorter. For a moment all she feels is despair. Her vision fades, but as it does, behind her eyelids she sees not just darkness, but a focused, bright-white light. It's a mere speck against the total darkness, but a noticeable one. She opens her eyes wide as Mark continues to squeeze the life out of her—so she thinks.

"Please," she chokes out, "please, Mark. Let go."

She closes her eyes again, seeing the speck of light. She reaches for it, then lets her hand drop. The star. She tries to open her eyes again, but her eyelids will not move.

⊱⊰

Craig shuffles around the jail cell, murmuring to himself about the things that have befallen him recently. He tries to make sure he keeps moving, because the moment he stops, the pain of his injuries catches up with him. He knows his injuries aren't truly serious; still, he wonders why he hasn't been taken to the hospital first. He paces in laps along the edges of the cell. *This is it,* he thinks. He looks around the cell, noticing he is completely cut off from the outside. There are no windows, so the only light he gets is from a single recessed light above him smack dab in the middle of the confined space. Opposite of the cell is a concrete wall, and it seems the cell is down a hall. He has no idea if there are other cells next to him because there are concrete walls on both sides of the space.

He doesn't know how long he was out upon being thrown in the cell, but based on the decreased noise as time went on since he's awakened, he would say it's nighttime, maybe even early morning. He stops walking the edges of the cell to walk to the middle of it. He stands, listening for something, though he doesn't know what. All he hears is a low humming. He looks above him to recognize the humming as the ballast of the fluorescent light. He plops down to sit on the cot.

Suddenly, he hears a beat of some sort faintly above the humming. The longer it goes on, the louder it gets, to a point where he recognizes the sound to be footsteps; bootsteps, to be exact. A few moments later, a large officer steps into view in front of the cell. Craig simply looks him in the eyes, trying to read him. The officer doesn't say anything, but is the first to break the staredown. He looks to his side.

Another person steps into view in front of the cell. He can tell by the walk that it's a woman. She wears a hoodie and has the hood up covering all but one facial feature: the bruise she got from her abusive husband, on the bottom of her jaw.

Craig still doesn't say anything, but the officer walks past the cell and pops back into view with a chair. He sets it in front of the cell and disappears back to the front of the building.

"Thank you, Mac," Addie says. She takes a labored seat and pulls her hood back. Craig continues to stare as she fluffs out her hair. Once she's settled, she stares at Craig, but it is Craig who cannot hold her gaze. He looks down.

"Why are you here?" he asks.

"Are you mad at me?"

"Shouldn't I be?"

"Of course you should. You should be infuriated." She places her hands in her lap. "But I still see that sadness. That same depressed look in your eye I saw when we first met. That sadness,"—she looks down at her hands—"that sadness seems to overtake everything."

"Well, I don't exactly have much to be happy about."

"I understand. And I am sorry. Craig"—she waits for him to look her in the eyes—"I am truly sorry." Craig nods. "I didn't know who to turn to. And I was scared."

"You don't need to apologize. If anything, I'm sorry I couldn't help." He stands with difficulty.

"Were you taken to the hospital?"

"I don't think so. I'm fine, though. Just a little sore." He gets to the bars and holds on. Addie stands. "How long has he been abusing you?"

She looks down, having difficulty with the question. "A long time. Too long."

"What exactly did you need me to do? Like, why did you carve 'help me' in the cucumber?"

"I don't know exactly. I just wanted . . . I wanted to be away. I wanted to disappear."

"And you thought I was the one to help with that?"

"You seemed like it. You seemed trustworthy. And you came out of nowhere. I just thought . . ."

"You thought I was your sign or something."

"Something like that." She sits back down. The wince she tries to wipe away from her face leads Craig to believe her husband did it again. "I want to be free . . . but all I did was drag an innocent man into my mess."

"What did he do?"

"Huh?"

Craig grips the bars tighter. "What. Did. He. Do."

Addie stares at a spot on the wall past Craig. Her face turns red as a sheen of tears glistens on her face. She stands, still not looking at Craig, and pulls off her hoodie. She starts to shake as she tries to squelch a sob that is making its way out. She turns her back to him and lifts up her loose-fitting t-shirt.

Craig's eyes fill with water as he stares at her terribly marred back.

"He just got back in the house after arresting you and—"

Craig hears the bootsteps coming again until the large officer is back in front of the cell, staring at Addie. She lets her shirt fall back down and stares at the man, wiping away tears.

"Addie." He flexes his jaw muscles a bit before grabbing her hand and looking at her wrists. "Was it him?"

She looks down and nods vigorously.

Craig watches as the man checks her, and for the first time, notices the bruises and marks up and down her arms.

"Mac," she says, but he silences her. He continues looking at the bruises and marks, and scars on her battered body. He gets to her back and stops.

"What is this?"

"A cord."

The man she calls Mac squints. "What else?"

"Mac, please. If I tell you, I know you are going to do something rash."

"Just tell me, Addison. Tell me."

Craig looks back and forth, trying to understand who this "Mac" is to Addie.

"He cuffed me to the bed." Tears drip off her chin. "Belly down. He tore my shirt off and took the cord to me. He hit me everywhere; I don't know how many times. I lost count at twenty-three." She sits back down. "I must have been screaming too much, because he gagged me. I could barely breathe. And . . ."

Mac stops her and kneels down before her. "Why did he do this?"

"Teaching me a lesson, he said." She looks Mac in the eyes. "Mac. Cassidy was there."

Mac looks like he's been slapped. "Wh-what do you mean Cassidy was there?"

Her face twists up in pain. "He was there . . . watching. Brad was teaching him how to . . . control his woman."

"Did Brad . . ." Mac looks down at Addie's lower body.

She shakes her head vigorously. "No. Just the cord."

Craig leans on the concrete wall and slides down, the weight of what was done to Addie settling on him. Mac stands and looks around in a rage. He turns toward the concrete wall and punches it. The sound his fist makes on the wall is unsettling to Craig. Mac continues on, punching the wall until Addie places a hand on his shoulder.

"Mac, please."

Mac stops and places his hands on the wall. It's silent, but Craig can see the man is crying, his hulking body shaking heavily with each sob. He pushes off the wall and takes in a deep breath as he turns toward Craig. Craig gets back to his feet. Mac grabs at the set of keys hanging from his belt loop and jams a key into the cell door, yanking it open.

"You get her to safety. You get her out of this town."

"Mac, what are you doing?"

He turns toward Addie. "This can not, this will not happen again. You need to get out of this place."

"And then what? I can't just up and run."

"You can, and you will. Isn't that what you called him for, anyway?"

Addie looks down, then at Craig. At that moment, Craig decides to take charge. He steps out of the cell and gently grabs Addie's hand. "We have to go." He looks toward Mac. "I need a car."

"Your truck is parked out back. We still have the keys up front." He moves quickly for a large man, headed toward the front of the building. Craig eyes the blood on the concrete wall before gently urging Addie to follow him and Mac. Mac gets to a desk, the second one closest to the side door in a single row of desks, and goes into the drawer. He pulls out a set of keys and throws it to Craig.

"What are you going to do, Mac?" Addie asks.

"Don't worry about that. You go be free." He looks to Craig. "You take care of her. And don't let her back into this town . . . at least not until things die down."

Craig nods. "Thank you."

"No. You are braver than I. I should have done something a long time ago." He looks down at his shoes. Slowly, deliberately, he walks to Addie and holds her face in his hands. He places his lips on hers for a few long seconds. He releases her and says to Craig, "Take the side door." He points in the direction. "It will take you to where we have your truck."

Craig nods and pulls Addie along out the side door. It takes a little bit of searching around, but he finds the truck and helps Addie in. He gets in and starts the engine. He waits for a few moments before turning the headlights on. He pulls out of the police parking lot and makes a sharp left, driving past the giant rock, and eventually out of the town. A chill goes up and down his spine for what he just witnessed.

♋

195

Mark pulls up to the front of his house and into the driveway. Joanne pulls up in front of the garage next to him. He gives her a solemn smile before turning toward the kids and trying to sound as chipper as possible.

"Okay guys, you ready?"

"I guess," Kalina says.

Charles doesn't answer.

"Charles?"

He simply nods, but is looking past Mark, into the house.

"Okay. Let's get you settled in your own rooms again, huh? That sound good?"

Neither says a word.

"Okay," Mark says as he gets out the car and starts unloading the kids' things from the trunk of the car.

Each time he goes back out to the car to grab another bag or suitcase, he looks at them still sitting in the car, not having even unbuckled their seatbelts. Once all their things are in, he walks back out and gets into the driver's seat of the car. For a few minutes, he remains silent. He looks back and forth at them, trying to read their faces. They don't even really acknowledge his presence, but rather stare at the front door of the home. He opens his mouth to say something, but quickly closes it. Joanne, holding Amber, appears from the house and looks at Mark. He gives her a look he hopes she understands: one that says the kids are having a tough time at the moment.

"She's not coming back here, is she? Mom, I mean."

He turns toward Kalina but is at a loss for what to say. He can't tell her the truth right now, not at this moment, but he feels so bad for lying to her. But, for her sake, and for Charles' sake, he has to tell them something he doesn't believe to be true.

"She is. She will be back soon."

"Then why are we coming back now? What makes now so significant?"

Mark sighs. He finds this to be more painful than he thought it would be. "We need to get life rolling like normal again . . . so when she is a hundred percent, and she does come back home, it isn't too much of an adjustment for everyone. We can all just fit again, you know?"

"Is that the truth?"

He swallows hard. "Why do you ask?"

"Because you don't look like Dad anymore. You're someone else. I know when you muster up fake smiles and fake happiness for our sakes. And it all makes me wonder . . . if Mom was really getting better . . . why would you have to fake happiness?"

Mark leans his head on the headrest and sighs. "We are going to have to talk later, all of us. But, for now, we need to get in the house."

"So we can start to move on without her."

"No. That's not what I'm saying."

She looks down at her hands. "Fine." She flips off her seatbelt, swings the car door open, and leaves the car. Mark looks in the back seat to see Charles fast asleep.

⊂⊃

Later in the night, after dinner, everyone sits in the living room awaiting what Mark has to say. He sits in front of the kids, with Joanne next to him. Mark notices her eyes are already glassy.

"Alright, so . . . I really don't know how to say this. I . . ."

Joanne taps him on the shoulder and brings him to the kitchen.

"You sure?" she whispers.

"What do you mean? What choice do I have? They should know."

197

"I mean are you sure there is no chance . . . no chance she will . . . make it."

"I only know what the doctors tell me . . . and they tell me that it's time."

"But do you believe that?"

"What choice do I have? This isn't one of those miracle shows you watch during the day. Faith isn't going to work here. Faith didn't help us from getting into this mess."

"What are you saying?"

"I'm saying"—he looks out at the kids—"I'm saying I can't lie to them and give them false hope."

"What . . . what happened to you?"

"With all due respect, that's a silly question."

"Have you talked to Pastor lately?"

"Yes, we've talked."

"He told me you haven't been to him like scheduled."

Mark closes his eyes. He feels a sharp pain on the left side of his head. When he opens his eyes again, he sees Alicia standing in the laundry room, just barely visible in the darkness of the room.

"We're going to have to tell them something. What exactly do you suppose that should be?"

"That everything is going to be okay," Joanne says. "But they just came home. They need a little bit of time to adjust. Let's not hammer them with this."

"Fine. I—"

He sees Alicia creep out the laundry room, holding her hand behind her back. He just stares as she lets her hand fall to her side, showing a handgun. As if he were hypnotized, he watches her lift the gun to her head and hold it to her temple. He slowly shakes his head, but realizes Joanne looking at him strangely. She looks toward the laundry room, but he knows she sees absolutely nothing. He turns away from what he knows will happen next.

He doesn't jump at the muffled crack anymore.

"I'll talk to Pastor tomorrow. I think we have an appointment anyway."

She nods and reaches for him. Before she can get to his shoulder, he turns away. "I need a breather, if that's okay with you."

"It is, Mark. Take the time you need."

"Thank you, ma'am."

He walks to the front door. "Kids, I'll be back in a few. Okay?"

"Where are you going?" Kalina asks.

"To get some air, that's all. I'll be back soon."

"Can I come?" Charles asks.

"Not this time, Buddy. I'll be back before you go to bed, to tuck you in."

Soon after, Mark is on the road, driving to run away. He quickly realizes, though, there's nowhere for him to run. A place comes up in his mind, a place where he wouldn't be seen, a place where he knows he won't be pestered by anyone wishing well but not knowing how to do well. A place where no one cares how much or how little faith he has. A place where he could be no one.

Before long, he is parking his car in front of the bar where he met Eleanor Bixby.

CHAPTER FOURTEEN

"So, what happens then?"

"Well, his son Solomon takes over. He becomes one of the greatest rulers the world has seen."

"But he wasn't perfect either, right? I heard of Solomon before . . . he was the guy with all the wisdom, but he had a thing for many women."

"This is true. I think that's the point, though. All imperfect people, leading up to a perfect God who died on the cross for our sins."

"If you believe that could actually happen."

"If you believe."

Berta and Jennifer sit in the kitchen talking about God, about life, and everything in between. Berta usually relishes in the moments where she is able to teach others about her faith, but she loves this moment with Jennifer, her half sister, even more.

"All of what I said is what I believe," Berta says as she taps the kitchen table with her pointer.

"And I don't necessarily have to believe the same thing, right?"

"You don't. I'm not forcing this on you. You just asked a few questions. I'm here to answer. You are my sis, right?"

Jennifer smiles. "Only partially."

"Well, that's enough for me."

Jennifer's smile doesn't leave her face.

"So, I was thinking about something you said," Berta says.

"Hey now, I opened your eyes to something here? I'm definitely all ears for this." She nudges Berta jokingly in the arm.

"Well, I never thought about this, at least not until you mentioned it to me . . ."

"Okay . . ." Jennifer frowns, wrinkling her forehead.

"I do wonder if I can truly have any successful relationship. In a way, we *are* damaged goods. The things that happened to us . . . the things we still are going through. No good man is going to want to be around all of that."

"Well, that's not wholly true. Craig knew mostly everything, right? And he still married you."

"I said no good man."

"Ouch," Jennifer chuckles. "So I'm guessing you are the one who is leaving him?"

"Filed not too long ago."

"Hmmm." She looks down. "Serious question. Why *do* you think he asked you to marry him, even knowing all your bad parts?"

"Because he loves me, I guess."

"But love isn't enough for you?"

"I'm not saying that." She sighs. "There's more to this situation than you think."

"But it shouldn't be. It should be very simple here. He loves you. You believe or believed that. He knows you, even at your worst spots. He still loves you."

"But again, there's more to it than that. Who *is* he? I have no idea who he is."

"You do. You know him well. Otherwise, why did you marry him? You know him well. He has a past, sure. So do you. But who is he now? Who are you now?"

Berta taps her finger harder on the table. "Why does it even matter? I'm getting the divorce. Either that or he is gone forever."

"Just asking. I might want to ask him out."

"Stop playing."

"No, I'm being serious. He knows all this about you and he *still* stayed. I don't know too many men who would stay . . . too much baggage."

Berta looks away and thinks for a moment. "So what are you saying? I shouldn't get the divorce?"

"Well, I think that decision is already made, like you said."

"I could stop it."

"Yeah, but . . . would he want to come back after you shooed him away?"

"I don't know." She looks at her cell phone, the little light in the corner shining. "Did you hear my phone ring?" She asks Jennifer.

"No. Not at all."

She goes and grabs her phone, noticing it lights up because she has an unheard voice message. She listens to it once, then twice, then a third time before setting the phone down gently. Tears start to fill her eyes.

"What's wrong?"

"I—I have to—my friend—she—she isn't going to make it. That was just her husband calling me telling me they are taking her off life support in a couple days."

Jennifer looks down. "I'm sorry to hear that."

"I ought to be there with them. I need to call Craig."

She dials Craig's burner phone, not caring to go through Ramses, but she gets the voicemail. She leaves a message, trying to avoid breaking down into tears. Afterward, she calls Mark but gets his voicemail as well. She leaves a message for him, almost begging him to call her back, then sets the phone down, distraught.

"You okay?"

"No one picks up their phones anymore." She wipes at her eyes. "I'm likely going to be gone for a few days. There's enough food and stuff here for you, so you won't have to go out anywhere. You'll be safe."

"That's fine. Take whatever time you need. I'll be here."

ᏚᏏᏚ

Craig pulls the truck up to the ranch and into the garage. After a silent ride that seemed to take forever, he parks and shuts the truck off. For a while he looks straight, trying to understand what just happened. The ping-pong sound the truck makes as it's cooling off is the only sound in the area. That and, Craig notices, Addie's quickened breathing.

"So, we are here," Craig says, simply to cut the silence.

"This is where you live?"

"Well . . . this is where I'm staying for now, yes."

"And you would jog all the way down to my stand?"

"Sure. Good exercise." He pops open the car door. "Listen, I'll show you around and—" He looks at her for the first time since leaving the town. She's definitely been crying, her eyes puffy, her face red. He shuts the door and lays his head on the headrest. "This is a stupid question. And I know it is, but if you want to tell me so, that's fine." He turns his head to the side to look at her. "You okay?"

She swallows hard. She turns her head to look at him and says, "That *is* a stupid question."

Craig, still looking her in her eyes, chuckles. He sees a glint in her eye as she starts to giggle. They share a quick laugh, but it fades quickly.

"So, who was he?" Craig asks.

"Mac?"

203

He nods.

"The man I should have married. Instead, I fell for his brother. And well, you know the story from there."

"Mac is your husband's brother. Have you two ever . . ."

"No. Mac is too respectful. What you saw before we left . . . that's the furthest we ever went."

Craig winces. "Why didn't he do anything about the abuse? I mean, he's a big guy. He could take your husband easily."

"If only that were true. Mac owes Brad his life. Mac was in a lot of trouble years ago. He got involved with drugs and, well . . . he wanted out. He got out but lost everything. Had nothing. Brad brought him to Silver Rock, where he helped him back to his feet. Got him a job. Got him inclusion into the group. He's their heavy."

"Wait. So there *is* a group? That crazy old lady isn't crazy?"

"No. Miss June isn't crazy. There is a group twisting events of this town. Rewriting history such that it slants in their advantage. Brad is a part of the group. So is Mac. Then there's Reverend Sally and the so-called mayor. Drubbins is his name. They meet somewhere—I was never able to find out where—and discuss ways to add to their power . . ."

Craig thinks for a moment while Addie speaks. The dots are connecting slowly for him. He interrupts Addie. "So I was a scary entity to them. I am the unknown."

"Sure you were. It has been years since an outsider even set foot in Silver Rock. Most people can't find it, and even if they could, there's no reason to show up." She shakes her head. "So there wasn't much Mac could do, especially if Brad swore to him on their parents' graves that he wouldn't harm me again. But, the abuse became worse. Before, it was only when Brad was drunk. Later, after that, it became at all times, to teach me a lesson. Because I was the one who ran to Mac." She looks at her hands, which are shaking, then at Craig with a look that startles him. "He said he would kill me if I told anyone, especially Mac. I believe him. And I believe if I ever end up near him again, he will kill me. I cannot go back."

"You're safe here. You are safe—"

"With you?"

He clears his throat, which hurts at the moment. "You are safe in this house."

She nods and looks back down. "Why are you helping me? Why have you helped me?"

He thinks for a few moments, wrestling with what to tell her and what not to tell her. He starts and stops a few times before saying, "You need it. I saw it. So I helped."

"That's more than your friendly good Samaritan. You put your life on the line for me. And you don't know me. You were almost thrown in jail for the rest of your life. I don't get it."

He sighs. "You know how at my cell you apologized for bringing an innocent man into your mess?"

"Yeah."

"Well, maybe I'm not so innocent. I probably deserve to rot in that cell. I'm not . . . I'm not a very good person."

She looks into his eyes in a way that makes him shy, but he knows she's searching for something. She places her hand on his.

"Well, you could have fooled me," she says and pats his hand. "It's late. You want to show me to a room?"

He looks at her strangely. "Sure. Um." He looks at the clock in the dash. One thirty-three in the morning. "Yeah, it's been a long day. Let's rest up and tomorrow . . . tomorrow."

"Is tomorrow. And we'll worry about that then." She gets out the truck gingerly.

Craig rushes out the truck to help her, but she waves him off.

☙

Mark opens the door to the shady bar and is immediately greeted by a moist heat that is in complete juxtaposition to the chilly air outside. The air is so thick, he chokes. Still, he makes his way to the bar first and grabs a glass of whiskey. He decides against heading all the way to the back as he once did, and takes one of the tables around the other side of the bar. He looks toward the corner on that side to see only a single person under the dim glow of a pendant light, downing shots. There are already several empty shot glasses in front of her.

He hesitates for a moment, not knowing whether he should approach or simply pretend he doesn't see her. Either way, he knows for sure he sees Eleanor Bixby drowning something in quite a few drinks. He decides to sit at the table with his back toward her. Maybe if he is quick enough, she won't notice. As he shifts to sit, he catches her stare, and for a moment, is frozen. He can't move, so he stays for a few seconds in an awkward squat position, hovering just above the wooden seat. She holds a shot glass in front of her mouth, not moving, either. He holds his glass up in salute, nods his head, and sits down, his back toward her.

He takes a sip of his drink, finding it sharp and bitter. He takes another just to stop thinking. One more sip and he sets the tumbler down. He hears his rational self talking, saying there aren't any answers in the deep brown liquid. His rational self tells him he needs to be home with his family or even by Jade's side.

He takes another sip to quiet his rational self.

He sits, his hands wrapped around his glass, his fingers folded together. He's tired of thinking. He's tired of struggling. He's tired of . . . living. He doesn't even consider this as living anymore. The brown liquid doesn't take too long to work its evil magic. His vision slightly blurs, then comes back into focus. He feels numb, and he realizes his vision is blurred because he's crying. He roughly wipes his tears away and sniffs a couple times.

Another sip.

He feels a burning in the back of his head, and adjusts in his seat so that his back is against the wall. He glances toward Eleanor to see her staring right at him. Her face is flushed, but she otherwise looks well put together. She looks like she just came from work, her professional attire still on. She stares at him, though he isn't sure she isn't staring through him. He looks down at the shot glasses in front of her, then looks away. A few moments later, he hears the clocking of dress shoes on the wooden floor of the bar. Eleanor walks past him and to the bar. She grabs two more shots and starts on her way back to her table. She walks right by him, leaving a trail of sweetly scented perfume behind her. Mark watches her walk back to her table and too carefully sit down. She downs another shot and slams the glass on the table.

Curious, Mark gets up, initially losing his balance, and walks to Eleanor's table. He sits on the wooden chair at her table.

"So, what are you drowning in shots?" he asks.

She stares at him, her eyebrow slightly raised. "Who says I'm drowning anything?"

"That's a lot of alcohol not to be."

"Well sure, for a lightweight like you. I saw you stumble off a few sips."

"I don't drink."

"So what are *you* drowning in your curious brown liquid?" She smiles.

Mark sighs before taking another sip. He can no longer taste the bitterness. "I have to pull the plug."

She looks confused at first. Her face shifts once she figures it out. "Oh. I'm sorry."

"No, you're not."

"A harsh and bitter misjudgment of my character."

"You can talk around it. But I know what you think. You think I deserve every last bit of misery that is coming to me."

She looks down and doesn't say anything. He finishes his drink and sets the glass down.

"So, I . . ." She bites the corner of her lip. "My fiance called it off."

He looks at her, reading her face. "Why?"

"Well,"—she laughs a mirthless laugh—"he ended up finding out about that stuff I was trying to keep hidden."

"Why do you laugh?"

"Because if I don't, I don't know what I would do."

"So, laughing is a defense mechanism?"

"What?" She leans over the table and places her hand under her chin. He can't help but glance at her cleavage, but immediately regrets doing so. He squints in an effort to regain focus. The small bit of liquor is really working on him now.

"Mr. Cooke, are you attempting to analyze me?"

"No."

"Then what's with all the questions?"

Mark shrugs. "Just making conversation, I guess." He looks down. "I'll go back to where I was. Shouldn't have disturbed you." He gets up and walks back to his table, empty tumbler in hand.

He plops down and sits, simply looking at the empty glass, not wanting to get another. At this point, he decides to wait for his quick buzz to wear off before going home. Lost in his thoughts, he doesn't immediately notice Eleanor carefully sitting down in front of him with two more drinks in hand. She slides one across to him and makes a *clink* as one glass hits another. He stares into the cup, then up at her. She looks unsure of herself, a look he hasn't seen on her before.

"So, my fiance called the whole thing off. He broke up with me. I —" She stares into her cup. "I cheated on him. But it was a long time ago." She shakes her head. "Whatever that crooked detective said must have sparked something for this guy. He came storming back into my life, wanting to be something more than a fling. Ruined everything."

"Why did you cheat in the first place?"

"Why did you?" She stares Mark down.

"I was hurt. And confused. I wanted the pain of things to stop. But instead of talking to my wife about it, I ran to Alicia. Alicia be-came . . . a drug to me. You?"

Her lips curl slightly into a snarl. Mark is unsure if it is directed at him or herself. "I was drunk. No pain, no confusion, just plain old drunk and stupid."

He nods. "I'm sorry. I know what it's like to have your past come up and completely ruin everything you thought to be good in your life."

"At the end of the day, was that what she was? Your past that ru-ined everything?"

"In some ways. But she was only able to ruin stuff because I let her. Because I gave her the tools and the room to do so. I'm still at fault."

She takes a quick sip of her drink. He watches her move elegantly even after taking back so much. "Maybe."

"What do you mean 'maybe'?"

"You've made some crap decisions, yeah. But Alicia was sick. She really was. And just the fact that she went through all that trouble to find you . . . even if you didn't entertain anything, I feel like she would have pushed the issue anyway. This woman sat there for years trying to find ways to get near you." She sighs. "That's what I believe."

"Is that the alcohol talking?"

"What? No? Why would you ask that?"

"Because when we first talked, you seemed to believe this was all my doing."

"I did, didn't I? Well, again, you made some really bad decisions. But this is not *all* your fault."

He sits with her for a few silent minutes, taking in what she said, but still sipping on his drink. He doesn't know what clicks in his head, but something shifts. He downs the rest of his drink and gets up to grab another.

"Another?" he asks Eleanor.

"Sure. Why not? I'm going to the ladies' room first." She gets up.

Mark purchases two more drinks and sets one at the end of the table, in front of the glass Eleanor emptied. He waits for her return while emptying his glass yet again. It doesn't take long for the drink to settle in on him, and when it does, he ends up hunching over the table, exactly like the man he saw the first time he came into this bar. He doesn't know how much time passes, but he gets a feeling it's quite a while. At this point, he knows he is sufficiently drunk, remembering this feeling as an ode to his college days. He looks around the bar, noticing only a few people. *How late is it?* He doesn't think to look at his cell for the time because his focus shifts to where Eleanor is, or rather where she isn't. He stares at the untouched cup and looks around again. He gets up on wobbly feet and looks back at where she sat. The entire table is cleared of all glasses and bottles. He almost waltzes to the bathrooms and bangs on the ladies' room door.

"Eleanor." He has no idea how loud he is. "You alright?"

After hearing nothing, he thinks he sneaks in, but actually barges in, pushing the door so hard it slams against the wall behind it. He looks under stalls but finds no one. Suddenly concerned about getting caught in the ladies' room, he slinks out. He walks to the front of the bar and stumbles out the front door. The bartender yells something out to him, but he ignores him and heads to his car to sit.

His mind is spinning, and he knows he can't drive anywhere, so he sits in his parked car in almost total darkness, feeling like he's on a roller coaster. He closes his eyes and finds Jade, perfectly healthy and smiling. She speaks to him, but he has no idea what she says. It's like watching her on TV with the sound muted. Her lips move, but no sound comes out. Stepping from behind her is Alicia and she holds a gun to Jade, who doesn't seem to notice. Jade just keeps mouthing something to him. Alicia lifts the gun and in simple fashion shoots Jade down. She then turns the gun on herself and pulls the trigger again. Still no sound is heard. He opens his eyes wide to stare out in front of him but finds his vision blurred. He paws at his eyes, observing the glistening of tears on his fingers. He rubs the liquid with his fingers until his fingers are dry.

Startling him is a feeling of a cool and hard object against his head.

"Don't move," a familiar voice says.

He freezes instantly after hearing a clicking sound.

"You've taken my baby away. My baby girl. Gone. All for this crazy woman who ended up blowing her own brains out."

Mark hesitates at first, but eventually says, "It's not like that. It's not like that at all."

"Even when a man has a gun to your head, you still can't tell the truth, can you? This gun I have pressed against the back of your head, that's the one Jade should have shot you with. You put your hands on her. I should have killed you myself."

"Sir, I—"

"SHUT UP." Jade's father's voice comes out strained.

Mark remains silent.

"Here's what you're going to do. You are going to start this car. You are going to turn left coming out of here, and you are going to drive. Ten minutes down the road, there's an empty lot. We go there, now."

"Sir, I've been drinking, and I'm not good to drive."

"Then, you better concentrate. Ten minutes down the road. Now."

Mark starts the car, trying to sober up quickly. He puts the car in reverse, then pulls out of the bar parking lot. He turns left and ends up on the highway. No other cars are on the road, and he counts himself lucky, because concentration is next to impossible.

"Listen, sir, I have no idea what you plan on doing. But please, let's just talk things out."

"Drive, Mark."

Mark remains silent for the rest of the ten-minute drive, though it seems to have taken much longer. He pulls into the empty lot that is half paved and half dusty ground.

"Shut the car off. Lights out. Step out of the car slowly."

Mark does as he is told and walks out into the chilly air. The only light he sees is from the full moon.

"Keep walking. To the dirt road section."

Mark walks as he is told but eventually stops.

"Don't do anything silly here, Mark."

"I'm sorry."

"What?"

"I'm deeply sorry for what I have done. For what I have done to Jade. I have an idea on how this is going to end, and I am ready. But before you do anything, I just had to let you know that I am sorry. Jade in many ways saved me. And it was a privilege and honor to be her husband. And though I failed on many accounts, sir, I need you to know I truly do love her, and I would do anything just to have her around." He thinks to himself, quickly realizing that what shifted in his mind was his will to live. He realizes now he no longer has the will to live. He feels a stiff jam in his back.

"On your knees."

Mark plops to his knees and he feels the stiff barrel of a gun in the back of his head.

He sees a bright flash of light.

Then darkness. Plunging into eternal darkness.

CHAPTER FIFTEEN

Mark's eye flutters open. The other doesn't open at all as he lies in the dirt, his cheek pressed against a jagged rock. His head feels like it's been split in two, and the rest of his body feels churned up. He blinks a few times before attempting to move. He slides his arm across the dusty, gravelly ground, bringing his hand to his head to somewhat shield his one eye from the beams of the rising sun.

He finds enough energy to flip around on his back, though the cold morning wind makes lying there unbearable. He stares up at the sky, trying to understand what exactly happened last night. A light breeze blows up a dust cloud just over him. He shields his eyes again. After a few more moments, he gets on his feet.

The shift in gravity makes him nauseated, and he winds up hunched over, vomiting into a ditch. When his stomach doesn't lurch any more, he saunters to his car and almost throws himself in. The cold makes him shiver, and the shivering makes him hurt, so he starts the car and turns the heat on full blast. After a few moments, the car is toasty, and he puts it in drive to make his way back home.

Once he turns onto his street, he pulls the car over and waits. He looks at the clock, knowing Kalina is walking to the bus stop and Joanne is probably taking Charles to school. He knows he should have been there to do that for them, to be their support. He hangs his head in shame.

Flying past him is Kalina's bus. The bus comes to a stop with all its lights flashing. In the distance, he thinks he sees Kalina climbing onto the bus. Before stepping up to the bus, she turns and looks in his direction. He knows she can't see him, but somehow, he believes she feels him nearby. He ducks more into the seat of the car. She eventually gets onto the bus and it pulls away. Once it does, he waits a few more minutes to allow for the house to be totally empty.

He pulls the car out onto the road again and heads home. He's thankful he timed it right, as he doesn't see Joanne's car anywhere. He pulls into the garage and turns off the engine. He then wills his aching body to move quickly into the house, into the bedroom, and into the shower. He turns the water up high and makes sure it's scalding hot. He wants to wash away all of last night, but more importantly, he wants the water to sting as if by some ritual. Punishment for what he has done. Punishment for what he has become. He cleans up and shaves, trying to appear as if nothing happened. He hurries to get dressed and rushes out the door to make it to his meeting with Pastor Brentwood.

⋘⋙

"So Mark, how have you been?" Pastor Brentwood asks.

"I've been hanging in there." He averts his gaze. "My ribs don't hurt as much. Still a little twinge here and there, but nothing near what it was a little while ago."

"Where were you last night?"

Mark freezes. "Pardon?"

"You left; never came home."

He sighs and closes his eyes. "What did she do? Call you first thing in the morning?"

"She's worried about you, Mark. We all are, and we all want to help in any way we can. But you have to accept that help. You've agreed to set up these recurring meetings so we can take this to God in prayer, so we can take the steps in making sure you are okay. You've missed three already. And now you're here obviously planning on ducking and dodging around the real issues that plague your spirit." He takes a slow, deep breath. "So, if that's the way it's going to be, you may as well cancel the rest of the appointments. There's no need for them if no real progress is going to be made, if you aren't going to be forthright and honest with me."

Mark looks down. He knows Pastor Brentwood is right, but he finds it difficult to simply empty his soul to him. A strange and random thought enters his mind. He sorely misses Craig. He nods.

"So are you ready to talk, to really talk?"

Mark nods again.

"Good." He sits in a chair in front of Mark. "So, how much sleep have you been getting?"

"Not a lot. A couple hours a day."

"Still taking the pain meds?"

"No."

"Eating well? Drinking plenty of fluids?"

"This sounds less like spiritual counseling and more like a psychiatric visit."

"Well, you've mentioned a few things that have me concerned."

"Like seeing Alicia."

"Yes. Do you wish to talk about that now?"

"No."

Pastor Brentwood eyes him curiously.

"I'd rather talk about last night."

"Okay. By all means. What happened last night?"

"I died. At least, I thought I died. I thought I was shot and I just fell."

Pastor looks confused.

"I went out last night to this bar. I don't know what I was looking for. I guess just to numb the pain. But then I saw someone I knew there and we were talking."

"Someone you knew . . . in the bar. On a weeknight."

"Yes, sir. I think she—"

"She?"

"It wasn't like that. It wasn't like that at all. I wasn't meeting up with her. I was trying to hide, to be alone, but she was there, downing shot after shot, trying to numb the pain of something as well."

"And who was this woman, exactly?"

"Alicia's psychologist."

Pastor Brentwood's mouth hangs slightly open.

"So I've been on this mission, I suppose. A search for understanding, even. I needed to know why this happened to us . . . why did Alicia do all this? I asked the detective who was on the case for help. He directed me to this woman, Eleanor Bixby, Alicia's psychologist. I met up with her before, in the same bar. Just didn't think I would see her again."

"Wait. So this detective led you to Alicia's psychologist for what? Legally, there's nothing that can be said."

"Yeah, well, I didn't quite say everything was legal here. We ended up having a long talk. I learned more about her motivations. Found out she was pregnant."

"Who? Alicia?"

"Yes, sir. She lost the baby, though."

"That's a shame."

"So, here's where . . ." He rubs the top of his head a few times. "The psychologist seems to believe the baby was mine."

"And why would she believe that?"

"Because that's what Alicia told her. She told her that I was the only one she was with."

"But . . . you've never slept with her."

"That's what I *said*."

"That wasn't the truth?"

"It was not the truth. I wanted to—I needed to be with Jade. So, I changed that detail, also because I couldn't admit how far I had fallen. It was embarrassing."

"You were ashamed."

"I was the old me. The one I ran away from." He looks at Pastor with a solemn look. "And now, I won't get the chance to tell Jade the truth."

Mark lets silence fill the air.

"So, you were at this bar, drinking with Alicia's psychologist . . ."

"Yeah." He shakes his head, trying to shake the feeling of dread away. "She disappeared on me, so I went to my car to sober up a little. That's when I felt the gun at the back of my head."

Pastor lets him continue.

"Jade's father held me at gunpoint, told me to drive to this abandoned lot. He told me to get out and walk to this dusty part. He forced me to my knees and jammed the gun to the back of my head. Then a flash of light and everything goes dark. The next thing I know, I'm lying flat in the dirt with the sun beaming in my eyes."

"A hallucination."

"Another hallucination." He adjusts in his seat. "The scary thing is, I was hoping it wasn't. I hoped it all wasn't a hallucination, some drunk story to tell people later on in life. I actually wanted . . . I wanted to die. I don't want this life anymore."

"What about your kids?"

Mark says nothing.

"They need you, don't they? What would happen to them if you decided to leave this place? You may think there's relief, but do you believe there would be any relief for them? If you left, especially now, do you think they wouldn't be irreparably, almost irrevocably damaged, forever changed by their father's decision to quit?"

"I think about them all the time."

"Do you? Be honest with yourself. Do you consider your children as much as you think?"

"I'm not a bad father."

"I'm not saying that. I'm saying do you consider them in all this *soul searching*?"

"But why does it seem like you are mad at me?"

Pastor chuckles. "I'm not mad at you, Son. I just know you are better than this. And I need *you* to know you are better than this."

For some time, Mark simply looks down at his lap. He fidgets a little.

"Mark. You. Are. Better. Than. This. You control your thoughts. You are strong. You have real power. You should not be ashamed. You will get through this. You have the uncanny ability to survive. That's what you do. You survive. Not only that, you thrive. You make things out of nothing. Look at your kids. Look at how well they do. Look at Kalina. For a while it was just you and her, Mark. Don't you see? Don't you see it?"

Mark feels the pre-cry pressure build up in his sinuses. In an instant, he is crying, but not just crying—mourning, grieving. Sobs from deep within force his body to shake in uncontrollable ways. He cries to a point of not breathing, but the sobs continue on with fervor. He cries for Alicia, for his and her unborn child. He cries for Bernard. He cries for everyone close to him, for him pushing them all away. He cries for himself, because he feels a part of him has already died.

He cries for Jade, not knowing if he will ever see her smile again.

⚘

The sun shines brightly through his eyelids, turning the black darkness into gold. He struggles to open his eyes, squinting a few times before giving up and burying his head back in the pillow. He groans as he feels a soft touch on his bare back.

"Berta, just a few more minutes," he says lazily.

The soft touch moves along his back, along the scar of his past. He falls into a state of semi sleep where he is neither awake fully or in a deep sleep. A wonderful memory fills his mind, one that seems a lifetime ago.

They were on one of their many vacations, in a small hotel in Madrid. The night before, he and Berta spent the entire night at a flamenco restaurant. They both observed intently the art form that is flamenco. He remembers watching the women twist, turn, and stomp in seductive yet joyful ways. The men, singing and strumming their guitars. All of it combined in a powerful melange of movement and music. That night, they made love so passionately for most of the night into the early morning. After their night of lovemaking, the sun rose on their bodies, urging them to awaken. He couldn't move then. He didn't want to. He was mostly awake, but kept his eyes closed and watched the darkness turn to gold. When he finally did open his eyes, he saw Berta, smiling at him. It was one of the best moments of his life, seeing her smile in that exhausted but satisfied way, her body glowing under the beams of morning sunlight.

He opens his eyes barely so they become slits on the front of his face, noticing a shadow moving in between him and the sunlight. It takes a few moments for him to adjust before he realizes it's not Berta who stands at the window smiling at him, but Addie. In a flash, memories of last night come rushing in. He pops up, being sure to keep himself covered and not show what happens to every man in the morning.

"Addie, you okay? Something wrong?"

"No," she says, still smiling. "I woke up today without the feeling of a weight pressing me into my bed. I woke up without hoping the weight on me would just press me further into the darkness until I died."

He takes a few more moments to adjust his vision. "Wh—What are you wearing?" He notices the black, yellow, and gray floral-print sundress she's wearing.

"I found this in the closet in the room. It's a little loose on the straps, and around the waist, but . . . anything is better than what I had on when I came here."

He looks down.

"So, who's Berta?"

Craig vaguely remembers saying Berta's name. "Someone important."

"And what's with the scar on your back?"

"I don't want to talk about it."

"But you know my scars." She turns around. Some of the marks peek out at the top band of the sundress.

"Look, Addie—"

"I need to know who you are. I am very sure you don't own this place and all this land. Pictures in one of the rooms tells me so. Your parents, I'm guessing? Anyway, I need to know how all this happened. How did you end up in my life? How did you end up in some part of the US that most people don't even know about? How did you end up saving me?"

Craig looks at her, not knowing what to say or what question to answer.

"I made breakfast," she says.

Craig thinks for a few seconds before nodding. "I have to take a shower first."

"You didn't take one before you hopped in bed last night?"

"No, I just passed out."

"Ewww. So when you're done, strip the bed and take the sheets to the laundry room. You have to show me where that is, by the way. I'll wash some clothes and those sheets."

"Addie, what are you doing?"

"Trying to move forward," she says as she leaves the room. "What else is there to do?"

Craig again is at a loss for words.

☙❧

Craig carefully steps downstairs. The warmth of the shower did some good in dulling his aches and pains, but his body still groans in protest. Immediately he picks up the scent of good food, a scent that hasn't really entered the ranch since his arrival. He sees plates set out that are full of food.

"When's the last time you ate a meal like this?" she asks, leaning slightly on a chair.

"It looks great, but—"

She waves her hand to cut him off. "Not yet. Just enjoy a warm meal with me." She sits in front of one of the plates, taking her time to make sure she doesn't rub her back on the chair.

Craig sits, still looking at Addie strangely. His stomach growls loudly enough for both of them to hear. He nods, blesses the food, and starts to eat. He doesn't remember the last time he had a warm home-cooked meal, but then, the ranch isn't home for him, nor is it for Addie. He sets his fork down.

"Was that you rubbing my back?" he asks.

"I was trying to wake you." She glances up at him. "Noise wasn't working."

"Look. I don't—"

"We both have scars. On our backs, no less. We both have deep, seemingly violent scars. I just wondered where yours came from. Then I wondered where you came from. Like, why am I not running back home right now? Some stranger comes out of nowhere to buy fruits and vegetables, ends up at my home, but then goes to jail because I asked for help. And . . ." She murmurs some to herself. "You could be a serial killer. You could actually mean to harm me." Her southern drawl becomes more pronounced.

It takes everything in Craig not to smile. "I mean you no harm. And I am not a serial killer." He slightly shakes his head. "If I did mean you harm, why didn't you try to run? Take one of the cars you saw in the garage. Drive away as far as you could go?"

"Because I figured"—she looks down at her plate and starts poking at her eggs—"either you're truly a nice man, and I'm safe . . . or you are a serial killer planning to kill me . . . and right now . . . death isn't so bad, either."

Craig feels a tinge of sadness poke him deep in his belly. "You are safe here, Addie."

She nods and returns to eating her food. Craig does the same. For some time, the only sound heard is the clanging of metal forks on china plates.

"I took the tour," Addie says. "This place is wonderful."

"Took the tour? How long have you been up?"

"I never really went to sleep." She brushes a few strands of hair behind her ear. "There are a lot of rooms. Just . . ." She wriggles her nose. "There's so much land going unused."

"No one here to work it."

"I walked to the barn out back."

"There's a barn?" Craig chuckles.

"Are you being serious?"

He nods. "I never knew there was a barn. But hey, I didn't really venture out, either."

"I tried to find as much as I could. Still couldn't find the laundry room, though."

"Yeah, let me show you." He gets up from the table, grabbing his plate and walking to the kitchen sink. "But you're still not doing my laundry."

"Fine." She gets up from her seat, wincing after brushing her back against the chair.

"Hey, did you go to the hospital after? Like, did you get any medical attention for your back?"

"No. I couldn't."

"Let me see."

"No, I'm fine."

"Addie, you aren't fine."

"I am. I really am."

"Tell that to the blood coming through on Miss Janice's dress."

She stops and stands there, almost embarrassed.

"Just let me take a look at it. Looks like there are some parts that need to be bandaged up. A quick check, clean, and bandage. That's all."

"Do you know what you're doing?"

"I know enough."

She seems to think for a moment before nodding. He goes to the drawer in the island and pulls out a first-aid kit. Spotting his burner phone, he grabs it and jams it into his pocket. He looks around for a place for him to do his best doctor impersonation. He looks at her.

"I'm not sure where we can do this, but I'm going to need you to slide down the dress. And—hold on a sec." He runs to the laundry room and comes back with a towel. "You can use this to cover your front."

She nods. "The chaise there." She points into the living area. "Will that work?"

"Sure."

They walk over to the chaise and Addie sits with her back turned toward Craig. Craig grabs a chair from the kitchen and pulls it up to her, being sure he isn't too close. "I'm closing my eyes, so tell me when you're ready."

"Okay," she whispers.

Craig waits in the chair with his eyes held shut, listening to the rustling of the sundress moving along Addie's skin.

"I'm ready," she whispers.

Craig opens his eyes and scans her battered and bruised torso. Crimson lines stretch across her back, and some cross each other. At the welted intersection of the wounds, blood slowly seeps out. She starts shaking.

"I'm going to need to clean it again. Looks like you already did."

"In the shower."

"Okay, so I just need to disinfect the open parts. Then I have a lot of gauze and tape here—"

"You don't need to talk me through it. I've been bandaged before."

"I'm sorry. Just . . . wanted to make you feel comfortable."

"None of this is comfortable, Craig."

"Understood."

He takes her comment as his cue to shut his mouth. He begins cleaning her wounds with rubbing alcohol and cotton swabs. She flinches a few times, but he is sure to be as careful as possible. She presses the towel harder to her chest. Craig places the first strip of bandage on her upper back. Swiftly he moves, placing the bandages on her back, covering wounds that still clearly hurt her.

"You are very gentle, and very kind to do this."

Craig still doesn't say anything until he finishes. "All done." He gets up and takes a bunch of the soiled items to the trash while she pulls the dress back up. He fumbles with the trashcan in the bottom part of the island. When he has everything put away, he finds the towel sitting on the chaise, and Addie nowhere to be seen.

CHAPTER SIXTEEN

It has been a long few months for Craig, and at this very moment, he feels things are at an all-time low. He just finished listening to the two voicemails he has received, one from Ramses, the other from Berta. The one from Ramses was disappointing, simply stating he cannot come home yet, and that there may be a hidden danger somewhere.

Killer blow to the gut.

The message from Berta explained to him what Mark told her: that Jade isn't going to make it, and that they are taking her off life support in a few days.

An uppercut landing square on the chin for the knockout.

For most of the morning, Craig sat outside, looking out at the field, praying.

Lost in his thoughts, he doesn't hear Addie walk outside and sit next to him.

"Is everything okay?" Her voice comes out timid.

"No. No, it's not."

A long silence fills the air, but Craig feels no need to fill the silence with anything but the sound of a gentle breeze swirling about them. He looks down at his hands.

"I can go back."

Craig glances at her. "What do you mean?"

"To Silver Rock. I can go back to *him* if all this is too much."

"It's not you. And I would never ask you to go back to that. Like I said, you are safe here. We are safe here." Tears start to mar his vision. "But I should be home."

Addie nods in understanding.

"So, I guess it's only fair that I tell you why I am here. I know you asked, and I somewhat avoided answering." He sighs. "You called me a nice man. I am not. You said I was innocent. I am not. In fact, I'm likely one of the worst people you will meet in life."

"I don't believe that."

"You should. You really should." He blinks away a few tears. "I'm here running from the law, running from prison, running from my past, running from my mistakes, just . . . running."

"What did you do?"

"When? To land me here directly, or in my past?"

"To get you to be here."

"I killed a man." When Addie doesn't move, he looks her in the eyes. "I put myself in a bad situation . . . but I felt I had to . . . to help a friend—my best friend. The problem is . . . besides the obvious . . . I opened up a door to my past that I should have kept shut. That guy . . . who I was . . . ruined my present life. It ruined my marriage . . . my job . . . my friendships. The scar on my back is from years ago. I tried to kill myself, essentially. Right now, I wish it worked." He stops, fearing he has said too much. He snaps his head forward, his gaze returning to the field in front of him. In his peripheral vision, he sees Addie move closer to him. A few moments later, he feels her hand on top of his.

Her hand is smaller than Berta's, much daintier. She grips his hand and with her cold fingers gives a soft squeeze. He squeezes her hand back.

"Tell me more," she says.

"I can't. I'm not supposed to. I've already blabbed enough."

"Craig, it's safe here."

"I know it's s—" He looks at Addie and understands just what she means. It's safe here, with her. She is saying he is safe with her. He nods and faces forward again. "What more can I tell?"

"Whatever you need to get off your chest. You were here all this time by yourself. I can't imagine that was healthy for your mind."

"It was supposed to be a retreat-type hiding."

"Maybe for monks."

Craig chuckles. "I guess you're right. Turns out this place is more punishment for me than anything. That's a large reason why I kept going to your stand. Maybe even why I went to Silver Rock. I needed to be around people. Can't be alone. Never could, though I'm much better at it than I was years ago."

"Hmmm," Addie says thoughtfully. "Why is being alone such a difficulty?"

"Ahhh, that's a long story. The short of it is this. I was thought to be a demon seed when I was little. My biological parents couldn't control me so they tried to *church* me. One day they took the lessons too far and locked me in the closet with a Bible. Made no sense because it was dark in there, so I couldn't read it." He swallows hard. "They gave me no food . . . no water. I was in there, and I could hear nothing. At first, I kicked and screamed. I tried so hard to knock the door open, but they must have put something in front of it. Not that I would have had enough strength to open it, anyway. I was just a kid."

"How old?"

He avoids all eye contact. "Eight. I was eight years old."

"I'm so sorry."

He shrugs. "So, in that closet, I swore I heard voices, but later I realized they were in my head. Voices that would tell me how worthless I am. Voices that would say . . . much worse. So take that all the way into my adult life. It's tough to be alone. Again, not as tough as before, but still. There are whispers sometimes." He chuckles. "And that makes me sound crazy, right?"

Addie shakes her head vigorously. "Not at all. That makes you a survivor. I never would have guessed something so bad happened in your childhood."

"My life is full of bad happenings, Friend."

Addie looks down and smirks. "You called me friend."

"Well, you are my friend now. I don't tell this stuff to people, otherwise."

"I see." She brushes a loose strand of hair behind her ear. "So how did you get out?"

"They let me out three days later. Said I was fasting so that the demon that was in me could leave my body."

"That's horrible."

"Yeah, well, that's some of my childhood. From that point on, it was a struggle to be someone. I struggled to be a good Christian. I struggled to be a good person. I struggled to be a good husband."

"You seem to be very self-aware."

"I've had more than enough time to think on these things." He realizes her hand still covers his and he goes to move. She gently pulls her hand away.

"I see." She turns her body toward him. "So you were married? To Berta. Is that her name?"

"Yup." He shifts in his seat. "So, tell me about this evil group of Silver Rock."

Her face shifts slightly and it takes a moment for her to adjust to Craig's sudden change in conversation. "I see. Secret for secret. Scar for scar."

"Not quite. I'm just not ready to go that deep with you."

"I understand." She sighs. "So, yeah, this group—I'm not sure how it started or with whom. I just know the day my husband became a part of it. He came home drunk. It was the beginning of the abuse all over again. In his drunken slurs, he would mention things like he didn't mean to kill him and he's unstoppable now. The next day the whole town was abuzz about the brutal shooting of Mister Holland. He owned a small antiques shop at the edge of town. Then ensued a three-month long manhunt for someone who I know for a fact didn't do it. Little by little, more strange things would happen, with the church . . . in the streets. Just weird stuff. Then Mac comes along and confirms all of my suspicions. He never wanted to be a part of the group, but he couldn't say no to his brother. He knew what would happen to him if he did. Whenever someone needed some convincing, Mac was there."

"So what were they? Like a mob, a gang? I don't get it."

"They are worse. They did whatever they could to make sure the people stayed under their control. So, if that meant killing one or two off, they would. If that meant twisting some of the sermons at the pulpit to make people more vulnerable, they would. If it meant causing events to incite panic—or even rage—they would. Reverend Sally looks like a saint to the people, and they lay their lives down for him, but he is no saint. My husband is supposedly a decorated cop for fifteen years. People lie at his feet, thanking him for the protection. He actually is a scumbag. Drubbins, the so-called champion of equal opportunity, has incited more racial and gender tension than anyone, just so he can come in and ease their concerns. Yes, women can do what men can do and should get equal pay for it. Sure, let's give the blacks a few jobs." She looks down, then at Craig. "Sorry. I know that sounds . . . harsh."

"No, please don't apologize. This Drubbins would prey on our differences at night, but come in like a hero and supposedly solve all the problems during the day. He would solve the problems he started. I get it. That's what they all did, right?"

She nods. "All but Mac. He didn't want to cause anything, he just wanted to do the right thing. But that turns out to be a tough matter for him. They designated him the heavy. Essentially he is their tool to use. He does all the tough manual stuff."

"Tough manual stuff?"

"He did the dirty work. The planting of evidence . . . the murders."

"And you knew all of this? Why didn't you tell anyone?"

"Tell who? The authorities? They have at least two high-ranking cops. How about I pray about it? Talk about it in confession? Wait, no, the church is off limits, too. The local mayor's office? How about that? I can see if he can invoke some legislation or something like that to see . . . wait . . . yeah, they're a part of it, too. I only know of the four main people. Who knows how many others there are under them."

"I get it. So, there's nothing you could do. But Mac . . ."

"Now that he believes I'm safe, who knows what he will do."

They both sit in silence for a few moments.

"What's the long term here?" She asks. "In the immediate future, I stay here with you, but you are going home, aren't you? Like, you aren't staying here forever."

"Yes, I'm going home soon. For you, I don't know. Is there family you can stay with?"

"I don't know where they are. They left Silver Rock years ago. I should have went with them. But I chose Brad." Her face turns red. "I chose Brad."

"It's okay. We both sit here as imperfect people. What did you call me? A survivor?" He looks into her eyes. "You're a survivor, too."

"Thank you." She avoids his gaze. "I have a confession to make. It's pretty bad. You may not think the same of me from here on out."

"I'm all ears."

"Well . . . I knew you taking me back to Silver Rock would be trouble. Outsiders never do well there. And I knew you were an outsider because . . . well . . . all of my customers at the produce stand are from Silver Rock. In fact, outsiders are usually the number-one scapegoats for stuff . . . as you were. That's why I had you drop me off in front of Miss June's home. I couldn't risk you going too far into town. And that's why I cut off all communication. But, you showed back up into town. I tried to push you away." She looks him in the eyes. "But you showed up at my home."

"I connected the dots some time ago. For you to know so much on how this group operates, you had to have known what my appearance was going to do. No hard feelings. None at all. Look at the end result. Sure, we're a little beat up, but you are free. What's it like to sleep in a bed knowing you're safe from harm?"

"It's wonderful."

"And what is it like to have the best company in this part of the US?" He points at himself.

Addie chuckles. "It's also pretty great."

Craig feels his spirits lift ever so slightly. "Hey, I have a confession, too."

"Oh. Worse than being a not-so-nice person with a scarred child-hood?"

"Yes. Much worse."

"Okay." She takes in a deep breath and exhales slowly. "I'm ready."

"Okay, so here it goes." He rubs his palms on the front of his pants. "I am a huge sucker for your accent."

"What?"

"Your accent. That southern belle thing you've got going. The light and dainty talk with a southern twang. You could ask me to do anything in that voice and I would do it."

Addie's chuckles erupt into a full, hearty laugh that Craig shares with her.

"It's my weakness," Craig says.

"Well, no worries, sir. You've already done everything for me. Ah could ask no more."

Craig smiles so hard his cheeks hurt. "Okay, now you're laying it on thick."

She smiles. "Come to think of it, there is one more thing I need to ask."

"Oh, boy. Here we go."

Addie smiles and takes to her feet. "Can you assist me in cooking dinner tonight?" She places her hand out for Craig to take.

"Of course." He grabs her hand. She intertwines her fingers with his and leads him back into the ranch house.

◦◦◦

Berta sits in her car on the phone, in front of Mark and Jade's home.

"So, what Marcella and Jennifer have done is collect highly detailed information. I mean, stuff that maybe even the government isn't privy to. Much of it still needs to be validated," Ramses says.

"What do you mean 'validated'?" Berta asks.

"I mean, we need to make sure this is all accurate. Initially, it looks like it all is. It looks like it is all of Courtland's network and years' worth of history. Still, there's a lot to sift through. I have people on it, of course, but they have only gotten through half of what's on that drive."

"What exactly is his network? Like, what does that mean?"

"It means it's everything he needed to run his dirty operations. Account numbers, names, events. It's as detailed as the home address of the dirty cop who was paid off two years ago for a one-off. The amount paid, crime committed, everything. It's actually pretty scary."

"I don't understand. Why would he even record something like that?"

"No idea. He was paranoid, for sure. But I'm thinking he needed this stuff as leverage, or he was saving it for leverage at some point."

"And the stuff that's on there about me . . . about Craig."

"Too detailed. He had someone tailing both of you for years. Still can't figure out why."

Berta shivers. "Well, is there anything you can do about it?"

"Certainly. Once we get through it all and validate everything, we could . . . we could send it all crumbling, we could start revealing cases, maybe even release some info to the media. Though, most of the people he worked with moved on after his death, it seems." Ramses clears his throat. "Marcy was playing with fire here. She should have never contacted any of them. She should have left well enough alone."

"But then there would be no drive."

"But she would have been alive."

She pauses in thought, somewhat ashamed she considered the cache of information more important than Marcella's life. "So, what of Jennifer?"

"We can protect her. And when we get through the drive, I'm thinking we would know who attacked her and her mother. We could . . . eliminate the threat at that point."

"You don't have to go into the details." She shakes her head.

"Sorry. Listen, we can send someone by to get Jennifer and take her somewhere."

"Why would you do that?"

"It is entirely up to you. I just didn't want this thing to become any more of a burden for you. I'm sure it's already more than what you thought."

Berta considers it. "I actually like having her with me. Though, I'm not home right now and—" A thought presses itself upon her mind. "Can I ask you a question?"

"Sure."

"You said they were tracking me and Craig. You have no idea why?"

Ramses hesitates enough for Berta to notice. "None."

"Put yourself in his shoes. Why would you?"

"Knowing I kept tabs on every contact for leverage . . . there really wouldn't be a need to keep tabs on you and Cr—" He stops speaking and lets silence fill the line.

"But Craig *was* a contact, no?"

"He was. He sure was." His voice is grim. "So it's likely Courtland kept tabs on Craig for leverage, and by default—"

"He kept tabs on me, because if there was ever a point in which Craig posed a threat—"

"He would go after you."

"But then . . ."

"He would have to go through me and potentially the entirety of Raul's network. It would be a war, one he would lose easily."

"But Raul's network is done, I thought. I thought it was just you."

"There are plenty of people who would come out of . . . *retirement* for you and Craig."

Berta looks as the Cooke residence's front door opens and Kalina comes rushing out, dashing toward her car.

"We have to continue this later. I'm staying with a friend tonight, so . . . can you make sure everything is good at my home?"

"I will."

"Thank you. Talk to you soon." She rushes off the phone with time to get out the car and catch Kalina in her arms. The girl wraps her arms around Berta's waist and holds tightly.

"Hey, Sweetums. You okay?"

"Yeah."

Kalina finally lets go of Berta, allowing her to grab her bags and stride to the front door. Kalina follows closely behind. Once she's just inside the house, Mark greets her with a hug and takes her bags from her.

"Thanks," Mark says.

"For what? We're family, Mark."

"I know. It's just—" He looks down. "Have you spoken to Craig lately?"

She hesitates. "I left him a voicemail updating him on things. But I haven't spoken to him in some time."

He looks away, distracted. "You think we can talk later?"

"Of course."

"Cool." His voice noticeably shifts. "So, you are in the guest room."

"Where's your mother–in-law staying?"

"Our room."

"So that puts you . . ."

"On the couch down here. I prefer it that way, so don't feel any type of way."

She nods. "Hey, you . . . okay? I mean, I know in many ways you aren't . . . maybe that was a stupid question. It's just that . . ."

"I look bad. I know. I . . . have quite a few things I need to work through."

"Well, if you need someone to talk to . . ."

He gives a curt nod. "Thanks. I'll take your things upstairs."

And like that, he is gone upstairs, with her bags in hand.

⚬⚬⚬

Mark drops Berta's bags in the guest room and makes sure he sets out towels and things she might need for her stay.

"Mark."

He turns around to see Joanne. "Ma'am."

"Just wondering if everything is okay."

"Sure it is." He refocuses his attention outside.

"We never talked about what happened."

"What happened?"

"You never came home two nights ago."

"I'm fine. There's nothing to talk about."

"Please don't play this game with me."

"I'm not playing any games." He sighs. "Look, I kept my appointment with Pastor Brentwood and we're working on things." He looks back at her. "Trust me."

"So, when are we going to talk with the kids?"

"Tonight. I've been working on something to say." He turns on his heel and walks toward her. He places his hands on her shoulders gently. "Trust me." He smiles a weak smile and walks downstairs. He feels awkward for telling someone to trust him when he can barely trust himself.

◁❦▷

Later in the night, Mark sits in his comfortable chair with Amber in his lap. Kalina and Charles sit on the couch in between Joanne and Berta.

"Okay, guys. There are a few things we must talk about." He looks at the two children and his heart almost breaks right there. "So, you know that Mommy is in the hospital."

"But she is getting better, right?" Charles asks.

"If she were getting better, there would be no need for this dramatic talk," Kalina says.

Mark looks down for a second. "We are entering a point where our faith is going to be tested a little bit more."

Both kids look confused as he tries to find the right words.

"We are stepping into Mommy's next stage of recovery," Joanne says.

"What stage is that?" Kalina asks. Her face is blank, but Mark notices something in her eyes. He isn't able to place what it is at the moment.

"Well, right now Mommy needs to start breathing on her own and —"

"Wait. Mommy isn't breathing on her own? What the heck does that mean?" Charles says.

"That's what life support is, stupid," Kalina says.

Charles snaps back. "I'm not stupid, you idiot."

"Hey, both of you, cut it out." Mark cuts in. "It means that she needed machines to help her breathe. But those aren't needed anymore."

"So she is getting better?"

"Well . . ." Everything he planned on saying just flew out the window.

"In order for her to get better, this is the next step to take." Berta chimes in.

Mark sits, staring at Kalina, gauging her reaction. She stares a hole into him. It is at this moment he realizes what her expression is.

She knows he's lying.

"Daddy," she says, "please tell me the truth. Tell me what you really think."

Everyone's eyes land on Mark. He stares only at his daughter, unable to hide his true feelings on what is going to happen.

"Sweetheart," Joanne says, "that is the truth."

Kalina stares at Mark now with pleading eyes. Mark glances at Charles to see him stunned into silence.

"Her brain activity is diminishing," Mark says, much to the chagrin of Joanne. "It was suggested by her doctors that we take her off life support."

"Which means she's dying . . . or going to die . . . when we take her off life support."

He clears his throat. "Yes. Well, sort of."

"Which means she wasn't getting better." She looks at her grandmother.

"This is true. But there's still a chance. There's still . . . hope."

"Hope for what, Daddy?"

"Hope that she pulls through. So, your grandmother"—he looks at her—"she's right in telling you that your mother is getting better. Because she believes that. She has hope."

"Do you? Do you have hope?"

Mark holds her stare for a few long moments. "Of course. We have to hold on to that because . . . the alternative stinks."

Kalina nods resolutely. "If you have hope, I have hope." She grabs Charles' hand. "Is there anything else to talk about?"

"No, Dear."

"Well, we would like to go upstairs." She stands and Charles stands with her, still clutching her hand.

"Of course."

Mark, Joanne, and Berta watch as the two siblings trudge upstairs. Joanne then takes Amber to get her ready for bed. She gives Mark a look of indictment before she disappears upstairs. Mark looks down at his hands for a few seconds before heading to the kitchen. He stands in front of the sink, peering out into the darkness through the window.

"You did the right thing."

He turns around to see Berta leaning on the frame of the doorway. "It doesn't feel like it."

"She would have figured it all out. She's a smart girl."

"Yeah." He turns to lean back on the edge of the counter. "Plus I don't think it would take too much to figure out that her mother isn't here." He sighs and looks down. "I just don't know what to do anymore. I've run out of options."

"There's always prayer."

"I've been praying. Nothing's changed. Maybe it's just time I accept it."

"Accept what, exactly?"

"Who I am. My part in all this. Jade's fate." He shakes his head. "Anyway, it's been a while. I just wanted to talk to see how you were doing . . . to see how Craig is doing."

She nods. "I haven't really talked to him lately. But when we last spoke, he mentioned he was thinking of you and Jade, that he's praying for you two."

"Yeah?" He folds his hands in front of him. "You know, this is all my fault. I asked him to . . . go back there. I asked him to reach out to some of his old contacts."

"It's not your fault. He could have said no."

Mark shakes his head. "No, he couldn't. It's not in his makeup. You know that. And I knew that then. Craig is an intensely loyal person. And I was desperate."

"Craig is a grown man, a grown man who makes his own decisions. You didn't hypnotize or brainwash him or anything like that. He still made the choice to go back."

"Is the divorce simply over that?"

"No, it isn't." She doesn't look him in the eyes. "Did you know?"

"Know what?"

"My past. Did he ever tell you about my past?"

He squints, looking at her in confusion. "Why would he do that?"

"Could have come up in conversation over the years."

"Well, no. He never told me anything about your past. All I know is that you were his assistant who beat him into shape every now and again." He smirks. "Slapping your then boss was a great move. I mean, how many people on Earth can get away with that and still have the job?"

She smiles, but it is a visibly pained one.

"I think he fell in love with you right then. It's weird. Those years ago, he was looking for love . . . but the one woman who cared . . . the one who cared the most was right there, the whole time."

"Mark, what are you doing?"

He shrugs. "Talking."

"Why about this?"

"I don't know. I guess I feel . . . I feel partially responsible for the divorce and . . . I just can't stand to see this happen to you two."

"Mark, he knew things about me, important things about my past, and he lied to me about all of it. He even tried to redirect me away from finding out. Like, I can't trust him. How does a marriage continue without that foundation of trust?"

"You ever think of why he never told you?"

"Does it matter?"

"It some ways it does."

"I thought about it tons. But at the end of it all, I still can't get past how easily he jumped back into his old life. I can't get over how close his old life is to him such that it is easy to jump back into. I can't get over the fact that he is a murderer, a cold-blooded murderer."

Mark tightens his face. For a while, he says nothing.

"I understand, Berta. I really do. Just make sure this is definitely the right thing to do."

"You think I'm making a mistake?"

"I can't quite tell you that. I just know the best of us has something wrong with us. And if this divorce is in efforts to eventually find the perfect man . . . well . . . let's just say you are setting yourself up for a lot more heartache."

"Why do I get the feeling you know a lot more than you're saying?"

"Because I do know a lot more than I'm saying. It's not my place to say most of this stuff. Just, do me this one favor: Talk to him. Talk to him before this whole thing is finalized." He starts to leave the kitchen but stops in front of her. He places a gentle hand on her arm and gives a squeeze. "Don't be so consumed with the past. It will strangle out any life you have left."

"But his past is filled with so many land mines."

"I'm not talking of his past. I'm talking of yours." He gives her one last look before leaving the kitchen and going upstairs to check on everyone before going to sleep.

CHAPTER SEVENTEEN

"How many times have you seen her lately?"

"None, sir."

"And any others?"

"Nope."

"Well, that's good. That is very good. And how have you been feeling?"

"Fine, I guess."

"Truthfully?"

"Maybe a little numb. I think . . . I think I've come to terms with everything."

"That's a lot to come to terms with."

"It is. But I have to, right? For the kids."

"Well, yes and no. For yourself as well. You don't have to rush the process of healing."

"Yeah." Mark adjusts in his seat. "Do you mind . . . if I start performing my church duties again? I have to form a routine again. I . . ."

"No problem, Mark. You can do as much or as little work as you desire."

"Thanks." Mark sighs. "So tomorrow is it, huh?"

Pastor Brentwood looks solemn. "Indeed it is."

"Is it too late to pray for a miracle?"

"It's never too late. In fact, a group of members were camping out front of the hospital for prayer."

Mark nods. "We need a miracle. We definitely need a miracle." He sucks his lips in and takes in a deep breath through his nose. "If not, we should at least pray . . . for her peace."

"Agreed. Have you talked to her doctors recently?"

"Yeah, I called to see if anything improved." He shifts uncomfortably in his seat. "Obviously things hadn't. She's not on this steady decline with her brain activity anymore . . . but still. They're having a tough time finding anything that would keep her vitals going."

"Meaning she would be on that forever if you all decided so?"

"And be brain-dead. She deserves better than that." His face turns grim, but noticing the tightness of his face, he forces a smile. "So, that miracle. We could really use that miracle."

☙

Later that night, Mark drifts in that gravityless land between reality and dreaming. He sits on the couch, his head rolling about, still trying to fight off sleep. He hates sleep as of late. All he's had are nightmares. But this dream starts off on his wedding day.

He stands at the front of the church, awaiting his bride. He looks at Pastor Brentwood, who wears a permanent smile. Mark turns his attention to the pews, which are completely empty. He frowns a bit, but the organ starts playing and he forgets about the empty church and focuses on the entrance, waiting for Jade to arrive.

She comes out wearing a white dress that seems to illuminate everything around her. Her smile is wide and true. Tears are already in her eyes. The closer she gets, the more the church seems to . . . fall away. When she stands right in front of Mark, they stand in darkness illuminated by her dress. He can't see much of anything past her.

"What's going on here?"

"Mark, the machines won't help."

"What?"

Her smile quickly turns to a frown. "Just listen. The machines won't help. I'm trying to make it back." She hugs him. "Will you wait for me?"

"Jade, I have no idea wh—"

"Will you?"

"Of course. I love you."

"I need you to remember. Promise me."

"I promise."

"Say the whole thing out loud."

"I promise I will wait for you."

In an instant, he wakes up.

⊂ℬ⊃

"So Jade is close to me. Very close. And in a day or so, they are taking her off life support. We didn't get to her in time. I went to the proverbial dark side to come up short in the long run. But it's not about me. It's about her. It's about Mark." Craig and Addie continue their excursion into each other's pasts, with Craig finally landing on the reasons for his jetting to the ranch.

"I am sorry."

"I should be there. I should be right next to my best friend helping him through what is likely the worst time in his life. But I'm not. I'm here. Running."

"But you don't have to run anymore. You're free, aren't you? That detective is off your back now, isn't he?"

"I thought so, but I'm still not allowed home."

"I have to admit," Addie says, "it would suck for you to leave, but I would call again if I were you. I'd press the issue."

"Well, I have. Mr. Ramses is not answering my calls anymore. If I were here by myself . . ." He looks down. "Maybe I should thank you."

"Thank me for what?"

"Thank you for being here with me. You have made this time much more bearable."

"You saved me, remember? I should be thanking you." She relaxes on the chaise in the living room. "Maybe this was the point, for it to be healing for both of us. Maybe this encounter is of the divine sort."

"You mean you believe God set this up?"

"Maybe. I don't know. I just know things just don't happen for no reason."

"True. I'll agree to that."

She sits up and crosses her legs under her. "So, tell me about Berta."

Craig shifts in his seat but doesn't say anything.

"C'mon, Craig. You told me about everything else, about the scar, about Mr. Valencia, about jail. I opened my entire life story to you, including the bad parts in my marriage. Your wife is a topic of conversation we skipped over repeatedly. Why?"

"Because I still don't know what to say. She's divorcing me. There's no changing her mind. That's all she wrote."

"Why is she divorcing you?"

Craig stares into Addie's cool blue eyes. She stares at him with an intensity that only makes his heart race. Her stare says she wants to know more, more about him. "Because I lied to her. I lied to her about something for a very long time."

"About what?"

"It is a really long story."

"Most divorce stories are." She inches closer to Craig. "But I want to know. Who is Berta?"

He rubs his hair back against the grain. "She was a friend for the longest time. She was my assistant. She . . ." He shakes his head. "She is the most beautiful woman I'd met, but I don't mean physically. Though she is physically attractive, her state of being is attractive. Her presence . . . her essence. Just beautiful. And I thought it was me and her forever. But some things came along and shook that perfect state of being. She changed. And I changed. Then, when we look up, we no longer match. And that scared me. She scares me."

"Those are some pretty powerful words."

"Well, truthfully, there are only two people who know me on such a level. One of them is Mark. The other is her. I trust Mark. I know he wouldn't sell me out or anything like that. We're cut from the same cloth. But Berta. She knows the smallest details about me and with that she could send me soaring . . . or crush me as if I never existed. Right now, she's choosing to crush."

"I'm sorry."

"It sounds like you're apologizing a lot."

"It does, doesn't it?" She stands and slides on a pair of flats. "C'mon." She holds her hand out for Craig to grab. This seems to be a normal thing now, and Craig seems to be less uncomfortable with it as time goes on.

They walk to the back of the ranch house and out the back door.

"It looks like it's going to rain," Craig says.

"It's not. Don't worry. Just come with me."

She grips his hand tighter as she pulls him deeper into the wide-open field that seems to stretch on forever. They walk hand in hand, not saying a word, for fifteen minutes before Addie stops. She turns to face him and gently grabs his other hand, holding them both in front of her.

"What do you see?" she asks.

"Pardon?"

"What do you see, Craig?"

He looks around. "I see cloudy skies. But the sun is peeking out just a little."

"What else?"

"Field. I see a lot of field."

"C'mon, Craig. What else do you see?"

"I don't know." He looks around, eventually stopping at her. "I see a strong and beautiful woman whose eyes . . ." He clears his throat. "What exactly am I supposed to see?"

She clearly has been caught off guard as she stares at him, her mouth agape. Her face turns pink as she lets his hands fall to his sides. "Potential." She turns around to look at the peeking sun. An orange glow fills the area. "We have no idea of the long term. We just know of the here and now. But looking out at this field . . . it tells me anything is possible. You just have to plant the seeds and nurture them until they grow." She snaps back around as the sun hides behind the clouds again. "What is your vision? Do you have any?"

"No. Right now, it's hard to see anything for the future. Too much is uncertain."

"Well, what do you want?"

"To be happy."

"That's too vague. What do you want?"

He feels a smack of water on his forehead, then another. As if someone turned on a shower, full blast, the skies open up to pour huge drops of water on them. He tries to talk, but the sound of rain hitting the ground is loud. He squints to see Addie pointing toward a spot deeper in the field. Then, she dashes toward where she pointed. Craig sprints to catch up, but Addie is fast, her lithe legs moving faster than Craig thought was possible. She cuts behind a few trees to a clearing and that's when he sees it. A giant white barn. They get to the door and he helps her open it. They rush in, laughing, out of breath.

"Oh, no, it isn't going to rain," Craig says in a goofy voice. "Don't worry."

Addie laughs a deep laugh that comes out louder than her petite body would lead one to believe. "So I was wrong."

Craig catches his breath and looks around. The barn is in incredibly good shape, though he can hear a few leaks somewhere. He wipes his forehead with his hand, still observing the barn. When he turns around, he sees Addie, wringing some of the rainwater from her hair. She tilts her head to the side and stares right at him. He quickly scans the once-loose blouse that now sticks to her skin. Her tight jeans are a few shades darker because of the rain. He watches her chest heave slightly as she tries to catch her breath. She smiles.

"What?"

"Nothing," he says. "Just wondering. What do you want?"

With her head still tilted to the side, she looks down at the ground. When she looks back up at Craig, she gives him a look that completely freezes him. "You."

She takes a few lazy steps up to him, exuding a confidence he has never seen in her before. She slides her hand in his. "I want you, Craig."

"Addie, I—"

She moves her other hand up toward his mouth, placing her fingertips on his lips. His heart quickens as he breathes in the sweet smell of her hands. He grabs the one hand and gently kisses her fingertips, then the back of her hand. The rainwater that's on her hand mixed with whatever sweet perfume or lotion she has on causes the little drops he kisses to taste sweet. He leans in and stares her in the eyes before gently kissing her on the lips. They kiss for a few long moments before Craig realizes exactly what he is doing. He pulls away gently.

"I want you, too," he whispers. "But I still love Berta."

Like that, they remain in each other's arms, seemingly frozen in time. Neither wants to be the first to move. He nuzzles his face into the crook of her neck, realizing the only sound he hears is her breathing. The rain has stopped.

"We better get back to the house before it's too dark."

She nods. She steps backward away from him and holds her hand out. Craig tries to process all of the things that have gone unsaid before sliding past her outstretched hand and to her side, wrapping his arm around her waist. She presses closer to him, grabbing his hand and wrapping his arm around the bottom of her ribcage. She leans in, her head gently tapping his chest. When they leave the barn, he separates from her to close the barn door. He stops, his steps making a squishing sound in the soaked ground. The setting sun now shines unabated, making everything seem like gold. Addie turns into a silhouette, her hair still matted to her face. He can't see her eyes, but he knows she's looking directly at him. As he inches closer to her, he determines now, more than ever, he may be in trouble. He wraps his arms around her and gives her a hug. He jumps slightly at how easily she fits.

"We have a lot to talk about," he says.

"I know. I know we do. But can we do that after the walk?"

"Of course. For a second there, I thought you were going to try to race me back."

"Awww, you didn't want to get beat by a girl again?"

"I thought I was fast. Man, you move at lightning speed." He realizes that somehow, his hand is holding hers again.

CHAPTER EIGHTEEN

Mark drives, turning into the lot of the hospital where Jade rests. He sees them from pretty far away, the various members of the church who trekked all the way to New Jersey to stand outside for a few moments in prayer. He has the kids with him, Kalina in the front seat, Charles and Amber in the back. They all remain silent and have for the entire ride. Even Amber has been unusually subdued, but that always could be because she's tired.

The sun is nearly gone and it has been retiring for the night earlier and earlier as the days go on. As he gets closer to the hospital, he sees what room Jade is in, and feels a wave of panic.

"Daddy, why are all these people here?"

Mark glances at Kalina. "Prayer, Sweetheart."

"But why? It hasn't helped us so far."

"Don't say that. You know that isn't true."

"I guess. Are they all people from the church?"

"I believe so. A lot of people care about your mother."

"They're acting like she's dead. Everyone is acting like she's dead already. She's not."

"I know." He takes a breath. "You okay back there, Charles?"

He doesn't respond.

"Charles." He glances back but catches enough to see a sheen on his face.

Mark parks the car but waits for a second before looking back at Charles. He watches his son's eyes dart back and forth in a panicked state. The wave of panic Mark felt, Charles clearly felt as well.

"Hey, Buddy. Things are going to be okay. We're going to be okay."

"But Mommy's not," he says. His voice is strained to the point of whispering. "Mommy isn't going to be okay."

Mark glances at Kalina as she simply looks forward. "No matter what happens, she will be okay."

"But you can't promise that."

He looks down. "I can't. But I can tell you—all of you—that if we stick together, we can make it. We will make it."

He says nothing more.

"You two ready?"

Charles starts crying more. Mark gets out the car and squeezes into the back seat with Charles. He lifts his son and holds him tightly as he sobs. He pats his back, trying to soothe him, but the sobs shake his little body. He looks up toward the front to see Kalina curled up in a little ball in the passenger seat. He reaches for her, tapping her leg. She startles, but when she sees Mark holding out his hand, she reaches and slides to the back seat as well. There Mark sits, holding Charles and Kalina as they cry more tears than he thought possible, all the while holding on to Amber's hand as she plays with his hand like it's a toy.

Out the corner of his eye he sees Joanne pull up in her car with Berta in the passenger's seat. They get out and freeze when they see him crunched up in the back seat with the kids, with two of them curled into little balls under his arms. He motions for them to go ahead of the kids and him, and they nod and move along. After a few more minutes, things settle down.

"Da-da up."

Mark glances over. Kalina pops her head up. Charles remains still. "Hey, Sweetie. What did you say?"

"Da-da up." She smiles and points toward the hospital. "Da-da up. Mmmm. Ma. Ma-ma."

Mark stares and smiles. "Give me a second, Sweetheart." He looks down at Charles. "Hey, Kiddo. You okay?"

"No."

"I'm not, either. But, having you three around makes it much better. You have made my life so rich . . . so . . . worth living. I draw strength from you."

"We're not very strong," Kalina says.

"You're stronger than you think. You're braver than you think. Believe me when I tell you this: we can face this."

"And what about all those people out there? It's bad enough to get all these weird looks in school . . . now we have to go in there and . . ." Charles trails off.

"Say goodbye?" Kalina asks.

"I'm not saying goodbye." Mark says. "I've thought about this a lot in the last few days. And surely someone is going to say this is bad parenting for not having prepared you two better, or I'm just prolonging the pain"— he shakes his head—"but I'm not saying goodbye. I can't. I will not."

"So we don't have to say goodbye?" Charles asks.

"I will not force you to."

"Even if . . . even if she dies after taking her off the machines?" Kalina asks.

"I . . . I honestly don't believe she is going to die . . . not tonight." His face is stern.

They all sit in the car for a few more moments before Charles sits up and stares at Mark.

"Can we see Mommy now?" he asks.

"If you're all ready. Kalina?"

She stares out the window and nods. She opens the car door and steps out. Charles climbs over Mark and steps out behind her. Mark unstraps Amber from her car seat and secures her in his arms. He slides out the car and closes the door. Then, they all walk toward the hospital, Kalina and Charles hand in hand, Mark trailing a bit behind them. He makes eye contact with a few of the church members as the entire group parts to make way for them. He gives a few curt nods and before long they are in the hospital on the elevator heading up to the floor Jade is on.

They get upstairs and Mark notices everything is unusually quiet. He sees all the normal nurses, including Jade's nurses. Everyone's face hangs. Their eyes are red and puffy. Even some of the male nurses look like they had a few bouts with tears as well. And in an instant, all of their eyes are on them. Kalina and Charles slow their pace, allowing Mark to move ahead so they can follow. He stops and turns around.

"Okay, guys. I need you to be brave. Mommy . . . may not look exactly like Mommy. Okay? There's just . . . a lot going on at once and . . ." He looks down.

"Can I give her a kiss on the cheek?" Charles asks.

"Of course you can, Buddy. But don't feel like you have to. If it's too much, we can go outside. Just let me know."

"Okay," he says.

Kalina simply nods. Mark looks up to see Roz staring at them and smiling a warm smile. He notices she looks tired, worn almost.

"Good luck," she mouths.

Mark nods and leads the kids to the door of Jade's room. He takes a deep breath and gently opens the door. He sees nothing but family, close ones, loved ones, and though there is one glaring omission, he feels this is what Jade would want. Joanne comes over and grabs Amber from Mark, giving him a loving pat on the arm. He looks behind him to see Kalina and Charles stuck at the door. Both sets of eyes are locked on Jade in the bed and the various machines that surround her. He places his hands out in front of him. Charles is the first to grab his hand. Kalina, still keeping her eyes on Jade, places her hand in his.

Mark walks both of them into the room and everyone else makes their way out, out of respect, just to give them all time and to not crowd the room. They take their time inching their way to Jade's side. The closer they get, the more he hears Kalina crying. She lets go of his hand and wraps her arms around his waist. But she keeps inching forward. Charles stares stone-faced and eventually lets go of Mark's hand and moves right up next to Jade.

"Hi, Mommy," he says. He starts to fidget. "I miss you."

Charles has a whole conversation with her, but Kalina refuses to let go of Mark. Mark has no issue with that, of course, and he has no plans of pushing her further than she is comfortable with. Eventually, they inch closer to Jade, and she touches her hand gently.

"She's so skinny," she says, but says nothing more.

Mark lets the kids have a few minutes with Jade before saying, "Why don't you two head outside for a few moments? I just need to speak with her alone for a few seconds."

They both look at him with a look of deep sadness. Kalina grabs Charles' hand and leaves the room. Mark turns his attention to Jade. He tries to find balance, a silent moment to spend with his wife, but beeps and the humming of the machines don't allow that to happen. He gently takes her hand. He notices it's much frailer than he last remembered.

"Jade. I know that was you. I saw you. I heard you. I felt you. But I don't know what to do. What do you mean, wait for you?" He pauses, trying to feel her response. He leans in, close to her ear. "You said the machines won't help. So, what will?" He waits again, this time giving her a kiss on her forehead. Then, he slowly backs away and heads to the door. He opens it to see everyone staring at him. He looks to Pastor Brentwood and nods. Pastor Brentwood directs everyone back into the room and everyone files in. Mark looks at his watch, noting the doctors will be there in about fifteen minutes. Once everyone is in, Roz gently closes the door behind them. He looks around, observing everyone.

"So, here we all are," Pastor Brentwood says, "to pray for Jade in this . . . strenuous time. There are a lot of thoughts concerning this day, this very moment. But, at the end of it all, God still has final say. And—"

A knock on the door.

Everyone pauses and looks up at the door. Roz peeks her head in.

"Someone saying he is Jade's father?"

Mark looks to Joanne as her face virtually melts into tears. She nods, and Roz opens the door.

Jade's father, dressed in slacks and wing-tipped shoes, walks in.

"Grandpa," Charles says and skips over to give him a hug.

"Hey, Little Guy." He gives him a tight hug. He looks at Kalina, but she doesn't move. Her focus is entirely on Jade. Her vice-like grip tightens even more around Mark's waist.

Jade's father gives a curt nod toward Mark, and Mark returns the greeting.

"Joanne," he says.

"Harold."

He greets Berta and Pastor Brentwood before turning his attention to Jade. His face is stern but twitchy. He places a hand on Jade's and gives a soft, fatherly pat. "Pumpkin." He lingers for a few moments before leaving Jade's side to stand next to Joanne.

Pastor Brentwood continues speaking. "We have only a few minutes left. A few minutes I hope to spend in prayer. Agreed?"

Everyone nods.

"Let us pray. Lord, Father, God, we humbly come to you first and foremost, thanking you for all you've done, and for all you continue to do. We thank you for the life that you have bestowed upon Jade here. We thank you for the role she has played in all our lives: wife, mother, daughter, friend. Lord, we gather here calling out to you simply asking that your will be done. Of course, Lord, we all desperately want and need to see Jade smile again. We desperately want and need to hear her voice. If I may get a bit personal, I realize how you have used Jade as the glue that keeps us all together . . ."

Mark opens his eyes with his head still bowed and looks to the side while Pastor Brentwood continues praying. He sees another set of feet by the door. Slowly looking up, he sees Alicia right by the door. He shakes his head while she looks at him plainly. He tenses a bit but closes his eyes again, this time tighter. After a few more seconds, he opens them again to see that she is gone. When he goes to look down again, he notices someone staring at him and looks up to meet their gaze. Harold bores a hole into Mark and doesn't flinch when Mark stares back. For the rest of the prayer, Mark and Harold glare at each other and even after the prayer is finished, they continue on. It's a long and awkward moment for Mark that he doesn't fully understand. Harold looks away when Roz and one of the other nurses knock and enter the room. Dr. Chalmers enters after them. Roz gives Mark's arm a squeeze as she passes him and lines up on the IV side of Jade's bed.

Dr. Chalmers, looking ready to go, says, "We will remove all the tubes, shut the machines off. She's been on a slow morphine drip for the pain." He doesn't say any more.

Mark nods and watches Dr. Chalmers remove the tubing. Kalina and Charles turn their heads away while still holding on to Mark. Dr. Chalmers finishes relatively quickly. When the doctor and nurses are all done, an eerie silence settles over the room. Everyone stares at Jade, almost in the vein of expectancy.

Jade sighs once, but breathes no more.

Dr. Chalmers gives a last solemn look and starts to leave the room when Jade gasps in air. The doctor stops and turns, staring at Jade. He squints and waits.

Jade takes another labored breath.

"Doctor?" Joanne says.

"This is normal. The problem is, there is no way of telling when she will . . . move on. In most cases I've seen, it's been ten minutes. I had one person who continued on for three weeks."

"Anyone longer than that?"

"No, ma'am."

Everyone remains silent, allowing that notion to sink in. Mark stands there holding Kalina and Charles. A smile creeps onto his face. "She will make it," he says. "We just have to wait for her."

Chapter Nineteen

Another day without a call from Ramses or Berta, another day of revealing himself to Addie, another day of Addie revealing herself to him. Today, Craig told her more about his and Berta's marriage, about how rocky it was, but how the great times were truly great. She revealed her entire marriage to Craig, starting from the beginning, answering the question of how she ended up with her husband in the first place. It was a difficult time for her, he knows. He watched her face as she relived everything she was talking about. He saw the pain. He saw the fear. He saw the regret.

He finds he has more in common with Addie than he originally suspected.

After a wonderful dinner they made together and a quick shower, he heads to the study. It's a cozy room with bookshelves full of books. A large fireplace stands at the back wall.

"How about cranking that thing up? It's cold."

He glances behind him to see Addie in a fluffy white bath robe. He turns on the gas fireplace and gives it a few moments before sitting down in a leather chair, presumably Ramses' reading chair. He grabs the book sitting on the table next to the chair and flips it open.

"Is there enough room for me?"

Craig smiles, knowing his answer to that question. He smiles harder, because he knows she knows the answer to that question. The chair is just a physical representation of what he has already done in his heart. He tells himself he's in trouble again.

"Sure."

She slides in right next to him, her bare leg dangling over his. Again, she fits perfectly into the curves and corners of his body. The warmth shooting from the fireplace puts Craig at ease. She looks him in the eyes in that way which he has figured out means she is reading him. Her blue-gray eyes dart back and forth, scanning each eye. He senses an intensity in her gaze that forces him to look down.

"I see you're used to Miss Janice's clothes, huh?"

She smiles. "I'm just happy there are some things here in my size. The people who vacation here . . . the Ramses . . . they're loaded, huh?"

"Something like that."

"Well, most of the stuff I'm wearing still had the tags on them." She tilts her head back. "Thank God the underwear still had tags and were in packages, because . . . you know . . . another woman's underwear." She frowns. "Ewww."

Craig chuckles. "I'll tell you what, though, those jeans you wore yesterday. Everything seemed to fit just right." His eyes get big after realizing what he just said.

Addie's mouth hangs open for a few moments before she smiles. "Are you being fresh?"

"No. I'm sorry. I didn't mean to make you uncomfortable."

She gets up from her spot next to Craig. "Craig, were you checking me out?"

"I mean. No. Yes. We kissed and you know, I was feeling stuff and . . ."

"I have never been so offended in my life. I don't know how I can stay here with you anymore." She smiles.

"Sarcasm. Cute. Real cute."

"Not cuter than your face when you said how well my jeans fit." She sits in Craig's lap. "You don't make me uncomfortable. In fact . . ." She looks down.

He watches her face as she works something out in her mind. Holding her, sitting in front of the fireplace that is now putting off an astronomical amount of heat, he realizes what she is trying to say. It doesn't scare him, though, as it actually urges him to be free and admit to himself, and her . . .

That he has fallen for her.

"Addie." He waits for her to look up. She looks at him with her piercing eyes and he finds his confirmation. But the way the fire dances off her eyes reminds him of one person, and as soon as he thinks of that one person, memories flood his mind. Emotions bubble up and before long, tears are streaming down his face. Memories, too many memories, punch him in the gut and leave him breathless.

Now he cannot stop thinking about Berta.

Addie wipes away his tears with her thumb, but then needs to use the back of that hand to wipe hers. "You still love her, I know," she says, and gets up from his lap.

Craig wonders how she can tell that's what he is thinking. How can she be so in tune with what goes on in his mind, with what he feels in his heart? It took so long for him to even feel open with Berta. How is it that with this woman, whom he hasn't known ten weeks let alone years, seems to know him—all of him?

She's just about to turn away and leave when he grabs her hand. "Addie, I think I love you."

She gasps and her hand becomes shaky in Craig's. "You don't mean that. You can't mean that. You don't know me. I don't know you."

"None of that was about to stop you from saying it. I saw it on your face. I heard it in my mind. You were telling me you love me, too. And it's weird. And I don't know what to do with that because we're both married . . . and I love my wife . . . but she . . . she isn't going to be that anymore. She doesn't *want* to be. And I know something must be wrong with me to say all this . . . love is such a strong word . . . and everything we've been through in our lives . . . I just . . . I just . . ." He lets her hand go. "You are special. You are someone very special."

She brings her hand to her mouth, failing at trying to cover her quivering chin. "I think you—" She swallows hard enough for Craig to hear. "I think I've fallen for you, too. And that's scary. We both are so close . . . we are virtually still in two very bad situations. There are things wrong with me. You don't go through what I've been through without something being . . . loose. And you . . . you've been through a crap ton more . . . But, I can't think of any of that. When I'm around you, I just want to . . . take care of you. Because you . . . you are very special, too."

They stare into each other's eyes and for a long while, the only sound heard is that of the crackling fire in the fireplace.

"So, what do we do now?" he asks.

"I don't know. Keep learning about each other. Keep growing to-gether. I mean,"—she wraps herself with her arms—"You aren't leaving yet, are you?"

"I . . . I don't know." He dips his head in thought. Does he just run back home when Ramses gives the green light? Does he stop "chasing" Berta and let her be with the decision she's made? "I guess there is a lot more we need to discuss."

"Sounds like there is." She looks unsure of herself. "I guess I'll go to bed. You should, too."

"Okay. Fine." He looks at the floor and listens to her bare feet slap the tile floor. *What an awkward way to end that conversation.* He gets up and tries to catch up with her before she gets to her room, but he cuts around the corner to see her at the steps standing, waiting. He slows his pace until he is just a few feet in front of her. He puts both his hands out, palms up. As if magnetized to him by their hands, she closes the gap and places her hands in his. He lifts her hands so that she can wrap her arms around his neck, and he leans in. He leans in, but stops just in front of her face, mere millimeters from her lips. He looks into her eyes and starts talking without saying a word. She nods at the words he spoke in his mind and that further solidifies how he truly feels about her. He finally kisses her, lightly at first, but after a few moments, she turns up the intensity.

Breaking Craig out of his trance of passion, Addie stops abruptly. She pulls away from him, panting. "I think . . . I think we should get our sleep," she says.

"We should."

"Good night, Craig."

"Good night, Addie." He waits for her to get to the top of the stairs before heading to his room. After a moment like that, he doesn't want to risk touching her again because he knows it will lead down a path he cannot turn back from. *Maybe it's already too late,* he thinks.

Chapter Twenty

Mark sits up in the hospital chair seated next to Jade's bedside. He checks her every so often to see if she's still breathing.

She is.

He had not slept at all last night, and it seems most of everyone else hadn't, either. Pastor Brentwood left early in the morning, a few hours after all the church members had left their camping area outside the hospital. Joanne and Berta left with the kids first thing in the morning, after sleeping on hospital cots.

Only he and Harold are by Jade's bedside now. He glances at Harold to notice him staring right back at him.

"So, where have you been?" Mark asks.

Harold scoffs. "You don't get to ask me that. In fact, you don't get to ask me any questions."

Mark chuckles through a sneer. "You just up and leave. Joanne was dealing with all this—"

"There wouldn't be anything to deal with if it weren't for you. No crazy ex. No ridiculous kidnappings. No Jade in this . . . bed, hanging on for dear life."

"This is not all my fault. I played a part. We all played a part, though. Even you."

"How dare you?"

"I'm not going to sit here and be everyone's whipping boy. I owned up to all of my shortcomings, but somehow people think that's the end of it. Ask yourself, what part did you play? Could it be, your lackadaisical attitude about *everything* had a part?"

Harold laughs. "You're getting a little too big for yourself here. I think you should stop now while I can stay calm."

"An idle threat." He sighs. "Look, I understand you don't like me. I know you may never like me. I don't care. I'm here for Jade."

"Is that right?"

"She chose me." Mark waits for a moment. "She chose me. So, when she wakes up—"

"When? I talked to the doctors. She could be like this for the rest of her life. Chances are, she's going to be sitting here breathing . . . and not wake up. She's a vegetable now."

"Get out."

"What?"

"Get the hell out of this room. Get out or I will put you out."

"So you're a big man now?"

"Nope. I'm just tired of hearing you talk. I am waiting for her. She told me to, and that's what I will do."

Harold chuckles. "She told you to wait for her? And how did that happen?"

"I don't need to explain anything to you. But for now, if you would leave."

Harold looks at Mark for a few long moments. He pops up, still staring at an unflinching Mark. He snatches his jacket off the back of one of the seats and leaves.

Mark looks at Jade. "I'm sorry, Babe. We just don't need that kind of negativity around. Now, keep fighting, okay? I'm right here." He sits back down. "Not going anywhere." He presses her call button and waits for someone to show. After a few minutes, Roz appears.

"Be real with me, Roz," he says. "What do you think is going to happen?"

She looks to be caught flat-footed. "Well . . ."

"My wonderful father-in-law just told me that there's a great chance she's not waking up. That we are still all just waiting here for her to pass . . . or be a vegetable for the rest of her life."

"There's that chance, yes."

"And why didn't anyone inform me of this?"

"Dr. Chalmers was waiting until a few more tests came back. But . . . I asked him not to. Not yet."

"Why?"

"Because you have hope. Hope, Mark. Hope is something you didn't seem to have for such a long time. I couldn't stand . . . I couldn't stand the thought of your losing that again."

He looks down.

"I know we overstepped some of our boundaries here. I do. But—"

"You didn't. I do have hope. But even with knowing there's a great chance this won't end well . . . she told me to wait for her. I'm waiting for her."

"What do you mean?"

"It sounds crazy. I might have lost it, Roz, but she told me to wait for her. She was there, and she was real, and she felt real . . ."

"She was where?"

Mark pauses for a second. "In my dream." He doesn't care too much to elaborate for fear of looking crazier than he already does.

Roz nods. "I actually think I understand." She looks away for a moment before asking, "Do you need anything?"

"Actually, Roz, I am okay. I am better than okay." For the first time in a long time, that statement isn't a lie.

She smiles and makes her way out the room. Mark takes a deep breath and leans back in his chair. "I'm right here, Babe," he says. He shuts his eyes to relax. "I'm right here."

◌

Jade opens her eyes.

She opens them with ease, noting the abundance of darkness that still surrounds her. She sits up and feels around her neck. The last thing she remembers is Mark choking her until she passed out . . . until she . . . died. She looks around but is unable to see nothing.

Quickly, she pops to her feet.

She looks around and stops at a bright dot in the darkness. The star. She starts toward the star again, not really finding any solid footing but somehow feeling like she is getting closer to it. Though she is moving toward it, she knows she isn't moving fast enough. She stops and looks around.

"Hello?" she calls out, but hears no answer.

She feels alone and scared. She just wants to give up.

"Hello," she cries out. "Please, anyone. Please."

She falls to her knees. Out of the corner of her eye, she sees another bright light. She shudders a bit thinking it's the flame angel, but the light is too bright. She rises again and turns toward what she believes is a real angel. It doesn't take long before the angel is right in front of her.

"Toward the star. You know this now. Why don't you move?"

"What just happened to me?"

"A plot devised to steal time."

"For what?"

"Not important. You must go. The enemy is near."

"That wasn't Mark."

"True."

She shakes her head. "He's hurting right now, isn't he? The kids are, too. I know they are. I can . . . feel them. I hear them faintly. I hear their cries."

"They are hurting . . . and losing faith."

"No." She starts to pace. "Can . . . is there a way to contact him, them, anyone?"

"No."

"I don't believe that." She looks with grim determination. "I have a better understanding on where I am . . . but at the same time, I don't. Help me. Help me understand. Help me get to them again. Please."

The angel stands there. Jade is unable to tell if the angel is looking at her or through her.

"Fine. Don't help." She starts toward the star again.

"You died. But you were revived, and that's how you came to be here, another layer of your world that is formless and void, yet more solid than anything you have experienced. You are now physically dying," the angel says. "You are currently hooked up to machines meant to keep you alive. But the machines cannot help. You can only help yourself by getting to that star. God has cleared the way."

"Cleared the way? I'm under attack."

"The sooner you realize a way to train your focus on the star, the sooner you will be able to get back. The enemy is simply trying to stall you. The prison, the fear of the messengers, your home . . . it was all devised to stop you from getting to the star."

"But why?"

"Look at what is happening to everyone close to you . . . they're losing faith. They are losing hope. Imagine what that would be like if you died, if you left them."

"They would eventually find a way to move on."

"Not everyone does. For some, it becomes a permanent scar on their soul. Many turn away from God then."

"I don't want that to happen to them and—" She looks at her hand. Her vision is blurred such that she sees multiple images of her hand, each becoming more transparent. "What is going on?"

"You have less time now. The process is beginning."

"Process? What process? This isn't my eyesight?"

"No. You must go."

"Can I make it?"

"Can you?"

Jade thinks for a moment. "I will." She starts toward the star, but feels something like pressure in her gut. "What?"

"He is reaching out to you."

"He who? God?"

"Mark."

She falls to her knees again, and quickly an enclosure forms around her. Quickly walls form around her and they are decorated with paintings of landscapes, landscape scenes she has seen a thousand times. She's at the church. She stands and notices her wedding dress on, fitting perfectly, though her wedding dress never fit that well in real life. She walks to the sanctuary and opens the doors. At first glance, no one is there, but looking down at the end of the aisle, right in front of the altar, is Mark. She tries to move faster, but is unable to do so. Her body simply will not move faster than a casual walk. She is almost brought to tears seeing him in his wedding-day tux. The closer she gets to him, the more her dress seems to light up, until it becomes so bright all she can see is Mark. She keeps moving toward him. When she is finally able to speak to him, she tells him that the machines won't help, and made him promise to wait for her. Just as soon as he agrees, he disappears. The walls of the church are gone, and her illuminated dress fades away. In a mere few seconds, she is back surrounded by darkness, the faint light from the star, and the angel who has helped her.

She stares at the star again before breaking out into a sprint. "Lord, help me," she says.

Berta, Joanne, Kalina, Charles, and Amber all pack into Joanne's car to get back home. Everyone is groggy and silent once in the vehicle. Everyone but Amber, that is. She, being oblivious to much of the hardships everyone faces, bounces and kicks in her car seat. Everyone else seems to be lost in his or her own thoughts.

They all get back home with most of the day still to go. Berta goes up to the guest room and starts to pack her things.

"Alberta."

Berta turns from her suitcase to see Joanne leaning on the doorway.

"We never really had a chance to talk," Joanne says.

"Oh," Berta says, a little confused by the statement. "Is there something you wanted to talk to me about?"

"Nothing in particular. It's just that you seem really close to Mark, and you are obviously good friends with Jade. You're considered family."

"Am I? That's comforting."

"It's just strange that I've never actually met you before."

"Yeah. I guess that is strange." She looks at her watch. "We can sit down for a few minutes."

Berta zips up her last suitcase and meets Joanne downstairs in the kitchen.

"So, things are looking up, huh?" Joanne says, with her back to Berta.

"It seems that way. I suppose there are still a few more hurdles to jump."

"Of course. Did you see Mark's face when she took that first real breath?"

"I did. We were all in some form of shock."

"Yeah. My baby is going to make it. She's a fighter."

"For sure. Jade is one tough lady. I'm glad to call her friend."

Joanne turns around and leans on the island. "And what's your relationship to Mark?"

Berta frowns. "Pardon?"

"You two seem to have an air of familiarity about you. As I said, you seem close."

"I think I get it. We seem too close."

"I never said such a thing. I'm just trying to understand the nature of your relationship."

Berta smiles. "Ah, I see." She grabs a stool to sit at the island. "Mark is a friend. Nothing more. Never wanted to be more. Never will want it to be more. We all know each other well because I married his best friend."

"Craig?"

"The one and only. But now I am in the middle of an . . . interesting divorce."

"Oh. I'm sorry to hear that."

"Yeah. We just weren't meant to be, I suppose."

"Is anyone?" Joanne wonders. "Is anyone meant to be with another, really?"

"I take it there's some tension between you and your husband? At least it seemed like there was. There was even more tension between him and Mark."

"When all of this happened . . . he up and left. He just disappeared and I had no idea where he was, or if he was okay. I got nothing. Like I didn't matter."

"I'm sorry."

"So he shows up last night at Jade's bedside. And I know you're wondering how he knew what was going on. I called him. I called him multiple times, but this one seems to be the one he answered."

Berta thinks to herself that she wasn't really wondering at all how Jade's father showed up.

"And that tension between him and Mark; he hates Mark. Always has. It's likely he always will, especially after all this. Mark was never good enough for his little pumpkin, and after all this . . . I fear there isn't any going back now."

"So what is going to happen with you and him?"

"Me and Mark?"

"No, you and your husband."

"He's going to come back home. We move on."

"Are you sure he's coming back?"

"I'm positive. We've been through so much already. There's always been only one place where he was truly comfortable . . . and that's with me."

"Interesting. Do you care about what he's done while away?"

"Nope."

"What if he cheated?"

"He didn't."

"How do you know?"

"I just do. Again, we've been together for almost thirty years. I know that man. I know what move he is going to make before he even gets the thought of making it."

"Sounds manipulative almost."

"It may sound that way, but really it's just knowing your spouse. The good, the bad, the downright terrible." She pulls up a stool to sit at the island as well. "So, why are you and Craig splitting?"

"Well, it seems I don't know my spouse as well as you know yours. He's a liar. He's a deceiver and I can't be with someone like that."

"How long have you two been married?"

"Two years. Getting close to three."

"Child, please. That's not even enough time to get to know the fake him. So he told a few lies. Did he cheat on you?"

"I don't think so."

"Don't tell me what you think. Tell me what you know. Did he cheat on you?"

"No, ma'am."

"So he's done what every human being on the face of this planet has done. He's told a lie, maybe even a few lies?"

"A few, yes. But these are major ones. Just . . . you wouldn't be able to understand and I'm not fully able to explain."

"Okay. But you still love him, don't you?"

"What? Why do you say that?"

"Because it looks like it pains you to talk about it, about him. If you were so gung-ho about the divorce, I would expect anger . . . or nothing. You're not so sure about the divorce, though, are you?"

Berta simply shakes her head.

"Then why not try to reconcile? You young kids don't want to work for anything good these days."

"I can't."

"Why not?"

"Because he's not here to reconcile with."

"Elaborate."

"I can't. He's in some other state." She looks up. "He ran . . . kind of like your husband . . . just under different circumstances."

"I see. Well, when he gets back—and he *will* come back—you talk to him. You work things out. You're a nice girl. And I've known Craig to be a nice man."

"Thank you, ma'am." She gets up from the stool. "I have to get going. A bunch of things to tend to this weekend."

"Of course. Just this one last thing: Have you ever heard of a thirty-year marriage that was easy?"

Berta thinks for a few seconds. "I guess not."

Joanne smiles. "It was good talking to you, Alberta."

"Yes, ma'am, it was. Could you . . . call me to keep me up to date on things?"

"Sure, Sweetie. What's your number?"

⊂ॐ⊃

Berta gets home in time for the setting sun to give one last bit of light before retiring. She sits in her car thinking about her conversation with Joanne, about Jade, about Mark, about Craig. She grabs her phone and calls Craig, but his phone goes straight to voicemail. She leaves him a message detailing Jade's condition and, finally, telling him she misses him and that she thinks they should talk. She hangs up and holds her phone in her hand. Her phone buzzes and she immediately looks to see who it is, but is disappointed when she knows it isn't Craig. She picks it up.

"Yes, Mr. Ramses."

"Alberta, we cracked open another part of the drive."

"Great." She simply cannot muster any excitement for this mission she was tasked with.

"Simms. That detective."

Her ears perk up. "What about him?"

"He was on Courtland's payroll."

"What? What do you mean?"

"He's dirty, Alberta. And you need to stay away from him at all costs. I'm sending a detail to you as we speak."

"Wait. Hold on. What is happening here?"

"I don't fully know. But I have a really bad feeling about this whole thing. The cases, all of it."

"But the monster is dead."

"I know. My fear is someone else has taken up his mantle. And if that happened . . . it would make sense why there was a play on Marcy and Jennifer's life. They leaked a still-active network to everyone, really."

Berta sighs. "I just can't wrap my head around this. Not right now. I just got back from the hospital and . . ."

"Is she okay? Your friend. Is she okay?"

"She's breathing on her own again."

"That's good news."

"But she's still in a coma."

"Oh. I wish her a speedy recovery."

She hangs her head. "Me, too. Okay, so Simms is dirty. We figured that, right?"

"In some ways, yes. His connection to Courtland is disturbing."

"Okay. Just keep me updated on what else comes from that drive."

"Will do. Alberta."

"Yes?"

"Be careful."

She gets off the phone and lazily trudges to her building and to her condo. She jams her key into the door and twists the door open. She drops her bags at the front.

"Welcome home, Berta."

Berta's face drops. "Where's Jennifer?"

"Who? I don't know who that is."

She doesn't move. "Why are you here?"

"Close the door."

"No."

"Jennifer's life depends on it. I think you should."

"But you don't know who she is?"

"Look, we could verbally jab all day. But I'm running out of time. Ramses is sending his guys over, no?"

Berta is stunned.

"Don't say another word."

"Jennifer," Berta yells. She dashes toward the back rooms, but finds nothing. She pops open the bathroom door to see a sight so horrifying, the image of it will be permanently on her mind. She gasps.

Jennifer lies slumped in the tub, covered in blood. Berta screams but feels a tight grip around her mouth and another grip on her wrist, twisting her arm back. Her screams get muffled in the palm of Simms' hand.

"Don't scream. Don't say anything. All I need you to do is follow me out this door and to my car. That's the easy way. Please don't choose the hard way. Nod if you understand."

She nods, breathing heavily through her nostrils. Her eyes are wide and wild, jutting back and forth over the gruesome scene.

"I'm going to let go now. But you do as you were told. If you decide not to, God help you."

"Why? Why, Simms?"

"I said not another word." He grabs her arm. "Let's go. Act casual."

Simms and Berta walk out of the condo and out of the building. Before starting the car, Simms says, "It was never supposed to be like this."

☙

He holds her close to him, wrapping his arms around her, securing her, protecting her. He looks into her eyes for what seems like hours at a time. He kisses her lips and realizes that's what he wants to do forever. But there are doubts. There are many doubts.

"Addie," Craig says, "what is this?"

She moves slightly to sit up, removing her head from his chest. She turns to face him, smiling. "What do you mean?"

"I'm trying to figure out . . . our future. If there is one."

Her face drops slightly. "I don't know, honestly. I feel for you things I have never felt for anyone . . . not even my husband when things were good. And I see a future with you . . . but that's here at this ranch—that neither of us own." Her eyes light up a bit. "But can you imagine what it would be like if we could live here forever? Just us?"

"I have thought of that. But what would happen when it isn't new anymore? Will we feel the same? Will we be the same?"

"Of course not. We're healing right now. We're dealing right now. We're grieving right now. But as we get through this together, we grow together . . . we grow stronger, together. Right?"

"I suppose. I still have quite a few things to handle back at home."

"Things like with Berta?"

He nods.

"What are you going to do? Beg her to want you again?" She looks down, biting her bottom lip. "I'm sorry. I know this is tough for you, and I shouldn't have said that. I just don't want you to leave. I don't want you to leave me."

"I understand. But I made a commitment to her. She is my wife."

"But she no longer wants to be that and told you as much. She set the whole divorce up and pressed it forward. She was helping the detective *find* you. She flat-out told you she doesn't love you anymore and her actions say the exact same thing. What more do you need?"

Craig stays silent, considering what she said.

"I mean, you have a past, and so does she. But her love for you seemed to be contingent upon you making her feel good about stuff that's done and over with. But here I am, in front of you right now, knowing the worst side of you, and still loving you. I love you without condition, Craig. You can jump through her hoops to never meet her standard, or you can be yourself, and be free, with me. We can make it work somehow. We can just go and start somewhere new. Me and you. Forge our own path."

"So what are you saying, exactly?"

"Simple. I want to be with you. I love you. But you need to let her go."

"That's not simple at all."

She pats his hand and gets up from the chaise, leaving Craig to his thoughts. Craig doesn't move but wonders a few things about Addie. *Why hasn't she run?* He thinks that Addie likes the guys with a little bit of edge, but that's a problem. He also wonders if she truly has fallen for him, or if she has fallen for what he has done for her. And the most pressing question in his mind is why he has fallen for her. Does he truly have a need to "rescue" those he's with? Does he have the need to be someone's knight in shining armor? He leans his head back, his mind swirling in thoughts, and closes his eyes. Over and over again in his mind, he replays Addie saying she loves him until slowly, her voice turns to Berta's. Now, he hears Berta telling him she loves him over and over again. He hears her saying it, but there is also a buzzing noise that increasingly gets louder. He snaps his eyes open wide, but still hears the buzzing. He looks toward the kitchen island and sees the burner phone slowly creeping toward the edge of the countertop. He jumps up and rushes toward the phone.

"Hello?"

"So, we are going to keep this very, very simple, okay?"

"What? Who is this?"

"This is Detective Simms."

Craig freezes and remains silent.

"I told you I would catch up to you somehow. But here's the deal. The chip. I want the chip."

"I have no idea what you are talking about."

"You do. But I can hear by the tone of your voice you need some convincing."

He hears some rustling over the phone. Then, he hears a voice he hasn't heard in a long time.

"Craig?"

"Berta!"

"Craig, he killed Jennifer." Her voice becomes strained. "He killed Jennifer."

More rustling.

"I had hoped it never came down to this." Simms again. "So, this is what is going to happen. You are going to catch a plane, and come home. Call this phone before you leave the airport. At the airport, someone will be there with a sign that has your last name on it. You get in the car with them and they will take you to where you need to be.

Have the chip and all will be well. Bring the chip and you get Berta. Otherwise, she's done."

"What do you mean 'done'?"

"C'mon, Craig. Don't play stupid. You know." Some rustling. "The chip. No games."

The line goes dead. Immediately, he calls Ramses, who picks up after the first ring.

"He's taken Berta."

"He who? What are you talking about? I just spoke to her not even twenty minutes ago."

"Simms. He just called me. Told me to deliver a chip."

"Damn it." Craig hears a loud bang, forcing him to pull away from the phone a bit.

"I have no idea what he's talking about. A chip?"

"I have an idea. You know what I'm staring at right now?"

"What?"

"I'm looking at decrypted folders and files detailing Courtland's entire operation."

"Okay."

"Raul had something similar."

"What files and folders on his operation? Why? And why would it still exist?"

"It's too much to explain now, but the pieces are coming together. I think this detective is trying to take over Courtland's operation. In the process, he's trying to take Raul's."

"He made threats. And he's killed someone named Jennifer."

Long pause.

"He gave me specific directions. Call first. Catch a plane. Hop in the car with the person with my name on a sign. Have the chip. But I don't have any chip."

Ramses sighs. "You have the chip. You have to. Raul wouldn't have given it to you as just a chip. It would have been a part of something."

"Why would he give it to me at all?"

"Probably the same reason why he made me promise to look after you and Alberta: just in case."

"Look,"—Craig starts to pace back and forth—"I have no idea where this thing could be. I—" Addie comes to the kitchen and peers at Craig with a concerned look. He turns away. "I only brought a few things with me, remember? Most of everything else, you took away."

"I know. I know."

"What the heck am I going to do?"

"I don't know."

"Well, we need to figure out something before Berta gets hurt."

He continues to pace but stops when Addie places her hand on his arm. "What's wrong?" she asks.

"Craig? You have to go." Ramses says. "You have to play into his hands for now."

"Without this chip?"

"For now, yes, without the chip. I'll have a few guys follow you from the airport."

"Fine." He quickly gets off the phone, staring at Addie intently. "I . . . have to go."

"What do you mean, you have to go?"

"I . . . it's a lot to explain, but Berta . . . she's in trouble. She's in some serious trouble. And I need a chip. I have no idea what that is." He feels his heart racing. "All I have with me are some clothes and my everyday stuff, but this detective that's been on my butt this whole time . . . he's dirty. And I just have . . ."

"Craig."

"I just have my clothes and . . . the watch. The watch that doesn't work that I've held on to for years." He leaps to the bedroom he has been sleeping in and to the dresser the rustic box sits on.

"Craig, slow down."

He gently opens the worn box and pulls out the watch. He sets it to the side and dissects the box, pulling and examining each individual piece. When he finds nothing, he turns his attention to the watch itself. He fiddles with it, but finds nothing that would seem strange. He sets the time on it, turning the dial, watching the long hand go around and around.

Still, nothing happens. He looks toward Addie, who looks at him with concern. In an instant, he settles and realizes what he said to her, and what it means for them.

"I'm sorry. I have to go."

"You said as much." She nods and wraps her arms around herself. To Craig, she suddenly looks so vulnerable.

"I know what this seems like."

"Do you?"

"Actually, I don't." He walks up to her and grabs her hand. "I'm not leaving you hanging here. We'll get this all sorted out. I just need to get home . . . quickly."

"Craig, I'm not stopping you. Just, if this is goodbye—"

"It's not. I will see you again, and soon."

"Yeah, but you will see me as what? Berta's husband?"

Craig doesn't know what to say.

"I can come with you," she says.

"No. Too dangerous."

She nods and looks down. Moments later she steps her way to him and kisses him deeply. When she pulls away, she says, "So this *is* good-bye."

"I'm not saying that."

"You're right. *I* am." She sighs. "You don't seriously think it's completely done between you and her, do you? Even now, you're bailing her out of trouble."

"You don't understand."

"I understand enough. Listen, thank you for all you have done. It will take me a couple days, but I'll clear out of the ranch."

"No. Don't."

"I think it's best that I do." She pats him on the chest. She lets her hand linger for a few seconds before leaving him alone.

CHAPTER TWENTY-ONE

Jade continues her sprint toward the star, not worrying she isn't going to make it in time, but believing she will. She is tired, and because of that, she doesn't hear a group of messengers chasing her down. One gallops up behind her and claws at her feet, causing her to trip and fall flat. She gets to her feet in a hurry. They all form a circle around her, screeching at her, calling her all kinds of names. She takes a step toward the star, but they don't move this time.

"Move," she says.

They don't budge. In anger, she rushes one of them, grabbing it by its legs and slamming it to the ground. The other messengers jump on her, digging their claws into her back, sinking their teeth into her skin. She feels no pain, but she's becoming increasingly more tired. She frantically searches for the star. Once she has eyes on it, she starts in that direction again. She can only take a few steps before the weight of the messengers causes her to collapse. She reaches her hand out and surprisingly, the angel in white flame grabs it. With a quick flash of light, the messengers are almost burned off, just like they were in the prison. She takes the angel's hand and help up. Once to her feet, she says, "Thank you."

"Let us go," the angel says, and starts running toward the star.

Jade catches up, but notices the scratches and marks on her body oozing a dark substance. She finds she's having difficulty keeping up with the speed of the angel.

"Hold on for a moment. I'm . . . I'm tired."

"No rest here. No rest needed."

"Yeah, but I can't keep up." She stops.

"What are your limitations?"

"What?"

"What are your limitations? There aren't any physical ones . . . so what holds you back?"

"I don't know. I feel tired."

"Then let your faith drive you."

She looks down. She doesn't have time to waste. She starts again, walking into a jog, and eventually at a sprint again. She looks at the star.

It actually seems like she is getting closer to it. This excites her to move faster; so fast it feels like she is flying. She looks to her left, thinking it's the bright angel by her side, but comes to an abrupt stop when she sees the orange flames of the flame angel. The flame angel stops only a few feet in front of her.

"You can't stop me," she says. "And I don't fear you."

"I can get you to do anything I want," it says in an angry choir of voices. "You've let me into your heart."

"I'm going."

"No. On the contrary, you are going to sit."

"What?"

"Sit, Jade."

Jade struggles a bit, but she plops down on her behind to sit on the ground. "No."

"You shouldn't have opened those doors. Though, it was wonderful to see what hidden secrets and resentment you have in your heart."

"I set them free, everyone that was in there."

"I saw. That was mighty big of you. A wasted effort, still, but it was amusing."

"I am"—she struggles to her feet—"better than this."

"You are not. Come to me."

She walks lazily to the flame angel, crying because in order to do so, she has to turn her back on the star.

"Don't cry. This was all inevitable."

She stands directly in front of it.

"Aren't you tired?"

She says nothing, but notices again that she is completely naked. She wraps her arms around herself because she hasn't felt as ashamed as she does now.

"Why would you want to go back?" it asks.

She closes her eyes as it touches her. "I have a family. People I want . . . I need to get back to."

"And how does that help you? More pain, more suffering. More people who will resent you, use you. You could just stay here. I will make you feel good for the rest of time."

"You're just stalling. Trying to slow me down." She tries to turn away, to just get a glimpse of the star again, but the flame angel grips her chin and snaps her face forward. She turns away again, now being able to turn her entire body away. She sees the star, and that's all she needs to start into a sprint again.

The flame angel growls and chases after her, eventually jumping on her back and pinning her to the ground.

"I'm not letting you go," it says.

Jade senses some fear in the multitude of voices that sounds from the flame-engulfed being. She laughs.

"*You* don't have a choice. Release me."

"No."

She laughs even more. "I never let you into my heart. You know who I have?"

The flame angel's grip loosens.

"Jesus."

The flame angel jumps off her and staggers back. It gags as if what Jade said was terribly disgusting. She scurries to her feet as the flame angel gags and gasps.

"You wanted me to forget, didn't you?" She hears a rumble similar to thunder. She starts toward the star again, but notices the flame angel oozing something that looks eerily like lava. The next moment, another set of arms comes out of its sides, then a head comes, and eventually legs.

Two flame angels stand before her now.

She doesn't take any more time to observe, and takes off running. She hears the two flame angels chasing her, and she thinks she hears the messengers again. She dashes forward with what sounds to be an entire army chasing her.

The rumbling gets louder and bright flashes of light illuminate the area. It sounds like she's in the middle of a thunderstorm.

Lightning strikes down in front of her, forcing her to dodge to the right. She notices many more lightning strikes, hitting ground all around her. She slows, squinting, trying to make out an image at the spot where one of the bolts of lightning struck.

An angel is standing there, glowing with a bright light. She picks up the pace again, finally seeing the star closer. It looks like a bright-white sun setting on a pitch-black horizon. More lightning strikes ahead of her and she starts smiling. The amount of angels she sees in front of her increases until she is running through a crowd of angels.

And they all start cheering. The sound is not unlike an army of old cheering after a victory.

This pushes her closer to the star, which now looks like a bright hole in the darkness; a floating doorway. She is only a few feet away when she yells out to all of her brightly lit helpers, "Thank you."

She rushes into the light.

⋘⋙

Mark stands from his seat, again trying to stave off sleep. He stretches his legs out after having fallen asleep in the middle of his prayer.

Earlier in the day, Dr. Chalmers came in and explained Jade's condition after more tests had been run. Most of it wasn't necessarily good news, but it wasn't bad, either. She's stable, and has enough brain function to breathe and operate on her own, but she may never wake up. Still, Mark's smile reached from ear to ear.

He looks down at her and smiles. What Doctor Chalmers doesn't know is that Mark feels her again. Mark knows he couldn't explain it to a doctor, but he feels Jade again—he feels her presence. "She's going to wake soon," he says to the silent room.

Furthermore, after everything he has been through, he finds it increasingly difficult living tragedy to tragedy. It's not living much at all, he realizes. He refuses to continue to live his life according to tragedy, because the way he's been living it thus far is killing him from the inside. He sits back down in the seat that seems to have grooves now from so much use. Almost immediately, the seat lulls him back to sleep. His head droops to the side a bit.

"Mark."

He dreams again of Jade. She is running through this field, the sun shining on her, her eyes glistening in an almost heavenly fashion.

"Mark."

He hears her whisper his name. It sounds sweet. It makes him feel good.

It sounds real.

Mark opens his eyes and just glances at Jade to see her looking directly at him, wide-eyed.

"Oh, my God." He pops up. "Jade. You're . . . you're . . ."

She blinks a long blink. He thinks he sees the beginning of a smile tugging at the edges of her mouth. He hops out the room and swings open the door.

"She's awake."

All the nurses at the station look at Mark in shock, a few in disbelief. He turns back around to see her eyes closed. He frowns and rushes back in.

"Jade?"

She opens her eyes again, slowly. She whispers something and Mark has to move his ear and nearly press it to her mouth for him to hear. Just as he is leaning in, Roz comes by the door. She looks for a second before leaving and saying, "I'll get Dr. Chalmers."

Mark refocuses on what Jade is saying. He suddenly hears it clear as day, as if she didn't need to say anything at all.

"I love you," she says.

Mark lifts her delicate hand and kisses the top of it. With tears in his eyes, he says, "I love you, too."

Chapter Twenty-Two

Berta sits on the edge of a hotel bed with Detective Simms sitting in a chair, staring right at her. She looks at him, trying to understand what the look he gives her means. She doesn't say anything. She is afraid to. Simms gets up and turns the TV on and takes his seat in the same position as before. Her hand trembles slightly so she grabs it with her other hand to stop it.

"I'm not going to hurt you," he says.

"You . . . you killed her."

"She pulled a gun on me."

"Why were you there in the first place?"

He adjusts in his seat. "You sure you want to know?"

"I already know quite a bit."

"Is that so?"

"How long were you working with the monster?"

He chuckles. "'The monster,' as you call him, was how I became detective in the first place."

"But I thought you believed in justice. I thought you believe in the right thing."

"You don't know me too well. Everything I've done, I've done in the name of justice."

"So what was Jennifer's death? What is kidnapping me? Are you that desperate to bring Craig in?"

"You don't get it. You don't get it at all." He throws her cell phone. "Call him."

She simply stares at the cell phone sitting next to her.

"Call him." He looks at her, wide-eyed.

"Tell me what is going on. I don't get it? Tell me, then."

"Screw it." He jumps up, causing Berta to jump as well. He grabs the cell phone and scans through it. He taps the screen a few times and holds the phone to his ear.

"So we are going to keep this very, very simple, okay?"

Berta listens to Simms make demands and he puts her on the phone. All she could say was that this "detective" has killed Jennifer. And she knows Craig has no idea who she is. Simms hangs up and sets the phone in his pocket. He looks at her. She averts her eyes.

"So what happens now?" she asks.

"We wait."

"And if he doesn't come?"

"He will."

"And if he does without this chip?"

He turns away and looks out the window. "Then I'm going to be forced to do something I don't want to do."

The way he says that sends chills up and down her spine. She doesn't ask any more questions for now, but thinks about everything she knows, trying to make sense of what is going on. *Simms is after this chip. Chip of what, though? He's killed Jennifer, which is easy for him because he used to work for the monster. He's dirty. That also means anything he told me before is up for scrutiny. He killed Jennifer.* She stops her train of thought as flashbacks of the scene in her bathroom take over her thinking. She shudders and before she can stop it, tears drop from her eyes and into her lap. *She thought she was safe with me. And I told Ramses not to take her somewhere safe . . . because I liked having her around.* She begins to sob. *She would be alive if it weren't for the decision I made.*

She feels sick to her stomach and holds her midsection. Simms continues to look away from her. She looks at him through her tears. He stands at the window, probably not looking at anything in particular, but avoiding looking at her, she believes. She feels sick, but she also feels a burning in her stomach. Quickly realizing it's anger, she gets up. Simms hears her shuffle and snaps around, but it's too late. Berta is already leaping toward him, her fists balled. She lands a hard hook on the bottom part of his jaw, and swings the left to land another, but he dodges with ease.

"What are you doing?" He grabs both of her wrists with a vice-like grip. "Stop."

Since her wrists are restrained, she uses her legs, kneeing and kicking with as much strength as she can muster. She knows she landed a few good hits as Simms becomes more mindful of covering up. He swings her by her wrists to the floor and she lands with a thud. As she tries to get up, she feels a hard knock on the side of her face, then little sparkling worms take over her vision. She slumps at first, but tries to get to her feet again. She's pushed down and her arms are pulled behind her. Finally, she feels a hard wrap around her wrists. The clicking tells her that she's been handcuffed. Simms plops to his original seat, out of breath.

"Bad idea. Really bad idea," he says. "Berta, I did not want to harm you. I was told specifically not to."

She lies just staring at the dust on the carpeted floor. "He's not coming."

"What?"

"Craig isn't coming for me. I already have done too much to push him away."

He sighs. "I hope . . . I hope that isn't the case."

"Why does it matter? None of it matters anymore."

He pinches the bridge of his nose.

"He abused me . . . when I was little. The monster did. Did you know that?"

"I didn't. I've never been in the position to inquire of his family."

"He abused his second family, too. Jennifer . . . the girl you killed . . . she was abused, too. She's had a rough life. We both have. And it's all because of the monster. Your previous employer."

"He was a criminal. I suspected he's done his fair share of dirty deeds."

"So why did you work for him? Why are you trying to take his network now?"

"I'm not. I didn't." He closes his eyes. "This is what you don't understand. I don't want his network. You and Jennifer have done more than enough to shake the foundation. You two have shaken it so much, it can no longer stand. And I worked for him because I needed help in cleaning up crime on a greater level. Sure, I worked for one crime boss . . . but with his help, I took down so many more. It was a net loss for crime. Different cops and different organizations have snitches. I had Courtland."

She takes a few moments to process what he just said.

"There's a lot you don't know about this. I can only tell you this: the less you know, the better."

"But if I'm going to die—"

"Who said you're going to die?"

"You did. Isn't that the threat you made to Craig?"

"That was just the impetus. I couldn't . . . I couldn't kill you."

She scoffs. "Says the man who beat me and handcuffed me."

"You brought that on yourself."

"Whatever." She peels her face off the carpeted floor and rolls to her side. "Could you help me up, please?"

He hesitates for a moment, but leans down and grabs her arm at the bicep and lifts her to her feet. He moves her back to the edge of the bed.

"So you expect Craig to come here, out of hiding, with this chip?"

"He has to."

"How do you know he even has this chip?"

"He does. We checked everywhere else."

"We?"

He clears his throat. "Drop it."

∞

Craig sits in the airport with only a single carryon bag of clothes, his cell phone, and his watch. His flight for some inexplicable reason has been delayed, but not too long. He takes the few minutes to collect his thoughts. He thinks about Addie and how much he misses her already. He purposefully didn't take all of his things, to show her he would be back, but he isn't so sure that is enough to convince her at this point. He continues to fiddle with the watch, but finds it to be simply a plain old watch that he tried to steal years ago. He jams it into his pocket and grabs his cell to call Ramses and let him know of the developments. It lights up with a voice message he didn't know was there. He immediately accesses his voicemail box and listens to the message. It's from Berta and, judging by her tone, it must have been before she was taken by Simms.

"Hey, Craig. It's me. I, uh, just came from the hospital not too long ago. We were all there and the doctors . . . took her off of life support. But there's some great news here; she's breathing on her own. It was

rough at first, but then she started taking in air on her own. Doctors say she's stable, but we're still on watch, so to speak. They seem to think she could pass at any time. I don't think that's the case, though. I think she's fighting. I think she's going to make it. Mark thinks so, too. He's been pretty strong throughout this whole thing. He misses you, though. I can tell. Being totally honest, I miss you, too. I think about you almost every day and I regret some of the decisions I have made concerning us and our marriage . . ."

That's the first time in a long time he's heard her even acknowledge their marriage.

"Listen, when things settle down and you get back home . . . can we talk? I'm guessing there's a lot to say. Anyway, I better get off this phone. Things are a little weird here. But just . . . I know it seems like I gave up on us . . . and in some ways, I did. I can own up to that. But the one thing that has been consistent throughout—even when I didn't want to admit it—is that I love you. I love you, Craig. Talk to you soon."

The message ends, but Craig still holds the phone to his ear. He slowly moves it away and hangs it up. As if magnetized, he grabs the watch again and fiddles with it. Now, it has become some sort of a nervous twitch. He pops the little knob out and twists and twists absentmindedly. He thinks about Berta and how he is rushing into danger, not knowing the complexities of this danger. He just knows he has to get her out of that danger. He shakes his head, knowing this is the same thing that got him into this mess in the first place. First he was rushing blindly into his past for Mark, then into a garage to help Jade, now into who-knows-what to save Berta.

The watch clicks.

Craig looks at the watch, thinking he broke the little knob, but it seems to be completely intact. He examines the watch and notices a little slit behind the faceplate. He sticks his fingernail behind it and pulls up gently.

The watch pops open, revealing a small, square, black piece of plastic. He grabs it with his fingertips and sees metal—likely copper—on the other side of the square piece of plastic.

The chip.

He looks at the front of the watch again to see the time says seven forty-three. Immediately, Craig is drawn back to when he first received the watch. Mr. Valencia told him to look forward to seven forty-three. It wasn't crazy talk. It was a code.

He hangs his head. On one hand, he knows he should be happy in a sense that he has this chip to set Berta free. The more pervasive feeling is one of shame. Why would his mentor specifically demand that he stay out of the dirty-businessman life, but give him the exact means to be great (or terrible) at it? He sits up with tears in his eyes. *He always knew I would go back.* He grinds his teeth and closes the watch. He jams it back into his pocket and calls Ramses.

He picks up quickly, yet again. Craig wishes he answered all of his calls this way.

"I found the chip."

"Where was it?"

"In a watch."

Ramses chuckles. "In a damn watch. Raul."

"So, what's the plan?"

"You okay, Kid?"

"No. I'm not. Why would he leave this with me?"

"Listen, I already told you my thoughts."

"I know. Just in case. But does that make sense to you? Just in case of what?"

"I don't know, Craig."

"He knew I was going back. He knew I was weak."

"I don't think it was that at all."

Craig snorts. "Well, doesn't matter now. I have the chip. What's the plan?"

Ramses hesitates for a few moments before speaking. "For now, we follow along. I'll have a few men waiting for you to land. They'll stay behind, though, just enough to be able to follow the car you get into. From there, we would be able to survey the area, extract you and Berta. Eliminate all enemies."

"You make it sound easy."

"It's not. But I'm making it sound that way so you think that way."

"You really think he's trying to be Crime Lord Supreme?"

"That's what it seems. Why? You don't think so?"

"No. I mean, it's a possibility, but there are so many things he could do with that information . . . this information I have with me now. He could sell it." Craig pauses. "Make millions."

"That's true."

"He could be looking for something very specific on the chip, too. For what, I don't know."

"Possibly," Ramses says.

"I guess this is all speculation, right?"

"For now, yes," Ramses assents. "But I will say this, I believe the cases were brought up against you to get you out the way."

"Meaning?"

"I believe he drug up those cases to move you, either by warrant, or by you disappearing, and doing so in order to search all of your property."

"For the chip?" Craig's voice goes up a few octaves.

"Think about it. He searched your office, an office that was once Raul's. Found nothing. Then searched your home. Found nothing. I'm sure he's stumbled upon information on you because Courtland was tracking you and Alberta for years."

Craig starts at this remark. "Wait. He's been what?"

"Tracking you two. So, chances are, the detective who was on his payroll knows that you didn't have any safe-deposit boxes or anything like that; nowhere to stash the chip that's safe."

"But you forget, all of this started when my friend Jade was kidnapped. Otherwise, he wouldn't have been in the picture."

"You believe that? You really believe this was all by chance? Those cases were there regardless. They were a ticking time bomb this entire time. It, to me, seems like he just was waiting for the right time."

"How was this the right time?"

"His employer died, or, rather, he was killed by his second wife. No more extra money for Crooked Detective."

Craig considers what Ramses says. "It would somewhat explain why he did such a crappy job in finding Jade."

"It wasn't his focus."

"Then why take the case?"

"Good question," Ramses quipped.

"Forget it. All this speculation . . . what's the plan again, and how am I not going to get my brains blown out?"

CHAPTER TWENTY-THREE

"So what was it like? Like, could you hear us? Did you feel anything? Did you dream?"

Jade sits propped up in her hospital bed, talking to Mark. She revels in the fact that she can have a conversation with him again and smiles. She takes a deep breath and even though it smells like somewhat stale hospital air, she thanks God for it. She turns her attention back to Mark.

"I don't really remember. It was dark. Really, really dark."

"Well, I dreamed of you. Often. There was this one in particular . . ." He looks away as if he were embarrassed. "It was our wedding day. And I was there waiting for you to come out and walk down to the altar. When you came out, you were . . . glowing. And the whole church fell away until it was just us. You shone so bright, your light consumed everything. And you told me—"

"—to wait for me," she says. "I told you to wait for me."

Mark looks stunned.

"I remember . . . I had that dream." She looks into his eyes. "There's more. I just don't know what that is."

"It's okay, Dear. You're back. And we're going to get you strong again."

She nods but knows getting back to the way she was before may be impossible.

"So, I know I wanted to lose weight," she says. "But not like this, of course."

"You look great."

"No, I don't. Don't lie. I look like I did some crazy crash diet. Nothing looks proportional."

"That's not a real concern, is it?"

"No. I'm just saying." She looks down at her skinny but surprisingly tone legs. "So when are the kids coming by?"

"Your mother is bringing them later today."

"Just my Mom?"

Mark's face twists slightly. "Yeah. Just your Mom."

She reads his face. "What happened?"

"He left."

"What do you mean, 'he left'?"

"When everything went down . . . the pressure was too much. Your Mom told me she wasn't much help, either. So he left."

"And went where?"

"No clue. No one knows, really. He showed up when we went to . . . remove you from life support. He was . . . pretty upset with me." He clears his throat. "And I him."

Jade doesn't say anything, lost in a number of thoughts.

"Babe, listen . . . there's a lot we need to talk about. The things that happened . . ."

"I know." She feels a quickening in her pulse. "So, Craig and Berta."

Mark's face drops a little. Most people wouldn't notice, but she has known him for years. She spots it easily. "Look, I know there are a lot of hurdles for us now. I really do. I just don't want to think of that right now."

"I understand." He sits up in his seat. "So, Craig and Berta . . . I'm not sure there's much good news there."

"They're still having trouble?"

"Berta filed for divorce."

Jade gasps.

"I talked to her and she seemed pretty . . . steadfast in her thinking."

"Where are they? I want to have dinner. All of us. Don't care what it takes."

"Well, that may be hard. Craig . . . I don't know where Craig is."

"What? Did he just up and leave, too?"

Mark looks at her, contorting his face.

"Sorry," she says. "I just. What the heck happened? Wait. I don't want to know yet. Just—" She looks up at the ceiling. "Can you try? Try to get them together for dinner."

"I can."

"Thank you."

They both sit in silence for a few moments. Jade has a bunch of swirling thoughts, but none of them makes much sense to her at the moment. She has a daydream about a person who is on fire but remains unharmed by the flames.

The flames are bright white.

"Mark?"

"Yes, Dear."

"I'm ready for you to tell me." She looks him in the eyes. "Tell me everything."

◌◌

After a long and nerve-racking flight, Craig finally lands. He moves through the airport, quickly reaching the pickup area. He visually combs through the number of people holding up signs, but doesn't notice anyone holding up a sign with his name on it. He becomes nervous, thinking he just walked straight into a trap. He stops and considers his options, though he already knows he is down to very few.

He grabs his phone to call Ramses, but just as he goes to dial, he sees a man in a black suit, standing in front of a stretch limousine, holding a posterboard with his name on it. He slides the phone into his pocket and heads toward the man holding the sign. He observes the man's face as he gets closer. The man's face twitches with recognition. Craig gives the man a curt nod as he takes Craig's bag and puts it in the trunk. He slides into the limousine as the man opens the door for him. The slam of the door sounds abnormally loud to him. He watches the man briskly walk around to the driver's side of the vehicle and get in. A few moments later, they are off. To calm himself, he thinks of Berta at first, but later settles into a blank stare, eventually thinking about nothing.

Little shards of sunlight break through in between the buildings, but the inside of the limo remains dark. Craig recognizes the streets they travel, feeling slightly nostalgic. He is home, finally, but he knows there is no real homecoming party for him. At least, not one he wants to be a part of. The limo enters a parking garage he has pulled into at least a thousand times.

He twists his face. "What the—"

The limo driver reaches the top of the garage and parks. Craig sits there for a few moments, even after the limo driver opens the door for him. He doesn't want to take this walk, but Berta is in danger. And he is still very loyal to her no matter what is going on. He shivers slightly, knowing there aren't many ways Ramses' men can get to him. He knows it is likely he will be escorted to the twenty-sixth floor, and what he will find there scares him. He steps out the limo as the driver walks to the trunk and grabs his bag.

"Sir?"

"Yeah, thanks," Craig says as he grabs his bag from the diver. "You're not taking me up?"

The driver looks strangely. "I was told you would know where to go. Is that a mistake?"

"No." He shakes his head. "No, it's not. Thank you."

The driver swiftly moves back into the limo and drives off. Craig notices he drove off in a hurry. Again, he looks up at the top of the building, feeling someone looking at him. He knows why the driver dropped him off here.

It's incredibly easy to see his arrival.

He walks to the edge of the parking area to a glass-enclosed walkway. He has rarely taken this way, as he had always parked in the lower, private sub area and taken the elevator straight up. Walking through the glass-enclosed walkway makes him feel like a stranger, which surprises him.

Because he has worked in this building for more than a decade.

He gets inside the building to find it mostly empty, which he expects for a Sunday night. He walks to the elevators and jams the "up" button, taking the first one that opens. He plugs the button that says twenty-six and the elevator smoothly starts its ascent. He takes a few deep breaths to calm himself before the doors open. When they do, he freezes. Part of him expects to see Berta at her desk, typing away, calming Mr. Rustinsky before Craig spoke to him. Part of him expects to go to work and take a break every hour to look out at the cityscape. Part of him expects to walk into life the way it was before. A greater part of him longs for that time.

He steps from the elevator and to his left, noting the emptiness of what once was Berta's desk. He has a quick thought, wondering if Ted is doing well, and determines to find out, if he makes it out of this situation alive.

The large double doors that lead to his office are closed. He sets his hand on the door handle, steeling himself for what is to come. He twists the handle and opens the doors, walking in. He looks around for Berta, for Simms, but finds no one. It's difficult to see as none of the lights is turned on and the sun has almost completely set. He leaves the door hanging open slightly and takes in the office. It looks nothing like what it was before. The whole interior has been redesigned. The desk is now in front of the large floor-to-ceiling windows. The sitting area has been moved and all new furniture has been placed. The heavy woods of old have been replaced with white and cream velvet. He shakes his head. He walks to the desk and eyes the tall executive chair that has its back facing him. Slowly, he moves to its side, but finds no one in the chair. He turns on the desk light. For a little more light.

"I've done some redecorating," a voice calls out from one of the corners. The lights come on.

Craig looks to where the voice came from and instantly freezes.

"Don't be so surprised, Kid." The man walks surely, confidently, even though he has a cane. He has white hair and a stone face. His eyes send chills up and down Craig's spine. "Put the bag down. Have a seat. Let's talk."

"What is this?"

"A business meeting," the man says.

"But you're dead," Craig says, feeling dumb for having said that.

He smiles. "What can I say? It's hard to keep me down." He sits in the executive chair. "Like the phoenix, I rise from the ashes of a burned-down and desolate world. Wait, you're Christian, right? So, like Jesus, I rise with all power in my hand." He chuckles. "Or does some other God suit you? Osiris? Tammuz? Dionysus? Whatever." He folds his hands and places them on top of the desk. "I don't want to go too far down that rabbit hole. So, the business at hand. The chip."

"Where's Berta?"

"She'll be here."

Courtland DeVries smiles with a devilish grin.

Cঙৎৎ০

Berta has tried a number of times to get more information out of Simms over the past few hours. Each time, she has been met with stone-cold resistance. She knows he's operating with someone else, but who? Her phone rang earlier and Simms immediately took the phone. It was apparently Craig about to take off and come home.

Hours later, the sun is setting, and she knows it's almost time. She doesn't really know what for, exactly, but she knows the way Simms acts now is different. He's more robotic. His cell phone rings. The speed with which he answers frightens her a little. He gives a quick "okay" and gets off the phone.

"Time to go," he says. "I'm going to take the cuffs off. If you try anything, it will mean trouble."

"What does that mean, exactly?"

"It means I will push you as close to death as possible. Don't test me."

She looks him in the eyes. "Could you really do that?"

He looks away and reaches behind her. "Just don't do anything stupid. You go back to Craig. He hands over the chip. Everyone goes on with their lives."

"Do you really believe that can happen for us . . . for me? You think I will be able to just continue on as if nothing happened?"

"I don't know."

She feels the handcuffs release. Simms pulls them off and Berta rubs around her wrists, trying to massage out the pain. "You know there isn't a normal life for me on the horizon."

"It means nothing to you right now, but I am sorry for that. I'm sorry for all of this."

His gaze lingers a few moments too long, long enough to make the exchange of words feel awkward.

"Let's go."

He takes her to his car and she gets in without a fight. He gets in and starts the car. The sun has now completely set and the sky is a cool blue. In a few more minutes, it will be dark. He pulls off, away from the hotel and into the main street. Berta remains silent for the entire ride until she sees where they park. She looks at her old work building and shudders.

"Why here?" she asks.

Simms doesn't answer.

"Logan?"

"C'mon. Let's go."

She examines his face under the fluorescent lights of the parking garage. She notes his face is determined, but there is something else there that gives her pause. She thinks she sees regret. She's led to the front lobby she has walked through a number of times and to the elevators. She knows exactly where they are going. They step onto the elevator. Once the doors shut, the area feels surprisingly more closed off than she last remembers. They go to the twenty-sixth floor. When the doors open, she hears talking. She steps off the elevator and Simms grabs her by the arm. He stops her and looks her in the eyes.

"I'm really sorry for this," he says, and he pulls her into the room.

Berta gets yanked into the office. The very same office that once was Craig's office; what once was Raul's office. She looks around to find it completely different. Simms lets go of her arm. She looks to see Craig stand up quickly and start toward her. Simms moves in front of her, blocking him from getting to her. She looks around Craig to see what she believes is her worst nightmare. She can't believe her eyes.

"Hello, Alberta," Courtland says.

She looks at Craig with a pained expression. Such a range of emotions she feels at this moment. She is excited to see Craig again for the first time in a long time. She's ashamed for what she has done to him. She is angry with Simms. And scared, sad, shocked, and angry at seeing for the first time in ages the man whom she despises the most. She stands there in silence for a while, trying to compute what is going on.

"Looks like you have a shiner there. Logan, I thought I told you to bring her unharmed."

Simms looks sheepish. "She was trying to get away."

"Of course she was." He steps from behind the desk and toward her. Each step he takes, she feels her heart quicken. He walks past Craig and comes up next to Simms, merely a few feet in front of her. She cannot stop the trembling. Her body is doing nothing of what she wants it to do. She wants to run, either away from the monster or through him. But she remains still. When he puts out his hand, she wants to grab it and break his arm, but she stays still, allowing him to gently touch the swollen skin on the side of her face. He shakes his head, but she doesn't quite know what for. She snaps her face away from his cold and smooth fingers. He looks, shrugs, and walks back toward the desk.

"Have a seat," he says and pats the chair next to Craig. Her thoughts become jumbled, but she moves to sit. That is the only way she can keep the room from spinning. Once she's seated, Courtland moves back behind the desk and takes a seat. He motions to Craig to take his seat again as well. Craig doesn't sit until Simms is standing next to Courtland.

"How have you been, Alberta?"

She cannot move her mouth to form any words. She just sits there and stares at him, with tears forming in her eyes.

"I see. Me? Well I've been well. Well, not actually. I've been . . . dead." He chuckles for a moment before realizing he is the only one laughing. His face turns grim. "Seems both my daughters have been pretty active. Trying to destroy my name even after death? I thought Jennifer could have done something of the sort, but you, Alberta. That's unbecoming of you."

Berta blinks back a few tears and finally gets enough courage to speak. "You are a terrible . . . despicable, sorry excuse for a human being. You self-serving son of a bitch."

"Is that the real Alberta coming out? Could it be? Craig, have you met Alberta, the real one?" He motions his hand toward her. "There's the real her. Not this holier-than-thou church lady she's been masquerading around as. The real Alberta is the one who beat this one girl to within an inch of her life. Carmen was her name. You remember that, Alberta?"

She feels heat rise to her face until she knows her face is flush. Anger begins to consume her. She looks to her side at Craig, shocked that he stares right at her. She stares at him, wondering why he hasn't said much.

"Shall we?" Courtland cuts in. "I'm sure you have busy lives to tend to."

Berta continues to stare at Craig, almost communicating with him without saying a word. Slightly, she shakes her head. Craig blinks, seemingly not understanding. She puts her head down, knowing at some point, they were so connected they could speak without speaking. They no longer have that luxury, it seems.

Through the jumbled thoughts, something becomes very clear. She stares at Courtland as piece by piece, everything comes together.

"I've seen that look quite a few times over my lifetime," Courtland says. "It's one of realization. I've seen it before a man dies when he realizes what he's done wrong. I've seen it in others when they realize they lost. I must ask: what did you just realize?"

She goes to speak but looks at Craig. She then turns to look at Simms and shakes her head. Simms looks away.

"This was a play for power. And once you started on this path . . . there was no turning back. You've set this all up. You've set us up."

"Oh please, do elaborate. I think some others are slow to the draw." He nods toward Craig.

She looks toward Simms. "You never wanted to bring him in. That was never your goal. Your goal was to get him out of the way. It didn't matter if he ran or not. You would have arrested him to move him. But you knew Ramses was looking after him . . . after us. So, you knew he was going to run. And that gave you prime opportunity to search all of his property. Legally. You did it legally so you didn't raise any suspicion. You looked for the chip but didn't find it. So, you determined Craig had it with him. I just . . . can't figure out how you knew there was a chip in the first place." She turns toward Courtland.

"Does it matter?" he asks.

She looks at him.

"It was Marcy. She wanted power. She thought she had power."

"But you had her killed."

"She killed me. I was returning the favor."

"You're disgusting."

He motions with his hand in a circular motion, showing lack of interest in her insults.

"So, Detective," Craig cuts in, "You were never trying to find Jade, were you?"

"I was a little . . . distracted." Simms doesn't say any more.

"And what about Angelina?" Berta says.

Simms looks back and forth between Berta and Craig, finally keeping his gaze on Berta. "I did it for you." He looks down, embarrassed.

She redirects her attention to Courtland. "So you make a play on this chip because if you got it you would have . . . all of Raul's network. And mostly everyone thinks you're dead . . ."

"So I would be a legend. I could rule from the shadows."

"And Detective here was doing your bidding the entire time?"

"Of course."

She looks at Simms. "Justice, huh?" She looks away, disgusted.

"Can we move on now? Craig? The chip."

"No," he says. "I don't have any chip."

Courtland freezes. Berta watches his somewhat light demeanor melt into a darker one. For the first time ever, Berta sees that shadow settle over him, the shadow Izabel told her about.

"I don't think you understand. You are well past the point of no return."

Craig looks at Berta again. This time, she knows it is for confirmation.

"Sounds like there's no deal," she says. "And from the sounds of it . . . you are well past the point of no return, too."

Courtland looks back and forth between the two. "Detective?"

Simms pulls out a gun and aims it at Berta. She doesn't flinch, but she looks at him with soft eyes.

"Is this justice?" she asks.

"Kill them both." Courtland says.

Simms aims a shaky hand at Berta, but she stays firm. "We aren't criminals, Simms. You cross this line, you become one of them."

"What choice do I have? If I don't, we're all dead, anyway," Simms says.

"How do you figure that? You know there's only one criminal in this room right now. And you have your gun aimed away from him."

"Dammit, Simms." Courtland pulls out a gun of his own and quickly pulls the trigger after jamming it into Simms' side. The crack sounds muffled. Simms hunches over to the side. The pain in his face before he falls is something Berta will not soon forget. Simms lands on the floor with a thud, the kind of thud someone makes when they're not able to brace for the fall. Simms disappears behind the desk. Courtland trains his gun on Berta.

She stares at the gun, realizing this is only the second time in her life she's had to stare down the barrel of one. The first time just happened with Simms, and he is now dead. She grips the chair armrests with a white-knuckle grip. The hairs on her arms stand on end as a cold sweat starts on the nape of her neck. She knew Simms wasn't going to shoot her before, but she knows for sure the monster will. She flexes every muscle in her body, trying to stop it from shaking.

She struggles to speak, feeling that if she opens her mouth a scream will escape. She forces air into her lungs and out her mouth. "You were going to do that anyway, weren't you?" She barely gets the sentence out.

"Eventually. So, Craig," he says without looking away from Berta, "You have one last shot. The chip. Now, think about this before you say another word. Are you willing to die over this? Are you willing to risk Berta's life over this?"

"I—"

CRACK! CRACK!

Berta is pushed to the ground as Craig's body flies on top of her. Her ears ring as everything becomes a blur. She looks at Craig, whose eyes are closed. A few seconds later, she notices he opens his eyes. They dart back and forth, searching hers. She turns her head to the side and looks at a set of feet walking from behind the desk and toward them. Craig scurries to his feet, hovering over Berta. She looks up from the floor to see Simms holding his side.

"Go. Get out of here," Simms says.

Craig helps her to her feet. She looks at Simms, who seems to be losing a lot of blood.

"You need to get to a hospital," she says.

"No. There's no way this goes well for me." He looks at the blood in his hand. "I'm sorry for all of this. I . . . I once wanted to do the right thing. He called in his chit, though . . . and I had to pay up."

She looks at the desk. Courtland's upper body lies flat on the desk, blood pooling under his head.

"You did it, Logan," Berta says. "You've just taken down one of the most notorious crime bosses ever."

"Ever, huh?" Simms laughs a weak laugh. He sits back onto the desk. "Let's just leave out the part where I helped make him, alright?"

She smirks, but it shows through a face of concern. "Of course."

"Listen, Craig, I'm sorry. I know that means nothing to you. And it shouldn't. I just needed to make sure you knew that I never wanted to go down this road. What you did to help Mark . . . that type of loyalty is far beyond anything I've ever seen. Far beyond anything I'm capable of."

Craig gives a curt nod.

"But I tried . . . I really did try to find Jade. There was only so much I could do with that guy breathing down my neck. I hope you understand."

Craig still says nothing.

"And please tell Mark that I am sorry . . . and that I hope that info I gave him helped." A helicopter sounds above. He smiles. "Ramses sent a freaking helicopter?"

She frowns and looks at Craig.

"Not surprising," Craig says.

"Seriously, you two better get out of here."

"No," she says. "We can't leave you here. Not like this."

"You don't get it." His breathing becomes labored. "It's all over for me. I've made my bed."

"Berta, let's go." Craig sounds annoyed almost. She looks at him as he turns and heads to the elevators.

She gives one last glance at Simms before turning and following Craig out.

CHAPTER TWENTY-FOUR

It has been two weeks since Mark was at Jade's bedside when she woke up. He almost couldn't believe it when they received discharge papers from the hospital. When he wheeled her out to the car, he nearly broke down in tears because he never thought the day was going to come. They did get a chance to talk, and as requested, he told her everything that happened, everything he found out. He told her about Bernard, about Alicia, about the hallucinations. For the whole day afterward, while still at the hospital, they said nothing to each other. He felt she wanted it that way and he knew she needed time to process. The next day, she laid her hand on his and told him she loved him. For the rest of that day, it seemed like all they did was cry.

CঽৰৎD

Mark helps Jade set the table for the large dinner she wanted to have. She had not been able to do much cooking, so Joanne came over and did most of it, with Mark helping where he could.

"Anything else you need me to do?" he asks Jade.

"No, Love." She seems short of breath. "I think we're good."

"You okay?" He kneels before her.

"I am. Just lost my breath for a moment. I'm fine."

"Are we going too hard with the physical therapy? Too much too soon?"

"No," she says quickly. "I'm not going to be in this chair much longer. And I'm not carrying that cane wherever I go."

He sees a fierce determination in her eyes. He just nods and lets her be. She maneuvers herself back into the kitchen.

"Give her a little bit. You know she's dealing with a lot." Joanne pats him on the shoulder.

"Of course. I know. I just want to—"

"Do something?"

"Yeah." He exhales. "I know part of her is still reeling from everything I told her. I don't want her to resent me. I don't want her to leave. I don't want to go back to where we were those years ago. We fought too hard."

"You worry too much. Come here." She opens her arms.

Mark hesitates for a moment before falling into Joanne's embrace. He plops his head on her shoulder as she pats his back.

"You're a strong man, Mark. I don't know many men who can go through what you went through and still stand . . . and still be around. And Jade loves you. Just love her back. That's all you need to do. It will all work out just fine."

He straightens up. "Thanks."

"I mean it. Don't worry. It will all be okay." She looks toward the kitchen. "Now let me get back in there before Jade jacks up my roast." She smiles and gives Mark's arm a squeeze.

⊗

Jade shuts the oven door when her mother appears.

"What are you doing?" Joanne asks.

"He's worrying again, isn't he?"

"You should worry if you keep messing with my roast."

"I'm serious, Mama. He's worrying again."

"Of course he is. But he will be okay."

"I'm not going to leave him."

"You don't have to explain that to me."

"I don't know how else to explain it to him." She wheels away from the stove. "You think he still sees her?"

Joanne goes into the refrigerator and pulls out broccoli and cauliflower. "I don't know. Does that make you feel insecure?"

"A little . . . but not enough to leave . . . or not trust him."

"I think there are still some things he has to work through, Dear."

"Yeah." She looks down. "You think Daddy is coming?"

"I don't know. I called him and left him a message. Mark told me they had a sort of falling out recently."

"So what are you going to do?"

"I'm going to do the same thing you should be doing: Enjoy this time with loved ones."

The doorbell rings and it seems like everyone in the house moves toward the front door. Mark gets to the door and opens it to let Berta in. She steps in, giving hugs to everyone. Jade smiles at seeing her.

"Hey, Girl," Jade says.

"Hey, Lady." Berta smiles a big smile.

"Thanks for coming." She looks at her. "Everything good?"

"You know. A lot of things going on." She smiles again. "What's new, right?"

"I guess."

"Nothing I can't handle. Anyway, the real question is, how are *you* doing?"

"I'm hanging in there. Thanks again for coming. We were supposed to do this . . . before everything happened and you know . . ."

"We're doing it now. That's what matters." She looks around. "Craig here yet?"

"Not yet." She gets to the kitchen with Berta following closely behind. "Mark filled me in on what's going on."

"Yeah?"

"I wish I could have helped more."

"It's fine. Nothing is finalized. We just need to talk, that's all." She goes to wash her hands. "You have to let me help cook. I couldn't bring anything because, well . . . I don't have a stove right now to cook on or anything."

"Sure. I was cutting up some vegetables. You can chop and cook those if you want." Jade looks with a frown. "What do you mean you don't have a stove?"

"I moved most of my stuff to storage and have been living in a hotel for the past couple weeks. I'm thinking of selling the condo. Just another thing on the list to talk to Craig about."

"Where are you moving to?"

"Nowhere yet. I have options, but . . . I don't know."

"Depends on what comes of your talk with Craig?"

"Depends on what comes of my talk with Craig."

Jade nods. "Well, I won't pester you any more about it. Just let me know if you need me. Okay?"

"Of course. Hey, Jade. It's really good having you . . . back. And I know you don't care about this . . . but I'm sorry for not visiting you more. I'm sorry I wasn't all the way there for you like I know you would be for me."

Jade, not expecting Berta to pop up with such raw emotion, squelches a small gasp. She smiles. "I was just taking a nap." She chuckles. "But I get it. You had—you still have—a lot going on. That's not something I would take to heart, anyway."

"I know. But I did. And I just had to let you know." She continues cutting the vegetables. "Did you dream?"

"You mean while I was out?"

Berta nods.

"No. Well, if I did, I don't remember."

Jade smiles when Joanne comes back into the kitchen. Berta and she have a conversation about something or another Jade doesn't pay much attention to. She sees their mouths moving, but what they say dissipates into an echo in the ambient noise. She thinks about Berta's last question. Mark asked her the same thing and she has told everyone who asked that she doesn't remember a thing. But that's a lie. She remembers everything. She remembers the darkness, and the bright star. She remembers being trapped in a cell of what was called her own heart. She remembers her other self, the one with more doubt, the one with more fear, the one whom she had to leave behind. She has sat back and thought about everything that happened in that *dream*. She has analyzed everything. The self-hatred, the doubt, the resentment of those she loves, the corrupted angel, the saving angel, she can recall each as one increasingly vivid memory. She keeps everything to herself for now, but she doesn't plan to forever.

Just long enough for her to make sense of what happened.

☙

Berta has been living in a hotel since being kidnapped by Simms. There's really no way she planned on going back to where Jennifer was killed. She's had one conversation with Ramses since, simply talking about what went down. He insisted that he got people to clean everything up, but she could never scrub down the images in her mind. Instead, she asked him to put all her belongings in storage, minus maybe a bag of stuff to live out of for the time being. She bought some new clothes and Ramses had someone deliver a bag of her familiar belongings. That was only one part of the conversation.

The other half dealt with some of the finer details as to how all this happened. Ramses finally had decrypted the rest of the drive. Lo and behold, everything she surmised was correct. Courtland faked his death, causing everyone to let their guard down. For years, Marcella built files on his network and thought she had the power; enough power to kill Courtland. At the end, she was killed and the info she had contained some information of Raul's network. This info was on the drive as well. Thus the search for the chip began.

Detective Simms, who has been on Courtland's payroll for years, unwillingly turned his sights on Craig, but simply to move him out of the way. This was to search all of his property, but when they came up empty-handed, they knew he had to have it on him somewhere. They assumed he knew about it. At that point, they had to take her because they knew she would be one of the only two people who could bring Craig out of hiding, the other person being Mark.

She got a call from Mark (a few calls, actually) checking up on her, and telling her about the upcoming dinner. He asked her to relay the message to Craig, as his cell seemed to be out of commission. She did, of course, but only through voicemail. She hadn't been able to actually speak with him, either.

She also made a few phone calls to her mother, letting her know everything that happened. She only doled out that information in pieces. There was only so much her mother could take at one time, and there was only so much Berta could talk about before breaking down in tears. She broke down a number of times in mourning, in anger, and a few times in fear. Each time, she called out to Jesus, just looking for understanding and peace.

෴

Berta pulls up in front of the Cooke residence and hops out of her car. She is excited and when she rings the doorbell and the door opens, she nearly bursts through. She hugs everyone she sees, and when she comes upon Jade, all she can do is smile. For a moment, Berta forgets what happened and enjoys being in her friends' company. They talk while cooking. Joanne comes in and joins the conversation and all three talk until the dinner. For a moment, she notices Jade zoning out, but she makes nothing of it. Just as quickly, Jade is back in the conversation. They finish all the cooking while Mark plays with the kids. She notices a few drops of tears coming from Jade's eyes as she watches them play. It almost makes Berta cry herself. She clears her throat and pretends to busy herself with things on the dining table. She looks outside to see the sun setting. She wonders where Craig is, if he's going to show up at all.

Then the doorbell rings.

෴

Since the incident at his old office, Craig has lain low. He wanted to separate himself from everyone, hoping in the time of decompression, he would find peace. He did; however, the peace he found in his giant hotel room pales in comparison to the peace he found at the ranch with Addie. There were plenty of unheard voicemails on his phone, but the ones that got his attention were the ones he got from Berta and Mark.

෴

He sits in his car just a little bit down the block. He watches as Berta goes into the Cooke residence, but he doesn't move. For some strange reason, he is planted in his seat, unable to move, paralyzed with fear. It's been quite a long time since he's seen Mark and Jade. He wonders how they will react to him. And he's been avoiding Berta on purpose. He listened to her voicemail a thousand times, to a point where he can hear her voice, and the truth in it, without even picking up his phone.

He leans his head back to relax. In the moment, he begins to pray. He prays, but turns out chuckling at himself. These are his friends. He hasn't seen them for a while, sure, but they are the closest people he knows. But then there's Berta. He's just as afraid to see her, but for different reasons. They never talked about what happened two weeks ago, and never had a chance to talk about her message. He knows they will have to soon. He takes in a deep breath and restarts the car, driving only up the street, parking behind Berta. He puts on a smile to cover his fears and gets out the car.

He walks to the front door. He hears the screams and laughter of children before he even gets to ringing the doorbell. When he does, his throat tightens and his palms sweat. He wipes them off on the front of his pants. The door swings wide open and Mark stands at the open doorway. Craig looks at Mark, noticing the little patch of gray hair at his temple. He opens his mouth to say something, but his throat is closed tight. Mark puts out his hand. Craig looks for only a moment before clapping his hand into a handshake. They pull each other into an embrace.

"You good, Man?" Mark asks.

All Craig is able to do is nod.

"Welcome home, yeah?"

"Something like that."

"Berta told me everything is clear."

"Yeah. About that—"

"Uncle Craig!" Kalina slides past Mark and wraps her arms around his waist.

"Hey, Little Lady."

"Little Lady? What is this? Some western?" Kalina asks.

"I don't know where that came from," Craig says.

Mark and Kalina pull Craig inside as Mark closes the door. Charles comes running up to them and gives Craig a handshake.

"He's getting big," Craig says to Mark.

"Don't say that out loud. The boy thinks he has muscles now. Wants to start going to the gym with us."

Craig chuckles but instantly is frozen in place when Jade wheels her way from the kitchen. All he can do is stare. She smiles brightly at him. And before he knows it, tears are sliding from his eyes. He holds a balled fist to his mouth to stop his mouth from trembling.

"Uncle Craig?" Charles says.

"Just give him a second, Bud," Mark says.

Jade sits right in front of him and puts her hands out. Craig leans in to give her a hug. She grips him tightly, as if she is trying to force more tears out of him. He cries into her shoulder. He hears her in his ear with a trembling voice saying, "Thank you."

He stands tall and wipes away the tears, but more fall. "If I could only stop crying like a little punk . . ." He feels a hard pat on his shoulder.

"Seriously. Without you . . . she wouldn't be here," Mark says. "I appreciate you, Bro."

"You aren't going to start crying, too, are you?" Craig says while trying to laugh away his tears.

Mark laughs but then gets quiet. Craig looks at why. He sees Berta leaning on the wall in the small hallway. Her eyes are bloodshot; her eyes puffy. She's been crying, too. He can't help but think that maybe it's out of some kind of guilt or shame. Here they all are, two people he cares about deeply, thanking him for making a decision for which she is divorcing him. Still, seeing her that way bothers him. He wants to console her. To tell her everything will be fine.

But he is unsure of even that.

"Okay, everyone's here," Mark says. "Can we eat?" He looks at Jade.

Craig notices there's some hesitancy in her voice, but she agrees that it is time to eat, admitting herself that she is hungry. As everyone moves toward the dining room, he catches up with Berta. He smiles at her and she returns a half smile.

"Hi," is all he can say.

"Hello, Craig."

"How . . . are . . . you?"

She curls her lips a bit. He's always known that to mean she's holding something back. "I'm fine. You?"

He sighs. "I'm as good as I can be right now. Listen, there's a lot for us to talk about, I know. Can we just put all that aside while we're here?"

"I was thinking the same thing."

"Good. Good. So . . . time to grub?"

She nods.

Craig and Berta enter the dining room together. He sees bowls and pans of food; a well prepared meal for friends.

"Everything looks delicious," he says.

In a matter of minutes, everyone is seated and the food is prayed over. Craig digs in first and tears through his food, not realizing he's eating like he hasn't eaten in years. He pulls off a hunk of bread and jams it into his mouth. Moments later, he looks up to see everyone looking at him.

"I'm guessing it's been a long time since you've had a real meal," Mark says.

"It's been a little bit." He sits up straight. "This food tastes great. Kudos to the cook."

"Well, I think the ladies all pitched in."

"Well, Jade, Mrs. Joanne, Berta, my stomach thanks you." He smiles.

Everyone around the table chuckles.

"So where did you go?" Mark asks.

"Texas. I was at a ranch in Texas."

The table falls silent as he looks down into his plate. "The real question is"—he looks up—"where did that patch of gray hair come from?" He points at Mark's temple.

Mark laughs. "I was thinking of keeping it. Makes me look distinguished, doesn't it?"

Craig looks with a smirk.

"Jade?" Mark says. "Don't I look good with this?" He rubs the hair around his temple.

"Of course you do, Babe."

"See." Mark smiles. "My boo likes it."

Craig looks at Jade and smiles. "Hey, you guys remember the haircut?"

"No one wants to hear that story," Mark breaks in.

Jade laughs out loud. "I remember the haircut. I could never forget *the haircut.*"

"What's the haircut?" Berta asks.

Craig leans in to Berta. "Right around the time Mark first met Jade, he got this haircut. He was trying to impress Jade."

"That's not true. I just wanted a fresh cut before dropping Kalina off again."

Craig glances at Jade and smirks. "Anyway. He was in a rush, so he went to a new barber. Just picked this random spot and thought it was a good idea to pay for a haircut there."

"I easily know where this is going," Berta says. She leans in closer to Craig.

"Well, this new barber cut off all of his hair. Now look at him." He turns toward Mark. "Imagine *that* guy bald. Lumpy Head USA. I mean, there are some guys who can do the bald head thing and be fine. Mark is not one of them. And all Jade could do was laugh, I bet."

"No. She couldn't laugh because I wore a hat. Went to the K-mart down the street and bought a cheap cap."

Craig laughs. "Poor second graders. You wore that cap all day, didn't you?"

"I did."

"A baseball cap with a suit." Jade laughs. "He was *my* cutie in a cap and a suit."

"I bet you weren't thinking that then, though," Craig says. "I know what you were really thinking. The same thing I thought." He looks at Berta. "I desperately needed to know how he got a cap big enough to fit that noggin'."

The whole table erupts into laughter.

Mark rubs the gray patch of hair. "I'm dyeing it tomorrow." More laughter rumbles across the table.

୧୫

After the dinner, Craig explains he has to go and goes around giving everyone hugs. He says his goodbyes and heads out the door. He feels lighthearted for a moment while walking out. He walks to his car and waits there, his hand on the door handle. He looks up at the sky to see it is clear. A full and bright moon casts a glow over the entire area.

It's chilly, but he waits. A few minutes later, Berta comes walking out the Cooke residence. She walks to the front of her car.

"There's this diner a few minutes away," Craig says.

"I know where. Meet there?"

He nods and gets in his car. A few minutes later, he gets to the diner to find it mostly empty. He parks and gets out, waiting for Berta before entering. When Berta gets to the door, he opens it for her and enters. It's brightly lit, and the only others there are a bunch of college-age kids, joking and laughing, having a good time. Craig moves toward a booth that's farther away from them, so he and Berta can talk uninterrupted. He waits for her to sit first, and he sits. For a moment, they sit and stare at each other like star-crossed lovers. He halfway wants to order a milkshake so they can share it. But what this really is, is a feel-out process. Neither of them wants to be the first to speak. Craig builds up some courage to start.

"Everything been okay?" he asks.

She shrugs. "I suppose. There's a lot to wrap my head around. The monster alive, Simms . . . Jennifer . . ." She waves her hand. "But that has nothing to do with this talk, I guess."

"Well, sure it does. It has to do with you. It has to do with me. But, I have to admit I don't have much else to say about that night. Other than you seemed to be really . . . close to the detective."

"I wasn't close to him at all. It's just he seemed to believe strongly in justice. He believed in it like I do . . . like I did."

"Is that what you thought tipping him off was? Justice?"

She looks down. "I'm sorry for that. I really am and I hope you can forgive me." She looks up at him. "Do you forgive me?"

"I do. No grudges or anything. It's all done."

"I'm glad. That was one of my fears . . . that you never would."

"Well, you can rest easy on that." He looks around. "So, what a crazy world we live in, huh? One of crime bosses and dirty cops and detectives and . . ." He looks down at his hands. "It all sounds so ludicrous."

"It does sound silly. Or from some story."

He nods slightly. "Listen, I'm sorry for . . . all of the situation . . . dealing with Mr. Valencia and how he got you. I knew. I knew this entire time, but it simply got pushed to the back of my mind. I pushed it there because he asked me to. He asked me not to say a thing." He looks her in the eyes. "He didn't want you to look at him differently, even after he died."

She nods. "I can understand in some ways why you didn't. But it was a betrayal nonetheless. That hurt me. That hurt me more than the news itself. We were on the same side . . . and I felt like that changed then."

"Again, I'm sorry." He places his hand out. When she places hers in his, he squeezes slightly. He looks her in the eyes. "I'm sorry. I never meant to hurt you. Please forgive me."

She wipes a few droplets from her eyes with her free hand. "I do."

For a few moments, they hold hands, each staring at their hands together. He uses his thumb to rub the back of her hand.

"Did you get my message?" she asks.

"I did."

"I meant it. I really do . . . miss you."

"I miss you, too."

"And if you are willing . . . I am willing to try this again. We can start over. Gonna need a new place and all, but . . . we still have some time before any court hearings. We can just . . ."

Craig looks down and away. He tenses his jaw a few times. "I . . . I miss you. I do. But I miss the you . . . from before we got married. I miss talking about our terrible dates . . . I miss those times years ago when we would be in the office late, eating dinner, working on another a set of new clients. I miss joking around with you at any given moment. I miss *that* Berta."

"What are you saying?"

"I'm saying . . . I'm saying I think we made a mistake. I think we should be . . . friends."

She snaps her hand away, shocked.

"I'm sorry, Berta. I'm just in a completely different head space now. And I know there was that promise we all made to one person or another . . . but none of those people is here now. And I want peace."

"You're saying there isn't any peace with me?"

"No. Not that. I'm saying that I found real peace at that ranch." He doesn't say any more.

She looks like she understands. "Too much has gone wrong for you to think differently."

"I'm sorry."

"No need to apologize. I'm a big girl. I had to be open to this when asking. I just . . . I just never pictured life without you." She looks down at the table, but it looks like she's somewhere else.

Craig doesn't know what to say, so he remains quiet, allowing Berta some time to process.

"So, I guess this is it?" she says, the tears in her eyes betraying her calm voice.

"It doesn't have to be. I will always be here for you."

"But what does that mean? That's just something someone says when they want to ease away from someone."

"No. I really mean it. If you are ever in trouble or anything . . . you can call."

She shakes her head while moving her jaw. "It's fine." She looks at her watch. "It's getting late. I should get back."

Craig nods. Berta quickly gets up, and he trails behind. When they step outside, they are greeted by a chilly breeze. He watches her hold herself, then rushes ahead of her to open her car door. She stops for a quick second to give him a weak hug and gets in her car. He walks back to his car somewhat dazed but stops. *What was that?*

He turns around to see she still sits in her car, looking forward. He cautiously steps up to her car and knocks on the window. She looks at him like he's someone else, but he opens her door and places his hand out. She looks at him, confused, but places her hand in his. He pulls her from the car and into an embrace. He holds her tight, rubbing her back with his left hand. He hugs her because he knows he still loves her. He hugs her because he knows he's hurt her. He hugs her because he needs to be away from her. She begins to sob. Her cries become more intense such that the noise of it reverberates throughout his entire chest. He holds her throughout, wave after wave of her sorrow. The young kids walk out the diner and look at them but say nothing. Eventually, they go along their way. Once she calms, she pulls away slightly.

"I got snot all over your shirt," she says.

"It's fine. Not the first time that happened."

She chuckles in between sniffing. "Guess not." She wipes away tears with the back of her hand and looks up at him. "Goodbye, Craig."

He tenses up. Goodbye doesn't work for him here because he knows he will see her again, and likely somewhat often. "I'll see you later."

She chuckles. "Will you?"

He squints, not knowing what she is getting at. He has plans in his head on what he's going to do, but he knows he's never revealed any of that to her. He looks into her eyes and somehow he understands. She waited for years for him to "see" her, as she said it. It was on their first real date on the rooftop of what was her condo then but turned into their home later. She said she waited years for him to "see" her, but he kept going woman to woman looking for "the one." He understands what she means.

"I suppose not."

"So, again, goodbye, Craig."

He hesitates, but says, "Goodbye, Alberta."

He notices neither one of them actually made a real move to leave. He lets his hands drop to his sides. She seemingly takes that as a cue to step back. She gets into her car. The door has been open the entire time. He steps away from her car, this time turning away and not looking back.

Final Chapter

Jade sits in her wheelchair, staring out their bedroom window. She thinks of how much fun the dinner was, but even more pressing is how different everyone is. Everything that has happened to them shows. Mark seems worn, and has become full of worry. Even the kids seemed to age a bit, like they've been forced to mature a bit more because of what happened. She saw the deep sadness in Berta's eyes and regret in Craig's. She feels bad for them, and for not being able to help more. She closes her eyes, letting the rays of sun warm her.

"Lord," she says, "I thank you for everything you have done, and everything you continue to do. I thank you for my family, and for finally being able to get back to them. I thank you for the help you have offered me even when I had no idea where I was. I know, Lord, that what I remember is too elaborate to be a dream. It felt real. And I may be crazy for thinking it was . . . or is real. But there was something there . . . for me to learn. I know my work here isn't finished. Thank you for at least giving me another shot at finishing it."

CʒʘƆ

"Lord, I pray for Berta. I hope she finds a way through that sadness I saw in her eyes. And though she and Craig may not end well . . . I hope she holds no bitterness toward him. I hope she doesn't end up resenting him, as I know firsthand what holding that type of stuff in your heart can do."

CʒʘƆ

333

"What do you think, Mom?" Berta asks. She unpacks a few boxes and sets plates and cutlery in the kitchen.

"It's wonderful, Dear," Izabel says. "You sure about this, though?"

"I better be. I sold the condo to get this place." She grabs her hand. "So this is why I called you over. Follow me."

Berta takes her mother up a set of wooden stairs and down a hall. She opens the door to show a large bedroom with a modern look. The skylights above are open and rays of sunlight shine in.

"This is a nice master suite."

"Check out the en-suite." She pulls her mother to the master bathroom. When she opens the door, she hears her mother gasp. She smiles.

"This is huge," Izabel says.

The entire bathroom is marble with a huge soaker tub and Vegas-worthy stand-in shower.

"So, what do you think?" Berta asks.

"I think you made the right choice in home. You can get a real peaceful sleep in here. Love the furniture, too. Nice picks."

"Thanks, Mom." She can't contain her smile. "I'm really glad you like it . . . because this is your room."

Izabel gasps again. "What are you talking about?"

"My room is down the hall. This is your room."

"You mean to live in? You want me to move in with you?"

"Well, yeah. It's better than living in that small apartment."

"But . . . this is all so much . . . especially for someone who wasn't much of a mother to you."

Berta sees the tears forming in Izabel's eyes. "We have a ways to go before we're a super mother-daughter team. But I would love to get there." She grabs her mother's hand. "And we can travel."

"Travel?"

"Yeah." She pulls her along, back downstairs. "You haven't seen that many places, have you?"

"No . . . but wait a second."

Berta stops.

"Are you sure you're okay?" Izabel asks.

Berta ponders on her question. "I think I am."

"Even with the impending court date."

"Yeah. I am." She thinks some more. "Don't get me wrong, I cried for weeks after Craig left. Saying goodbye to him was one of the hardest things I ever had to do. But it's for the better." She walks to the kitchen with Izabel close behind. "I woke up one day with a single question on my mind. Who am I? It's funny because I was able to answer that in some way before, but never fully. You see, I've been somewhat defined by Craig, and before him, Raul, and before him, the monster. I wasn't just defined by them; I was defining myself by what they all did to me. It was a silly way to live life."

Izabel looks down in thought. "I understand."

"Anyway, we're still close to the library . . . not too far from my job. This place is perfect." She looks at Izabel with bright eyes. "So, are you in?"

A smile forms on Izabel's face. "Of course. Of course."

Berta jumps to Izabel and hugs her, holding her tightly.

She hears her phone ring and goes to see who it is. When she looks at it, she sees it's her bank. She immediately picks it up, fearing the worst.

"Hello?"

"Hello. Mrs. Barlow, please."

"This is she."

"Hi, this is Paul Fervante from Cyrus National Bank. I'm the branch director for the branch you have gone to for some time now."

"Hello, Paul. Is there an issue? I don't normally get calls from my bank. I just bought a house, so I'm a little nervous on what this call could be about."

"No. No need to worry. This is actually a call to inform you that one million dollars has been deposited into your account. I wanted to let you know that it is not a bank mistake."

"What?"

"Yes. We went over everything with a fine-toothed comb. All of it is legit. I just wanted to give you a call before you went into your account online and saw that amount there and thought it was a mistake."

"Who deposited that amount into my account?"

"Well, Mr. Barlow did."

Berta freezes. "Okay. Thank you, Paul. I appreciate the call."

"No problem. Have a good day, ma'am."

Berta gets off the phone and sets it down on a counter. She looks at Izabel with a slight smile.

"Lots of vacations, Mom. Lots of vacations."

She walks to the front of the house to open up her makeshift curtains. The first thing she notices on the quiet block is the black Honda Accord with tinted windows parked across the street. She stares for a few long moments before the car starts and drives away.

⊗

"I also pray for Craig. He's spent so many years looking for someone to be the one for him and he thought . . . we all thought it was Berta. It seems maybe it just wasn't to be, but I hope and pray that there is someone out there . . . and that he finds her. Craig is a great man who would easily make any woman happy. I pray for the right

one to come along his way. He has a lot of demons of the past that he must contend with. Give him strength, give him courage, but most of all, give him peace and a sound mind . . ."

☙❧

"I'm glad to see you haven't just completely cut me off," Ramses says.

"No, sir. I just needed a little more time to think." Craig sits in a chair in front of Ramses' desk. "I hope you understand."

"Of course I do. Just . . . was starting to worry about you a little."

"You? Worrying about me?"

"C'mon, Craig."

"I'm joking. Just a joke."

"I can't tell anymore." He folds his hands and sets them on top of the desk. "Listen, Alberta informed me of . . . the decision. I'm sorry to hear that you two won't be continuing on."

"It's fine. It's for the better. At the end of the day, I believe this is what would make her happy."

"And you? What would make you happy?"

"Peace."

Ramses looks at him thoughtfully.

"Which I why I would like to ask you to sell me the ranch."

"What?" He smiles a knowing smile. "That time there really helped . . . or was it that woman?"

"What are you talking about?"

"Don't play coy. I know about her staying with you, especially because it was on my ranch."

"I meant no disrespect. She needed a safe place to be and . . ."

"No need to explain. I'm sure you wish you were with her now."

"Well. When I left, so did she, so she probably isn't even there. Not after all this time."

"So what were you going to do?"

"Move into the ranch and find her."

Ramses smiles. "Well, I guess you will be pleased to know she hasn't left. I've just had some food delivered there and some of my people said they saw a slender woman living there, and well"—he chuckles—"Janice isn't necessarily skinny."

Craig's face remains still for a moment, but a small smile creeps onto his face.

"So I'm giving you the ranch."

"You have to let me pay for it."

"No. I won't hear of it. Call it a gift."

"That's a pretty hefty gift."

"Well, it's the last thing I can do to make sure I fulfill the promise I made to Raul. I told him I would look after you two. That the entire network he built would be focused on your and Berta's protection. It turned out to be more, but at this point . . . there's no threat to protect against."

"So, what are you saying?"

"I'm saying I'm out. I'm already in the middle of collapsing Courtland's network. What's left of Raul's, I'm completely disbanding."

Craig leans in. "So you decoded the chip?"

"I have. Well, it wasn't encoded to begin with."

"And it was everything?"

"Actually, no."

Craig stares. "What do you mean, 'no'? They were wrong?"

"They were, in part."

"Make it plain."

"Raul left the numbers to two accounts . . . and a letter."

"What?"

"Yeah. You see, Raul was never as paranoid as Courtland was. He didn't leave you with details of his network . . . that would be silly for him to do . . . of course I think this after knowing he didn't do it. I wasn't so sure at first. Anyway, he didn't leave you the network as a just-in-case measure; he left you an inheritance."

"What?"

"And a letter. I printed it off, but I didn't read it." He hands him a folded piece of paper.

Craig grabs the paper and folds it again before sliding it into his pocket. "I thought he left Berta with everything. He left me with the business. There was nothing more than that."

"Apparently there is."

"Well, how much is in those accounts?"

"You ready for this?"

"Well, I'm sitting, so yes, I think I'm ready."

"You've become real sarcastic as of late, you know that?"

"Ramses."

"Okay. He left you a combined total of three point two five million dollars and growing."

Craig smiles. His smile turns into a slight frown. "You know, I've been crying quite a bit as of late, too."

"It's okay for a grown man to cry."

"I'm not saying it isn't. It's just I'm tired of it."

"But these would be tears of joy. No?"

"True enough."

"So, it seems he didn't leave you the chip because he thought you were weak. He was making sure you were set for life."

"And he made sure I remembered the conversation we had when he gave me the watch." He chuckles. "Hey, you still won't take my money for the ranch?"

"Won't hear of it. We'll work out the finer details later."

"Then can you do me a favor? Before you shut all of everything down?"

"I suppose. What is it?"

"Mark and Jade Cooke. They have a joint account."

"And you want me to give them the whole thing?"

"No. Can you wire a million to them? A million to Berta? And I'll take the rest back to the ranch."

"Done." He gives a perplexed look. "What of your job?"

"I'm done. I was giving everyone a two-month notice, and suggesting them to a few other advisors."

"You're giving it up?"

"Yup. All of it."

"Are you going to personally call Patrice Stafford?"

He chuckles. "Yeah. And I'll let her know. What's your angle here?"

"No angle. Just strange that you risk getting caught just to talk to her, but then when you are actually able to perhaps pursue something with her, you find yourself going the other way." He leans back. "This Addie must be something."

"She is." He smiles while holding out his hand. "Thank you, sir." Ramses takes it with a strong grip. "It has been a pleasure."

"I'm glad I could be of some assistance." He looks down. "You take care of yourself out there."

"I will, sir." He starts toward the door. "Sir? What happened to the detective?"

"He wasn't there. But no worries, we'll find him. He and Court-land must have had an escape route somewhere. Don't know how he reached it before we got there. Either way, he will be dealt with accordingly. We'll see how he likes being on the run."

"You think he is going to bother us?"

"I get the feeling he won't. He helped you two out, no?"

"He did."

"I think he will just disappear."

"I hope so." He gives Ramses a salute goodbye. "Sir."

Ramses nods. "Don't be a stranger, Kid."

Craig smiles and leaves the office.

◦◦◦

"I pray for my family: Mark, Kalina, Charles, and Amber. I pray for them collectively and individually. I pray that you continue to form Mark into the husband and father you will have him be. Allow him to be of a sound mind. I pray that we both are able to lead our children in the right direction. Many things have happened to our family in recent memory. I ask that you don't let those negative things turn into scars on our very being. We are all alive, and in relatively good health. I thank you for that. Our hope is to get stronger in you. Again, I thank you for bringing me through a tremendous storm. I thank you for bringing us through a tremendous storm, Lord. I bless your name. I love you. It is in Jesus' name I pray, Amen."

◦◦◦

Mark sits at the dining-room table staring at various hospital bills from Jade's extended visit. He's totaled up what it's going to cost them and stares at the number on a filled piece of notebook paper. He's not too concerned as the severance Jade received from Raynard Pharmeceuticals is enough to cover, but that somewhat leaves them stranded.

Without a well paying job for either of them, ongoing health coverage for them and the kids will prove to be an issue. And Jade's physical therapy will be another drain to that amount. He collects all the bills and puts them in a neat stack, tired of looking at the numbers. The doorbell rings and he jumps up to answer the door.

"'Sup, Man?"

Craig stands at the door with a huge grin on his face.

"Doesn't look like you're ready for the gym. And why are you smiling at me like that?"

"She's still there," he says and walks in. "Where's Jade?"

"Upstairs. Why, what's up?"

"We have to talk."

"Yeah. Sure. Jade."

Mark goes upstairs to their bedroom to hear her seemingly ending prayer. He just peeks his head in. "Craig's here."

"Okay, Dear. Don't hurt anything at the gym," she says.

"No. He came to talk. Asked for both of us."

"Everything okay?"

"I don't know. He seems okay. He's smiling."

She gives him a strange look. "Help me down?"

"Of course."

He enters the bedroom and helps Jade to her feet. She leans on him with one arm and grabs her cane for the other.

"You're getting stronger," he says.

"I am. Only another month or so. You know, pretty soon, other things could happen, too." She gives him a sly look.

He immediately knows what she's talking about. "You sure?"

"Boy, if I don't, I think I might explode."

"Well, I never wanted to push the issue."

"I know." She starts to lose her breath. "And I appreciate you for it."

"Hey, you want to break?"

"No. If we take breaks just going downstairs, Craig will be here until nighttime."

"Just let me know."

"I will. Now back to the main issue at hand."

"Issue at hand?"

"Yeah. Like I said, if you don't handle this soon, I'm gonna explode."

Mark chuckles.

"There he is. There's the Mark I've been looking for."

"What do you mean?"

"Too serious lately. Too worried lately. I'm here, Babe. Fun. That's what we should be having."

Mark doesn't say much more. He abruptly stops in the hallway, holding her. He leans in and kisses her. He goes to pull away, but she cups her free hand and hooks it around the back of his head, pulling him in for more. He falls into a state of bliss, kissing his wife, holding her for the first time in what seems like forever. She finally pulls away, out of breath. She pats him on his chest.

"Soon, Big Boy. Soon. I'm going to wear you out."

Mark can't help but laugh again. "Saving the universe?"

"You got it, Buddy." She giggles. "I'm doing my part."

"You good?"

"Yeah, I'm good. Let's go."

Mark helps Jade downstairs to the living room where Craig paces the floor back and forth. He seems to be deep in thought.

"Hey," he says, stopping dead in his tracks. "How are you doing, Jade?"

"I'm well, Craig. So, what's going on?"

"Well, I wanted to talk to the both of you. Mega important. A little bittersweet. But still."

"Craig, what are you talking about?" Mark asks.

"Sit. Both of you."

Craig waits for Mark and Jade to get to the couch and sit down. Mark glances at Jade, and she catches his eye.

"Okay, so I don't really know where to start. But as you know, when in hiding, I was at this ranch in Texas."

"Right," Jade says.

"So, I'm going to come out and say it. I bought the ranch." He looks down. "Well, was given the ranch, but he's not going to get away without my giving him something in return." He looks back up brightly. "But anyway, I bought it and I'm moving in soon."

"Congrats, Man." Mark says. "Wait. Permanently? You moving in . . . to start a new life?"

"Here's the bitter part." He sits. "It's where I plan on being for a while . . . so, yes. Permanent."

Mark feels like he's been punched in the gut. Jade grabs and holds his hand. He looks at her in disbelief. He then looks at Craig and notices how happy he looks, not in delivering the bitter part, but in explaining the new life.

"But I'll always be around. You know? Like, if y'all need me, and by now you should know for anything, just call. The holidays are coming up. Thanksgiving is next week. I'll be around for that, obviously. And Christmas, I was thinking you and the kids come down. It would be a good time to . . . introduce you to someone."

Mark doesn't know what to say.

"Introduce us to someone?" Jade asks. "Someone like who?"

"Well, Berta and I are done. I hope we can be friends again, but I don't know if that is in her plans at all. Knowing her, she's going to move on. But that's okay. I just . . . while at the ranch, I met a woman. And she's great. I mean . . . she's great. And I'm not rushing into anything. I just want to see where it goes. But it would be really nice if you met her."

Mark still doesn't know what to say.

"Well, we are happy for you," Jade says. Mark feels her eyes on him.

"Yeah. I'm a little thrown off. But . . . I mean, are you sure you aren't rushing things? You're already with her? And are you sure this isn't just great and exciting because it's new? And who is she?"

Jade taps him on the arm.

"All very valid questions. And all I can say is when I'm with her, I am at peace. I've never been at peace with anyone. Ever. There's something about that ranch. There's something about that life. There's something about her. I spent all my time while back home, living in a hotel, thinking, dreaming about being at the ranch with her. I care for her on a level that came up so fast it's scary. You know what it's like, don't you? You don't want to be away from someone not because you simply don't want to be apart, but you can't be apart. You feel like physically, you cannot be apart from that person for too long because . . ."

"Because you love her," Mark says.

Craig looks up at Mark and nods. "And all you think about is how you can fill her up with so much love. That thought consumes you. You think of great things to do for her, things that would simply make her smile. You long to see her smile and . . . You get what I mean, right?"

"I do, Pal. And we got your back, too." Mark smiles. "I still don't like it that much, but I get it. Just call every now and again."

"Oh, you guys are gonna get sick of me. I'm not just gonna disappear. You all mean too much to me to do that."

"So when are you leaving?" Jade asks.

"As soon as I leave here. All my stuff is still at the ranch. Car is packed with other things. Taking a private flight out. But there's one more thing I need to tell you, but I'm running out of time." He gets up and Mark helps Jade up. He heads to the door.

"I love y'all." He hugs Jade.

Mark stands at the doorway, not wanting to say anything like goodbye. Craig goes in for a hug.

"Don't be weird about it, Man," Craig says. "Hug me back."

Mark laughs, but he knows it's to stop the beginning of a cry fest. He sees Jade already has a few tears in her eyes. "Whatever, Man." He hugs Craig. "Jerk."

"Tell me how mad you are about it tomorrow."

"Yeah, yeah. You better not get fat. I don't keep fat friends. Find a gym down there."

Jade hits Mark on the arm. "Stop playing, Mark. Tell him what you really feel."

"It's okay, Jade. I've been through this for years. He's as hardheaded as they come," Craig says.

"He is," she says.

"Whatever, the both of you," Mark says. "Listen, Man, seriously. We're going to miss you. But I hope for nothing but the best for you. I owe you . . . everything. I owe you my life, Bro."

Craig looks down and smiles. "Y'all don't owe me a thing." He looks at both of them. "Y'all pulled me out of so much stuff. Just be well, okay? I'll be checking in." He clears his throat. "And check with your bank tonight, okay? I know the hospital bills must be outrageous."

"What? Why? What did you do?"

"No worries. I gotta go." He pops out the door and trots to his car, giving one last look and wave before driving off.

Mark rushes to his computer and turns it on. He logs into their bank account online and checks the balance.

"That bastard," Mark says.

"Mark, language. When did you start talking like that?"

"I don't. It was the only thing I could think of saying." His eyes are full of tears. "Look at what he did."

Jade walks over to the computer and gasps. "What? Oh, my goodness. Chair. Chair."

Mark pops up and helps Jade to sit down. She holds her hand to her mouth. Her voice sounds muffled. "He bought a ranch. He just gave us a million freaking dollars. Mark, how much money did Craig have?"

"I don't know. I knew he made a good living, but I never knew how good. It never mattered."

"Well . . . we're going to have to send him a thank-you card or something."

Mark laughs. "What? Who sends a thank-you card for that? I'm sure somewhere there's a greeting card that says 'Hey, Friend. Thanks for the life-changing money.' Yeah, no. No such card."

"I don't know. How do you thank someone for this?"

Mark looks. "I think we already did."

They both continue to stare at the screen. Mark grabs her hand and kisses the top of it. "Possibilities," he says as he kneels down beside her.

She grabs his face and kisses him deeply. Then she pulls away slightly.

"Possibilities."

∞

After a flight that seemed to take forever, Craig gets chauffeured back to the ranch. As soon as the car stops, he's jumping out to grab his bag from the trunk. He hoists the strap of the bag on his shoulder and gives the car a soft tap. It turns around in the drive and speeds off. He hurries to the front door, halfway expecting to see Addie rushing the door, but when he opens it, he sees no one. He drops his bag at the door and listens. He hears nothing as well.

"Addie," he calls out. He waits a few moments but still, nothing. He runs all around the house, checking each room, but finding no one. It doesn't even look like anyone has been in any of the rooms. He searches the lower level but finds more of the same. Impeccably clean rooms. He walks back to the living room and sits on the chaise, looking befuddled. He thinks for a moment. *She's back in Silver Rock. I gotta see if she's good.* He stands up, but as soon as he does, he hears a noise at the back. A few seconds later, Addie comes walking in with gloves that are covered in dirt. She pulls one off, but stops in the middle of pulling the second off. She sees him standing there, frozen. She seems like she doesn't believe her eyes, either. He takes a step toward her.

"Hello, Addie."

She finishes taking her second glove off. He notices she has on similar clothing to when he first met her. Torn jeans. A button-down with the sleeves rolled up. A large straw hat. He isn't able to tell what her expression means. She sets the gloves on the counter and pulls off the straw hat. Her hair falls gently to the sides of her face. She simply continues to stare.

"I've been working some things out in my mind these past few weeks," he says. "When I was leaving, you said you were clearing out. That you were going back to Silver Rock."

"I never said I was going back to Silver Rock. I said I was clearing out of here, sure. But I wasn't going back there."

Craig smiles. "But you did. You went back to Silver Rock. You didn't have those clothes with you." He looks down. "You went back to him?" He takes a few steps closer.

"You already know I didn't." She looks down and away. "He wasn't there. The town . . . it's different now. The group . . . they're gone. Just gone. And no one would tell me what happened. I'm an outsider now."

"What about Miss June?"

"She didn't know anything. She knows just what I told you." She looks at him. "You know I waited for you. I waited a week before I packed up and started on my way. I was about thirty miles out, going the opposite way of town, and I just pulled over. I cried for the longest time, because in my gut I knew you would come back. So I came back and I stayed for another week before I went to town. And I went there to see if I could grab some things. Went in the middle of the night. Found my entire house packed up in boxes. Grabbed as much of my stuff as possible and was about to go when Miss June popped up." She shuffles her feet. "So now it's your turn. You go back to her?"

Craig finds himself enjoying the conversation. He smiles.

"Why are you smiling?"

"Because you're gorgeous."

"Stop it, Craig. I'm being serious."

"I am, too." He chuckles. "I didn't go back to her." He moves a couple more steps closer, and when he sees she doesn't move, he takes a few more. He is now close enough to reach and grab her, but he doesn't. Not yet.

"So, what happened?"

"I'll tell you over dinner."

"You were gone for almost a month."

"I know. So much was going on and I had to take some time to think. I had to see if I was crazy. I know you did the same."

"What, think I was crazy? Yes, I thought that. I still do."

Craig laughs.

"There's nothing funny, Craig." She starts to laugh as well.

"I get it. I do. But dinner. I will explain everything. Everything down to the smallest detail. Please."

She stops and seems to think.

"Please say yes so I can kiss you. Lord knows I've been thinking about that for a while."

A smile creeps onto her face. She still doesn't say anything.

"You know you're gonna say yes," Craig teases.

She purses her lips to stop herself from smiling even more.

"Addie." He waits for her to look at him. "I'm yours."

"Okay, fine. Dinner tonight. I'm feeling all these butterflies and stuff."

Craig nearly leaps to her and pulls her in close to him. Longing to feel her lips on his, he finally kisses her.

EPILOGUE

"Kalina, hurry up," Jade yells upstairs. "Never heard of someone being late to their own graduation."

"Oh, Mom, it's happened before," Kalina yells back downstairs.

"Not when they're Valedictorian!"

Jade dashes to the kitchen to make sure Mark is on task as well. She gets there to see him stuffing the last little bit of his sandwich in his mouth while avoiding messing up his shirt.

"Ready to go, Babe," he says. "Kalina ready?"

"She better be."

Charles walks into the kitchen wearing slacks and a short-sleeved button-down shirt. "Mom, I'm hungry."

"You're always hungry. I'll have snacks in the car. Mark, did Craig call you?"

"Yeah, he did. He and Addie are going to meet us out front for their tickets."

"Okay. And I talked to Berta this morning. Ka—"

She turns to yell upstairs again when Kalina comes running down, holding her cap and gown in her hand.

"Sorry. Sorry."

Jade looks at her daughter and admires the young woman who stands before her. Kalina stands just a little bit taller than Jade and is only an inch or so shorter than Mark. Kalina smiles at her with a knowing grin. Jade returns the smile, noticing the gleam in her eyes. "You ready?" Jade asks.

"I am. I have my speech ready, too."

"Good. We have to hurry."

Jade rushes everyone to the garage. "Let's go, let's go. Into the van." After everyone rushes in, she jumps in the passenger seat.

"Everyone buckled in?" Mark asks.

Jade listens to the chorus of answers all saying yes. She places her hand on Mark's over the gearshift. He looks at her and smiles. Jade realizes at this very moment, that she is where she always wanted to be. She turns to look out the window.

The last three years have been the best three years of her life. Sure, a portion of that time was spent recovering from physical wounds, from mental wounds, from emotional wounds, but what she found on the other side of all those negative things was real freedom. She's found real freedom in her marriage. She's found real freedom in her walk with God.

Eventually, she did tell Mark in as much detail as she could remember what it was like being in the coma. She told him about the angels and the demons, and about the resentment she had for many of those she cared about. He was floored at first, but still helped her find balance through the experience. For a while after, she thought he was going to dip into a depression because it all seemed to be too much for him. It seemed like the more she told him, the grayer his hair became. The more she cried about the pain she was having as her muscles came back to form, the more pronounced the bags under his eyes became. The more sleepless nights she had because of a revived fear of darkness, the more he seemed to lose his bounce when he walked. She tried to tell herself it was his new schedule, having gone back to school, that caused his elevated stress. She would ask if he was alright, and he would always answer yes. At the end, looking back, he never wavered on his support for her, and she is beyond grateful for that.

She turns to look back at him. While the kids who aren't so small anymore talk about some song she's never heard of, she leans in slightly to get to his ear.

"I love you," she says.

When she pulls back, she sees that he still focuses on the road, but a huge grin forms on his face. She looks out the window, satisfied.

⟨⟩

Craig pulls a rental car into a parking space at Kalina's school. He looks around the parking lot.

"They said they would meet us at the front of the school." He un-buckles his seat belt and moves to get out the car.

Addie looks at him and smiles, but doesn't move. He notices and pauses. "What's wrong?"

"Nothing." She unfastens her seatbelt while asking. "It's just . . . Is Berta going to be there?"

"Yeah. Why?"

"Just asking. You seem nervous."

Craig sighs. "Are we talking about this again?"

"No. No, we're not." She places her hand on the door handle.

"Look, Ads." He gently grabs both of her hands in his and kisses them. "I love you. You know I do."

"I do. But there's a lot to be said about how you change when you're around her. I wouldn't be so concerned if it happened once. But it's happened every time we've been around her. Every Christmas. Every Thanksgiving. Every birthday." She pulls her hands from his. "You still love her?"

"No." A bead of sweat forms on the back of his neck and trickles down his back. "I am totally and wholly in love with you. I'm sorry if I made you feel otherwise. I just can't seem to find balance. And maybe that doesn't make sense, but she's my ex-wife and . . ."

"Look, I get it. There's always going to be something there."

"No. There's nothing there."

"I know you, Craig. I know your heart. You still care about how she is. You still care about who she dates and when she is eventually going to get married. You care about what she does in her life."

Craig plops his head against the headrest.

"You still have her in your system."

"It's been years since the divorce."

"What's your point?"

"I don't know."

She places her hand on his leg. "You remember those years ago when you asked me where could this, meaning me and you, go?"

"Yeah."

"And what did I say?"

"You said you wanted to be with me. That we could be together. Learn and grow together. We could forge our own path."

"And by you coming back to the ranch after you handled what you said you needed to handle?"

"I was saying I wanted to forge a new path with you." He turns his head. "And I still do. I've found the peace that I so desperately sought out all these years. And I found that peace with you."

She stares at him for a long time. She blinks multiple times and says something with her eyes. He swears he falls in love with her every time she looks at him like that. But this time, he knows she is looking for truth. She's looking for truth in his eyes.

"I believe you," she says.

Craig internally breathes a sigh of relief. He can't imagine his life without Addie. In every way he can think of, she fits him like a glove. He believes he was and is meant to be with her, but he knows she may be onto something. There still may be something for Berta, though he doesn't want to admit it; that something may be the desire to be more than just acquaintances.

"And I love you," he says.

CB&EO

Berta stands in front of Kalina's high school waiting for everyone to arrive. She been outside waiting for some time, but that is only because she's excited. She's excited to see everyone, though she visits Mark, Jade, and the kids regularly. Her real excitement stems from knowing she will have another chance to see Craig and she knows she shouldn't be excited at all.

"Hey, Berta."

She turns around to see Jade storming up with two cameras around her neck. Behind her is Mark, holding Kalina as they walk side by side. He says something to her she is unable to make out.

"'Sup girl," Berta says. She greets and hugs everyone before asking; "Craig and Addie pop up yet?"

"Not yet. They better hurry up, though."

"Mom, I gotta go in," Kalina says.

Jade flips around and grips Kalina tightly. "I love you, Baby. Go. Go." And she pushes her along.

"See, Addie, I told you we should have broken out into a sprint."

Berta turns around to see Craig and Addie walking up to the group. Berta smiles brightly at seeing Craig. She looks at Addie, notic-

355

ing the curious way she eyes her. She gives a warm hug to Addie first, then Craig.

"How are you two?" Berta asks.

"No complaints," Craig says.

Berta looks to Addie when Addie responds, "We're good." She notices something in Addie's expression that makes her second-guess that notion.

"Alright, we better get seated," Jade says.

"It's such a beautiful day," Mark says while giving Addie a hug. "Maybe we can stroll the—"

"No time for sightseeing," Jade says.

"Shouldn't I be the overkill one?" Mark asks.

Jade shrugs and starts toward the school front doors. She grabs Amber's hand and nudges Charles on. Everyone starts to follow.

"Hey, Berta, can I talk to you for a second?" Addie asks.

Berta looks at how serious her face is. "Sure."

"You go ahead, Sweets," Addie says to Craig. "I won't be long."

Craig looks at her strangely. "What are you doing?" he asks.

Mark grabs Craig's arm. "Let's rock, man. Let the ladies talk."

Berta looks back at Jade, finding her expression to be the same as Mark's, like she knows something that she isn't saying.

Jade hands her and Addie their tickets and before long, the rest of the group is striding toward the building.

"What's on your mind?" Berta asks when everyone is out of earshot.

"He's still in love with you," Addie says plainly.

"What? Who? Craig? No, he's not."

"And I think you may still have something for him."

"Okay. So where is this coming from?"

"Where do you think? Did you see how much you lit up when you saw him? I did." She shuffles her feet. "I also saw how hard he tried to cover up his excitement to see you. I've seen it for every holiday for the past three years. And don't think I haven't noticed the secret phone calls. He thinks I didn't notice. I've noticed all of them."

Berta thinks for a moment. She was excited to see Craig, and she knows her excitement reached a bit past simply being happy to see a friend. She thinks of those aforementioned phone calls. She's called Craig on many occasions just to hear his voice again, just to be friends again.

"Listen, if you are concerned about me trying to take Craig or something like that—"

"I'm not. That isn't my concern at all." She crosses her arms. "My concern is that he would just up and walk away."

"But he loves you."

"I know. But again, he still loves you."

Berta sighs. She watches a few people stride by to get to the ceremony. "What do you want me to do? Stay away from everyone during the holidays?"

"No. That's not fair to you. But those calls have to stop."

"What exactly is *fair* to me?"

Addie shows signs of frustration. "Berta, I like you. I like you a lot. But at the end of the day, you left Craig. You filed for the divorce. It's not *fair* to *him* to even give him an inkling of an idea that maybe it could work between you two. It's not fair to him or you for either one of you to hold on to something that is gone." She looks down. "And it especially isn't fair to me." She snaps her gaze up to look at Berta with a fire in her eyes. "He hasn't brought up marriage or kids or anything like that with me. And I'm scared that just means that I'm—"

"A placeholder. You're afraid you're nothing more than a place-holder."

"And I love him too much to even think of what that path means."

Berta and Addie stand in front of the school for a few clicks, letting the sounds of anxious parents and their excited children fill the void in between them.

"Do you think it could work between you two?" Addie asks. "If you tried again, I mean."

Berta looks at her, noticing a tear drop from her eye. "No. I don't think it could work."

"But you care about him, right?"

"I do. Always will."

Addie nods. "Then I think you already know what you must do."

"What I *must* do?"

"If you really care about him like you say, yes, what you must do." Addie starts toward the stadium. "We better get to our seats."

Berta agrees and starts toward the school as well. As they get into the auditorium and to their seats, Berta trails behind a bit. She sees Craig and steels herself for something she realizes she's never really wanted to do.

She has to let him go.

She gets up to their seats and whispers in Craig's ear. "We need to talk."

He looks at her strangely. "Everything is about to begin."

"It will only be a few minutes."

She walks back out of the auditorium and waits for him. One of the younger high school students, acting as an usher, asks her if she needs help finding her seat, but she declines. Craig walks briskly toward her.

"What's up?" he asks. "And what did Addie want to talk to you about?"

"Insecure, are we?" She smiles. She motions toward the courtyard in front of the building and Craig follows.

"Oh, well, there's nothing I like more than having my current girl-friend have deep conversations with my ex-wife. That's what guys like, you know."

"Your sarcasm is cute."

"Yeah?"

"So listen, that talk with Addie was interesting."

"Look, I'm sorry if she offended you or anything; if she made you uncomfortable, whatever. I'm sorry."

"She did none of those things. She opened my eyes a little, though."

"What do you mean?"

"Craig, why did you pick up?"

"Huh?"

"When I first called you; why did you pick up the phone?"

"Because you needed me."

"But you're not mine to need."

"Come again."

"Does Addie know about the calls? Rather, have you talked to her about still speaking with me on the phone?"

"No." He takes in a deep breath and exhales slowly through parted lips. "I couldn't."

"Why?"

"I don't know."

"Do you still love me?"

"Is that what she said?"

"Just answer the question."

"I mean, I always will be here for you. That's what I told you, isn't it?"

Berta smiles, but her insides are a churning mess. "You're messing up, Craig."

"What are you talking about?"

"Addie is so plainly and so clearly the one for you. She fits you in ways I could never fit. You two are meant to be with each other."

"Why are you saying all this now?"

"Why haven't you married her yet?"

"What. Whoa. Berta, slow down."

"You want to, don't you?"

"I haven't thought about it."

"You lie. You have." She sighs and looks into the sky. "Craig, I care about you. I have since the day I met you. And I know you still care about me. But we have to let go of us. We have to let go of the idea of us even as friends like we were before. We can't be friends. Not anymore. Not"—her breath catches—"not like we were when we first fell in love. It's just not fair. It's not fair to anyone involved."

His expression is plain. She can tell he's processing everything she's said. Moments later, he nods.

"We really should get going," he says. He starts back toward the school without so much as another word.

Berta follows and they reenter the auditorium. He stops to look back at her and smiles. He moves to the side to allow her to sit first. She moves past Mark, Jade, and the children to sit at the end of their group, and he takes his seat next to Addie on the opposite end.

Faintly, over the ambient chatter in the auditorium, she hears Craig talking to Addie. She tries for a few moments to hear what he's saying, but gives up when another family takes their seats next to her. She gives a courteous smile and faces forward.

She feels a tap on her shoulder and looks to see Mark reaching his arm over Charles to tap her. Charles acts as any teenager would: annoyed at the slightest things.

"You okay?" Mark asks.

Berta looks in Mark's direction, but looks past him. She watches Craig and Addie act as if they are the only ones in the auditorium. She tries to remember if she and Craig were ever like that. She nods.

"I'm good, Mark." She gives him a resolute look.

As the ceremony begins, Berta finds herself sliding into deep thought. She respects Addie for doing what she's done, and is even more convinced that Addie is the one for Craig. The change that occurred at the moment Addie spoke to her, she realizes, was a simple one, but one that will surely mean some changes in her life.

She simply let go. She's let go of Craig, of their past, of her past. Tears form in her eyes as she breathes a breath of cool, light air.

She feels so free.

∽◦∾

Mark stands holding Kalina in his arms swaying back and forth in a soothing motion. He hugs her hoping that somehow through his extra-long hug, she understands how proud he is of her.

The graduation is over and everyone already sat and enjoyed a barbeque at the Cooke residence. Kalina was on her way out the door to get to another graduation party to celebrate with her friends when he grabbed her. She hasn't said a word, though. She just continues to hug back. When he finally lets her go, he holds her on her shoulders and stares. He stares so long, she becomes shy under his gaze.

"I'm being weird, I know," he says.

"No, you're not," she says. "Plus, if you were, you're my Dad. You get a 'be weird when your daughter graduates' pass."

He smiles. "You better be off. And don't stay out too late tonight."

"I won't." She gives him one last hug and heads out the door.

Mark heads to the backyard, where Jade, Craig, Addie, and Berta all sit, relaxed on patio furniture. He finds his seat next to Jade and rejoins the conversation.

"I didn't think you were going to let her go," Craig says while chuckling.

"Oh, leave him alone," Addie says. "It's his firstborn. Of course it's gonna take a little bit to let go."

"Thank you, Addie," Mark says. "And Craig, you take a hike."

"Hey, man, I'm just saying. When my firstborn graduates, I'm not going to be all sappy and emotional like that guy." He looks at Jade and points toward Mark.

A silence falls over the area.

Mark stares at Craig for a few moments before scanning the faces of everyone else.

"When your firstborn graduates?" Jade asks.

Craig looks around at everyone. "Yeah. What did I say wrong?"

"Nothing," Jade says. "It's just . . . I don't think anyone has heard you talk about kids before."

"I have. I must have." He looks around but stops at the only person he's ever talked about kids with.

Mark notices the looks exchanged between Craig and Berta, also noting how quiet Berta has been since the graduation ceremony.

"I guess I haven't really said anything to anyone about that." He looks down.

"Well, Addie," Berta says, "it sounds like you've changed him for the better. Because none of us have heard him talk about kids before."

Mark looks at Berta, and at Addie, then at Craig.

"Yeah. Anyone need anything to drink?" Mark asks as he stands back up.

"Wine," Jade says, almost too quickly.

Mark doesn't wait for anyone else to say anything and calls out to Craig to help him out. Craig snaps up and follows Mark back into the house.

"What was that?" Mark asks.

"Foot in mouth. That's what that was. I thought something different in my head and I was just, you know, poking fun, but . . ."

"You stepped in it this time."

"You have no idea," Craig says as he grabs a pack of wine coolers.

"What do you mean?"

"So, I've been talking to Berta." He looks at Mark as if he understands.

"What do you mean talking?"

"Talking. On the phone. Somewhat regularly. We're still good friends."

Mark nods in understanding. "How good of friends?"

"Probably too good."

"Why? And does Addie know?"

"I don't really know why. I'm sure Addie knows about the calls now, or at the very least has an idea." He sets the wine coolers on the counter. "I guess I miss her, Berta, I mean. And maybe I haven't really let her go."

Mark pops open a bottle of wine and grabs a wine glass for Jade. "Best advice: get your mind right. Addie is a good woman and you two have something going here."

"I know. I know. Don't worry about that. Berta and I had a talk after she and Addie did. I'm not sure what Addie said, but at the end of the day, Berta and I found it best to simply be friends, but not as close of friends as we have been. It would just open the door to too much."

"That's smart. Because let me tell you, Jade and I noticed all the unsaid stuff between you two. And if we noticed it . . ."

"Yeah." Craig sighs. "I want to do right by Addie, man, I really do."

"I know."

"I'm thinking of asking her to marry me when we get back home."

"Well, you know what I'm going to say about that."

"What? That I should have made that decision a long time ago?"

Mark smiles. "I was just going to ask you who you were getting to preside over the wedding."

Craig pats Mark on the shoulder. "Of course you, Pastor Mark Cooke." He laughs. "Still trying to get used to that one."

"Assistant Pastor, but still, I'd be honored."

"Hey, man, before we get back out there, do you still see"—he lowers his voice to a whisper—"Alicia?"

"Nope."

"How did you get her out of your head?"

"You asking for ways to stop thinking of Berta?"

"Of course."

"I got her out of my head by taking it one day at a time. That's how most things are. Big things change incrementally. There's always something smaller leading up to the bigger. I didn't stop seeing her as soon as Jade awoke from that hospital bed. It didn't stop when Jade was recovering, either. It slowed little by little over the years. I kept moving." He balls his fist and taps it on Craig's chest. "Don't get stuck in your own head. Don't get stuck in the past, in what was or could have been. Keep moving. You have someone in front of you who deserves all of your attention, all of your love. Give it to her. Hold nothing back."

Craig smiles. "Are you about to preach, sir?"

Mark laughs. "Let's get back out there." He throws his arm around Craig's shoulders and they walk out to hear the ladies laughing and talking.

"Mark," Jade says, "I'm sorry. I had to tell them."

"Tell them what?"

"The naked Mark fiasco."

"The what?" Craig takes his seat next to Addie.

Mark smirks and puts his head down. "And why would you tell anyone that story?"

"The real question is why you haven't told *me* this one," Craig says.

"There's nothing to tell," Mark says.

"Oh, I think there is," Addie says, unable to hold in her laughter.

"Jade, could you please fill me in?" Craig asks.

Mark looks over at Berta, who seems to be trying to contain her laughter, too. "She embellishes a lot of that story, you know."

"I'm sure," Berta says and lets out a hearty laugh.

"Okay, okay, for Craig," Jade says. She clears her throat in dramatic fashion. "It all begins with your homeboy, a bottle of maple syrup, and a pillow . . ."

www.ingramcontent.com/pod-product-compliance
Lightning Source LLC
Chambersburg PA
CBHW072012110726
47910CB00005B/1737